THE ESFAH SAGAS:
SECRETS OF THE SHADOWLANDS

BY
CHRISTOPHER D. SCHMITZ

A DRAGON DICE NOVEL

PUBLISHED BY TREESHAKER BOOKS

THE ESFAH SAGAS

Rise and Fall of the Obsidian Grotto
Cast of Fate
Army of the Dead

The Relic Quests
Ashes of Ailushurai
Rise of the Champions
Drakuwar

The Cyrean Songs
Chill Wind
Eye of the Storm
Secrets of the Shadowlands

STAY UP TO DATE ON THE WORLD OF ESFAH!

Get a free book from in the Esfah Sagas by visiting:

www.subscribepage.com/getfreedragondicenovels

Subscribers who sign up for this no-spam email list will get free books, exclusive content, and more! You'll get *a free ebook* immediately… if you would like more details or want to follow the author, you can find his details at the end of this book.

BACKGROUND

Dragon Dice™ was originally created by Lester Smith and produced by TSR in 1995.It is an Origins Award winning strategy game where players create mythical armies using dice to represent each troop and is one of several collectible dice games that emerged in the 1990s. The game combines strategy and skill as well as a little luck.

After several years, TSR, now owned by Wizards of the Coast, had put Dragon Dice™ on hold to work on other projects. In October of 2000, SFR Inc. purchased the rights to Dragon Dice™.

Most of the races and monsters in original TSR Dragon Dice were created by Lester Smith and include some creatures unique to a fantasy setting and others that are familiar to the Dungeons & Dragons role-playing game. While the world of Esfah, where Dragon Dice™ takes place, has many similarities to that of Dungeons & Dragons, it is distinctly different in many respects. In some ways, there are greater unknowns and its history is both newer and older all at once.

Around the end of 1995 I was a teenager and avid board gamer who had a burger slinging job (which gave me a disposable income) and a car (that took most of my disposable income.) In addition to many other games I played as part of a regular quartet of gamers, Dragon Dice™ was one that we all enjoyed.

I fondly remember how the four of us would cut out of elective classes, study halls, and independent learning periods to meet up for gaming sessions. Dragon Dice™ came in a pocketable carrying bag which made it perfect for that.

We also had a mutual acquaintance. An older gentleman in town owned a new and used bookstore that also carried a limited supply of gaming products. Though he did not stock Dragon Dice™, he had a copy of *Cast of Fate*, the first Dragon Dice™ novel which included a special promo die; I snapped it up right away as the most avid reader of the foursome (which lent itself to me become the dedicated DM for our role-playing game sessions and solidified my path as a story-teller.) The included promotional die was our bright and shiny object for months.

Cast of Fate by Allen Varney was not the only book set in the world of Esfah, though it remains one of the few. As I write and publish more and more fiction (both Fantasy and Science Fiction,) I tend to write the stories that I've always wanted to... and I've always wanted to have a voice in a shared universe. Creating a story within the Dragon Dice™ universe is something I've always wanted to do, so I give a special thanks to SFR, a company composed of true and like-minded fans who have kept alive a product that was one of the gems of the 1990s.

—Christopher Schmitz

FOREWORD

In eons past, when time was young and creation malleable, the four powers of Nature -- earth, air, fire, and water -- the children of Nature, gods in their own rights, brought forth two races of beings to care for their fledgling world, created by the all-father, Tarvanehl. One race, the selumari or coral elves, was created to husband the fluid forces of air and water. The other race, the vagha, a dwarvish race, embodied the stability of earth and the tempering power of fire. Together, these two peoples worked to nurture their infant world into something glorious and beautiful.

But Nature had a nemesis in Death, the spirit of entropy. In imitation of Nature, Death brought into being its own races: the morehl, or lava elves, who worshiped fire and destruction, and the trogs, a race of goblins, who sprang from earth and corruption. From the moment of their creation, the morehl and trogs sowed conflict, defiling the very world that gave them life and corrupting the other races who tended it. War sparked over land and possessions. Soon, hordes of dispossessed selumari, vagha, morehl, and trogs swept back and forth across the lands of Esfah, locked in endless battle.

In their struggles for supremacy over the fledgling world, the First Races pressed other magical beings into their service. The morehl were the first to do so, bringing up fire-breathing hellhounds and web-casting driders from the deepest caverns below Esfah. The trogs followed suit, leading trolls, harpies, and other monsters into battle. In response, the selumari called forth coral giants from the ocean and swarms of sprites from the skies. The vagha enlisted gargoyles, androsphinxes, and other creatures of the crags.

Conflict raged across the face of Esfah, and Death delighted in the carnage.

Back and forth across the world, darkness battle against light. Each side pushed harder yet for victory and the battles grew ever savage and desperate. New races arose, each pressed into the fray of the bloody struggle that seemed to have no end in sight.

Saddened by the bloodshed, Nature, the goddess-mother Ghaeial, dealt death to preserve life. Death, the bastard child Malgrimm – son of Ghaeial and Selurehl, the god known as Void – reveled in the chaos, terror, and pain that war brought.

A time of champions arose to safeguard the realm. Wars continued and an entire age passed. Pockets of tenuous peace grew from apathy – a new trick engineered by Death to soften the resolve of Nature's troops, almost seeming to abandon his playground for the comforts of the Abyss – but his attention never truly waned.

Esfah has never known true peace. It is not in the planet's makeup: this is where the children of gods war on their behalf. Both old and new races struggle ever onward – creatures inspired to greater ends, forever in search of either an end to the bloodshed, or carnage renewed, as each is bent towards his or her own ends.

Esfah cannot know peace. Malgrimm, the god known as Death, will not allow it. Only a few know his true name – and to speak it aloud is to court Death himself.

For a short video overview of Esfah's origins, visit

https://youtu.be/JhF8RPFkF9I

For up to date information on the world of Esfah, and all things related to the Dragon Dice universe, including products and specials, check out:

http://www.sfr-inc.com

ACKNOWLEDGEMENTS
AND
DEDICATION

Joe Joiner, the author of Chill Wind, passed away in 2014. Nearly a decade after Joe released the original version of that story, the literary world of Esfah finally comes into its own and I would like to dedicate this version of its sequel, Eye of the Storm to Joe, his legacy, and to the Joiner family.

Joe left behind notes and some story scraps that were compiled, revised, and added to, posthumously helping create a Chill Wind prequel titled Thunderfist & the Dragon. He also left behind a few details in the final notes of Chill Wind: that he ahd hope to write a series following the children of Geril and Thrag. We learned of a very young Ra'al who stayed behind in Icehome via the story and his notes revealed Geril's future child who was to be named Coryn.

Aside from the title and those two names, this was all we had to go on, and so we hope we did a service to Joe and all the other denizens of Cyrea.

—Christopher D. Schmitz

The Shadowlands
Maris Sea
The Shining Sea
Gyrea
Brixey Main
Faeleise
The Feylands
Maris Coast
Lemeliandor
Tarvenish Ocean
The Birthlands
Doban
Renvan Sea
Dereb'Liandor
Talvat Sea
Far Seas
Charnock
Sontarra
Menloe Sea
Cape Iris
Hiriath
Scattered Isles
Tarvenish Ocean
Onothe Home
The Broken Crown
Lost Diadem Isles

PROLOGUE

Year 1140, of the Second Age

Avaryth tightened a wool coat around his human form and shuddered as the chopping of oars made rhythmic noises in the water; members of his crew tightened their coats. Seldom did sailors make it this far north. But Ry'Ober, the notorious pirate queen and Avaryth's sometimes-lover, had sent him on this errand.

As a human, he was nearly as adept at sailing as any of the selumari, the coral elves of Esfah who claimed the gods of wind and water had made them. But few rivaled the high seas skills of Ry'Ober, though Avaryth thought himself a possible contender. His skiff was anchored a short way behind them, far enough out to keep from damaging its hull on the jagged rocks that dotted the nearest patch of Shadowlands coast.

Members of Avaryth's crew rowed the dinghy through the rough waves and angled for the area of the shore where Ry'Ober had directed Avaryth. Her deal had been simple and to the point: row in and steal a treasure horde, which Ry'Ober's contact had left there. Some shifty dwarf named Harol had uncovered a trove of Magestorm weapons down on the warmer side of Cyrea and left them to rust in the desolation. Any single item could fetch a hefty sum and Harol had dumped loads of them upon the beachhead.

Ry'Ober had promised to let him keep a third of the profits. It was not a good deal by normal metrics, but there was an additional value in pulling favors for Ry'Ober.

Freezing spray splashed against the dinghy until the scraping sounds of land against the boat's bottom welcomed the sailors to the shore. In a flash, Avaryth and his men sprang onto the beach and pulled their boats beyond the tide's reach.

Nothing but gray shores extended as far as the eye could see and icy plinths and frosted stone jutted out from the shore. They only had to scour the beach for a few minutes before they located the horde piled a few hundred cubits up from the stony outcropping on the shoreline. Further inland was only more gray. Wastelands spread across the expanse and scrubby trees and copses of bracken and sickly growths dotted the landscape.

Avaryth and his men looked in every direction, but heard no sounds except for breaking waves. No birds sang; no animals made noises. It was a desolate and lonely place.

"No wonder superstitious folk have always thought this the Death god's domain," he mumbled. Then, he waved to his sailors. "Alright, boys. Let's load it all up and get it back to the ship."

The pirates gathered around the mound of treasure dazzling their eyes. It seemed to radiate promises of power and wealth. A pile of sightstones mounded against the body of a deactivated blade golem: a massive humanoid with a solitary eye mounted in its head and blades affixed to both limbs and body. Black swords gleamed as if they'd been freshly forged, and a bale of enchanted arrows waited to be launched against any enemy. Rolled carpets, arcane boots, wayfare orbs—

Avaryth's breath caught in his lungs. His eyes could scarcely take it in.

A man behind them screamed and Avaryth heard the sickly *slurch* sound of a blade penetrating flesh. The humans drew steel and whirled to face the threat, eyes searching for the source of the sound.

Shoving a dead human off his blade, a skeleton stared at them with unblinking, baleful red eyes.

"It is the bloodless!" a sailor cried.

More skeletons emerged from the thickets as if they'd been lying in wait. Avaryth cursed, wishing he'd brought a spell caster with him who could have summoned a veil of fog to retrieve their plunder within. *Of course! They saw the ship when we entered the bay.*

Two more sailors fell to the bloodless. They hacked at the undead, but as soon as the fiends were chopped down, they reassembled and stood again. Before they could be caught off guard by a superior force, Avaryth shouted, "Fall back!" He and the crew hurried back toward the dinghy.

A dozen skeletons carrying swords and scythes emerged from the near-freezing sea, barring a retreat by water. The pirates faltered, and one by one, the bloodless soldiers cut them down, splashing crimson against the black, white, and gray shoreline.

The skeletons closed in around Avaryth, the last one who remained alive. They raised their blades to strike, and the human dropped his arms, resigned to his fate.

"Halt," spoke a gravelly voice. It came from a massive creature wrapped in once-fancy silks and armor that had long ago faded and lost its luster. "Keep this one alive in case the master has need of him. Bind him and drag him along with the rest."

The minions leapt upon Avaryth. Subduing him and tying his wrists, the dead hobbled his legs with a short rope tied between his ankles. Avaryth watched in terror as the death knight produced a crystal vial and dripped a dot of black ichor upon each of his fallen companions. Soon after, the dead sailors crawled to their feet jerkily, revived in zombie form.

"Back to the Crag," the death knight ordered.

As if they were one, the undead forces, picked up an armload of the precious loot left behind by Harol and began their trek deep inland, dragging the bewildered Avaryth with them.

"We are waiting for you, Dragonsbane," Captain Taerlon said. The blue-skinned coral elf looked somewhat anemic below ground, where he attended a meeting in the dwarf's quarters. A plain desk in the center of the unassuming subterranean apartment was where most of the important business in Balgavarr Reaches was conducted.

Geril sa'Ghuren, Lord of Balgavarr, the dwarven kingdom of the Cyrean continent, held up a finger to stall the elven sky ship captain at bay one moment longer. Taerlon stood in silence, and Geril dipped his quill in the inkwell and finished a document before stamping the wax seal with his signet ring.

"I must ensure a chain of command and appoint a successor in case everything goes tragically awry," the dwarf said. He was only king in a sense. The Reaches did not have a monarchy like many of their neighbors; their civilization was more nuanced and ancient, resembling the vaghan clans in diaspora who followed a Warlord's rule. But Geril had earned the right to lead for his heroism and aptitude in civic matters. Folk in Balgavarr even called him *King* at times, which rankled Geril's political enemies.

"You are leaving the crown to your daughter, Coryn?"

Geril shot the blue-skinned selumari an apprehensive look. "No. I would not wish this burden on her. And besides, the council would never accept her. They are a contentious lot, with a few bright exceptions. I was the youngest ruler ever, and she is younger than I was, then—quite a bit so, in fact." He sighed and passed off the sealed document to a page, one of Geril's Hydrak Clan kinsmen named Drommie. "Besides, such a role would kill her spirit. Politics are no place for the adventurous sort… and I just hope she would understand that if the worst comes to pass."

Geril swallowed at the thought of causing his daughter pain. Hopefully she would not think he chose a different successor because of her mishap in Tulgesh. She'd been used by one of Geril's enemies, who stole the hidden Magestorm weapons there and committed several murders, spinning the dwarven citizens into such an uproar that they nearly went to war with their elven hosts.

Taerlon walked abreast of the vaghan king as they exited the broad gates of the once-hidden city. He appeared more visibly comfortable with the rays of Soll's light cascading down from overhead. "Who, then?"

"By our tradition, it cannot be a member of the council." Geril held the sealed parchment. "I am appointing Warlord Kile to the task. I have every faith in him. Truth be told, I could use him in the coming war, but his injuries will take some time to heal."

Geril scanned the vale where a hellish battle had only just recently occurred. Beneath the shadow of the low-hovering sky ship, bodies of fallen dwarves and gwereste, the feral folk, had been stacked in preparation for memorial. Another heap of them, the corpses of the undead soldiers who had come down from the snowy Shadowlands, had been piled and awaited immolation. The priests would ask their matron goddess Firiel to annihilate them in this life and torment them in the next.

"Kile's injuries are physical, but his mental faculties are still sharp. He will serve well as steward," Geril said. "And his reputation will earn him many allies."

Elder Lordan, one of the few council members Geril truly trusted, approached and received the sealed scroll from the page who carried it. "Your succession line?" he asked.

Geril nodded. "Let's hope it does not come to it, but I fear the worst. I tried to keep the Magestorm Cache from falling into evil hands because of this very sort of thing," he said and waved around at the carnage. "But the dark hour has come upon us. I've already spoken with Kile. If something should happen to him as well, the council will decide the best course of action."

Lordan nodded and bowed to follow protocol.

The dwarven king clambered up the hanging rope ladder and onto the sky ship. They had little time to spare if they were to aid the northern kingdom of Icehome against the frozen dead. Balgavarr's frostwing allies would need all the help they could get against such a bitter enemy, and Geril knew he risked overtaxing the coral elf spell casters who summoned winds to propel the ship. He'd promised Taerlon that the furry areosa in Icehome could aid them once they were in range—they, too, could command wind magic. A coral sky ship was the fastest route to helping Queen Rashingot... and if her kingdom of Icehome fell, the buffer between the dwarves, and all the kingdoms south of Balgavarr, would become susceptible to whatever dark forces had driven the bloodless hordes from the Heimdarl Crag and caused them to attack the south.

Ra'al finished speaking with Hennedy, the only other frostwing on the coral airship. Hennedy was about the same age and was a messenger sent by Ra'al's mother, Queen Rashingot. The areosan prince stalked through the ship looking for Coryn, his dwarven best friend.

He and Coryn had practically grown up together, and she was like a little sister to him. Ra'al liked to emphasize the *little*; Coryn was short even for a dwarf, and even more of a spitfire because of it.

With the air bladder inflated overhead, the sky ship had elevated to a hovering distance, which would afford them a clear path through the mountain vales of the Kafnysan Range, despite the craft being short-staffed when it came to selumari casters. Captain Taerlon needed more magicians who could summon the winds from the goddess Ailuril to reach top speeds. But as it was, the ship remained the fastest way to deploy forces to aid their northern allies.

During the siege of Balgavarr, Ra'al's mother had sent Hennedy with the message that Castle Ice was under attack. Geril and the others feared the worst: that the undead's movement against the vagha was a diversion. *Perhaps the same was true for Icehome*, Ra'al wondered. *Maybe all is well and we will arrive to relative serenity? Perhaps the undead had some other prize in mind... or perhaps they were so disjointed that everything they did was totally random?*

Ra'al knew he had a bastard's luck. The army they'd fought only days ago had simply wandered off. But not until after their spies stole the maps that functioned as keys to the secret Mist Stones in the far northern Shadowlands. Undead were not exceptionally fast, but they moved tirelessly—they'd learned that fact from Bastawr, the tigerfolk who they'd sent to track them all the way across the northern tundra after the first map was stolen in Frostshoal. The gwereste had nearly wasted away during the journey.

Balgavarr's forces, paltry as they were, had to leave immediately if they hoped to arrive in Icehome at about the same time as the army they had just repelled from the mountains. A larger force of dwarven troops headed north by the road and would arrive afterward. Ra'al and his company hoped to provide critical information and help Rashingot resist any undead. They'd fought these fiends before and knew they could not be destroyed by conventional means.

Ra'al scanned the deck of the ship again, searching for Coryn. He did not spot her, but he did note that a selumari rolled a rope ladder over the side and Coryn's father, Geril sa'Ghuren, clambered up it. He was the final passenger to board.

Coryn must be here, somewhere. I know she'd hate to miss watching the launch, Ra'al thought, walking the length of the craft. He found Garesch, the morehl prince, standing alongside Marnash, his adviser and the small cluster of red-skinned lava elves. A long-standing enemy of nearly every other species aboard, they looked somewhat uncomfortable standing on the shifting deck boards of their newfound allies.

"Garesch, is Coryn with you?" Ra'al asked.

He shook his head. "No, but I believe I saw her a few minutes ago. I know she is aboard."

Ra'al turned and nearly bumped into Bastawr.

"You are looking for Coryn?" the gwereste asked. "I can help you find her." A fugitive could hide on ten square leagues and the tigerfolk could find him.

Ra'al followed Bastawr, who sniffed the air and walked below decks. The tigerfolk sniffed around and walked through the ship's interior. "Her smell is stronger here."

"Yes. She was exploring the ship while I spoke with Hennedy. He said my mother seemed agitated when she had dispatched him to Tulgesh... she is normally high strung, but this was different. Queen Rashingot knew that the gathering undead in the Shadowlands was more than a rumor. She told me as much before throwing me into our now moot diplomatic mission."

"Then let us hope we arrive with the blessing of Ailuril," Bastawr said optimistically. He stopped. "The trail ends here."

Ra'al looked around. "Well, where is she?" He stubbed his toe on something metallic, which skittered across the floor. Wincing, he called out, "Coryn? Coryn, where are you?"

"She does like to play jokes," Bastawr said. "Maybe she is hiding from you?"

"Could she hide from your nose, Bastawr?"

The tigerfolk grimaced and shook his head.

Ra'al's gut sank when he bent to retrieve what he'd struck with his foot. It was the gnomish toy that Coryn had claimed from the cache of Magestorm weapons hidden beneath Tulgesh. She'd carried the golden cube of interlocking plates with her ever since, fiddling with it in hopes of learning its mysteries.

He took one more look around and his worry only grew. Ra'al asked aloud, "Where is that girl?"

Coryn squinted at her surroundings. They were bright, but she understood that the light did not come from daylight. It was much brighter than below decks on Taerlon's coral airship.

Whatever she'd taken from the Magestorm cache, it had been no gnomish toy. Once she'd managed to activate it, the thing created some kind of circle made out of pure lightning which had opened and closed like the blinking of an eye, sucking her in with it. She dusted herself off and cursed. "Damned gremmlobahnd."

She panicked momentarily, seeing no way out of whatever prison had ensnared her and fearing the puzzle cube may have been some kind of trap for the gnome's enemies. The other races of Esfah knew precious little of the gremmlobahnd, and a little knowledge right now would have gone a long way.

"Not that I'm much for studying in books," Coryn grumbled to herself, realizing scholars could have opined for generations, but she wouldn't have possessed any helpful knowledge, anyway. Her voice echoed off the smooth geometric walls of her prison; they formed a triangle of sorts. The side walls looked like mirrors and the floors looked like a kind of burnished metal. They felt solid beneath her clomping steel boots.

Coryn's breath caught when she saw what waited in the far, narrow end of the compartment. A clear pane of crystal contained what appeared to be a dragon. *No,* thought the dwarf, *not a dragon. Perhaps a drakufreet, one of the dragonkin? But this one is massive, a champion size at least. It's definitely a sukie.* She recognized that it had wings making it the suchia type.

"What's wrong with your color?" she asked it. If such a term could be used for a living creature, it looked... *new.* Like an oil coated blade fresh from the forge. The thing's scales looked more like polished gold leaf than the yellow and ochres of natural dragonkin.

She approached the holding pen and realized that the beast was awake... and aware of her. The creature's keen eyes followed her intently as she approached the singular plinth projecting upward in front of its cell.

Coryn touched the post bearing an engraved plate with a word written in several languages. In the common tongue, it read *Euhysaurom.*

"Do you know how to get out of here, Yoo-ee?" she sounded out the first part of his name. The thing gave a kind of growling squawk, as if it were just awakening to find the pint-sized intruder. She rested a hand on the post, and an apparition projected from it.

Yoo-ee's eyes widened as the astral figure of a gnome appeared like a ghostly light. It spoke in some unknown tongue which Coryn could not understand. The flickering thing stared directly at her, awaiting an answer to its question.

"I… I don't know what you want. I'm lost. How do I…" the gnomish light flickered out of existence and disappeared. Coryn waited several minutes, but nothing happened.

She touched the plinth again, and the creature returned. It followed the same pattern as before, asking the same question. Coryn realized it wasn't real; it was some kind of magical image projection, much like her father's wizard friend, Sheron, was adept at creating.

Coryn hissed another couple of curses after spending several minutes unable to locate a switch or mechanism to any door that would release her from this gnomish time-out chamber. She turned and kicked the glass wall with her metal boot. It rippled and hummed and she suddenly realized that whatever lay beyond it might be worse than her current condition. For all she knew, she could have been teleported onto the floor of the cursed Mertrician Troika, where the Autumn and Mertide Seas conjoined.

She paced a few steps, locking eyes with the great golden beast, and felt as if something *else* watched her. A shiver went up her spine, but it was not the massive, draconic creature whose eyes she felt on her. Yoo-ee's gaze felt more like a puppy watching its master. What she felt was something intelligent—and it was beyond the reflective walls.

Coryn placed her hand against the glass where the monstrous mount waited. "Do you want out of there, Yoo-ee? As soon as I find the durned door, I'll get you out." She turned a loop, hackles still raised. "But I've got to get *me* out of here first."

CHAPTER ONE

"Two days," griped Taerlon. The selumari captain was not happy about his craft's speed. "It was supposed to take us two days to get from Balgavarr to Icehome." He shook his head at the coral elf magician who stood on the forecastle with him. "It took us barely more than a day to get to the Kafnysan Mountains from Tulgesh *and that's twice as far...*"

"With so many of our casters wounded or dead," the magi mumbled defensively, "I suspected it would have been worse than this."

"Don't think me critical of your performance," the captain said, putting a hand on the magi's shoulder. "I know you're doing your best."

"Without the bladder, *Aguarehl's Envy* will fall from the sky," he confirmed, looking above at the balloon-like sack that helped keep the craft airborne.

Taerlon bit his lip. "It certainly might be easier if these panicking vagha hadn't torn the ship apart in search of one missing dwarf princess." He sighed. "But I know I'd do the same for my own daughter, were she lost."

They hadn't been traveling for more than an hour when the news surfaced about Coryn sa'Geril's disappearance. Oddly enough, Geril seemed to take the news in far greater stride than the rest of his company. It was mostly the vaghan warriors and Coryn's other adventuring companions who had practically torn the ship down to deck boards in search of her.

Geril had nodded approvingly, though with reluctance, when Taerlon ordered his crew to continue north with all due haste—with or without Coryn. They could not waste a minute more. The areosa of Icehome might need more of them than the airship could provide.

Two humans assembled a device made of tube and lenses. They had answered the war call of the gwereste and Taerlon thought they might provide only little service away from their chariots, but they proved themselves talented in many other areas. "We use these when scouting long distances," one human explained. "From the vantage of a ship, I expect they may be even more effective."

Taerlon looked through and blinked. "It's a scrying device? Like a long-look?"

The human nodded and left him to play with the adjustments to focus on the target. Taerlon gasped and then spoke aloud to the caster nearest him without pulling back from the lens. "The vision is murky, but I can make out the outline of Castle Ice. It is surrounded by black amorphous shapes like a cancer."

"It is the undead."

Geril's husky voice startled the captain. "Er, yes. And we should meet them by the morning."

"Then it is as we feared," Geril said, taking a step closer to use the apparatus. Taerlon motioned him to utilize it and traded places with him.

"The castle is surrounded, I think," Taerlon reported.

Geril squinted. "Most areosa have wings. They're *never* surrounded," he said. "But they won't retreat, either. It's not their way. Frostwings are tough. Hardy. Stubborn. They're also loyal, and Queen Rashingot takes seriously her people's duty as protectors of the north. She knows if something dark exists in the Shadowlands, it is her job to kill it before it can get south."

"And what about when it's already dead?" Taerlon asked.

Geril shot him a look. "Apparently you've never met Rashingot. She'll kill 'em again. And again, if necessary. Frostwings are formidable—there's a reason the faeli decided to encroach on the morehl's southern borders rather than come back and attack their old enemy, the areosa."

Taerlon cocked his head. "Then why such haste?"

"I said they were tough. Not invincible. And there are *a lot* of bloodless down there."

The captain remembered that Geril had risen to initial fame by defending Balgavarr Reaches from its myriad enemies... but at the cost of his best friend, Thrag, the frostwing king and father of a pup named Ra'al. The dwarf's bond with their neighbors was more than duty; they'd become family to him.

"Thrag is... gone." Geril said in a moment of fresh, honest pain. "Ghuren, my father, too. Coryn's mother as well. She died while I was gone... away on Council business. My last words to her were that I would be back soon. But she had passed before I got back." He turned and looked at Taerlon. "We *will* come to Rashingot's aid. I will not allow her to become the next person I've pledged to help and who dies because I showed up too late."

Taerlon held his gaze and nodded. "Well, then. Let us hope that we can help her... and that our efforts don't get *us* killed in the process."

Someone cried from behind them on the poop deck. "Incoming at the rear!"

Taerlon turned and searched the sky for his crewman's alert. His eyes locked on something in the distance.

"What is it?" Geril asked.

"Eagles."

Three eagles swooped toward *Aguarehl's Envy* with great speed. Two of them bore riders, while the third mount was empty. One by one, they alighted on the ship's rear and the two messengers dismounted, calling for Captain Taerlon.

Taerlon and Geril met the two selumari who claimed they'd been dispatched by King Matrek in Tulgesh. "Don't tell me there's an attack on Tulgesh, too," Geril grumbled. "We can't afford to send aid south—there ain't enough dwarves left at this point. If the undead have reached so far south…"

"Thankfully, no," said the scout. "At least, it's not the undead causing trouble back home." He shot his fellow rider a knowing look, which Geril understood: following a murder at the vaghan embassy, the local dwarves had risen up and caused more than a few riots.

"You have a message from the king, then?" Taerlon asked.

The scout nodded. "We were sent with a spare bird and told to retrieve Geril sa'Ghuren. Matrek has information which is only for the ears of the ruler of Balgavarr."

"There's no time for that now," Geril spat. "If Matrek wants me, he can bloody well get on his own damned bird and come to fetch me himself." Geril and Matrek had gone many rounds fighting both together and sometimes against each other. Even when they agreed, they often disagreed. They'd fallen out greatly over the usage of the arcane Magestorm weapons. Years after Geril thought Matrek had disposed of them, he'd agreed to provide part of those spoils to the selumari kingdom… provided they could be reclaimed from the traitor who stole them.

The scout shrugged. "He only told us that it pertained to Ki'Harol sa'Lahmyn."

Geril bristled at the name. The dwarven traitor. Harol, the son of a power-hungry elder on Balgavarr's council, had been the one to unearth and steal the Magestorm cache. He was a known acolyte—a worshiper of only one god—but that chosen god was Death—the one with the unspeakable, cursed name. Harol was a cultist and a murderer who'd been exiled from the dwarven kingdom long ago. Geril had sworn to end Harol's bloody reign of terror… just as soon as Icehome was saved.

"Matrek and Harol will have to wait," Geril said, his muscles tightening at the prospect of battle. "Icehome is already under siege and we are at the battlefront's doorstep."

The messengers looked at each other, hands sliding slowly to their belts and sheathed blades. "We were given orders, sir, not options."

Taerlon stayed the scouts. "Hold, men. I am always the first one to follow orders. And you can scarcely know how much I miss Tulgesh. My wife and children are there, but this bloodless cancer must be stopped here and now. There must be some secondary option. I'll not turn the ship around."

A scout shook his head. "Matrek was unsure *Aguarehl's Envy* would even remain operational. That is why we brought an additional bird, but the king claimed you would turn the ship back to Tulgesh at his command."

"I *would*, except I need the promised help of the areosa in order to make such a return. How many selumari do you see working the wind magics that drive this craft? Far too few, that's for certain! Without frostwing help, we cannot make it back."

Geril stroked his beard. "I'll make ye boys a deal. One of you can return and report to Matrek that I am on my way and that we'll return his ship post-haste as soon as it is able. But I'm going to arrive in Icehome first and drive these bloodless bastards back into their graves. I can give ye my word that I'll head to Tulgesh via a Path spell directly after Castle Ice is liberated," he said, referencing the spell that only casters of Earth-based magic could perform. It was functionally a teleportation spell, but with limitations that failed to affect a teleporter. "I might even beat you there," Geril continued, "and if I die in the battle, then the other one of you can use that durned bird and bring him my body. Matrek can tell my corpse all about Harol."

The scouts looked at each other and then at Taerlon, who appeared set in agreement with the dwarven ruler. They reluctantly nodded. "We have your word?" asked one as he mounted to return south with the message.

"*Rashingot* has my word," Geril stated. "And I intend to keep it. You have the assurance of my ever-burning hatred for Harol sa'Lahmyn. I *will* end that dwarf. And if Matrek has information that will lead me to him, you can be damned sure that I will seek him out directly… just as soon I secure Thrag's house."

That was good enough for the king's messenger. He mounted an eagle and nudged his bird forward and into the air.

Taerlon pointed the remaining coral elf toward the small pool of his species working their diminished magic together. "Meanwhile, you can join the rest in summoning the winds as best as you're able."

"I'm no caster," he argued.

Taerlon glared at him. "Everyone works. You're selumari, and that means you're a child of Ailuril. You'll have at least some draw on the spirits of the air. Now get to work."

Avaryth stumbled and collapsed. After the pirate's captors dragged him for nearly half a league, the death knight in charge of the dread parade shouted for a halt. With glowing crimson eyes, the skeletal warrior glared balefully at the exhausted human.

Shrill winds whipped as they gathered speed and shot across the wastes of the Shadowlands. They spun up snowy eddies that shimmered with a life all their own before dissipating and settling into distant drifts.

With a voice like grave dust, the creature leading the undead procession howled to the bloodless minions who followed him. "The prize must recuperate. He is weak. We shall wait for him."

"Yes, mighty Rorduk," several of the minions hissed.

Avaryth scooped a limp handful of windswept snow into his mouth to try and hydrate, but he paid a keen eye to their activities. One by one, the bloodless showed the items that they carried to Rorduk, who appeared to be some kind of undead general.

Finally, one of the minions carried something that caught his eye. Rorduk snatched an ornate blade with an equally gaudy hilt and quillons that were shaped like wings. Some kind of precious metal inlaid the sheath. The pommel, an ebon gem, sparkled, and the handle appeared to be made of some kind of ivory or bone. Though the ancient fabric that once wrapped its handle had long since moldered to scrap.

"This! Now this is one of the mighty blades that our lord has sought. It shall make a fine gift for the mighty Leisterbane." Rorduk looked around as if getting his bearings, or perhaps he heard the ethereal call of his master. "We have gathered all that our lord requires. The red traitor bears the maps to the stones. We must hurry to meet our lord at the Crag."

A skeleton yanked Avaryth to his feet. The pirate bartered for time. "I am still too weak to walk. I must rest."

Rorduk stared at him for a few moments as if weighing the man's words. He snatched a rolled carpet from a nearby minion and then flung it out before him. The carpet splayed out in the air and then fell to the ground. It stopped in mid-air, levitating at waist height. "Bind his legs, too. And gag him," Rorduk ordered.

The undead forces did as commanded and then threw their prisoner atop the floating platform. A few moments later, the bloodless were again on the move, the flying carpet carrying Avaryth along with them.

"We're picking up speed," Taerlon told Geril. He recognized Geril's inquisitive look. "I can feel it," the captain said.

Geril hunched over a drawing table where they'd sketched the layout of Icehome from what they'd seen in the long-look. "Natural air currents picking up? Or maybe that selumari messenger brought enough freshness with him to summon additional winds?"

"A little of both, I suspect," Taerlon stated. "And Ra'al, Bastawr, and Hennedy also joined the mages shortly before we came inside to discuss battle plans. I think they finally realized there were more productive things to do than fret over your daughter's disappearance."

Hearing his own voice in his pointed ears, Taerlon regretted his words, fearing Geril would take offense. He hadn't meant for it to sound callous, but they were entering a life or death engagement at any moment.

Geril kept his face neutral. "She's a big girl. I'm sure she's fine… wherever she is."

Taerlon sighed with relief, but still asked, "You're not worried at all?" His tone was fatherly and genuine, as if wondering how Geril could remain composed.

The dwarf kept his eyes on the map they'd drawn up and placed tokens on the table representing the hordes of undead. "Her fate is in the gods' hands now. I can't likely do anything to affect the outcome. And worrying over it at a time like this scarcely seems productive. Besides, whatever she's gotten up to, she's likely to make the best possible choice. She gets that drive from me—both to get up to trouble, *that's what we dwarves call adventuring,* and to do right whenever possible. That knowledge helps me focus on the battle at hand." He motioned to the table.

Taerlon cleared his throat and shifted his attention to the map. He wished for a slice of Geril's confidence in the gods and a positive outcome, even if the elf sensed that some of it was false bravado.

The captain added a few more pieces to the table as Geril identified what resources he knew the frostwings possessed at Castle Ice. Artisans from Balgavarr had helped build the fortress and vagha were notorious for adding secret access hatches and tunnels to projects just in case they ever had need of them. Geril knew of many, but at least one of them he knew about had to remain a secret, even from Taerlon. Not that it mattered; they would have had to be underground to use it, anyway.

A few minutes into studying the map, they realized they had few options. "We'll need to attack from the air as much as possible," Geril said. "Keep the high ground. There's more good we can do from here than is possible from the ground."

"But isn't there a great value in preserving the castle?" Taerlon asked.

"If we can manage it, but the people are the highest priority," Geril said.

"There we agree," said the captain. "But if Icehome falls, then Queen Rashingot will no longer hold power. She will have failed in her duty as protector of the northern region. That doesn't strike me as something she will allow."

Geril scratched his bearded chin. "No, I suppose not. Icehome has stood as a safe haven and capital of the areosa ever since they escaped the Death god's thrall thousands of years ago. I don't think she'll let it go as long as she still lives."

Taerlon moved a model airship across the field and into the fortress. "I think our best move is to gain access to the capital and figure out Rashingot's game plan first, provided it's not too late to be helpful. There are any number of options that open once an airship is in the mix. If nothing else, certainly the morale boost of Ra'al's return could have a significant impact."

After a few moments, Geril agreed. "But we can at least rain down some hell as we pass by."

"As much as possible." Taerlon grinned. "Of course, since most of the frostwings can fly, I assume they've got some kind of plan to deal with—"

Yelling from the deck interrupted him. Geril hurried out the door before the captain could finish.

Ra'al slashed at the air with his axe and roared, snorting loudly. "They are here," he snarled.

The crew and passengers above the deck hurried away from him, watching the winged prince flail with his weapon as if he'd lost his mind, batting at invisible things. They chirped with concern as Ra'al reached out a hand and formed an ice lance as long as his wingspan and took aim at the selumari magicians on the far side of the ship.

Ra'al hurled the spear with deadly force and it impacted something unseeable. The ice exploded into frozen shards and the invisible fiend burst apart in a flash of violet light.

"I smell them," Ra'al insisted. "There is death all around."

Sheron, an accomplished mage and member of Geril's entourage, took the prince by the arm. "I believe you. You have the sense for it. It's a blessing and a curse if you've not been trained in magic. Sit with me; perhaps we can dispel the invisibility together."

"Yes, he has a gift," said Marnash, who cast another kind of magic altogether, sharing one step of alignment between both of them.

Ra'al calmed himself and sat with the old dwarf and lava elf. They were aligned to different kinds of elements, for sure, but they were not casting magic. They were instead trying to open the others' eyes to a nature that Ra'al and a few gifted others could see.

As the frostwing warrior sat on his haunches, Garesch approached Taerlon and Geril. The lava elf leaned in close. "We made good time, given the conditions. I can see Icehome from the bow."

The captain and Geril strode up to the front of the vessel and stared off the front. Black masses of writhing bodies stretched in huge swaths across the white landscape. They'd formed legions around the frozen city, surrounding it with a total siege. Why the frostwings hadn't fled via the sky was anyone's guess.

Behind them, Ra'al suddenly roared as whatever ritual Sheron walked him through seemed to spread from him and to the rest of those aboard the ship. As if some mystic veil had been lifted, the rest of the crew could now see what Ra'al had sensed. Shimmering green apparitions soared through the sky, roaming to and fro and latching onto any being in the nearby sky to siphon the life forces off them.

Three men aboard the ship stood stiff, in the throes of being sucked dry by ethereal wraiths. Those nearby cried out and began attacking the undead, spectral creatures. The bloodless, surprised that they were discovered, burst apart with ectoplasmic light.

Other flying undead that patrolled the skies of the Shadowlands turned when they saw their companions suffer destruction. A wave of them shifted and angled for the airship like a tidal force, plunging toward *Aguarehl's Envy* like moths to a flame.

Taerlon gulped. "Quickly! Deploy the air fins and cut the air bladder! Employ falling maneuvers! We've got to beat these foul creatures to Castle Ice."

CHAPTER TWO

Dwarven Elder Fi'Lordan sa'Vibrahn stared at the body of a murder victim deep in the heart of Balgavarr Reaches. The victim's back lay exposed to the air with a ragged, circular wound that had blasted clean through the ribs and spine from the other side.

Lordan's lips curled with rage, mostly masked by his bushy beard. Balgavarr was often at risk from outside invaders, *but this?* This had been a cold-blooded murder… someone with access to the interior of the mountainous city had done this thing.

Members of an investigative team of enforcers combed through the dwarf's home. The victim had been moderately wealthy, at least, and his home was in disarray, as if there had been a struggle, but none of the valuables had been taken.

Lordan glared at a decorative family crest on the wall and his heart sank. The victim was a member of house Kiyh, Geril's primary political enemies on the council. Their clan was one of Balgavarr's oldest families and had long-since cornered a successful industry collecting the heavy leaves from the ironwood trees and refining them to harvest their metals.

House Kiyh had tried to wrest control of Balgavarr from Geril on more than one occasion and Lordan felt in his gut that this period of war was perhaps the most opportune moment for an attack on the Kafnysan towns, Balgavarr chief among them.

Detective Perdy, a dwarf perhaps a decade younger than Geril, rolled the body over. Lordan knew Perdy's reputation and trusted him as a neutral party.

"Yup. It's Harahsus alright," Perdy sighed.

Lordan frowned. He looked up and spotted Elder Lahmyn just exiting the home after giving a statement to investigators on behalf of Harahsus's relations, the Kiyh Clan.

Perdy continued thinking aloud and jotting notes in a tablet. "Looks like he's been dead for quite some time. I'd estimate since shortly before the undead's recent attack on the city. Maybe a day or two before."

Lordan moved closer and joined the detective. "What does that mean, Detective?"

Perdy lay the victim back down in his original repose. "I think the timing of it all provided someone with an opportunity. In all the hubbub preparing for the invasion, someone used the chaos to cover their tracks." He stared at the hole where the flesh had been torn away. "But what kind of weapon makes this kind of wound?"

A voice called out across the room, where junior investigators looked for clues. "I got something, Perdy." A dwarf stood from where he'd searched the nearby furniture and he held aloft a unique weapon: a morehl flintlock pistol.

Perdy took the weapon and analyzed it. Lordan, being far older, recognized it immediately from his studies of history. It was no ordinary version of the weapon. "You know what this is?" the detective asked.

Lordan nodded. "We all know. Until recently, the morehl of Uruzak have been our chief enemies."

Perdy turned the flintlock over in his hands and sniffed it. The pistol was gilded and ornate, far prettier than the utilitarian version of the weapons normal soldiers might carry. "It doesn't smell like gunpowder." His eyes widened when the clues came together in his mind. He almost dropped it when he realized what he carried. "It's one of those Karaktoan flintlocks!"

Lordan's lips stretched thin. "Aye," he said, hoping the detective wouldn't have arrived at that conclusion quite so soon. Now extremely rare, the flintlocks were made in the faraway forges of Karakto, which operated by magical means. They did not need to be reloaded with powder and shot. They simply worked, firing cursed bullets at will. So rare were they, that they were hoarded by the obscenely wealthy and had become a traditional gift of royalty, often passing from lava elf ruler to ruler. "May I? I am something of an amateur historian."

The detective nodded and turned the weapon over to Lordan. Perdy flipped through his notes as Lordan examined the gun's markings. Its barrel bore an inscription written in gnomish. As far as Lordan knew, only a few on all of Cyrea could interpret the ancient, dead language.

Perdy nodded. "I think I've got a solid lead."

Lordan beckoned for a leaf of paper and a charcoal stylus. He made a rubbing of the barrel's inscription before returning the weapon. The councilman recognized the one word inscribed in the common tongue: Hirthak, the name of one of the champions of the first age. "Who is your suspect?"

"I think it evident," Perdy said. "It is fairly well attested to that Coryn sa'Geril and Ra'al sa'Thrag had an altercation with Harahsus shortly before the bloodless attacked." He checked his notes again. "Apparently she threatened that 'her pet frostwing might eat him.'"

Lordan scoffed. "Surely you don't suspect Coryn or the frostwing prince over a mere jest. And most folk know that the areosa don't eat dwarves…"

"Oh, I know that," Perdy said. "But I also know who the members of Coryn's company are." He didn't need to state the obvious: Garesch, a morehl who traveled with Coryn and her company, was a lava elf prince. "Coryn's family has a long-standing grudge against house Kiyh, and vice versa." Perdy raked a hand through his whiskers. Kiyh was well known for their many political stunts through the course of that same feud, but to entertain the idea that one of Lahmyn's clan could have murdered one of their own for political gain was unthinkable—only Harol, the Kiyh clan's Death worshiper, could have been so evil, and he'd been excommunicated and banned from the city for decades.

"I'll bring my findings to the council soon," Perdy promised.

Lordan thanked him and then departed, wondering exactly what Lahmyn had told the investigators earlier. One thing he knew was certain, having met Garesch and fought alongside him in the recent battle, he knew such a person was no murderer... and having known many members of House Kiyh, they would twist this into a narrative meant to grow their political influence during a sensitive time for the city.

Returning to his home, Lordan sent a summons to a nephew he trusted. Vibrahn arrived shortly after Lordan finished his letter and sealed it with his signet stamp.

"I need you to take the fastest pony still left in Balgavarr," Lordan said. "Rent it. Buy it. I don't care; send me the bill and I'll see it paid, but I need you to put this message into Coryn sa'Geril's hand. Barring that, Geril sa'Ghuren will also do. It's a matter of utmost importance and secrecy."

Vibrahn bowed and accepted the letter. "I'll see it done, Uncle." He stashed the letter in his satchel, turned, and then departed.

Lordan watched him go and then spoke to the air, hoping the spirits and the gods might hear him and take notice. "Something stinks in Balgavarr, and I fear the worst for Geril and his daughter. Moreover, this evil couldn't have come at a worse time."

Sky sailors manning *Aguarehl's Envy* scrambled up the rope ladders and split a line of seams on the air bladder. Others flared the fins on the side of the coral airship's hull. Hundreds of the floating spirits rushed to the ship, but it angled toward the ground, rapidly losing altitude.

"All summoners," Taerlon howled, "I know you're tired—but don't let us crash!"

The blue-skinned elves who'd pushed them thus far blanched. Like runners hitting a wall, they had to push beyond their limits or they'd all wind up little more than wrecked scree cast upon the wastelands surrounding Icehome.

Moments before the apparitions reached them, the balloon above *Aguarehl's Envy* lost its buoyancy and the craft slid toward the ground in a free fall. Rapidly increasing speed, the craft cut through the air as it approached its terminal velocity.

Air cushions caught on the ship's fins much like the patagial membranes that formed ridges around the wingless wyrm dragons, giving them the ability of limited flight and resembled gliding. *Aguarehl's Envy* careened over the heads of the gathered, bloodless armies. Legions of bleached bone troops turned their head to watch Rashingot's reinforcements.

Passengers aboard the craft howled in terror. They clung to the rails and each other, fearful for their lives. Ahead of them, the central doors to Icehome had been overrun. Frostwings had barricaded them from within by freezing a layer of ice into a bastion wall behind them, meaning the undead couldn't even attempt to ram through.

Not to be outdone, the bloodless had pushed snow and debris against the outer walls and built a frozen ramp that sloped upwards and flushed to the edge. The fiends rushed upon it and hurled themselves over, overtaking the perimeter's curtain wall and forcing the frostwings back.

Aguarehl's Envy careened toward the interior of the city with a cloud of ghostly demons in pursuit. Taerlon piloted the vessel around a tower jutting up from Castle Ice and areosan mages, who wore ornate accoutrements and bright colors, before he spotted the enemy. They summoned a gale-force wind. The gust blasted through the creatures like fist through confetti, scattering them randomly.

Ra'al's voice called out, "Mother! Queen Rashingot, she is there!" He pointed.

A fighting force at the ground held back a wave of undead enemies. Frostwings held a hard line against the swarming masses, creating a kind of corridor for the weaker areosa to evacuate from the outer sections of the city. With the invisible threats, they could not escape, but they could flee deeper into the next layer. An interior wall still stood and within that, Castle Ice provided another zone to fall back within. Below the fortress lay one more retreat: a cavern where the original Icehome had existed when Ra'al was still just a newborn kit.

Selumari sorcerers groaned as they stretched themselves far beyond their capacity. They'd nearly burned themselves out with fatigue as Taerlon whipped *Aguarehl's Envy* around in a tight arc and brought it into a low hover directly above the heads of the bloodless as near to Rashingot as he dared.

Ra'al had already flung himself over the side and flew to his mother's aid.

Finally, the mages gave out and *Aguarehl's Envy* crashed down upon a horde of undead, crushing them utterly. Geril, Garesch, Bastawr and all the rest of the soldiers aboard surged out from the craft, hacking through the undead and separating heads from shoulders. They had discovered it was the best way to put down the fiends and keep them from reanimating. So long as the spot of necralluvium near the base of the skull remained intact, the bodies would eventually pull themselves back together upon inky black tendrils of death magic.

With Hennedy following directly on his tail, Ra'al glided over the top of the invaders and angled directly for Rashingot. Her closest guards had fallen to rusty, ancient blades clutched by soulless bodies long since dead. A cluster of them bore down upon the queen, who refused to yield the line and surrender the last group of refugees who scurried behind the protectors.

Rashingot hacked apart the skeletons nearby, but a mummified corpse evaded her blade with unsuspected skill and he thrust a blade into the areosan queen. The armor she wore at her chest bent the sword to one side, but the weapon found a seam and slid into her flesh. She roared with pain as blood spurted from the wound. Ra'al roared louder yet, though he was still too far away to help.

The nearest skeletons and several revenants, skeletal creatures whose flesh still clung to bone, grew in knots around Rashingot. Some joined the fray and others waited while reassembling. Ra'al summoned a hail of jagged ice lances from the sky and rained them down upon his enemy with practiced precision. The jagged spears pinned the desiccated bodies to the ground, allowing Rashingot time to recoil and catch her breath.

Ra'al and Hennedy dropped down upon the fiends before they could pull themselves free and hacked their heads clean off with sharpened axes. Hennedy beat back the nearest bloodless while Ra'al checked on his mother. He summoned a patch of ice to seal the wound on her chest until a healer could take a look at it.

"My son, you have returned," Rashingot said with a pained breath. "You... you have found the song of the wind?"

Ra'al inclined his head slightly. His greatest shame had been the sling of javelins he had formerly carried. Until days ago, he'd been unable to use the magic of their people, or even summon ice lances from the northern air as the youngest warriors were able.

"Yes, and I am here, mother."

Rashingot looked up as the dwarves fanned out from the fallen sky ferry. A force of them pushed their way forward. At their forefront, a dozen lava elves cut through the bloodless. "And your diplomatic mission was a success, then, too?"

Ra'al nodded, but gave her an askew look. "Your mission was never about forging diplomatic ties. Let's be honest now."

Too weary to mask her true thoughts, she flashed him a sheepish look. The mission had always been a thinly veiled attempt to force him out of the comforts of the castle and in search of what he lacked: a necessary trait for the next leader of Icehome. To follow in King Thrag's wind wake, Ra'al needed to hear the song of the wind for what it was. It was not a simple howl of nature—it was a divine calling that tied their people to the goddess Ailuril.

The last of the populace made it through the passage and into the interior curtain wall of the city with the support of Balgavarr's troops. "I see Geril, but where is Coryn?" Rashingot asked Ra'al. A hint of worry crept into her voice.

Ra'al helped bear some of his mother's weight and escorted her to the interior layer of Icehome. "That, I'm afraid, is a long story and I don't think anyone present truly has an answer."

Lordan paused near Elder Dusut, who he spotted in Balgavarr's general market. A dour mood had fallen like a pall across the great hall where most trade happened inside the Reaches.

Most elders knew where each other stood on a variety of issues, as was common for politics. But Dusut was one of the better known swing votes. His clan was not particularly beholden to any viewpoint.

The vagha stood near a ring of gossipers who listened to one of the lower casted members of Lahmyn's house. Lordan paused and heard the dwarf tell outright falsehoods.

"…saw it with me own eyes," the liar said. "Harahsus was murdered in his own home by the morehl prince. Did'in I tell ya they couldn't be trusted? And who brought 'em in here but members of Geril's household," he continued, stirring the pot. "This falls squarely at the feet of the Hydrak clan."

Some dwarves grumbled; others waved him off as crazy. His reputation was known, though few would remember the source of the rumor in a few days' time.

"Ask anybody from the investigation," the crier insisted. "'Twas a Karaktoan flintlock that done him in—the rare kind that only a wealthy or princely lava elf could afford. Hole the size of me fist coming out his backside, it did. One could almost think that those wicked elves brought the bloodless down on our heads just so they'd have access to the city and to poor old Harahsus."

That speculation was so wild that most of the crowd laughed and chalked the declaration up to wild-haired conspiracy. But it felt like a calculated move. While the undead's command by the morehl was a wild leap, it only reinforced the first point. The jump in logic validated everything up until that crazy assertion.

Dusut backed away and bumped into Lordan. "Oh. Pardon me, Elder Lordan."

Lordan walked alongside his peer for a short distance. "Do you really think that Prince Garesch could have engineered such a murder?" he asked. "It seems a futile venture. He and his people stand to gain so much more by adhering to the peace accords Garesch agreed to when the Council met with him in chambers… that is, provided he can wrest control of Uruzak away from his father as he claimed he could."

Dusut stroked his beard. "I dunno," he said. "It seems this is all the folk are talking about right now. And I say, let 'em talk; they need the distraction from all the death and loss we just suffered barely a tenday ago."

"But it's simply not true," Lordan said.

"Isn't it?" Dusut looked at Lordan skeptically. "I received a briefing just this morning. While that dwarf obviously embellished the account, Harahsus certainly *was* killed by a flintlock and the timeline fit their speculation. None had seen Harahsus since Coryn and her companions returned home shortly before the invasion."

Lordan tightened his jaw. "I'm well aware of that, of course. But I refuse to jump to such a conclusion."

Dusut shrugged. "I'd like to wait for proof as well, but public opinion is a powerful thing, my friend, and you might be in a minority position. It is certainly an easy thing to believe that the lava elves might assassinate an isolated vagha when all we've ever known from them has been bloodshed, heartbreak, and conflict."

"That's not all," Lordan said, trying to bring up Garesch's efforts to stave off the undead.

"No. Perhaps not. But I think scant few will remember small efforts of kindness among such a historical tide of rage." Dusut tapped him on the arm as a way of saying goodbye. "I shall see you when the council next convenes.

Lordan watched him go and cursed under his breath. Things had quickly worsened, and a bitter seed took root in his gut. He knew Lahmyn was a master of swinging public opinion, and without Geril here to interfere, he could foresee these anti-morehl sentiments quickly growing out of control in Balgavarr. It threatened all the diplomatic efforts Coryn had recently engineered, and the peace they'd brokered for a future with Uruzak could be undone in a matter of days.

Ra'al stood by his mother's side as the wounded frostwing queen spoke with Geril.

"It will take several days for additional support to arrive from Balgavarr," Geril said. "But I fear that even they won't be enough to punch through the line, now that I've seen the scope of the undead forces. We're better prepared now than when they attacked us in the mountain—but even having a few days to get better equipped, we could scarcely imagine the size of it."

Rashingot nodded measuredly. "Neither could I. It is almost as if they've been amassing this secret army in the Shadowlands for many hundred years."

"Bastawr sent a few of his kind searching for more troops in the Wilds of Dur'Sona. A few amazon nomads went with him, but I fear that will barely scratch the surface." Geril stroked his beard. "We may need to consider additional plans rather than a straight fight."

She looked at him curiously. "I too have sent out signals to the other areosa living in communities abroad. But tell me what you mean, Geril." The glare Rashingot fixed on him would have made a lesser dwarf whither.

"I know you have a vast network of spies, Rashingot. I'm sure you know what I mean."

"I do not," Ra'al said.

Geril sighed. He'd always been a doting uncle figure to the frostwing prince. He hated to admit unpleasant truths. "I know you've heard rumors in the past of a dwarven contingency plan for Icehome."

The queen's unrelenting gaze did not waver. Neither did Ra'al's, and so, Geril continued.

"It was not my choice, but it was partly how I got Balgavarr's council on board with the reconstruction efforts in Icehome. We built a failsafe into the sub-structures below the city, inside the ancient tunnels of Old Icehome. Hidden behind rock curtains that only vagha could find are a series of explosives that could bring down the entire city, incinerating everything in the old caverns and collapsing Icehome in upon itself."

Rashingot bared her teeth. "So, the vagha always assumed the areosa would betray them?"

Geril held his hands up. "Not I. You know as much, but the council swore me to secrecy. And you know I would never allow such destruction—my daughter lived more than half her life here," he insisted.

That admission calmed Rashingot's ire. She snorted her disapproval, but let her rage ebb. "I assume you also built secret tunnels to escape by, much as your builders did when they helped the reconstruction in Tulgesh?"

Geril bit his lip and nodded. "Nobody will ever accuse the Kafnysan clans of a lack of foresight." He shook away the fact that he'd just admitted to a dwarven plan of genocidal attacks against the frostwings if they ever betrayed their allies. He quickly got to the point. "If it comes to it, we can send the people into the old caverns. There are enough vagha that we can guide them to safety while the army lures the undead in after us. While the people of Icehome escape to freedom, we can detonate the bombs and destroy the army. I'd expect we could bury at least ninety percent of them in one fell swoop... but at the cost of Icehome."

Rashingot and Ra'al looked at each other. They conferred a few moments in their native hooting and growling language. It was clear they did not fully agree. "That is a last resort only," Rashingot said.

"But Icehome is a people, not a place," Geril insisted. "It can always be rebuilt—and this time with no failsafe. We taught your artisans how to craft structures like—"

"I am aware of that," Rashingot cut him off, barking slightly louder than she might have if not for the chest wound that sapped her concentration. "But I will not destroy the last remnants of the city that Thrag built and leave his son and heir with no inheritance."

Geril shut his mouth and nodded. A silence stretched out, and the dwarf said, "We'll rely on the reinforcements, then. But I will prepare a few of my most trusted lieutenants just in case we must evacuate in a spur-of-the-moment decision."

Rashingot nodded slowly, letting her fangs remain visible. "Fine." She reminded him, "This is a last resort, only. If it comes to it, I'll likely be dead… and if I'm gone, I expect you'll be dead as well and none of this will matter."

Geril nodded and left to make the arrangements, unsure if Thrag's widow was stating the obvious or threatening him. If such a moment ever came to pass, he figured Rashingot was right: none of it, even the reason for his death, would matter anyway.

CHAPTER THREE

The frigid battlescape of Icehome became a hell of hot blood spilling and freezing against cobblestone and the bony wreckage of destroyed corpse warriors. Days stretched into night in a cycle of unrelenting torment.

Frostwings and their companions who had been caught in the besieged city fought along the inner walls and gate to keep the undead at bay. Battle shifts stretched long between uneasy periods of rest, like the lulls of fever dreams.

Soldiers would barely fall asleep before bells would clang, rousing all those slumbering and calling them to arms in attacks that felt engineered to disrupt circadian rhythms. The battle stretched into one never-ending, gray smear of fatigue.

Near a small fire, Geril sat with a mixed company of his own trusted warriors and his daughter's companions. After the carnage of so many fights against the undead, skirmishes fought side by side with the small group of lava elves. Geril had become somewhat accustomed himself to the red-skinned elves' presence. They'd all earned a few hours of rest—and they needed it. Despite the strength of the walls, the continual pressure of the enemy's numbers would eventually break them like a hullifruit in a vice. Everyone knew it, and they wore their worry on their faces.

One of Geril's dwarves rushed toward the bleary-eyed and battle-worn company. "The walls… the walls, Warlord!" he yelled. The vagha used Geril's honorific when he was present on the battlefield.

Geril turned and blinked. He figured they'd have several days yet before the bloodless could weaken a wall so thick as Icehome's.

The soldier continued, "I'm an engineer when not conscripted," the vagha insisted. "I spotted the pattern just now. The enemy has consistently engaged us in order to distract us from their true intentions. They're burrowing and weakening the base of the bastion structures, much like they did around Balgavarr Reaches. It ain't a hammer they're using—they're just whittling away at the underpinnings and bein' patient with it!"

Geril snapped up Old Thunder, his axe which had killed the mighty dragon Morguus Ebraxus, and the crew surrounding him jumped to their feet, noticing the worried look in Geril's eyes. As difficult as the last few days of toilsome drudgery had been, if the wall fell, Icehome would quickly shift from siege to slaughter.

Garesch drew steel from his sheath and the ancient blade gleamed with a mark of high craftsmanship. It lit ablaze with a blessing of Firiel as Marnash, the lava elf sorcerer, drew upon his connection to the fire goddess. The undead, if immolated, did not rise again after being cut down.

Sheron, not to be outdone, cast a spell of his own and Geril's skin hardened like stone, which would, for a time, help turn away all but the most intense of the enemy's strikes.

The others scrambled to their feet and forgot about any need for rest. Ra'al looked sidelong at a shape that darkened the door, and Rashingot appeared. She held a broad, short blade with a long haft. It was more axe than sword. The prince could read the purpose on her face.

"This city shall not fall," she hissed, pouring her iron will into the statement, even though she winced as she walked. She had shed her breastplate so that her torso could be wrapped with bandages.

"You ought to stay here," Geril insisted. "Your people need you—that means staying alive." He was perhaps the only one with strong enough personal standing to speak his mind with the areosan queen.

Ra'al worked his mouth as if he might agree with the dwarf, but he shut it as Rashingot turned her head to him. The prince knew better; even *he* didn't have the stones to contend with the will of Rashingot.

"More than my presence, my people need a queen right now—a powerful leader. They need the office, not the person. And if I cower wounded in the back lines, then I am not worthy of the ice crown," she snarled, not to be deterred.

Garesch cocked his head, wondering about the crown. He'd never seen any frostwing wear one and assumed it figurative.

A horn sounded in one of the observation towers affixed to Castle Ice, which lay at the center-most part of the interior, a towering fortress just behind the party and hidden past one more layer of wall. The watcher in the elevated post pointed and shouted, but his voice was lost in the blistering northland winds.

Moments later came the harrowing sounds of crumbling stone and the shrieks of ice sheafs grinding against each other. Bastawr sprinted ahead of his friends, growling with feral ferocity.

The others caught up to Bastawr, who stood erect with his arms splayed out to keep his friends from running past. They slowed and stood abreast the gwereste—Ra'al and his mother, Geril with his vagha behind him, Marnash and Garesch with a dwindling number of his loyal morehl, and Taerlon with what remained of his selumari crew.

After a roar like thunder, the base of the interior curtain wall cracked sidelong and then gave away. It fell inward, crashing to the ground scarcely forty cubits before the company of heroes, fracturing their hopes along with what security the barrier had still provided.

A mass of writhing black and the bleached ivory of exposed bones protruded from soldiers clustered into the breach. Geril's heart sank, and he realized what the watchman had been signaling with his horn. The entirety of the bloodless army had rerouted toward their point of entry where they now trickled in, intending to wipe Icehome clean of any living thing.

Geril shot Rashingot a wild look. "My plan, Rashingot—the contingency. Use it now! We don't need to die here needlessly."

"Go, then," she shot back. "Let the vaghan charges take us all. But I will not back down in the face of the greatest challenge my people have ever faced. I will stay and buy you time. As Thrag once saved your people, *you* go now and save mine."

"Damn it!" Geril barked at her. She was a master of manipulation, and the dwarf knew it—he could scarcely leave her and be responsible for both Thrag *and* his best friend's widow being killed. His internal code of honor demanded he stay at her side.

"At least Coryn is not here to suffer with the rest of us," Geril mumbled a quick thanksgiving to the gods. He looked up and into the glowing eyes of an enemy devoid of all life or love—only ravenous purpose and devotion to the Death god remained. And there were so, so many of them.

Coryn's steel boots echoed as she clomped loudly around the prison chamber that held her. She felt oddly aware of the passage of time, but something about the place sustained her. There were no vents, tubes, or tunnels like the vagha bored into the mountain stone to allow airflow, but she didn't suffocate. Coryn also did not hunger, thirst, or tire, and suspected that the gnomes had some kind of stasis effect or enchantment in place.

She shuddered and gazed at the scaly creature locked away. Coryn had heard of some civilizations using such a spell to punish enemies or prisoners. Not many fates sounded worse than going into a time-locked stasis while famished. And she should be hungry by now, but something prevented it.

After pacing the length of the strange chamber for what was probably the seven thousandth time, Coryn sat glumly at the place where she'd first entered the gnomish room, the narrow corner of the angular shaped room. She sighed and tried to quiet her mind.

That didn't work.

"Festration," she cursed at the top of her lungs while resting her chin on her fists.

Coryn looked down. For the first time, she realized something was faintly etched in the floor. It appeared to be some kind of round shape. Maybe a magic portal or a caster's circle? The text that scrawled along its edge was written in a similar script to the gremmlobahnd words she'd found on the plinth near the strange drakufreet.

There were a few different gnomish phrases etched there, barely discernible unless one knew to look for them. The light glared off the polished floor and made them appear as little more than dust artifacts, even though there wasn't a speck of dust anywhere else in the room.

"Gods, I wish I could read gnomish right now. Maybe if Lady Naemyar was here. I bet she knows enough of it to translate." Naemyar was a powerful selumari, and the estranged spouse of a foreign king on the far side of Esfah. In addition to being a benefactor for Coryn's traveling party, she exuded all the appeal of a strong and independent female who had found success in a man's world. She was everything Coryn wished to be… that is, if Coryn had been born a coral elf. Naemyar's late father had been something of an amateur expert on the Magestorm Wars and on mysterious items related to it—mystic items like gnomish devices that were able to swallow unsuspecting vagha.

"Actually, I don't think Naemyar knows any gnomish. It's a dead language. But at least she'd be able to figure out how to open this puzzle. I'm sure of it."

She slouched and traced her finger over the weird script, drawing in bigger loops than the original. In a blank patch of space, her finger made new etchings wherever her fingers touched, as if she had dragged her fingers through sand.

Coryn raised her brows suspiciously and played with it several times. She discovered that if she left her drawing alone, it would erase itself and let her begin again. After entertaining herself with it for a while, she lost interest in the mysterious feature and then slid her hand across the area with frustration, wiping the reactive slate clean.

The edge of her hand caught the next bit of engraved text and it flashed after she'd touched it. Coryn cocked her head, certain she'd discovered some kind of gnomish puzzle or control input.

Touching the phrase again, it flickered and seemed to attach to her fingertip so long as it remained in contact with the floor, and it appeared to lift and follow Coryn's finger as she moved it along the edge of the circle. But when she lifted her finger away, the text returned to its original position.

"That's interesting," she said.

Yoo-ee snorted from his cage, where he watched her on the far side of the room. Coryn thought she detected a note of agreement in it.

She returned her attention to the puzzle, touched the phrase, and then flicked it, trying to bounce it to the next bank of text several hand spaces away. And then the light flashed.

More and more support arrived from Castle Ice as the heroes hacked and slashed at the enemy. Axes broke chitinous bone of skeletal soldiers and swords bit through decayed and zombified flesh. The remains of the dead shuddered and pulled back together as the necralluvium stitched the fallen ones' heads back onto their bodies, as if they were never severed.

Marnash and Sheron, both fire casters, did their best to hurl arcane flames at the heaps of bodies, but they were hard pressed to keep pace as the influx of the undead overwhelmed them. The grueling toll of the earlier days spent fighting had added up and areosa and their allies began falling in greater numbers. Worse, those same soldiers often came back later, now swinging weapons against their former friends and marked by hollow eyes and dusky blotches where the blackened unlife granted by the necralluvium had taken them. Somewhere, a bloodless general with a vial of the stuff meandered the battlefield in search of fresh troops to add to the cause.

Geril roared as a blade clipped too close and nicked his neck. The dwarf fought furiously, trying to close a gap that had developed between him and Rashingot. He'd pledged himself to keep her safe whenever possible in honor of his devotion to Thrag—and he'd meant it.

A dull roar sounded to the west as some unknown skirmish intensified between the undead and other pockets of warriors. Rashingot yelped as a carrion crawler burrowed up from the permafrost below. The flesh-eating worm resembled a massive larva with a mouth full of proboscis. It hung from its mouth filled with palp like ragged ropes and dripped with stinging saliva. One of the tendrils lashed out and struck the frostwing queen, whose agonized scream quickly quieted as she fell stiff, momentarily stunned by the monster's chemical poison.

Before the crawler could set upon his mother, Ra'al flashed his wings and glided above the clustered undead between him and her. His side suddenly burned in flashes of lightning and the pouch at his side erupted in what felt like fire.

Ra'al yanked the gnomish puzzle cube free before the thing could do any serious damage. It seemed to be malfunctioning. He threw it up in the air, unsure if it would electrocute him or his friends, and then he crashed to the ground to defend his mother without giving the thing another thought.

Before Geril could arrive to aid Rashingot and hopefully pull her to safety, *and talk some sense into her about a retreat*, Ra'al raked his claws across the thing's myriad eyes, blinding it on the left. He hacked at its dorsal flesh until it reared up, ready to strike.

Suddenly, Coryn fell from the sky, clutching her gnomish cube in one hand and crashing down upon the face of the surprised monster. She crushed its head with the sickly, metallic sound of her unnecessarily heavy steel boots. Coryn's axe was in her hand as soon as the strange cube quit shifting and collapsed back into itself to resume its original solid state.

"Hey Ra'al. Did you miss me?"

"It's about time you showed up, little sparrow," he called her by her pet name as he hacked apart a trio of zombies.

Coryn dashed below his taller strokes and cleaved dead enemies head from neck before the scramblers could crawl back to their feet.

Rashingot finally sat up, under her own power again. Geril arrived with two more of his men at his back. He helped Rashingot back to her feet. A sizzle of electricity seared through the knots of walking dead at their west flank. The corpses smoldered like overcooked sausages, some bursting like bangers on a hot grill, and then a corridor of them collapsed to reveal a company of coral elves. Several of them could summon magic and they blasted the dead to cut a path to the others. They used every resource and hurried into the heart of the fray, angling toward the others.

There were at least fifty selumari who shored up their numbers and brought temporary relief, though they still lost a regular step as the undead crushed in around them. The defenders formed a fence to hold back the enemy while the others regrouped.

Geril grabbed Coryn and squeezed her into an embrace. "I'm so glad you're alright..."

She immediately began telling him what had happened, chattering like the chirpy little sparrows Ra'al teased her about. But Geril held up a hand. "Later. After this fight, you can tell me all about it."

The leader of the selumari fighters looked from face to face and then noted Coryn's boots. "She said I could recognize you by the footgear," he said, grinning with pearly white teeth hidden under dark blue lips.

"Who?" Coryn asked.

He bowed. "Lady Naemyar of Tulgesh hired us and wanted us to arrive to protect Coryn sa'Geril. I am Fazayou of the Azure Company..."

Geril raised a brow. "You're mercenaries. I've heard of ye. Thought there were more'n this of you, though."

Fazayou gave him a sheepish look. "There *were*. We're barely more than fifty now. And against this horde? We stand little chance. Has the queen considered pulling back to Castle Ice?"

"Only as a last resort," Geril explained.

"We are nearly to that point," Fazayou noted. "I saw a landed coral airship outside the interior wall. Whatever is in the sky has undoubtedly forced it to ground. Something invisible. It withered our eagles and riders like grapes in the sun. It blocks the skies, and our horses did not fare well with the hordes."

"Horses?" asked a voice.

They looked up. Rashingot had been listening and now drew near enough to engage.

Fazayou nodded. "Eaten. Every last one. They shrieked and wailed as the dead tore them apart with tooth and claw. We fought through the weakest flank and managed to scale the outer walls. Figured we'd aim for the thickest concentration of dead with whatever fighting spirit we had left—then we saw the lightning and watched Coryn fall from the sky."

Coryn obviously wanted to talk about it, but Rashingot didn't give her a place. "I believe I am ready to fall back into the fortress and consider options... including your ultimate solution, Geril." She clutched her wounded side with an arm that bled from new lacerations.

"Are there reinforcements coming?" Fazayou asked. He looked from face to face, but none revealed anything.

"We sent for help days ago, before the fighting began— before Geril and company arrived," Rashingot said. "I fear that whatever is in the sky may have impacted them as well."

A voice piped up from a morehl standing near. Marnash's red skin shone, and he looked very out of place in the frozen city. "Ra'al and I were able to reveal them for a time. It was how we were able to steer a course through them and reach the city with minimal casualties."

He opened the thick robes he wore to ward off the cold and revealed his chest. Steam wafted off his exposed body as the frigid air hit his hot skin. He wore some kind of artifact on a lanyard around his neck. "I do not know what it is." It resembled a kind of mangled key covered in mysterious runes.

"I can't even identify the magic, except to say that it certainly *is* magical... well, *actually*, anti-magical might be a better word. I call it the Spell-Breaker."

Marnash found Ra'al in the small gathering and knew they were running out of time. The Azure Company would quickly tire. "It may be a lost cause now, but we could dispel the aura around the ghostly creatures we saw in the sky, Ra'al. *You* could do this. You could strip whatever spell gives them their invisibility." He put the item in his hand. "Keep this item secret, except from those you trust more than life itself. Something tells me an artifact this powerful could be more dangerous than the whole of the Magestorm Cache itself."

Rashingot looked proudly at her son. "If we can see it, we can fight it."

Fazayou's eyes brightened. "And if we can fight our way to Tulgesh's landed ship, we could attempt to reclaim the sky."

Selumari cries sounded, and the line began to waver, even with the addition of vagha and frostwing support. Icehome's forces had fallen back all the way to the gates of Castle Ice.

"That's a whole lot of 'ifs,'" said Prince Garesch. "But we came here to stop the bloodless or die trying."

As if in response to his bold declaration, the low peal of a war horn echoed like rolling thunder in the distance beyond Icehome. The fighters traded looks, all settling on Geril, but he shook his head. The horn's timbre was pitched wrong for it to be vaghan battle horns announcing their arrival.

Coryn tightened her hands on her axe. "I didn't escape an inter-dimensional prison just to die in the cold," she barked.

Fazayou winked at her. "Naemyar said you had spirit. Let us hope that the gods still have use of us this day."

Smoke wafted up from an incense bowl in Elder Lahmyn's home, giving it a spicy, pungent aroma that stretched the length of the long feast-hall table. The councilman's servant greeted the new arrivals with a bow. "Elders Hezoid and Umi. Welcome."

They headed into the hall and found Lahmyn seated at its head. A gray-skinned elf refilled his drink. Keeping frehlasuhl, the lowly gray elf bastards of nature were not a popular position amongst residents of Balgavarr Reaches. But Lahmyn had never been known as a populist. His strength came from his ability to manipulate.

Once the last two dwarves took their seats at the table, Lahmyn stood and raised his glass. "I promised Geril sa'Ghuren that he would pay, and the first phase of our plan has gone according to plan." He looked around the table and met each one's gaze. Trinean, Lodurli, Umi, Nazbaen, and Hezoid. "Our cabal is six members," Lahmyn continued.

Trinean drained his ale and spoke. "So long as we have quorum and seven votes, we can win any legal measures. I have identified three dwarves who might be friendly to our cause. Well, not friendly… but if we pitch an idea well enough, they might be amenable to it and ensure a vote is passed. Bakurun is typically under Lordan's thrall but he seems swayed by the news of your nephew's murder."

Lahmyn grinned deviously. Harahsus had been embezzling money for decades and the habit had only gotten worse in recent years. His nephew had to go, and this way, his death could be put to good service for the Kiyh clan.

"Dusut is also leaning across the middle and in support of us." Lahmyn puckered his lips into a sad face that verged on tears. He added sorrowfully, "Pity for an old dwarf who just lost his favorite nephew will go a long way."

"Detective Perdy is doing his job admirably," Umi said.

"Yes. And he doesn't realize how he's only dancing to the tune which we have played," Lahmyn said. "But we will still need to make more bold moves. Warlord Kile will always do what Geril instructed. The same goes for Lordan. We must plan for eventual moves against them. One cannot play a game of shadows when meddlesome vagha keep trying cast light upon it."

"And if they jeopardize our plans?" Umi asked. Female dwarves in high positions were typically not found among the Kafnysan vagha. She had proved herself a juggernaut in the world of politics and trade, brandishing the chip on her shoulder at any turn where it proved convenient.

"I promised you all power," Lahmyn said. "I ensured you that the rightful rule of the Council of Elders would return and that we would cast off this de facto crown that we've so often awarded wartime heroes. It is high time we returned the politicians to power. We will not allow one or two uppity dwarves to stand in our way."

Lahmyn raised his glass in salute. The rest of the cabal did likewise. "If they dare to interfere, we'll have to remove them from the equation. Permanently."

And they all drank.

CHAPTER FOUR

The distant horns grew louder, cracking sharply in the frigid air surrounding Icehome. Weariless undead troops paid them no heed, which only made the defenders' hearts sink low after the momentary joy of Coryn's return.

Marnash stood alongside Ra'al, who tried to focus his concentration.

"If you can do this, Ra'al," the lava elf insisted, "You'll be able to dispel the ethereal fiend's invisibility for far longer than I was able—because *you* have the gift. You know how to sense them. On the ship, I merely channeled your abilities *through* the artifact. Your connection is stronger."

The defenders had been beaten back and pressed up against the fortress walls of Castle Ice. Slowly, they trickled back within the bastion, yielding the greater city, but knowing that these walls would eventually fall like the others. Geril escorted a bleeding Rashingot to safety just as the horns pealed again and all eyes turned to watch the shifting mists part. This time, the dead did pause.

From the fog emerged a force of wingless areosa riding upon support animals. At the forefront charged the largest bear any had ever seen. Riding it, a huge, dreadlocked frostwing clung to its back. His red eyes locked their gaze upon the queen in retreat.

A murmur of hope rippled through those trapped in Icehome. Rashingot snarled and tried to surge back toward the battle, but Geril easily shoved her back inside. She was on the verge of collapse as it was.

"Let me go, Geril," she insisted weakly.

"You ain't gonna die on my watch," spat the vagha.

"You must. You don't understand—it is our way…"

Geril wouldn't hear it. "So long as I still breathe, you're not throwing your life away."

Directly above them on the fortress wall stood Marnash and Ra'al. The relative safety of their position allowed them to meditate on the magic at hand.

"But I'm no magic user," Ra'al insisted.

"You can hear the song of the wind, as your people call it?" Marnash said.

Ra'al nodded.

"It is like that. Find your calm. Open yourself to it," Marnash said. He watched the frostwing try to center himself and avail himself of the magics of the world. "Good… good," he said. "Now, keep that hold and concentrate on your gift that lets you sense the wraiths and ghosts and any of those sorts of nasties."

A few seconds passed and Ra'al wrinkled his nose in disgust. He clearly sensed them; his insight always represented itself as smell. "And now what?"

Marnash sighed. "Remember that song of the wind thing? We need to forget about it and listen for the *other* song. This next part is dangerous, and I'll not have you try it except that our need is dire. Listen for the Song of Death, that corrupt part of nature we both share."

Ra'al gulped and then his eyes turned a kind of milk white. "I... I see them. Ghosts. And the song... drums... drums and screams and the sound of blades upon infant flesh. All of it... worship of Malgr—"

Marnash clamped a hand over Ra'al's mouth before he could speak the forbidden name and curse himself. "Do not *succumb* to the song. But use it; bend it to your will. Command the magic... and more so, the anti-magic. Frostwings are resistant already, so this will be easier for you than for me. Strip the creatures in the sky of their invisibility. Break the spell."

Ra'al growled and then buckled. He collapsed to his knees, panting, but the sky glimmered as if the northmost lights, which often painted itself green in the skies of the Shadowlands, exploded in a cascade of colorful showers. Ra'al's eyes returned to normal, and the undead who guarded the airways lost their concealment.

On the far side of the bloodless hordes, the bear rider and his forces charged through the rear flanks.

He had brought more than just the gathered areosan warriors from the outskirt villages. A cluster of yetis swung heavy clubs and a tamed remorhaz rushed into the fray, scorching the dead with its internal chemical fire as it trampled them and bit others in two. The enemy blades bounced off the giant centipede-like beast's chitinous plates as it raced between them.

Coryn scrambled up the wall to join her friend. Her eyes were eager for battle, and she clutched her axe as she clambered over the top lip of the wall. "Are we gonna do this or not?" she asked enthusiastically.

Ra'al looked out over the battle. The dreadlocked newcomer had breached the outer city and his forces eviscerated the black hordes. But they were still too few, and now that they could see the airborne dead swooping through the sky, the battle looked all the more hopeless. He wasn't so sure that the bear rider had even helped the cause.

Coryn pointed. "Look! It's the rest of them."

Coming from the rear of the bear-rider's approach flew a host of winged soldiers. Finally able to fight in the sky, they hacked their way through the ethereal forces.

The Azure Company joined what remained of Taerlon's crew upon the wall and they summoned lightning and winds, clearing the worst of the patches of menacing sky. Gusts blasted some of the ghostly undead so far away that they simply disappeared beyond sight, as if eroded by the frigid air currents.

With the sky partly clear, the aerial warriors turned their attention to the ground and provided support. They cast volleys of ice javelins down into the pockets of the dead, pinning them to the ground where they could be casually dispatched. The rain of icy spears shifted the battle in favor of the defenders.

Many of the undead at the fringes of the vanguard simply turned and wandered back into the tundra, meandering circuitously through the rubble of the damaged city. Just as in Balgavarr, they simply walked away.

"Let's go, Ra'al!" Coryn looked ready to hurl herself over the edge and rejoin the battle. She hadn't been as wearied as the rest of her peers, whose last tenday was spent constantly beleaguered by a tireless enemy. He snorted once at her and then scooped her up.

With a flap of his wings, he escorted Coryn to the battlefront, where they joined old friends. Coryn plopped to her feet, adjacent to Garesch, whose blade flashed with trained precision. She'd watched the lava elf prince in action before. He danced like a song of swords with his enemies falling to pieces in his wake.

Coryn hacked the walking dead to pieces and used her heavy boots to stomp their necks and skulls. The act made them stay down. Ra'al used his reach to keep Coryn's blindside safe and destroy as many of the festering horde as he could. Behind them, Bastawr did likewise.

The remnant forces of Balgavarr, Tulgesh, and Icehome rallied the last of their energy and pushed ahead as the bear rider's forces did the same. A shower of bones suddenly clattered around Coryn. She looked up just in time to see them flung over the heads of the enemies she aced. A skull connected to a clavicle and an arm landed near her feet; they glowed momentarily as if some mystic effect burned the necralluvium off from the bones and then they darkened. The skeleton did not reform.

With a mighty roar, the bear and rider tore through the enemy line. Coryn took a step back as the tall areosa on the bear looked down at her. He had stark white fur except for the midnight black of his forearms and haunches. Between his dangling locks, his eyes glowed red like a snow ferret's and Coryn recognized him.

"Have no fear of Nanku, little one," he said, petting the bear on the side of his face. "I am Rawrgyld, and I've heard the cries of Icehome." He hefted a fancy heavy axe, twirled it in his grip, and then reached out to smash a bloodless fiend. The weapon seemed to hit like a shock wave and a clash of light. The light in the fiend's eyes extinguished immediately, and the necralluvium seemed to boil off it in an instant. "All the undead fall to power of Frostquake," Rawrgyld bellowed, and then he and his company pressed ahead.

The wearied defenders staggered back to the safety of Castle Ice as the zealous reinforcements pressed the defense of the city. Resting their weary muscles, they took a backup position while the newcomers did the heavy lifting. Within moments, despite retaining overwhelming numbers, the army of the dead dispersed. They slunk back into the snowy cover and drifts of the Shadowlands, abandoning their siege.

Coryn practically collapsed against Ra'al, who watched Rawrgyld ride his beast through Castle Ice's approach and hunt down whatever enemy lingered. Ra'al raised an eye at the impressive weapon. "I don't even know what that thing is," he muttered. "Some kind of relic, perhaps?"

"You don't recognize him?" Coryn asked with surprise evident in her voice.

Ra'al shot her an askew look. He clearly did not.

"Rawrgyld was at Lady Naemyar's ball when we arrived in Tulgesh all those months ago," she said.

Ra'al stroked his chin. "Interesting," he mumbled.

"Man. I'm hungry all of a sudden," Coryn said. Her stomach grumbled loud enough to be heard. "I haven't eaten since Balgavarr," she admitted. "I could really go for some burned hen right now."

Ra'al twisted his lips into a frostwing smile. The dish was little more than baked bird drenched with the dwarven fire sauce she loved so much. "Let's see what we can muster up in the castle's kitchens," he said, leading the way. Even though Ra'al was nearly always hungry, he had greater things on his mind. His mother was somewhere inside the fortress, and he had to tell her about the newcomer in case there was far more— or less—to Rawrgyld than it seemed. He may have been the eleventh-hour hero of Icehome, but something about him made Ra'al suspicious.

The residents of Icehome did their best to tend wounds and recover in the aftermath of the city's siege. A blanket of cold fell over the castle like a pall. Many of the defenders sighed with relief. For some, the rest came like a death rattle; the battle had overwhelmed them and until now, soldiers hadn't even had time to die.

Coryn walked the halls of Castle Ice and knocked on a door. She opened the chamber where Queen Rashingot reclined.

Geril was with her, and she saw the queen's wounds had been worse than she'd let on. So depleted were the magic reserves that the healers had not been able to fully restore her yet.

Rashingot waved her in. "Little Sparrow," she teased uncharacteristically, "Come in."

Coryn entered and saw the bowl of herbs on the bench beside her. She must have self-medicated to cope with the pain, not that Coryn could blame her. Something nasty festered in the gash that split Rashingot's hide.

Ra'al and Coryn had eaten already and the big frostwing had collapsed, taking a nap in his own bed for the first time since Rashingot had pushed him out of the palace. Coryn had helped, practically dragging him by his wing tips. But she'd had enough adventures now. At least for a little while.

"I wanted to check on you," she said.

Rashingot grimaced. "I am wounded, but I shall heal."

Geril stood and took his leave for the two to talk. "I've got to speak with what remains of my company," he said. "There's still that summons to Tulgesh I've got to deal with… and that bloody cultist Harol is still out there." He departed, mumbling about how they couldn't yet muster magic strong enough to send a proper traveling party to King Matrek until the rest of the forces arrived from Balgavarr.

After her father left, Coryn asked her about Rawrgyld and called him by name. "Ra'al and I saw him in Tulgesh during our diplomatic travels. Since the fighting ceased, all the people are talking about him as if he single-handedly won this war."

"Yes," Rashingot said. "I am familiar with him. He is no true hero, but he *is* a powerful areosa. There is no doubt of that. I tried to grant him a military commission many decades ago to draw him to my side—I feared he might want the throne. Instead, he chose to travel the world, which put my mind greatly at ease. I knew he had many connections to the outlying towns in the Shadowlands, but my last word of his whereabouts was that he had gone questing in Charnock, the continent far southwest of here."

"Well, whatever he was looking for, I think he found it," said Coryn. "Do you think he still wants the throne?"

Rashingot grimaced. "The throne was never truly mine." She fixed her eyes on Coryn and spoke with candor. "Tell me, Little Sparrow, as you know my son best. Is he strong enough to claim and defend his father's throne? Is he strong enough to hold it if someone like Rawrgyld wants it?"

Coryn gulped. Rashingot had never spoken to her like that before, like an equal. "I… I don't know."

"Frostwings follow strong leadership. Challenges are not issued fancifully, as the rite of leadership must pass by the elders. I know your father had the best intentions, and I am afraid that my retreat earlier today is likely to have shaken that faith the elders have in me. It makes me open to challenges, and they have not yet seen Ra'al prove his worth. I suspect Rawrgyld riding to the rescue was motivated by more than a sense of solidarity with Icehome." Rashingot's eyes pierced the dwarf to her soul. "I fear for my son and what comes next. He must be ready… for anything."

A full, frigid day passed marked only by wisps of gray wind. The bleary-eyed trauma of Icehome's devastation was worn on the faces of all those in Icehome. Especially by the common areosa who returned to their homes to discover them thoroughly demolished.

Rashingot kept her head held high, but she felt the weighty sting of eyes upon her. Her subjects looked for someone to blame, and the undead were senseless creatures of wanton destruction. They made poor targets for such nuanced rage.

Ra'al walked abreast of his mother, who had been mostly patched up thanks to the arcane healers. They toured the wreckage of the city, along with Ra'al's closest companions. The outermost sections of the city were nearly a total loss; all but the sturdiest of structures had been reduced to rubble.

Rashingot and Ra'al turned a corner and noticed many of the bears, wolves, and other mounts who had joined Rawrgyld's cavalry. The reinforcements had stationed their animals in the hollowed-out structures. The frostwing queen snorted through her nose, still unsure if Icehome was free or if she'd traded one enemy occupation for another.

"Hennedy has already informed me about the maps and the mist stones," Rashingot told those companions who traveled alongside her. Only trusted companions stood within earshot. "So long as the undead possess them, the Shadowlands will never be safe. And if the Shadowlands remain in peril, so too does Balgavarr."

Prince Garesch kept his face placid. "And whether Uruzak acknowledges it or not, if Balgavarr falters, so will the morehl."

Ra'al tightened his lips. He'd always suspected Hennedy was his mother's informant. That he'd kept her abreast of the details merely confirmed it. Ra'al noted, "The undead still outnumber us. They could have pressed the attack and taken Castle Ice."

"No," Rashingot almost snapped. "That they could never do." She glanced sidelong at Geril. "There is a failsafe to prevent that."

"A failsafe?" Coryn cocked her head.

"It's not important now," Rashingot said. "The most important thing is to understand our enemy." She lowered her voice and added, "The undead one. If we can guess their next move, we can try to circumvent it."

"They got to my man in Balgavarr," Garesch told her. "Used that black stuff to revive him and then scoured his memories before sending in a zombie version of him to take the maps and escape."

"This I heard," Rashingot said. Hennedy had been in possession of the maps and been fooled by the freshly turned lava elf.

Garesch continued, "Once he was away, the bloodless army quit the fight. They got what they wanted from us… the remaining maps to the mist stones."

"Whatever these stones are, or whatever they do, must not be allowed. If the undead have revealed themselves after so long, it will not be for some insignificant purpose. The times we live in have not been this dark since the days of Nekarthis the World Breaker," Rashingot said.

Geril bobbed his head in agreement. He looked at his daughter. "I will be called away shortly—I have a day or maybe two. I'll need to leave once the rest of our vaghan forces arrive. *This fight*, I'm afraid, is going to fall to you. Keep the north safe."

"I will, Father. Ra'al will help me."

Ra'al growled his assent. And Bastawr, who strode abreast of him, nodded as well. He'd already surveyed the frozen wastes and assured them he could lead a return trip to the mist stones, map or not.

A dwarf appeared on the horizon, riding a long-haired pony hard through the frosty air. "This one's early," Geril said.

The messenger arrived and dismounted near Geril. He brushed the snow out of his beard and then retrieved a sealed letter. "I am Fi'Vibrahn sa'Fliryl," he announced himself.

"Vibrahn… you're Lordan's nephew," Geril acknowledged and held out a hand. "You have a message for me?"

"Uh, no," Vibrahn said with mild embarrassment. "Lordan sent me with this, but it is for Coryn."

Coryn's eyes sparkled, and she hopped from foot to foot. She rarely got mail. "Don't worry, Father," she teased. "Lordan probably figured you'd have been killed by the hordes of bloodless and put me in charge of all dwarf kind since."

Geril shook his head and muttered through the teasing. The two vagha stepped away to read it. From their faces, the others could tell that the news was not good.

Rashingot left them to their own business and turned her attention back to the black threat. "This matter is perhaps more urgent than even the rebuilding of our city. The dead must be stopped."

"Whatever forces they used here," Bastawr said, "it was only a portion. I saw the rest within the Heimdarl Crag. The place was practically stuffed full of 'em." His face paled. "And that did not account for the forces already at the mist stone."

"We do not have enough soldiers to defeat them in the open. Not at present, and not with our interests divided," Ra'al said.

His mother nodded approval at his assessment. She beamed, noticing how much he had grown in the past several months.

"No. We cannot," Garesch said. "But we do not need to defeat the behemoth. We must merely turn its head. Destroy the maps to the mist stones. Whatever they are or, or whatever purpose they have, if we conceal their location forever, we can perhaps stop the enemy."

Rashingot scratched her chin. "That is the best plan we have thought of so far. A strategic strike against the desires of whoever controls these fiends…"

"You think someone controls them?" Ra'al asked.

Bastawr piped up. "From what I saw, some are intelligent, and others are more like worker drones… like insects."

Rashingot stiffened when she noticed outsiders approach their group. Five wizened elders of the frostwing community walked ahead of the tall hero of the recent battle. They remained aloof and stood as witnesses to the meeting.

Rawrgyld bowed and then shook back his dreadlocks. Luckily, he'd left his bear, Nanku, behind. "Queen Rashingot," he greeted. "I am glad I was able to assist the people of Icehome, but I am distressed by the city's condition. I was even more dismayed to find its leader in full retreat as the enemy razed the homes and livelihood of its people. I am here to issue a challenge for rule of the areosa."

Rashingot breathed out with composure and regarded him coolly. She turned aside from him and engaged the elders. "I am ready to abdicate. My son is ready to rule. He has proven himself in battle and made political alliances worthy of any leader."

One of the elders wilted beneath her gaze. The others remained strong. One said, "These are mere words. The son of Thrag has yet to prove he is his father's heir to the people. Perhaps there would be no need to defend if he had started earlier, but…"

Ra'al growled, "I will accept my father's mantle and also the obligation to defend it." He stood tall and turned to glower at Rawrgyld. The prince looked every bit the bear rider's equal.

The elders accepted his response. "In two days' time, then, we shall let strength of tooth and claw decide." They bowed and turned to depart. Rawrgyld spent a half second scanning his opponent to size him up, and then turned and followed the older frostwings.

Coryn hopped to her friend's side as she and the dwarves returned. "What was that about, huh, Ra'al? I think you can totally take that guy. You're young. You've got the wind on your side."

"I hope so, Coryn," Rashingot told her. "He's just accepted a challenge to the death from him."

Coryn's face fell, and she clung to her best friend's arm. "What? More bad news?" With a face full of fur, she turned to the lava elf. "Things get worse. The letter. There's news from Lordan in Balgavarr, Garesch. The council thinks you murdered someone."

"That's absurd," Garesch spat.

"You and I know that. Elder Lordan knows that. But they've got enough evidence to try and convict you if they want. Fabricated for sure, but it'll stick, according to Lordan. You'll need to watch your back. Elder Lahmyn has dispatched a squad of constables to take you into custody," Coryn said.

Geril grumbled, "Days like today are living proof that it could always get worse." He shook his head at the others. "Never tempt the goddesses of fate. They are not to be trifled with."

Avaryth cursed as the cold and bitter winds brushed against his skin where it lay exposed in open flaps of cloth. The pirate's hands and feet were both bound and so he could do little to bundle himself against the frigid climate of the Shadowlands.

The floating rug bore him ever onward in the middle of the bloodless pack that escorted him deeper into the mainland and further from the sea and Avaryth's ship. Certainly, his crew had abandoned hope that he or the others would return by now and sailed away.

Ry'ober would be displeased there was no prize, but his crew would keep their lives. At least, the undead couldn't harm them; Ry'ober was another matter.

He rolled to his side to block the wind, and the carpet adjusted to accommodate him. It was the only mercy he'd receive from his unfeeling enemies. As he shifted, a different patch of skin exposed itself to the elements where his shirt separated from his pants.

The general, who some had called Rorduk, looked down at his prey with eyes that glowed in mischievous glee. Avaryth felt certain that he knew of the prisoner's discomfort. But so long as the human's condition didn't prove fatal, he would do nothing to remedy it.

Avaryth swallowed with a dry throat. He was chaff to these beasts, fodder for some vile purpose that he did not yet know. Avaryth *did* know that he was dead already. It was all over but for the swinging of the final blade.

CHAPTER FIVE

Geril and Sheron the vagha spell caster stood at the edge of Icehome's ruined borders. Frostwing spotters had identified the approaching Balgavarrian force some time ago and alerted Geril.

Presently, an impressive array of dwarves trudged through the landscape littered with frozen remains of the bloodless army. Chunks of corpse meat froze hard as stone where they'd been heaped into piles of bones and husks of cadaverous flesh, which had so recently walked even as it decayed. Behind the vagha rolled their myriad support wagons, which arrived on the path to the main city.

Geril met a stout captain with a scar across one milky eye. The wound appeared fresh, still pink and puckered, and likely earned on the slopes of the most recent skirmish at Balgavarr Reaches.

"Captain Ringuld," he introduced himself to Geril, jabbing a thumb into his own chest. "And it looks like we missed all the fun."

Geril twisted his mouth. He was a renowned fighter and a bona fide war hero, but he found such wanton slaughter distasteful. The hate of war was anything but fun for him. Geril considered the whole concept of war to be something birthed in the belly of the dreaded Death god.

Ringuld understood the look on his face and recanted. "I mean, uh, I'm sure many of our fine soldiers were lost in the defense of Icehome. It's a pity we could not arrive sooner."

Geril understood the younger soldier's eagerness to put an axe to the enemy; he'd been that way once as well. He clapped him on the shoulder. "Don't worry about it. I'm just a crusty old miser who's seen too many of my comrades taken by needless conflict." He sighed and Ringuld fell into step with him as they entered the battered outskirts of the frozen city.

"Truth be told," Geril said, "I've got much on my mind… the unexpected movements of the undead, a ritual challenge for the frozen throne, and worst of all, a summons to Tulgesh."

Ringuld merely blinked at him. "Gods. It's a wonder ye don't explode."

"Don't tempt me. I hear there's a potion for that," Geril said. "On that note, what's the magician corps look like? I will need a spell to send myself and an escort to Tulgesh, and soon."

Ringuld raised his eyes. "More adventure? I could scarcely imagine the exploits ye might be called to."

"More like a probable death as we bring the traitor of house Kiyh to justice for a string of murders in the south. He is likely tied to the bloodless army that attacked our home," explained Geril. He waited a second and asked again, "The casters?"

"Uh, rested and ready," Ringuld explained. "Road weary is all, but we'll find them eager." He looked up as a frostwing angled through the sky on a path to meet them. The winged creature glided to a landing nearby. "Depending on the size of your escort, I can have them ready now," he assured Geril. "They'll be even more reliable after a night's rest."

Ra'al approached the two dwarves.

Geril introduced the areosan prince to the captain. "I assume the travel was unpleasant," Ra'al said, "but not likely as much as the siege which was just broken."

"I suspect you're right," said Ringuld.

Ra'al narrowed his eyes at a band of roughly fifty dwarves who wore red and gold arm bands. "Who are they?" he asked Geril.

Geril shrugged. But something on his face made Ra'al suspect he knew their true purpose: Coryn had filled him in on the Council's orders to apprehend Prince Garesch.

"I've no idea," Ringuld admitted. "I suspected they were a volunteer corps from one of the cities further along the Kafnysan range... except I recognize a few of their faces. Private militia, perhaps?"

Ra'al's voice purred knowingly. He anticipated the threat. "Something like that, I suspect." At least until the contest for Thrag's throne was decided, he could grant Garesch the protection of Icehome.

Ra'al followed the rest of the army and walked with Geril, assessing the strength of the army and its capabilities. He knew they were weary. They were all bone-tired. But if his mother and friends were right about the undead's vile purposes, he'd need to request that many of these vagha accompany him north to stop the army once and for all.

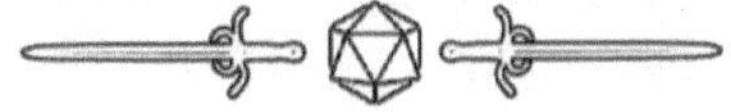

Geril grumbled beneath his breath as he sat hunched over an end table and stared at a sheet of military requisitions. The work of bureaucracy never ceased, and his eyes went bleary from reading through forms when a glimpse of blue passed through his peripheral and a pleasant aroma reached his nose. He looked up in time to spot two selumari wander past.

"Fazayou?" he asked, only barely catching a partial view of him.

The blue elf poked his head back and confirmed it. He bid his company a farewell and let the other elf depart. He was the king's messenger who had arrived with a bird meant for Geril.

They'd not had an extended opportunity to chat. Fazayou ducked into the study where Geril did his business. The blue elf was tall and slender, but well-muscled, and had a keen spark in his eye that Geril knew meant Fazayou was deadly if he chose to be. As a mercenary, he was less bound by the edicts of the King in Tulgesh than a military man was. Regardless, he was thankful the Azure Company had ridden to support them, though Geril found the motives confusing. He did not know any who would ride into certain death for mere gold.

Fazayou held up a bottle of wine as he swaggered in. "Can I pour you some?" He sloshed the bottle back and forth, but it was empty. The elf frowned and set it down before retrieving a fresh bottle, which he carried in a pouch at his hip.

Geril gave Fazayou a warm smile. "Sure. I could stand a drink."

Fazayou uncorked it and poured them each a glass. "Compliments of Lady Naemyar," he said.

"You and her… she's more than your employer?" Geril sipped from the glass to test its flavor and then gulped it down.

"She is…" Fazayou trailed off and then caught himself. "I'm not sure what you mean."

Geril caught the shift in the elf's eyes and confirmed his suspicions. "Nobody takes on the undead hordes for coin. You are her lover?"

Fazayou flashed a guilty grin. "Almost. She asked me to ride to rescue Coryn when she learned the bloodless were moving. I am not her lover…"

"But you wish to be?"

Another guilty grin.

"It has been many years since I saw her last, but she is an unforgettable woman and I had heard how she helped Coryn in recent months."

Fazayou nodded. "She was planning on coming herself if the Azure Company would not follow me into battle. I convinced them we need to be here if Tulgesh is to have a future. If Matrek was not a fool, he would have sent soldiers here to die with us."

"Naemyar, *here?* I wouldn't suspect she'd trade the comforts of Tulgesh for a frozen battlefront."

The elf poured them both another glass. "She was quite insistent about your daughter, actually. She has a great interest in Coryn and knew she would be here, in the thick of things."

Geril could only grin. "That certainly sounds like her."

"Naemyar sees greatness in her. A vast and important future, if she chooses to lay hold of it," the coral elf said.

"Aye. I never doubted that much," Geril noted.

Fazayou took another sip. "I am no fool," he sighed. "But I am foolish enough to risk my life for grand causes and beautiful women—even if I am a convenient option rather than a noteworthy lover."

Geril raised a brow.

The elf's neck flushed. "I don't mean I am a poor lover," he stammered and then blinked at the bottle. "This blend may have been stronger than I expected." He gathered his thoughts and chuckled. "I mean that Naemyar and I have become close, but she will never completely sever that tie to her estranged husband and the kingdom across the seas. If the Lady sees danger here or thinks Coryn needs protection, then addressing that is the call of my life."

Geril nodded. He understood that kind of devotion. His life would have been considerably different had Baeramie, his wife, not died so young.

Fazayou wisely put the cork back in the bottle and stood to depart for his bunk. "Geril. There is one more thing. I am sure Matrek has summoned you…"

Geril set his papers down and gave Fazayou his full attention.

"We both know how ambitious he is, and that he has desired the mystic weapons you had hidden for as long as he's been in power," Fazayou said. "Naemyar has always been grateful that he did not come into possession of them after what you and Thrag accomplished all those years ago."

"Matrek and I have a modicum of respect and understanding for each other, but that does not mean we trust each other," Geril said. "If I could, I'd keep them hidden away forever, but I have agreed to give him certain items in exchange for his help."

"Yes. I saw the coral airship outside. A steep price for sure," Fazayou stated. "I know Naemyar has concerns about Matrek gaining too much power. The Lady's door is always open to you and your daughter. Matrek's game delves too deeply into shadow, and I am sure Naemyar will show you the puzzle pieces properly."

"You mean she would hate for Matrek to upset the current balance of power in Tulgesh?" Geril grinned. The selumari woman owned Riechus Aqualines and controlled a great amount of power and wealth in the city. While Matrek had a firm grip on the military, Naemyar had vast influence because of her importance to the region's economy. Geril knew that she played the same game he and Matrek did, only she played it differently—and probably far more skillfully.

Fazayou grinned. "Something like that."

Geril crooked his jaw. "She has information Matrek might withhold from me, then. It must be related to the vaghan murderer, Harol sa'Lahmyn?"

Fazayou nodded slowly. "Just remember who owns seventy percent of the trading ships that pass through Tulgesh. Naemyar has many eyes and ears abroad. You will know if you need her when the time comes." The blue-skinned elf turned and headed down a corridor, searching for the barracks.

The dwarf recollected his papers, but he could no longer concentrate on them. He sighed and set them aside; the army would sort most of those details out. Orders, appointments, and transfers were usually like that. And most questions had only one obvious answer.

Geril stood and gathered his belongings. *Just like my Harol problem only has one good answer.* He'd already gotten word through Vibrahn, Lordan's nephew, of the political unrest that was rising. It had reached a new pinnacle in Tulgesh, where riots had nearly broken out by the local vagha after a massacre in the embassy. In Tulgesh, House Kiyh's excommunicated son had caused chaos, and in Balgavarr, its patron had disrupted public sentiment.

Harol was the key to both. He was sure of it. And the sooner he could remove that piece from the table, the more confident Geril felt he could play the game and stand a chance at winning.

Geril stopped at his temporary quarters and dumped the work he'd been dealing with. It was nothing more than busywork, anyway. He made up his mind on the next needed course of action. He'd leave for Tulgesh in the morning; but there were conversations he needed to have before then.

Prince Garesch strolled through the breezy corridors of Castle Ice. The palace had been built in such a way that the frostwings' beloved winds could enter the upper windows and blow through, creating an ever-present whistle through the main halls.

He shuddered and pulled his parka closer to him as he admired the craftsmanship. Lava elves were hot weather creatures, but even so, Garesch felt glad that Castle Ice had survived the ravages of the undead. It made him yearn to walk again through his native halls in Mount Uruzak, but he'd promised himself he wouldn't return without securing the support he needed to formally oppose his father.

So far, he'd aligned himself with all the major powers of the northern regions, but none had pledged military support. So long as Saugor, King of Uruzak, remained too weak to launch a meaningful offensive, none of the Cyrean communities were prepared to directly oppose his rule and sponsor an expensive war.

Prince Garesch knew that the bloodless threat could destroy all the continent if left unchecked. The same could be said for his father, but few could currently see that. If evil existed in Cyrea and it was connected to the Death god, Garesch suspected Saugor was complicit. And that thought weighed heavily upon him.

Garesch had gone this far north with his friends, but he didn't know how much further he could travel with them. Not only did the extremes of the north disagree with him, but he had to make for Uruzak and soon. At some point, a physician had to switch from treating open wounds and address the cancer plaguing his patient. Garesch was the specialist among competent doctors—he was the only one who could deal with Saugor.

He had other concerns as well. But presently, his father weighed heaviest on his mind.

A cluster of vagha stepped around the corner and stood several paces ahead of him. Their presence pulled him from his head space, as they clearly intended to block his way forward.

Garesch scanned them. They were part of the group wearing red and yellow arm bands whom Coryn had told him about. She'd received word that some of the council elders in Balgavarr had sent a squad to retrieve him by force and bring him back so they could lay false charges against him.

The morehl prince sized them up and then spun to go back the way he'd come. Another group appeared from around the bend where he'd come and boxed him in.

Garesch locked eyes with the leader. The dwarf sneered wordlessly, and the lava elf opened his long coat to reveal a sword hanging there. He didn't want to shed vaghan blood, but he would kill them all if they tried to seize him. "If you think you can take me quietly or without casualties, you are quite mistaken."

The silent knots of dwarves on both sides of him brandished weapons of their own. Garesch took a defensive posture and poised to strike as the vagha tensed and maneuvered into position.

A gruff and authoritative voice bellowed nearby. "Stop!" howled Geril, who happened upon the encounter. "Who are you? What in the Sha'la'dinan do you think you are doing here?"

The leader of the banded vagha, a dwarf with a missing incisor, turned to Balgavarr's ruler. He spoke with clear disdain. "Pardon, my lord. I am Skrathos, and we are just following the council's orders. We answer to *them, not you*." With his missing tooth, the sneer on his face looked even more menacing.

Geril narrowed his eyes. "You do *here*. Icehome is still a battlefield until the army has been recalled—and until that time, a Warlord has complete authority. Unless Balgavarr is in open rebellion to its own rule?" He maintained tight eye contact, challenging the dwarf to test him.

Skrathos finally flinched and backed down. He nodded to his crew, and they put away their weapons before departing. Looks thrown over their shoulders indicated that this wouldn't be their first encounter.

"Hold," Geril ordered with such authority that every vagha froze mid-step. "I want you out of Icehome. Don't care where you go, but the battlefield of our allies is no place for Kafnysan politics." He studied each of their faces, making threatening eye contact. The twitch in his eye reinforced what he would do to them if they tried to stay and threaten the elf who Geril considered a Balgavarrian ally.

The leader of the dissenters gulped, and then he and his coterie slipped away without another word.

Geril nodded to Garesch and walked with him a short distance. In a low voice, he told him of his plan to leave in the morning and insisted that he take greater care for his own protection. "You should go nowhere—even the halls of your allies—without an escort of your own morehl guard. We may be in the coldest part of the world, but things are beginning to heat up."

Garesch buttoned his coat against the chill and then split company with the dwarf, committing Skrathos's name and face to memory. "They are heating up indeed."

Geril twisted his lips into a grimace and stroked his beard. Uruzak's throne was always in contention, but now Balgavarr was in turmoil and Rashingot feared for her own seat. Trouble was brewing, and he needed to expand his circle of trust. *I've got to speak with Coryn.*

Coryn looked up from the table where she sat with Queen Rashingot, Ra'al, and her band of adventurers over breakfast. The gnomish puzzle cube lay on the table.

"I just know that it could help us, if I can get it out of there," she finished saying when she looked up at her father. Geril appeared ragged and worn down, as if he'd gotten very little sleep.

Behind Geril, a cluster of dwarves who followed him remained in the corridor near the dining hall. He held up his hand to stay his friends. "Don't get up. I just came to say goodbye." Geril turned to address Ra'al. "And good luck."

Coryn tilted her head. "You sound like you won't be here for Ra'al's challenge?" She gave him an askew glare. "And you look terrible."

"I've been up most of the night making arrangements." Geril shook his head somberly. "And I must return to Tulgesh. You know as well as I that things are getting sticky in Balgavarr. We can't untangle so many loose ends at once, and Matrek is notoriously high maintenance. If I can quell what remains of the bad blood in Tulgesh by bringing Harol to justice, that's one less front to wage war upon."

Despite her father's assurances, Coryn stood and embraced him. She pressed her face into his beard. "Be careful. Harol is an acolyte—a death cultist. Who knows what kind of traps he's laid?"

Geril looked down at her. "*You* be careful. The bloodless army is still out there and I'm putting you in charge of thwarting its plans." He used his head to indicate her peers at the table. "Perhaps your company can still find those maps before they are used. Regardless, you'll have an army of stout vagha and a fleet of frostwings, plus a few others who I'm sure will come in handy. More'n that, daughter, you have the favor of the gods."

Coryn squeezed him tighter. "And Balgavarr? I'm sure Lahmyn is behind most of this."

"Surely you're right. We'll get back there together when all this is over and set things right at home." Geril looked at Ra'al. "For now, you've got to overcome your first challenge and keep the throne. So long as those creatures are still out there, none of Cyrea is safe."

Geril put a rolled-up letter into her hand and flashed her a stern look. "Keep this one secret. I mean it," he said and winked.

She peeked through the end of the rolled tube and saw it was another map. Her cheeks flushed, knowing how badly she'd bungled the last map her father owned.

Hugging his daughter one last time, he separated. "I've issued orders making you the Acting Warlord. You're in charge so long as we remain at war, or until you get our kin back to the mountains." He gave her a look that she knew all too well. It was the same look he gave whenever he cautioned her not to be reckless. "Mind your supplies. An army cannot fight if it does not eat."

Geril had always been more of a bean counter than a soldier. He understood the tactical necessity of the little things. He was more like his father, Ghuren, while Coryn had always taken after his grandfather, Zephras. Though, looking at her now, he saw only her mother, Baeramie. Geril swallowed hard; she'd been gone now for more years than Coryn had been alive.

Coryn followed the cluster of vagha to the courtyard of Castle Ice, where a large gathering of dwarves assembled to summon enough magic to cast a major spell. She spotted Captain Ringuld and Sheron, the sorcerer among her father's entourage.

A faint golden aura radiated off the casters who combined their magic and focused on the gathered number of dwarves around Geril. They channeled that magic into a spell the dwarves simply called *Path*. It would allow them rapid travel to anywhere they wanted to go—faster than any bird or airship. They'd be in Tulgesh well before nightfall.

The soil beneath Geril's feet trembled slightly as the spell took hold and he took a final look at Coryn, hoping it wouldn't be the last time he saw her. His face fell when he recognized a sneer from the dwarf with the missing tooth; he'd taken off his red and yellow arm band and hidden among the caster corps.

Geril wanted to speak, but it was too late. An eggshell thin bubble of stone enveloped him and those vagha nearest Geril. The dwarves could feel the earth rumble all around the protective barrier as the sphere traveled through the earth; it fired toward Tulgesh like a morehl ball shot from a flintlock.

He had caught sight of Garesch just as the stone husk wrapped around him. The lava elf had noticed Geril's eyes— hopefully he'd also spotted the council's spy. Lahmyn's spy, most likely… *Skrathos.*

As the earth rumbled around him, Geril saw the irony that he trusted the son of his red-elf enemy, King Saugor, more than members of his own council of elders. Then another thought struck him. Could he really trust Garesch in the midst of such swirling intrigue? *Gods, I hope I can trust you, Garesch.*

Bastawr and Ra'al followed Coryn as she spelunked through the old caves that made up the sub-levels of Icehome. Some of these caves had once been the upper levels of the original Icehome, where Ra'al and Bastawr's ancestors lived for many generations. Until the feral folks' opportunity to fight back had arisen, King Thrag saw to it that his people protected the displaced gwereste who had been nearly destroyed when the lava elves overran Seshara long before Coryn was born.

"I still don't see why we didn't bring Garesch or Marnash along," said Ra'al.

"Because my father asked me not to," she shot back, eyes glued to a crude map her father had drawn on the evening prior. "It was in the letter."

"He specifically said that?" Ra'al asked.

"I read between the lines," she fired back.

"That hasn't usually stopped you in the past," muttered Ra'al.

Coryn stopped and shot him a glare that made his wings droop. She'd gone against his wishes earlier and opened the Magestorm weapons cache too soon. That had been a catalyst for all the chaos they found themselves in currently. The undead could not have been avoided, but Geril would be leading the army now, and Tulgesh might have even joined the fight had Harol not stirred up trouble with the selumari. The bad blood between Tulgesh and Balgavarr was her fault. "I've turned over a new leaf," she said and left it at that.

She didn't mention that her father's letter told her about the trapped sub-structure below Icehome, but also that he'd explicitly written to leave it alone. Coryn took great license with the meaning behind the wink he'd given her.

"I see no reason to distrust our morehl friends," Bastawr said.

"I don't either," Coryn agreed as they came to the rear of a cave where a wall had been scraped almost flat. "But it's more about respecting whatever it is that the old Council put down there than anything else." She shot her companions a look of trepidation. "I know what's down here, but I wanted to see it for myself. He called it a 'Final Solution.'"

Ra'al cocked his head.

"Oh, there it is," she said excitedly, almost bouncing toward the wall.

"We can't see it, Little Sparrow," Ra'al teased.

Coryn grinned. Dwarves could spot rock curtains easily, but the eyes of other creatures could not make them out. "Follow me." She stepped forward and slipped through the wall as if it were an illusion. Made from tassels of very fine stones threaded together, they functioned like a bead curtain, only much more advanced, and the party slipped through the wall with ease and into the hidden passage beyond.

A winding stair had been carved through the stone. It led far below the surface, descending so many cubits they thought it might never end. It finally terminated and exited into a large chamber that yawned out before them.

Coryn found and activated a sunstone set in a dwarven contraption. The rock glowed brilliantly, and she turned the mirrored arm, which clicked into place and reflected a light beam toward receivers stationed all around the cavern. Amplifying it, light cascaded downward, caught in dazzling displays where giant columns of ice scattered iridescent spectrums.

"Old Icehome… it's beautiful," said Bastawr.

"Except for that," Ra'al pointed. Pillars of frosty stone stretched from floor to ceiling. Casks of explosive powder, each stamped with morehl markings indicating their contents, were affixed to the support beam.

Ahead was another. More kegs of powder waited. Everywhere there were supports to shore up Icehome, there were explosives.

"This was what I meant," Coryn spoke softly. "It might be an insult to the morehl to know what the vagha had done after the lava elves lost the war. Before the prisoners were returned to Uruzak, they were pressed into service and forced to make these casks of powder."

"It is an insult to the areosa," Ra'al's voice was furious. "Did my mother know about this?"

Coryn hung her head, but said, "Yes. But she only just learned of it and did not know its location."

Ra'al stormed forward and began dismantling the first series of explosives. He cursed as he worked, so disgusted he couldn't even look at his dwarven friend.

"Come on, Ra'al," mediated Bastawr. "Coryn did not know about this. Clearly, she did not bring us down here to insult your people."

"Father told me he regretted the fact that they built in this failsafe, and your mother insisted they talk about it, but he had to go away first. I assume they'll have words in the future. But Father said he had argued against doing this, and the Balgavarrian Council insisted they build a failsafe."

"I like your Elders less and less the more I learn about them," Ra'al growled.

"You and me both," Coryn agreed. "Revealing this, and that he took part in the plot, however reluctantly, was a huge risk to my father. But he knew it was a resource we might need; he wanted us to have every tool in case we needed it. It shows exactly how serious a threat he thinks this Rawrgyld could be… or whoever this Skrathos guy is."

"Skrathos?" Bastawr asked.

Coryn shrugged. "Some dwarf stirring up trouble on behalf of Harol's father. He was sent back to Balgavarr, but he's trying to form a coup or something. My father wasn't sure what. But it looks like the undead are not the only knot he's trying to unravel."

Ra'al stared at the pillars surrounded with explosives and then his shoulders slumped. "Fine. It is good we know this is here. And we must keep it a secret, but when I am king, all this is getting safely removed." He turned the mirror piece, and the lights dissipated.

"Agreed," said Coryn as she turned toward the stairs.

Ra'al quieted the sunstone and glanced at the map Coryn held. "Why is it that whenever your father gives you a map, it leads to something capable of killing thousands of people?"

CHAPTER SIX

Ra'al had gone to spend the rest of the afternoon with his mother and with the combat instructors who had tutored him since he'd been a kit. That left Coryn to her own devices for longer than she desired. She'd rather battle the undead than be left alone with her thoughts.

Coryn shuffled through the halls, kicking her steel boots anxiously. Her father had departed earlier in the morning. That, and the exploration through the depths of old Icehome, had pushed away any thoughts she'd had about food for most of the day.

Her father's departure put her in charge of the dwarven army and their mission against the undead, but her best friend was about to battle a powerful fighter for rule of the areosan kingdom. While it wasn't necessarily a duel to the death, Coryn knew that was the most likely outcome.

Ra'al seemed to gain a new and sudden appreciation for all that his old combat instructor had taught him during his youth. While a younger Ra'al had often shirked his lessons to play with poetry and compose music, bards were nowhere to be found in the combat arena. He couldn't even take time for a snack with his old friend.

Through Ra'al and Coryn's travels, they'd realized the bards would only sing of them *after* they were gone. She thought glumly, *few knew of Ra'al's exploits leading up to this challenge, and none of those were even frostwings. And I think any of us would very much prefer to stay alive than to be sung about.*

Coryn could only watch her friend train for so long before she needed to wander. She'd spent half her life in Icehome and knew its history well.

The rite of challenge had been issued a number of times throughout the kingdom's history. Each time, it had ended with death for one party. Typically, the challenge came when a greedy frostwing saw an opportunity to seize power and wealth—which is how Coryn saw Rawrgyld—or a hero of the people that arose to tear down such a villain—and was how Thrag rose to power. The king in Thrag's day, a creature named Dassymus, had nearly driven the frostwings mad with starvation. Had Thrag not acted, Icehome would have eaten the gwereste they'd sheltered for protection, and the mixed army of frostwings and feral folk that saved Balgavarr would have never existed. Coryn's father would have died in the morehl onslaught or been killed by Morguus Ebraxus, the dragon who plagued the northern vagha for generations.

Coryn didn't know Rawrgyld. She hoped for the best possible outcome, should the wingless hero prevail, but she could not fathom anything aside from Ra'al taking his rightful place as ruler of Icehome. *I want Ra'al to kill the frostwing who'd saved everyone in Castle Ice*, and that thought made her sick to her stomach. If that was her default, did that make Rawrgyld the new Thrag?

The dwarf paused mid-step. Such a notion meant that Rashingot and Ra'al were the corrupt leaders who clutched thrones and crowns for selfish reasons, according to the historic pattern.

"They say that Avanna, one of the goddesses of fate, often weaves cruelty into the pattern of life," said a voice.

Coryn looked up. She'd been so preoccupied, she hadn't even noticed Fazayou standing in front of her. Cocking her head, Coryn wondered, *can he read my mind?*

"No," responded the selumari. "I can't read your mind."

"What! How did you do that?" Coryn blurted.

"I am very skilled at reading faces," Fazayou said. "I have spent much time in Lady Naemyar's company; it is a skill she insisted that I hone." His face softened. "Everything is going to be okay."

Coryn watched the elf, his mannerisms, and expressions, and briefly quizzed him on all things relating to the selumari queen. Fazayou scored perfectly and Coryn relaxed. Moments later, she dumped all her thoughts—the undead, the challenge for the throne, her father's trouble in Balgavarr and Tulgesh—onto her selumari visitor.

Finally, Coryn took a deep breath and realized how badly she'd needed to talk—even if just to vent all the anxiety she'd built up.

Fazayou gave her a warm grin. "Naemyar dispatched me to the north. She sent me here to find *you*, Coryn." He looked aside as Garesch walked into view. He was flanked by Marnash and two other lava elves. The red-skinned comrades joined Coryn, and Garesch greeted Fazayou with a deep bow.

Fazayou gave a stiff bow in kind and continued, "In Tulgesh, the Lady learned from one of Matrek's scouts that the battle looked unwinnable. Avanna aside, she insisted that if anyone stood a chance to overcome, it would be you and Ra'al." The selumari lowered his voice. "I know that Ra'al faces a serious challenge in the morning. Geril also faces hardship on multiple fronts." He locked eyes with Garesch. "You have your own challenges with Uruzak and I suspect its resources are not nearly as depleted as Saugor would have us believe."

Garesch was learned in diplomacy and remained perfectly neutral. However, the jaws of his guards stiffened and Marnash would not meet his gaze.

He did not intend to probe deeper into the lava elf problem, however. "Despite all of that, the single greatest threat is the undead army. You brought Naemyar into the fold in Tulgesh and she has information that is critical to your efforts. Were the distance not so great, she would have come herself. Instead, she tasked me with conveying her wishes on her behalf, once we could be alone."

"Um, okay," Coryn said. "Then give me the information."

Fazayou watched the dwarf for a moment. "I cannot. She did not give it to me. It is too private, and she would not consent to write it down."

"Then how are we to receive it?" Coryn asked.

Fazayou looked nervous. "I shall connect you." He looked to the morehl. "You must give us the room. This is only for those in my Lady's confidence… as intimate as my link is with her, she has not divulged this message even to me… and I will not be privy to it when she speaks it to you."

"I assure you, we are in her circle," Garesch said, "Marnash and I." The prince waved away his two guards. One of them questioned his orders with an apprehensive look, but Garesch insisted.

When only the four of them remained, Fazayou unstopped two small bottles and poured their contents into two tiny shot glasses. One liquid was red, and the other was blue. "When the conversation is over, make sure that I drink the remaining cup."

"What happens if you don't?" Coryn asked.

"My heart and lungs will stop, and I will die," Fazayou said very seriously.

Coryn nodded and the blue elf threw back the first of the liquids. The selumari slumped down onto his rump and shuddered as a kind of trance took hold.

"I have seen this before," Marnash said. He explained, "Magicians can use their abilities to speak to and through others over great distances. The greater the space between, the more painful and dangerous it is. For Fazayou to be a vessel, he must enter a deep trance. Essentially, he'll be blackout drunk. He won't remember a thing; he'll be too far relaxed to have caught any of the conversation... and yes, without the second drink, he'll slip into a coma and die."

Before Coryn could respond, Fazayou's legs jerked, and he stood, mimicking the poise and mannerisms of Lady Naemyar. Fazayou did his best falsetto impression of her voice. For all intents and purposes, Fazayou *was* Naemyar as she cast her consciousness across the continent of Cyrea.

"Coryn... is that you?" Fazayou blinked, staring into space.

"Yes, Lady Naemyar. I am here."

"Are you alone?" Naemyar asked. It was obvious that she could hear and speak but could not see. "I must speak with you. On your honor, these words are for you alone."

"I am here, too," Garesch said. "And Marnash is with me."

"It is only us three," Coryn said, "and your servant Fazayou."

Naemyar fell silent for a moment. "The morehl may remain. I trust them. And once you hear my words, you will know exactly how damning they could be. All of you have proved yourself worthy of that trust."

None of them quite knew how to respond to that. But the selumari continued unabated so that her hold on the difficult spell would not fail.

"I've studied much of my father's notes since you first left for Frostshoal—and even more so after the evil forces stole the Magestorm Cache. I am beyond concerned."

Coryn's adventurous spirit vibrated within her. As much as she feared the danger of her mission, the fact that fate had called her to such a task excited her. She'd grown up with a wannabe-bard for her best friend and been fed a diet of over-embellished tales of the ancient King Gundraokh and Zephras Thunderfist.

"What have you learned?" Coryn asked.

"I believe I know who controls the fiends: an ancient evil named Leisterbane. He was a great selumari general once and the royal protector of the coral elf princess Ailushurai. She was the selumari Champion of the first age. Ailushurai was Gods'own until her eldarim lover, Melkior, was corrupted by the Death god. You know the tale?"

Coryn nodded, though the morehl appeared hesitant. "Yes," she said. "The Lady of Lurneville is the name of the song, I think?"

"Melkior's memory has largely faded from memory, and it has become difficult to separate fact from myth, but he was Death's chosen one. The greatest of the threats against Nature so close to the Making. After Ailushurai's tragic death and the slaughter of an entire race, Leisterbane and his troops tracked Melkior down and the eldarim murdered them and made them into some of the earliest versions of the undead. He tasked Leisterbane with spreading the bloodless plague across the face of Esfah. Leisterbane did as instructed, even while the remaining Champions rallied and slayed their former companion, sacrificing themselves to finally end Melkior. Leisterbane survived. He left Charnock during the time of the Champions and was observed in the Birthlands before the fall of the Obsidian Grotto and the demise of Sshkkryyahr the Dread. Sightings all over the world were reported after; the most recent was in Cyrea around year eight hundred in the Second Age."

"That's nearly three hundred and fifty years ago," Coryn noted.

Naemyar nodded. "The sighting of Leisterbane is merely assumed. After so many generations, he, too, has passed much out of memory. And ascertaining one awakened corpse from another can be difficult. Let us hope that the report was wrong." She paused. "But I fear we may not be so lucky."

Coryn's throat tightened.

"If it is Leisterbane, he now has both an overwhelming force *and,* we can assume, Harol. He has probably delivered Leisterbane the gnomish weapons from the Magestorm Cache. Evil frequently fights amongst itself for power, but in my research, I found Harol's confession to the Balgavarrian council all those years ago. He admitted to becoming an acolyte of Death and a cultist. He said he was recruited by..." Naemyar paused and swallowed. Words became difficult for her.

Coryn champed at the bit to know. "Who, Naemyar?"

"I... I..." she glanced around the room even though the elf's eyes could not show her anything.

Naemyar took a deep breath. "Please believe me when I tell you that few know my darkest secret, and I expect you will take it to your grave with you."

The others nodded and then pledged with spoken word.

"It was tradesman Riechus. My father. While the vaghan elders banished Harol, my father was executed for separate, equally terrible crimes in Tulgesh that only the elite houses knew of. Matrek has kept that fact far from the public to preserve a political and economic balance. Even I did not know of Riechus's dark apprentice until you left to defend Balgavarr."

Naemyar sighed. "All this explains why my father's research is so accurate and focused on Harol and the Magestorm weapons."

"And what of the mist stones?" asked Marnash.

Naemyar shrugged. "He had no record of them. There were several references to a secret tree that was hidden by the sages. Apparently, it was the sages' duty to protect it. You received the maps from a sage, correct?"

"Something like that," Marnash admitted.

"Whatever the bloodless are searching for, whatever Leisterbane's mission, the mist stones are simply a means to an end. He wants whatever those markers protect." Naemyar's body language looked very serious. "Whatever each of our personal struggles might be, this battle has far greater repercussions. The result of our next steps will ring across all of Esfah, impacting all men and women, including those who sit on thrones or wear crowns."

Coryn gulped. "But if Ra'al loses the duel tomorrow?"

Naemyar wouldn't let her focus on that possibility. "We must simply pray that he prevails. Far more rests upon his success than gaining his father's title. I fear that without Icehome's support, the vagha stand little chance of overcoming Leisterbane's forces. They are significant, and each one that falls will only increase Leisterbane's army."

"If there is a chance to defeat Leisterbane at all," Coryn vowed, "the vagha will see it done."

Naemyar nodded resolutely. "Of that, Lady Coryn, I have no doubt. All of Esfah, those of us who know the truth of the black army in the north, are trusting you. The rest of us too far removed from battle will have to try to dispel whatever havoc the politicians are wreaking upon the populace in the meantime. I shall do what I can in Tulgesh."

"Oh good," Coryn said. "My father is on his way there now."

The coral elf sighed. "I hope I've helped. I fear I must now go. I feel myself weakening under this spell."

Before she could leave, Garesch interjected, "Lady Naemyar, might I have a private word first? At the risk of overtaxing you, I... need a favor that only you can provide."

"Of course," Naemyar said.

Coryn nodded and then handed the prince the drink Fazayou required to stay alive and then departed to give him some privacy.

Ra'al was hungry. The big areosa was *always* hungry, but never before had he yearned for a good meal like tonight. He'd trained most of the day with his former combat instructor. The frostwing had taught him all through his youth, but he'd never actually paid attention until now. Luckily, much of the lessons had trickled through over the years despite his lack of eagerness.

This time, with his life on the line, his eagerness was at an all-time high. In previous years, his master had bruised and pummeled him, hoping that pain would teach lessons the student's attention span could not grasp. This time, his instructor would not damage him and refused to wear him down physically. Those were dangers for tomorrow when Rawrgyld and Ra'al battled for supremacy. Today's lessons had been intellectual—he showed Ra'al as many looks as possible and demonstrated how he could counter certain maneuvers and tactics to stay alive and press his advantage. Because his enemy had no wings, it changed how the attacks would come.

Rawrgyld had more years' worth of experience, but Ra'al had his youth and vigor. Those didn't account for much. Rawrgyld was not advanced in years and Ra'al was barely an adult by frostwing reckoning.

Ra'al may have proved himself to his friends and comrades, but Rawrgyld was no lowly trog or faeli upstart. He was a highly skilled frostwing warrior who had traveled the world and been offered high positions in Icehome's military in the past. But Ra'al had the song of the wind on his side, and he felt the presence of King Thrag surging in his bones.

He was confident, but hungry. He entered his quarters late. Ra'al was exhausted, but more so mentally than physically. He knew what he needed more than anything else was a hearty meal and a long rest before the challenge.

Something tickled his nose, and he smelled the baked fish and roasted dove within his chambers. He'd not seen Coryn since she'd left him to train earlier in the morning, and that had been shortly after the excursion into the bowels of Icehome. He was still angry about that but had too little mental energy left to dwell on it.

Ra'al could sense his friend's hand in the surprise supper. A full spread was laid out in his room. Appetizers, drink, and primary dishes that were Ra'al's favorites had been placed upon trays in his room. Nestled between the dishes was a bottle of Coryn's favorite, spicy condiment, Kafnysan fire sauce.

He smiled and dug in. He'd thank his friend in the morning.

Ra'al knew his time to serve his people and his family had finally arrived. He knew Coryn's would come too, in time.

Until then, he was just glad to have friends he could rely on. Life or death, come what may, he knew Coryn would have his back. But for now, he needed to eat, and so Ra'al did.

Coryn looked up when someone knocked on her door, even though it hung ajar. Garesch waited for her.

"Come in," she insisted and kicked a path clear through supplies, laundry, and other discarded items. Her room in Castle

Ice remained much as she'd left it before she and Ra'al had departed many months ago on their diplomatic journey.

Garesch kept any judgment from his face and found a seat.

Coryn offered him some of the food that had been brought to her on a tray, but he passed. "You're sure? I mean, I can't seem to find any fire sauce in this Firiel-forsaken place, but the food's okay. I guess I should've brought some with me from Balgavarr…"

The prince shook his head. "I'm sure that many in the city are just glad they still have food, if not homes."

Coryn nodded slowly, realizing her slightest complaints were worlds better than the refugee frostwings currently living in the caves below them, or Old Icehome. The explosive-rigged pillars were only accessible from the secret passages hidden behind rockblankets, but the upper level of the caves provided ample housing for those families displaced by the undead's attack. Reconstruction would begin soon. Currently, Coryn needed to decide how many vagha she could spare to leave back and help guide building efforts while they went north.

"The plight of the refugees weighs heavily on my mind, Coryn. It is much the same in Uruzak. Many thousands of morehl suffer under the waste of my father's endless wars," said Garesch.

Coryn stared at him and picked at the food with her fingers. At their first meeting, she'd maintained a lady-like demeanor, hoping to impress the prince. Those manners were long gone now they'd grown close enough to become friends. "You sound like you want to get back to them?"

Garesch stared at her, and Coryn's shoulders slumped with recognition. "No," she said. "You can't go *now*. I need you with me when we go north to hunt down the undead. You heard Lady Naemyar… this is *Leisterbane* we're dealing with."

"There are barely more than a dozen of us lava elves," Garesch said. "We will scarcely be missed. And I have obligations to my people. Civil war brews in Uruzak as sentiments shift against Saugor. I must launch my campaign now, Coryn. I know my father. If I wait any longer, he will strike first, gutting the sympathizers before they've had a chance to prepare for them. He'll make such an example of the rebels that it will keep the rest in line for the next century."

Coryn frowned. "But Naemyar said that the undead are…"

"I know what she said," Garesch interrupted her. "But she actually agreed with my assessment in your absence."

Coryn crossed her arms, clearly displeased. "Fine. We'll have plenty of help once Ra'al is king."

"*If Ra'al emerges victorious*," Garesch said, cautioning her against presumption. "And I hope so."

Her brows knit with anger. "There is no other possible outcome," she snapped.

Garesch put his hands up. "I'm not trying to cast doubt on him. I have seen him fight and battled alongside him as you have. I am just saying that… how did Fazayou put it… the goddess Avanna is a cruel weaver of fate. The unexpected too often comes to pass."

She exhaled a blast of hot air through her nose and crossed her arms, unwilling to believe such a thing was possible.

"If there was more time or if circumstances were different, I would ride at your side to the Netherwold itself," Garesch said. "But if my support in Uruzak fails, then evil grows stronger and the Death god gains even more of a foothold on this world." He frowned. "There is the matter of the dwarven spies."

She had received word from Lordan about them, but this was the first she'd heard Garesch speak of it.

"Your father discovered them when they tried to take me last night. He banished them from the city, but I've seen them since. They will try again, and they will eventually succeed.

And even if they don't, surely my number will shrink below twelve," Garesch spoke with a heavy heart. "I really do have little choice, my friend. I must leave."

Coryn sighed and relented. "I know," she spoke softly. "But I'm still going to be angry about it."

They sat together in silence for a short while as the dwarf's emotions unraveled deep within her and she felt ever more alone as her friends and family went separate ways. Her course remained plotted directly into the heart of darkness. A course she dreaded walking alone—and if Ra'al lost his challenge, she'd be fully cast adrift on her mission.

"Nothing is going according to plan right now," she muttered, breaking the quiet.

"Avanna truly is cruel," Garesch said and then stood. He bowed formally to Coryn. "We leave under the cover of darkness. Please explain our absence to *King Ra'al* after the challenge. I do not want to burden his mind at a time like this, but Marnash thinks it best to sneak away when the council's hunters will have the most difficulty spotting us... and that means right now."

Coryn held her emotions in check long enough to return a stiff bow. "I shall see you again, *King of Uruzak*," she said with forced optimism.

Garesch returned the bow, turned, and then left.

CHAPTER SEVEN

Morning wind swept across the frigid circle of ice where the areosan elders had designated the challenge would occur. Five frosty pillars towered at the edges of a semi-enclosure and cast long shadows in the early morning light.

Coryn stood in the chilly air, bundled up in furs and hides, and of course, her boots. *Where* is *he,* she wondered… *where is Ra'al?*

She was one of the few invited to witness the challenge in addition to the elders. Coryn's gut quaked at the sight of the massive, wingless areosa approaching upon his mighty bear, Nanku. The creature lumbered with a fluid, powerful gait.

Rawrgyld dismounted on the far side of the arena and stepped into the circle. He looked from face to face and asked the elders the same question that everyone else wondered. "Where is Ra'al, son of Thrag? Does he intend to surrender the throne so easily?"

Rashingot turned her head stiffly, still dealing with recent wounds suffered on the battlefield. She snorted through her nostrils, obviously wondering about her son. The five elders gave her a disapproving look. They'd long encouraged her to take a firmer hand with the prince.

"This isn't like him," Coryn insisted to the queen. "He knows how important this is." She frowned, however. *This was* exactly *like Ra'al... the old Ra'al, anyway, the Ra'al from before he'd found the song of the wind.*

Rawrgyld spread his arms wide, clutching his magic axe in one hand. "If my challenger refuses to meet me, what is the elders' ruling?"

The elders, a group of the most aged frostwings from the community, traded confused glances. They were advisers to the throne first and foremost. Control over the rite of challenge was the only true power they wielded. It was a mighty check to the throne's balance and one which could be swayed by the will of the people and of public sentiment, but no royal areosa had ever refused to arrive and meet a challenge. There was no protocol in place for such an action.

"We will have to confer about consequences to the failing party," stated the oldest of them, "but we *can* render judgment for the prevailing party taking the throne."

Rashingot's lips curled, and she bared her fangs. Coryn nearly recoiled at their sight. Rashingot would not surrender Thrag's kingdom so easily to an outsider.

"Elders, we live in unique times, and I am sure there is reason for my son's absence. However, there is another unique feature of this challenge: though I had agreed to abdicate, my son has not yet been crowned, meaning I ought to still be able to defend the throne at my option."

Surprised ripples of fur on one elder matched the raised brows of another as they chatted briefly among themselves and then quieted. "We accept that as a fair interpretation," said the spokesman. "The original challenge *was* issued to the queen, after all."

Rawrgyld's face melted into a pleasantly surprised smile. Rashingot's strength was formidable, but her son had unknown potential. For all the elders and Rawrgyld knew, he might have possessed more of Thrag's legendary prowess than even the fallen king had.

"Wait!" howled a weak voice from the nearby Castle Ice. "I am coming." Ra'al loped from the gate with drooping, weary eyes. His wings were barely held to half height, and he practically dragged his axe.

Ra'al took five more steps and then doubled over, retching and emptying the contents of his stomach. He staggered and fell to one knee and then hurried forward again. The frostwing could barely run in a straight line and listed to one side like his inner ear was thrown off. He finally arrived, panting and in obvious pain.

Rawrgyld's surprised face turned to the elders. "Is this one drunk?"

Ra'al growled, "I am here and prepared to face the challenge. And I'm certainly not drunk. I haven't been able to keep anything down since my meal last night." The idea struck like lightning. "I believe that I have been poisoned. Someone must have dosed the food you sent me last night, Coryn."

The dwarf's face revealed her worry. "I didn't send you anything." Panic reddened her cheeks even more than the winter winds that bit them. She feared Ra'al would have to fight while ill and he would be killed for it.

"This is my birthright," Ra'al roared with as much vitriol as he could muster. "My father's throne must pass to me, and I am here to defend it. My travels taught me what it means to be areosa."

The elders stared at him as if they might be swayed by his commitment. And then Ra'al turned and fell to his knees, dry heaving.

"Queen Rashingot has already agreed to the challenge and stated she will not abdicate until the fight has ended... if she emerges victorious," they responded. "Perhaps the prince's illness is the verdict of the gods. Only the outcome of this fight can ascertain that."

Rashingot grabbed her son and hauled Ra'al to his feet. She pulled Coryn in, too, and hugged them both. "You are family as well, little sparrow. Something foul is surely at play, but we must be strong. It is the frostwing way." She touched her head to Ra'al's as a sign of affection. "I truly believe rule belongs to our line—to *your* line, Ra'al. You are your father's son." She touched his face and saw something in him that Ra'al had difficulty finding on his own.

"Even now, after learning the song of the wind, I feel unworthy," he said and nearly collapsed again, but his mother held him up.

"You have heard its song," insisted Rashingot. "Now you must prove it to the rest. Be strong like ice and as unyielding as a glacier. It is the way of the areosa. Promise me that if I fall, you will protect our people from the undead and from themselves?"

Ra'al nodded. "I promise," he said breathlessly.

Satisfied, the queen stepped away and into the ceremonial circle, where the others could not follow. She drew the broad blade from her side and stared at the impressive weapon her opponent carried. The enchanted axe had once disrupted the power of the necralluvium.

"The rite has begun," called one of the elders who struck a small, ceremonial gong.

The two combatants circled each other warily, sizing each other up.

"Do not worry over Frostquake," Rawrgyld said. "My axe will do no greater damage to you than yours, unless you are undead." He leapt forward and slashed at her.

Rashingot dodged backwards with a flap of her wings and soared just out of his reach. She snarled at him and then lunged downward with a might strike of her blade. Rawrgyld dodged out of the way just in time.

The challenger growled, "So much for this being a fair fight."

"You challenge my honor?" she roared, swinging her weapon twice.

Rawrgyld side-stepped and then batted a stroke away. "Merely making an observation. I, too, would do whatever is required for victory. It is the frostwing way."

"Without honor, that way is meaningless," she snarled, pressing her attack. "But I will not fly beyond your reach," Rashingot pledged.

Rawrgyld lunged at her with a wild, telegraphed stroke of his axe. Rashingot knocked it aside, sending Frostquake sailing through the air and disarming her opponent.

She did not see how he'd baited her and summoned a lance of ice in his off hand, keeping low. Then, he rammed it through the top-most part of her wing, impacting and breaking the bone.

"No. You certainly will not," Rawrgyld growled.

With her wing hanging limp, Rashingot hacked at him, shattering the ice spike he'd formed from the air. Rawrgyld created two more, and she smashed them as well.

The queen pressed at him, her rage sustaining her and momentarily masking her pain. Her enemy ducked beneath a horizontal stroke and stomped upon her injured wing where it dragged behind her. Rashingot stiffened, blinded by a surge of agony.

Rawrgyld summoned another lance and ran her through from the back side before leaping away. He failed to react fast enough, and the queen's claws raked across his face, slicing him open from brow to snout and spattering crimson across the white ground. It speckled Rawrgyld's snow-colored fur in red.

Rashingot anticipated him leaping to safety, and she flashed her arms outward, flinging jagged spears of ice like crossbow bolts in a full circle around her. The guests witnessing the duel ducked to avoid the wild cascade of deadly ice.

Rawrgyld leapt upon one of the plinths and scaled it vertically to stay beyond her weapons' reach. He did not have wings, but he was canny, and he leapt from tower to tower, angling for a perfect position while Rashingot tried to locate him and summon the strength to chase him.

Before she could muster such an offensive, Rawrgyld roared and summoned lances of ice from overhead. He called them down from the sky like the legend of the Daybringer's fall in Karakto, and the spears rained down upon Rashingot.

The queen raised her arms and good wing as if they might shield her from the fist-thick needles of hardened ice. They did not, and a barrage of frozen javelins rammed through her. At least a dozen of them slammed into her body, piercing her and pinning her to the ground while Rawrgyld relaxed his grip and lowered himself to the field of battle.

Ra'al yelled as the missiles struck his mother. He collapsed to his knees from both the poison running a course through his system and the shock of Rashingot's defeat. Coryn gasped as her best friend searched for her hand and squeezed it.

Rashingot lay bent half backwards, impaled by so many spikes. Her red blood oozed down and froze to the icicles that pierced and held her aloft like macabre legs of a table. Her head lolled to one side, and she locked eyes with Ra'al and Coryn. "Remember your promise," she gasped. And then an elder rang the gong to finalize the conclusion and Rashingot died with a final gasp.

Rawrgyld picked up the queen's blade and grasped it by the hilt, feeling the weight of it. "By rite, this is now mine." His lips curled, barring his teeth as he hefted the weapon and then brought it crashing down upon Rashingot, severing her head. It fell with a sickly thump. "As is the throne."

"At last, our lord Malgrimm has allowed me to reveal my presence." Leisterbane's voice boomed in the dark. It echoed off the cavernous walls of the frozen Heimdarl Crag and even the fiery apparitions of his three conspirators flinched.

Leisterbane had never bothered to learn their names. He knew them by the smell of their fears and the stink of their undisturbed flesh. Those things told more about any creature than a name.

The crazed vagha who had delivered him the cache of Magestorm weapons grinned eagerly, like a dog awaiting praise for its behavior. Leisterbane knew the dwarf was on his way to his next appointment and was nowhere near Cyrea. The other two paid close attention.

Leisterbane's eyes glowed as he fixed them upon the morehl. "Our deal has endured these centuries and my power has made you each a force to reckon with. How stands your task?"

The red elf said, "My spies assure me that the seeds of chaos have been sown. Our part in the operation is nearly complete. None of the races beyond the Shadowlands could stand against your might. And even if all the races opposed you, by the time they are aware of your true purpose in the Shadowlands, or your intentions upon what the sages hid beyond the mist stones, it will be far too late. But we shall continue the ruse all the same."

"And you, selumari?" Leisterbane shifted his gaze. "Tell me why I endure your presence and should make you a chief in the coming world of darkness?" The coral elf always smelled the least fearful of the three, and that fact had always disturbed Leisterbane.

"I have provided many secrets in my years of service," said the blue elf. "And you shall retain my company because I am the last surviving consort of the great eight-legged one. When Sshkkryyahr the Dread took me as her lover, she promised me that her position would pass to me. I represent the favor given to the elder monster since the First Age."

Leisterbane's eyes burned again as he reassessed the cultist. "And when have you last provided useful information?"

"I bring some now, great Leisterbane. In the house of a shipping magnate, a certain ambitious frostwing was spotted. That same creature was reported on by the brothers and sisters in service of Nekarthis. Rawrgyld recently attended a Wind and Fire auction in faraway Charnock… the same continent where my mistress finally lost her life to the child of the Adventurer King. Rawrgyld returned via a Riechus ship and traveled north to wait for an opportunity among his people."

The undead leader stared at the flaming effigy, waiting for it to continue. "What opportunity. What did this areosa purchase?"

"An opportunity to become a hero. Rawrgyld was the grandson of Dassymus, the former frostwing deposed by King Thrag."

Leisterbane leaned in, finally understanding the implications. Not only did Rawrgyld's presence aide in the discord among the cult's enemies, but he remembered Dassymus as a scourge upon his own people. He did not know the grandson, but the undead had complete freedom in the Shadowlands. With a weakened areosan people, his resurrected minions walked freely in the frosty wastes.

The blue skin continued, "Rawrgyld rescued Castle Ice from our southern army. He led the rallied forces of the outland frostwings and did so in such a manner that shamed the queen, may she rot. His purpose was never anything but a play for the throne and he has issued the ritual challenge. Rawrgyld is aided by a weapon he purchased from the faeli relic brokers—an enchanted hammer that hits with the power of Eldurim but quiets the necralluvium."

"Explain," Leisterbane commanded.

"It destroys us. Much like an intense amount of fire."

Leisterbane growled within the tattered remains of his throat. "How is such a thing possible?"

"The gremmlobahnd made many weapons, and they always aligned them with the power of the gods. Perhaps this is something new, or perhaps a gnome or other crafter learned to align the weapon with Ghaeial herself. No other god has the strength to so clearly dispel Malgrimm's blessing."

Leisterbane sat back and rubbed his chin. "Interesting," he said after a long pause. "And this descendant of Dassymus has no true intentions of playing the hero?"

"No, dread lord," the coral elf said. "Even were it so, he will remain too preoccupied with solidifying power rather than involving himself with new wars. We were a means to an end for him: an opportunity to acquire power. Shall I send an emissary to establish contact? Perhaps he could make a powerful ally in the…"

"No," Leisterbane commanded. "Icehome is no longer a concern. So long as we leave via the north side of the Crag, they will never spot us and shall never worry about the undead again. Their kind are too short-sighted to see the full tapestry we weave. As soon as we finish Malgrimm's task, we shall leave Cyrea in search of our next target."

He waved his hand, and the flame-wreathed visages of his minions dissipated in a wisp of smoke. Leisterbane stood and left the makeshift throne room where he had waited for centuries, amassing his army. Cracks in the floor seeped black ichor, where necralluvium bubbled to the surface in pools. Death's alchemy brewed here because of the festration established within the crag… a festration created by an old tool lost to time: a boon granted by Malgrimm.

Festrations, dead zones that projected an aura of evil death magic, were often strongholds that attracted all sorts of Malgrimm's minions. Typically, festrations attached themselves to places where great atrocities had been committed. But the Heimdarl Crag was too inhospitable even for the regular agents of Death. This festration was different—it came from a person, and what he carried: the darkhold gem, a precious stone which had been given to an ambitious, and psychotic, sorceress long ago.

She'd been defeated while the undead were still learning what they were. But after his lover's defeat which Peregrine had survived, he wandered halfway around the world with the crystal in his possession; Leisterbane found him wandering the wastes and given him purpose. A festration was permanently attached to Peregrine's darkhold gem. Wherever *it* went, the festration followed. It corrupted the land and amplified the death magic present. It also stirred up the necralluvium.

"Peregrine," Leisterbane barked.

The loathsome creature crept from the ranks of bloodless soldiers. A purple gem hung from his neck by a simple lanyard, glowing with a fell light. "I am here."

Peregrine had proved compliant and so Leisterbane had never attempted to take it from him. But if he chose to do so, Leisterbane was not certain he'd have been able to. Such was the power of those relics.

"We move out shortly," Leisterbane ordered, causing a shiver of excitement in the exposed bones of his myriad warriors. Some had awaited orders in this place for hundreds of years.

"Task the artisans," Leisterbane said, "and fire the smiths. We need wheeled carts and great cauldrons to transport the necralluvium. With it we shall poison the land and attack Ghaeial herself."

Peregrine bowed. "I shall make it so."

Lahmyn sat down inside the dingy hovel down the slopes of the Kafnysan range. The home belonged to Derihus, an old dwarven war hero who had long ago fallen out of favor.

Derihus was a soldier in his youth and lost everything in Saugor's war against Balgavarr Reaches, the same one that had propelled Geril to fame. When the lava elves first stumbled upon the suburban town of Downslope, they thought they had finally located the elusive entrance to the vaghan city. Derihus had been part of the forward battle group alongside Geril and several others. Those soldiers had later been summoned to Tulgesh, where many had perished or been taken captive by the morehl. Returning home in defeat, a much younger Geril crossed paths with the injured Thrag.

Ever since, Derihus nursed a chip on his shoulder and languished in the rural community after his return. While Geril had escaped back to Balgavarr, enduring a brief detour that allowed him to meet Thrag in a cave, Derihus and several other prisoners of war languished in detention pits run by the invading lava elves who had conquered Tulgesh. Derihus was one of the few survivors of those harsh conditions; they'd waited months, hoping for a rescue from Matrek, who was a mere soldier during the invasion—and an opportunistic one at that.

The reclusive vagha knew the truth: Matrek had been a product of multiple, rapid field promotions. He had the right pedigree, but it was the fact that his superiors kept dying during the operations at Little Tulgesh, the base of the coral elves' guerrilla warfare against the red-skinned conquerors, that positioned him as a leader. While Derihus hoped for release with his peers dying all around him, Matrek sent Geril back to

Balgavarr Reaches for aid, using the prisoners of war as bargaining chips for support.

Most of Derihus's and Geril's peers earned an early grave for Matrek's ploy. But Geril had claimed a crown because of it, and he let Elder Lahmyn know how much he thought that was unfair.

"I ain't disloyal, mind ye," Derihus insisted. "But I ain't a fan of Geril sa'Ghuren. He was merely a product of an opportune moment, and he was lucky enough to have avoided drawing a bead from the morehl ball shot." He turned his head and spat to curse the lava elves for their past villainy.

"As one who gave so much on the field of battle for our causes," Lahmyn noted with fake shock, "I would never assume anything but the highest integrity from you."

Lahmyn poured another cup of ale for the dwarf. "You've been in the military all your life, Derihus. It seems odd that you've never risen very far in the ranks."

Derihus accepted the fresh mug and chugged the brew through the foam. "It's all politics, is what it is," he muttered. "I'm a nobody from a dirt-scratcher family. What does it matter how I served Balgavarr during the great war? My father had no special connections to the Council, and we didn't own nothing but what Eldurim gave us: the stones in our walls."

The elder grinned. "You are quite unlike Geril, but you *are* a war hero and a strong soldier. That makes you much more than a *nothing*," Lahmyn said. "People *do know you*. Though you've never made it earn for you, as one of the survivors of the red elf camps, your name is known among the people."

Derihus's countenance shifted and Lahmyn continued.

"I need a dwarf of your skill and reputation. Someone who knows the military and has connections: someone loyal to Balgavarr Reaches and its interests."

The grouchy dwarf took another swig, albeit more slowly. "I'm listening."

Lahmyn mustered a false sense of concern as he leaned forward. "There are many things shifting in the shadows of Balgavarr's long halls, my friend. Geril sa'Ghuren is away, and he's appointed Warlord Kile in his stead as steward. Kile is Geril's man—he is merely a puppet meant to let Geril rule from afar—and that further restricts the will of the people."

Derihus polished off his drink and set it down. "I know Kile. And I can agree with your observation. Besides, he and Geril are from the same clan, Hydrak."

Lahmyn nodded. "As clans, each house can seat a member on the council and have their voice heard. Why is Geril's voice the only one with authority? And then he puts a warlord atop it to keep his power. I daresay conversations like ours could become illegal very soon."

"But we *need* warlords," Derihus said. "Not to make war, but to keep order. It's merely a title for the…"

"I know all that." Lahmyn waved his hand. "But do we need *this* warlord?"

Derihus raised a brow and his company slid him another drink.

"I believe the council will be appointing a new warlord soon. I am looking for potential vagha who might take on the role."

Derihus kept his voice even. "And you think another hero from the great war would fit the bill?"

"It would certainly help," Lahmyn said. "I need to find one who can command respect in the military. One who can muster a force that can act swiftly and work on behalf of the Council of Elders, the true rulers of Balgavarr Reaches—the elders who work on behalf of its people. We need such loyalty that they might disobey the steward, even if it became necessary."

The dwarf stared into his cup. "I can find the warriors. I know many of 'em… but siding against the steward is the same as disobedience to the crown. I don't know if I can get many patriots willing to disobey direct orders from the throne. Not unless its corruptions were glaringly obvious."

"What if it was in the best interest of Balgavarr?" Lahmyn asked. "What if the steward, or an elder, was caught up in treason? I have suspicions against Elder Lordan and his dealings with the morehl."

Derihus's face shifted. He'd been obviously displeased with the recent occurrence of lava elves being given access to Balgavarr Reaches when he'd sacrificed everything to win the war against them, and he suspected Lordan had tipped them off to his private hunters sent on the Council's behalf. Derihus absentmindedly touched an old scar he'd received when the morehl had tortured him in Tulgesh. "A traitor, you say?"

"Strong evidence," Lahmyn insisted.

Derihus nodded. "Aye. Perhaps, then, my Lord. I could certainly gather an army of loyalists."

"Excellent," Lahmyn said and smiled. "How soon can you contact them?"

CHAPTER EIGHT

Prince Garesch rode abreast of Marnash, his closest adviser, as they angled south and east toward the Wilds of Dur'Sona. Night drew closer all around them. A full day had passed, and they'd traveled all during the previous night as well. The crew of twelve lava elves felt they'd safely put the dwarven council's hunters behind them.

Midway through the day, they had stumbled onto a traveling band of humans who had many animals they were willing to trade. The human traders knew they'd be able to upcharge for the convenience of larger mounts and then resell the ponies to dwarven tradesmen the next time they passed near the Kafnysan Mountains. Garesch and his elves traded up to fresh horses, which were more suited to the morehl riders and exchanged them for the ponies they'd taken from their vaghan allies, plus a few gold coins. It gave them the added benefit of fresh mounts, which gave them an edge in case Skrathos and his men still pursued them.

Thankfully, the traders had given Garesch something else they wanted: concrete directions leading to a small village in the wilds. Lava elves lived in the wilderness all along the disputed borders between the morehl and the trogs of Big Wet, as well as the boundary with the vagha.

Garesch knew of the elves living in diaspora. His initial mission had been to barter the land disputes with Uruzak's neighbors to increase the integrity of their borders and solidify profit for the crown. In a way, he'd accomplished all that through his travels, even if he'd never located those displaced morehl. But part of the job meant surveying the borders, and he'd learned in doing so that many morehl outcasts, political dissidents, and anyone failing to walk lockstep with King Saugor tended to dwell at the fringes of the Uruzak kingdom, and often put down roots just beyond its reaches.

The prince realized what tasks his father had given him were really about. Surrendering those fringe lands at the borders would run off any of the king's political opponents. Those who kept their distance because of the danger Saugor represented would wake up after the treaties were signed and find themselves living in lands owned by folk who hated lava elves. If they survived and moved closer, Saugor's spies could watch them more easily.

Garesch bit his lip as he traveled. *Saugor is a calculating, evil bastard of a king... and an even worse father.*

Their horses' breath came in white plumes as the beasts navigated narrow trails where trees pressed in against them like crushing walls. Conifers densely packed this part of the Wilds and both cone and bristle gleamed white where frost accented them. Finally, a clearing opened, and the hidden morehl village sat in its middle. This location was not close enough to the border to be under Uruzak's control. The Wilds of Dur'Sona were free lands, but the vagha and others had agreed to act as its wardens. That meant the village would likely see any unknown visitors as a threat, including other lava elves. Given Saugor's atrocities, *especially* other lava elves.

Garesch realized that the faces of folk in the village had turned to watch them the instant they'd come into view. He assumed that he and his escort's arrival looked every bit like Saugor's scouts had come to kill or capture them. The prince held his hands aloft to indicate he was not holding a weapon; he guessed that more than one flintlock was already trained on him and had been from the moment he entered visibility.

The line of horses stopped and Garesch's followers came to the same realization. They paused, waiting for one of the villagers to approach.

Garesch watched frightened children scurry into their homes. Two young lava elves broke company with a pair of gray elves; the foursome dashed in opposite directions and Garesch cocked his head toward Marnash.

"There are more here than just morehl," he said, keeping his voice low.

"Frehlasuhl," Marnash noted. "There must be at least one selumari here, then. How very progressive." The grays were the children of forbidden romances—the offspring of coral and lava elf unions. They were rejected by most cultures as abominations and often became indentured servants or even slaves as a means of survival.

Slowly, red-skinned men and women began to show themselves, gathering into a group at least twice the size of the newcomers. As Garesch scanned the village, he spotted no fewer than four hidden marksmen with long barreled firearms trained on him.

The bravest of the forest dwellers took a few steps toward Garesch and his men. He shouted, "We aren't coming back to Uruzak and we won't fight for the king. You can't make us—you won't survive any attempts, so I don't care what you tell your masters. Tell 'em you didn't find us, tell 'em you killed us all. It doesn't matter to us. We'll have relocated by the time you get back here with any larger numbers; we just want to be left alone."

Garesch cocked his head. "You really have no idea who I am?"

The elf shook his head.

"I am Prince Garesch, the rightful heir to Uruzak, and I have not come to force you to do anything. However, I am afraid some of you may decide my coming causes trouble for your village, which is quite contrary to our purpose here."

Garesch saw that the marksmen had slowly lowered their weapons and turned their ears to listen. "Please, may we enter your town and speak with your local leaders?"

"He ain't no prince," shouted one unruly villager. "He's lying. This is one of Saugor's traps."

"I *am* the prince and will even confess some of the rumors about me to be true. While I am not in open rebellion, I am not friendly to the crown's intentions and as royalty, I am exempt from any repercussions my father might lay against me. Aside from attempting an assassination, that is. But I am also more than the heir to Uruzak."

Garesch held aloft his sword and sheath and drew it over his head for the morehl to see it. They stood rooted in place as they beheld its beauty. Every lava elf knew this legendary blade.

"Is that…"

"It is the Sword of Aeschere," he confirmed reverently. Garesch turned it so that the light caught the inscription that ran along the ornate blade. In four different written languages, it read, *The Right Hand of Firiel.*

Aeschere had been the morehl Champion: the chosen one of the gods, or Gods'own, who had helped defeat Melkior, the son of Death, during the first age. The sword's existence had passed into myth. It was not magical, but it was of eldari origin and craftsmanship, and the lava elves believed that it gave a morehl the right to rule. Not just to lead a kingdom, but *all lava elves,* and their patron goddess, aside from Death, was Firiel.

The town's spokesman stepped closer to get a better look. "How did you come by it?"

"Fate," Garesch simply said. "Avanna may be a cruel weaver, but her sister Evaquar often grants a kindness." He'd discovered the blade in a junk store in Frostshoal. The shopkeeper did not know what he'd had. Given how one looked at it, they could still see the hand of fate guiding that encounter. In truth, the moment he spotted the blade in Frostshoal, Garesch knew he'd been set on a course by destiny—a course that could only end in Uruzak.

An older morehl emerged from the crowd. He had a confident look about him and the others seemed to regard him with respect. Garesch knew he was the local authority in an instant.

"I am Sharsah and I lead the town," he admitted. "You may enter."

Garesch nodded to his company, and they dismounted, but left their weapons mounted at their packs to avoid accidentally posturing threats.

"Come. We have a village hall in the main square. We will bring food and discuss whatever it is that concerns you. Hopefully the town of Wildkeep can prove it is a friend of Prince Garesch?"

The prince bowed and followed. "I believe it more important to prove that *I* desire the support and friendship of Wildkeep."

"Then you intend to ask a favor of us?" Sharsah asked.

Garesch nodded slowly.

They arrived at a small plank building which had been arranged as a meeting house. Sharsah explained that the residents had fled from Saugor's ever-increasing demands. At first, they had built cabins in the wilds and then they eventually established a network of them and moved closer together for the benefit of community. They'd been helped significantly by human traders and occasionally by the gwereste. It was difficult to hide from the feral folk, and so human and gwereste visitors were the only ones they felt unthreatened by.

"The dwarves do not know we are here, but hopefully they can take a lesson from the others," Sharsah said. "Uruzak destroyed Thurisa before it eventually attacked the vagha. But the humans have shown charity, even though our kind murdered their Thurisan ancestors."

Marnash said nothing, wondering how long the memories of humans even went. He hadn't been alive yet during the destruction of Thurisa, but he *had* been present at the battle of Balgavarr and witnessed the sacking of Tulgesh.

"My father's reign must end," Garesch said. "I fully intend to put a stop to it. We are enlisting support for when that time comes."

Sharsah looked skeptical.

"The winds of change are on the rise," Marnash insisted. "Civil war will break out soon if Saugor continues to pressure the lower castes as he has done these last many years. We need factions we can rely on to help rally a call to arms."

The town's leader slumped. "Then you suffer from delusions of grandeur. We can never beat those in the city. They are too strong."

Garesch leaned in. "That is just what those in the city want you to believe, but there are so many more of *us* than there are of *them*. If we band together, we can end Saugor's tyranny."

Sharsah still looked unconvinced, but he shrugged. "I will bring the idea to the people. I dare not speak for any of them over such an important issue… but you hold the blade of Aeschere and that makes your words compelling."

Garesch nodded. "For a free town, that is the most I could hope for. I will not order free men and women to service which could cost them their lives."

Sharsah looked to the door. "Food will arrive at any moment. It won't be a banquet, but it'll be the best we can do on short notice. Have you visited any of the other secret, free towns?"

The lava elf prince shook his head and gave him a wistful look. "About that, I would certainly like to learn more."

Ra'al and Coryn kept their heads high as they entered the throne room where Rashingot had held court for so many years. The coronation ceremony would mean that Ra'al was no longer a prince, but his culture would leave every royal expectation upon his shoulders as if he were still one. Coryn knew the frostwing way, and she stuck by his side; Rashingot had been like a mother to Coryn in her formative years after her own had passed and her father dedicated all his time into creating a better Balgavarr.

Neither of the two would show weakness at the ceremony. They'd done plenty of that on the day prior when they'd laid Rashingot's mutilated body to rest in a glacial region to freeze it solid. Whatever toxin had affected Ra'al on the morning of the challenge had run its course quickly and he'd been well enough to memorialize his mother. Someday, he hoped to carry away her remains and inter them alongside Thrag, who was buried beneath a statue made in his honor on one of the Kafnysan peaks nearest Balgavarr Reaches.

They entered the long hall and took their place with the others who had gathered: important officials within their fighting ranks, family leaders, and mixed species company such as diplomats and tradespeople.

Coryn scanned the crowd, wishing she could spot Naemyar among them. She knew the selumari rarely left

Tulgesh these days except on important business and wouldn't have the time to make the journey, even if she could get away for it. Just like with Garesch, but Coryn would have found a seat adjacent any morehl if there had been one left in Icehome.

Ra'al muttered profanities as they lumbered to a pair of open seats. Neither wanted to attend, but it was a necessary part of protocol, and if Ra'al ever wanted to reclaim his father's throne, he'd have to first obey. They only hoped the ceremony would be over swiftly.

"My mother did not die for pomp and circumstance," Ra'al growled in a whisper. "We need to take the army north immediately. Every moment we delay, the undead gain an advantage. That was what her sacrifice was for: to stop the hordes."

"I fully agree," spoke a familiar voice behind him.

Ra'al turned to find Hennedy. He and the scout traded knowing looks. Adjacent Hennedy sat another areosa adorned with bangles and trinkets binding tufts of fur in ornate patterns. Ra'al recognized him from the prior battle; he was a high-ranking magi from the frostwing's arcana corps and he'd helped drive out the ethereal undead with his wind magic.

The magi dipped his head in respect. "I am Karou," he said. "The wind's song be with you, son of Thrag."

Ra'al copied the motion. "And also with you, magi."

"Likewise to you, daughter of Balgavarr," Karou told Coryn.

The dwarf tilted her head. "Do you know my father?"

Karou shook his head. "Only by reputation, but I spent time during the battle with his confidant, Sheron the caster, who wanted me to find you. There has not been an appropriate time. There isn't likely to be one; time is something that is running in short supply. We should speak. Soon."

Ra'al and Coryn traded glances, and then nodded as a horn blower sounded the call for silence. Rawrgyld entered the hall, and the coronation began. He rode aback Nanku and beamed proudly as the bonded animal bore him to the front.

As the incoming king passed Ra'al, he gave the prince a shifty-eyed squint. Rawrgyld had emerged victorious and perhaps taken more than he could have otherwise by murdering Rashingot. As if to prove it, he bore the queen's sword at his back rather than Frostquake.

Ra'al could not even challenge him by the same rite. Not now. He needed the backing of the elders to permit it. And that meant Ra'al had to perform some grand heroic deed—and Rawrgyld had to simultaneously fall out of favor, and that might not happen for some time.

The former prince did his best not to bare his fangs at the new ruler who had stolen everything from him. Ra'al had just returned home in a more heroic manner than the elders could have assumed, but frostwing memories were as short as those of humans who were notoriously forgetful of public affairs and political winds. With a few exceptions, areosa remembered the most recent of heroic deeds, and the bear rider's rescue of Icehome felt somehow more real to them.

Rawrgyld passed him by, and everything in Ra'al urged him to attack. He wondered if the entire thing had been planned. *Did Rawrgyld poison me? I bet he's been hiding Frostquake for years and just waiting for the opportunity to use it and take the crown. No—I bet he engineered* everything: *the undead, the mist stones...* Ra'al sighed and realized his mind had gone to a dark place. No frostwing could have engineered so many factors for such an outcome. That simply didn't make sense. *Except the poisoning. That part could still be right.*

The wingless areosa climbed off Nanku and turned to the audience. He roared as the elders placed a ceremonial crown of ice upon his brow. And then he snatched the crown and smashed it to the ground, where it shattered into pieces, ceremonially signaling that the crown was not important—only his duty to the people he ruled.

Again, the horn echoed through the hall, completing the ceremony. The crowd dispersed slowly as watchers greeted the new ruler and used the opportunity to make political overtures, but Ra'al and Coryn made an exit ahead of the rest.

Rawrgyld was now king.

Skrathos stormed up the remainder of the Balgavarr slope and toward the main gate. He'd commandeered the services of some younger vagha casters stationed in Icehome while that pup Coryn decided her next course of action. He had them cast a path spell on his behalf. The casters he'd found were still green and their focus hadn't put the dwarf quite as close as he'd like, but it was a far cry better than riding back to address his uncle Trinean, Lahmyn, and the rest of the Balgavarrian loyalists on the council.

Running his tongue along his teeth and sucking in on the hole where he'd lost a tooth during a fight, Skrathos stomped past the city entrance and into the familiar tunnels that eventually led to Lahmyn's home. He knew the Council Elder would be awaiting his report.

After a longer walk than he'd cared for, Skrathos hurried through the city until he found himself at Elder Lahmyn's. The politician welcomed him in and brought him into the drawing room where Skrathos reported on his efforts to subdue Garesch.

"I nearly got that red-skinned imp. Found him wandering the halls of Castle Ice, but Geril got there just in time to rescue him."

Lahmyn raised a brow. "A pity a scuffle did not ensue; it could have accidentally seen him killed," the elder said, maintaining eye contact. "A pity indeed. I'm sure one of your zealous men could have been so eager to carry out orders, he did not realize who it was that interfered with them until it was too late. Perhaps that poor vagha might take grief-stricken justice into his own hands and kill himself…" The ender looked down his nose at Skrathos. "Should such a thing actually happen in the future, I would be pleased. *Could* it happen in the future?"

"It is impossible," Skrathos said. "Geril has gone to Tulgesh along with his most trusted guards. I watched him go myself. He went by a path spell."

"Then there is no one to stop you from taking Prince Garesch?"

"He cannot be located," said Skrathos. "None of the lava elves can be found in Icehome."

"Then look elsewhere," Lahmyn stated. "I'm certain you realize the necessity of capturing him. Do you have a skilled tracker in your party?"

"We do."

"Good. Send him to scout for clues. And check the military supply register. Whoever is in charge may have granted a request to provision them. It's likely if Garesch and his company decided to venture deeper into the Shadowlands or into the Wilds." As he said it, Lahmyn realized that piece of information was important. "Who did Geril leave in command?"

"Who do you think?"

"His daughter," Lahmyn realized. With a sneer, he drew up an order with quill and parchment.

Skrathos nodded. "She is Acting Warlord until Geril revokes such a status, returns, or the war ends."

"I assume Geril is chasing my son with the intent to kill him; I don't blame the dwarf for that. But at least I can deal young Coryn a surprising hand in response." Lahmyn turned the parchment toward Skrathos.

"A military order for the forces to return?"

"It's more than that," said Lahmyn, grinning. "It's a verdict to end the war and declare that the undead threat is past. Certainly, many of the troops would love to return to their families and begin reparations on Balgavarr Reaches, their homes, and businesses."

Skrathos grinned, flashing the gaping hole between his teeth. "And if we aren't in an active conflict, the title of Warlord is impotent. She won't be able to force any soldiers to do *anything* unless they want to do it... and of course, they won't have access to the provisions of Balgavarr's military."

He melted a stump of wax and fitted his signet ring to add his seal to the bottom. "It will need at least seven elders' seals for this to be official, or one from Warlord Kile, but he's unlikely to give it. I will provide you a list of names," Lahmyn said. "They will follow suit as soon as they see my mark. Return when you have this document ratified. Meanwhile, I'll gather some of my theurgists to send you back swiftly. The sooner your scouts can react to our missing lava elves, the better your odds of finding them." He looked at Skrathos with steely eyes. "You *will* find them."

"I've a few tricks up my sleeve," the hunter said. "My uncle did not recommend me to you on a whim. I'll catch this rogue morehl for you and you'll see him suffer for what he did to your family member... for what he did to *all Balgavarr*."

"Excellent," Lahmyn said. And he handed over a list of names to visit next to override Kile, the appointed steward, and strip Coryn of any ability to perform the job Geril had left her to do.

Bastawr hurried after Coryn at a gentle lope. Together, they slipped into the deep tunnels and through the darkness.

"You're sure nobody is following us?" Coryn asked.

"I am certain. We are alone. But *why* are we going alone?"

Coryn nodded. They both knew they'd been under surveillance ever since Rawrgyld took the throne. The new king had his people watching all of Ra'al's known companions, or any who had been loyal to Rashingot.

"Ra'al is meeting with the *new king*," she spoke mockingly, "as we speak. I figured this might be the only opportunity to sneak away without being followed. I suppose Rawrgyld's bodyguards are on high alert since he's meeting Ra'al."

She led her feral friend through the rock curtain and to the stair that led to old Icehome. "Why are we going down there?"

"I've got a bad feeling," she muttered. "We're going up against the undead, and without the morehl. But it might come in handy if we had access to some of their firepower. I mean, there are *a lot* of undead, and we know that they aren't particularly keen on fire."

They arrived at the bottom of the descent to Old Icehome and activated the lighting mechanism. Coryn picked up the nearest keg of explosive powder that the red-skinned elves used in their flintlocks. They were large, and a person couldn't realistically carry more than two of them at once. Even that would quickly tire a person and they couldn't take anything else.

Bastawr hefted a cask and looked hesitantly back at the long, winding stair, not eager to lug two of them all the way to the top. "It seems like an awful lot of effort to get a few barrels of black powder to the battlefield. Plus, we've still got to take them north with us."

Coryn shot him a sly grin. "We'll need a lot of them. If we can get a hundred, I'll be happy. There are certainly far more than that here."

Bastawr's eyes bulged, and he balked at the thought of so many trips up and down the stairs, unsure how they could keep such an operation a secret. The vaghan builders had only been able to do so because the whole of Icehome was being overhauled.

"Leave the ones around the foundations for Castle Ice. But we can scavenge the casks from around the edges of the city, where the civilians live. I can't see any need to ever blow those pillars, anyway."

"But… but…" Bastawr wasn't sure how to explain to his friend that she was asking for the impossible.

Coryn sensed his worry. She produced a metallic cube from her pocket. "We're not hauling them up the steps. Don't worry so much." She activated the gnomish device and opened a portal to her secret space.

She motioned for him to follow. "We're putting it all in here. Come on, I'll introduce you to Yoo-ee."

She stepped inside and Bastawr asked, "What's a Yoo-ee?"

CHAPTER NINE

Ra'al refused to meet King Rawrgyld's eyes as he stood before the newly crowned ruler. Nanku laid behind the throne, watching over the king's court.

He had gone to the bear rider without Coryn. Ra'al knew he could control himself for the sake of his greater mission, but Coryn had a sharp tongue and that vaghan temper.

Rawrgyld seemed almost amused to entertain the frostwing who he'd challenged to a duel only days prior. Under different circumstances, one of the two warriors would have been killed by the other. Rawrgyld looked over Ra'al and maintained a superior air, knowing that the younger one was at his mercy.

"Son of Thrag, I am told you have a request of me?" Rawrgyld scanned him suspiciously. Vengeance from kin after ritual combat was not unheard of, and Rawrgyld half expected a trick.

Ra'al's fur rippled with agitation. He did not want to be here, not like this, but he had made a promise to his mother.

Icehome needed to be protected from the undead, and despite his skill for it, neither Rashingot, Ra'al, or any others trusted Rawrgyld to remedy it.

"I do not know how much of Rashingot's network of informants survived the undead invasion. I assume few or none because of how she spoke to me in the last days. The undead still threaten Icehome," Ra'al said.

"I have already defeated these fiends," Rawrgyld said. "Don't forget that me and my outland allies smashed them apart upon the tundra."

Ra'al grimaced. "They were repelled from here and Balgavarr, but they will return—or worse…"

"Worse? What could be worse than the rape of Icehome?"

"One of my company, a gwereste tracker, discovered their plans," Ra'al said, speaking evenly and retaining his composure.

Rawrgyld waved through the air and scoffed. "Plans? Bloodless are mindless creatures. Dangerous, but they have no mind or greater purpose except to feed."

"Perhaps that is often true, but this army is different. It is led by Leisterbane, an ancient knight, and the chief general of Melkior the Fallen," said Ra'al.

Rawrgyld cocked his head. "You know this is a fact?"

Ra'al nodded. He relaxed fractionally. The worry in Rawrgyld's voice indicated they could find common ground, at least in their enemies—though Ra'al would never forgive the king for Rashingot's death.

"It is fact. Leisterbane's southern attacks had greater purpose: to distract those of us in the know from his true activities. He has stolen secrets from the sages, secrets that could wound the nature of Esfah as much as Nekarthis the Worldbreaker did," Ra'al explained.

Rawrgyld stroked the fur at his own chin and kept his red eyes focused on the former prince. Finally, he asked, "What is your request?"

"That you direct the army to act. We must smash Leisterbane's army before it accomplishes their plans."

"You think that's possible?"

Ra'al scowled. "I don't know. He has gathered forces for hundreds of years, creating new bloodless minions. But with the dwarven forces from Balgavarr and our allies across the Shadowlands, we stand a chance."

Rawrgyld paused for a moment of thought. He grinned when he spoke. "If you lead the mission personally, then I will issue the order."

"I will accept the responsibility." Fingering the key-like amulet around his neck, Ra'al smiled. Marnash had given it to him, and he'd called it Spell-Breaker. To unassuming eyes, it looked like a simple decorative trinket, but the morehl caster had taught him to use it as a dispelling device. Ra'al knew he had to be present. Using Spell-Breaker, he'd be able to reveal any invisible wraiths and ghosts so that the army could avoid or eliminate them. Ra'al *had* to be present and so he'd made no actual concessions.

Rawrgyld motioned to a nearby recorder who would dispatch the required messages. "I shall make the orders then. But there is one more thing."

Ra'al cocked his head.

"You must swear here and now your allegiance to me, your king," Rawrgyld said. "I cannot hand over an army to a potential political rival, you see. You must bend the knee and acknowledge my rule."

Ra'al's guts twisted. Once again, he was glad he'd left Coryn behind. She'd have tried to gut him for such a demand. He remembered his mother's dying wishes and swallowed the distaste of it all. Deep down, as much as he'd avoided it until recently, Ra'al knew that Thrag's throne was his responsibility and his destiny. Now that he knew the song of the wind, he wanted nothing more than to accept his calling to it.

His mind urged him to summon a barrage of ice spears and murder the king. He could fight his way out of Castle Ice and flee… live as a refugee, but his mother would be avenged. If he did, the undead would succeed, but Rawrgyld would be stopped. A seed of temptation called from his gut.

Bending into a kind of bow, he forced the words, "I swear my fealty to Icehome, it's rites, and rule. I am its loyal subject." He looked up at Rawrgyld, having chosen his words carefully. They left room for Ra'al to have meant them of himself and his father's memory.

The king glowered, but he accepted the pledge and released him. As soon as Ra'al left the court, he thought it over. Rawrgyld must have wanted Ra'al out of the city. Otherwise, he would not have accepted such an obviously hollow vow.

Ra'al muttered, "He probably just wants me out of Icehome so he can solidify his power base." Ra'al didn't particularly care. He had to accept that his chance for the throne had passed him by and it would likely be decades before he could invoke the same rite which Rawrgyld had used to steal it.

It was the long game that Ra'al had to commit to. And for that to happen, Ra'al had to make sure Icehome was still around in the future; he had to obey his mother's last request and obliterate this undead menace.

Ra'al had to protect the people. It's what Thrag would have done: put the areosan population above any throne or crown.

He thought back to the shattered crown of ice. Ra'al did not know if Rawrgyld understood the significance of such an act. Ra'al only knew that *he* meant it, though he had no crown to smash… it was how he knew that Thrag's royal destiny truly called to him.

Deep within his throat, he growled his oath. This was how Ra'al would live—and he'd sacrificed greatly for it already—he was called to a hero's life, even one that might never acknowledge him for it. He had to protect the people.

Ra'al sighed and walked through the corridors, where the winds howled with their shrill songs. He hurried off to find Coryn and let her know they had the necessary permission to continue their quest.

The frostwing turned a corner and nearly bumped into Bastawr. Coryn walked behind the gwereste. Both looked as if they'd just been caught pilfering crabs from the fishmonger.

"Where have you two just been up to?" Ra'al asked.

Bastawr grinned. "Let us show you."

"I just realized I haven't even introduced you yet to Yoo-ee," Coryn blurted. "We also just grabbed, uh, a few supplies." She produced her gnomish cube. "Come on, I'll show you."

Ra'al raised a brow. "Who's Yoo-ee?"

Geril and his company emerged on the far edge of Matrek's castle, bursting gaps in the coral elf king's lawn before causing the stone bubbles to erupt up from the soil. The dwarves could not have entered the castle grounds via the path as a ring of warding stones prevented the dwarves' magic. At great cost, Matrek had buried dweomernull symbols to ward that kind of magic.

The vagha's stony bubbles shuddered and rose from the soil like eggshell thin cocoons. Finally, the dwarves broke free as if newborn chicks, aside from the axes and other deadly weapons.

Selumari guards immediately leveled blade and spear at them, and every bowman posted along the king's crenelated walls nocked an arrow. The ranking soldier cocked his head when he recognized the famous dwarf. "Geril sa'Ghuren?"

"The one and only," Geril claimed. "I believe Matrek is expecting me?"

"He is, though he'd hoped to see you several days prior."

"Aye. I was… previously engaged," Geril muttered. The de facto vagha king tapped Captain Ringuld and Sheron and nodded toward the gate. He knew the rest of his small battalion would have to remain outside. The way Matrek had warded the place only proved the selumari king's paranoia—and that was enough reason in Geril's mind to keep the mystic weapons cache out of selumari's hands.

Before entering the gates, Geril asked, "Is Naemyar in Tulgesh?"

The captain of the guard shrugged, but one of the bowmen on the wall reported, "I know she visited some of her operations abroad, but I saw her eagle return this morning…" he snapped his mouth shut when his superior flashed him a dirty look.

Geril pretended not to notice and took his two companions into the elven castle. He suspected Matrek had instructed the captain to keep his mouth shut, and Geril grinned. He knew he had options.

A blue-skinned elf attendant led them to a meeting room and promised the king would arrive shortly while a few grey elf scullions filled water and wine glasses and arranged for a small spread of fruit and bread. When Matrek arrived a few moments later, the frehlasuhl bowed low and backed away into the shadows as the invisible elves were so adept at doing.

Matrek held his head high, as if his height gave him some kind of superiority over the dwarves. "Geril sa'Ghuren," he greeted him stiffly and with a formal tone.

Geril merely bobbed his head. "Matrek," he acknowledged informally and grinned. He knew that his lack of decorum rankled the elf. "What have you got for me?"

The king smiled. "Information that will allow you to finally get your local vagha under control. Things have not escalated into a full-blown riot, but the vagha have been precariously unruly in the wake of your ambassador's murder. You need to catch this culprit and appease them."

"Yeah. I remember," Geril stated. Local dwarves in Tulgesh had initially blamed Harol's murderous rampage on the prejudice of certain selumari. "You have information on Harol, then?"

"I do. Harol was spotted recently, and I have a heading on his general direction. I can tell you where he was last seen." Matrek folded his hands. "But first, I'd like to renegotiate the agreed upon price."

"We already agreed upon terms," Geril growled, standing. "I don't have time for games, Matrek, and I certainly didn't just travel across all Cyrea for this nonsense." He signaled his companions to head for the door.

"Wait. Where are you going?" Matrek wore a mask of confusion.

"You're not the only information source I have in Tulgesh. And I'm certainly not giving you any more of the Magestorm weapons than I've already agreed."

"If you're speaking of Naemyar, your daughter's apparent benefactor, I wouldn't bother. She left Tulgesh several days ago on unknown business. Even if she *was* in the city, she won't be of much help."

Geril shrugged. "I've got it on good authority she's returned." He winked and walked out of the chamber with the coral elf king spitting and sputtering in his wake.

Coryn's face rested in her hands, and she stretched her skin as she tried not to fall asleep staring at the book. A frostwing wearing jewelry and tufted fur sat next to her.

"Ugh," she complained to Karou, the areosan magi. "Why do we have read all this mumbo jumbo? I'd much rather swing my axe at something."

Karou did his best to conceal any irritation. He was enamored far more by the books that Sheron had left for them to look over, particularly the one from the Yentosh library which Sheron had claimed as a leftover from the Magestorm cache remnants at Tulgesh.

Coryn recognized it as one of the few items she and her crew had taken from the cache below Tulgesh. She hadn't thought it very important *then,* either.

"Trust me, *Warlord* Coryn," he said, using her full title. "It will be worth it in the end. We must understand the magic if we are to deal with it. Magic always requires understanding, and it always extracts a cost."

"Just Coryn," the dwarf said. Like her father, she didn't put much stock in titles. Besides, hers was only a temporary commission. "And what do you mean?"

Karou turned the book to her. A drawing of the mist stones took up one entire page. "These things are certainly magical. It appears that one of our historians had a conversation with a sage once before, many centuries ago."

He turned the book back and deciphered the scratchy letters jotted down so long ago. "Not much is known about them except that they hide a great secret of Ghaeial."

"You mean the Great Tree of the north? One of the Worldtrees?" Coryn asked.

Karou shot her an amazed look. "How did you know what the book says about…"

"I've already heard it before," she said. "It's an obscure legend, but I luckily know some obscure people who like that kind of lore." Naemyar had speculated as to the undead's desires in the Shadowlands when Coryn and Garesch previously told her about the lost maps and Yarichek's defection. She knew the basic parts of the legend. "So, I know the mist stones create some kind of secret barrier, but what do these trees do?"

Karou furrowed a brow. "I… I don't know exactly. I only know that the sages had a couple primary jobs and that one of these was to safeguard the Worldtrees."

Coryn put her face back in her hands and sighed. "Another dead end then."

"No," Karou explained as Ra'al's shape darkened the door. "There is a footnote here that says the sage spent a great many years in the household of a frost ogre and under his protection."

"You think the frost ogre is still alive?"

Karou shrugged. "They are very long-lived. And if not, his clan may have clues that could come in handy… if we could survive the trek."

Ra'al approached, gleaning enough of the conversation to ask, "Where is his clan?"

"Skrilluk Peak," Karou said.

Ra'al clenched his jaws and Coryn gulped. The winds surrounding Skrilluk were so fierce that the journey would have to be made on foot. But luckily, it was not far out of the way. Ra'al had gotten the clearance needed to take the army north to stop Leisterbane, and this was only a minor detour.

The former prince nodded slowly and turned to Coryn. "Then we go to Skrilluk Peak. Prepare your army, Little Sparrow. I'll do the same for the areosa and I'll see if we can get Captain Taerlon to go a little further with us yet."

Coryn's face brightened.

Ra'al bobbed his head and commented, looking from Coryn to Karou. "I wonder if Rawrgyld thinks this mission might kill me yet."

Coryn put a hand around the handle of her axe. "Well, let's make sure that doesn't happen."

Geril followed Lotep, a shifty-eyed selumari who had been Naemyar's majordomo for many years. He'd always been suspicious of Lotep, who was typically the go between for Naemyar and often visited Balgavarr on her behalf. She did not often enter the mountains.

Lotep did not engage him with small talk. The dwarf did not mind. As far as he was concerned, Lotep was a security risk, but he was not about to broach the subject with Naemyar. If Lotep sold secrets from Riechus Aqualines or from Naemyar's more private business, Geril would not be surprised; he assumed Naemyar would not be either. The dwarf followed the blue elf, grumbling, wondering if there was any connection between Lotep and Harol. If he found proof of it, Geril would use Old Thunder to knock the elf's head clean off his shoulders.

Geril's two companions followed him, though the remainder of the vaghan company waited in the lobby.

Lotep stopped at the entrance to a room in his mistress's estate. "This way." He waved him through and remained behind, perhaps sensing Geril's hostility.

Inside, he found a very harried looking Naemyar, who looked like she'd just emerged from a week in the woods. Her hair was tousled and she spoke through chapped lips, but her smile was warm. "Geril. You made it. I assume you are here because…"

"Yeah. Matrek tried to put me over a barrel. I might have to keep his airship as payback."

Naemyar absentmindedly raked a snarl from her hair. "I only just returned, and I've been gathering information for you."

"I assume it's about Harol?"

She nodded gravely. "It was my ships that spotted him aboard *Chariot's Wake*... Ry'Ober's ship. When they saw it, they thought their cargo forfeit for sure, but when the pirates made no move to attack, they investigated. I usually have at least one spell caster aboard and they spied out the situation using magic. Harol was on that ship—along with many of the Magestorm weapons—he commissioned the pirate queen for a charter. They were headed southeast. Little else is known."

Geril stroked his beard and glanced back to the doorway that Lotep waited at, thinking it funny that the King knew about Harol's travels when the information should have stayed within Naemyar's house. "Do you know where he's gone? Maybe they mentioned it when your arcanist was eavesdropping?"

Naemyar shook her head. "Not specifically. But we can make an educated guess based on sightings of the ship and its course as it left Cyrean waters. Geril... this sighting was made in the Autumn Sea by one of my boats that ferried cargo from Dohan."

The dwarf gulped. There wasn't much doubt on his heading, then.

Confirming his suspicions, Naemyar said, "He is going to Dereh'Liandor. I suspect he will either dock in the bay of the Firequags or the Treglyteholm... either way, he must be trading the weapons to the faeli or the trogs."

"Maybe both," Geril grumbled. "And I think he's got bigger intentions. Some kind of sick pilgrimage to the World Wound?"

Naemyar's face darkened, and she turned as if she had a guess, but declined to share it. "He must be stopped… at any cost," the elf insisted.

"Aye. No argument there."

"I think that, if you hurry, you can catch him," Naemyar said quietly.

"Fat chance at that," Geril said. "Even if I could pry another airship out of Matrek, it'd take too long—and that's if the weather held *and* the durned scalders in the Plaguelands and the Firequags let us pass without incident, and I've never met a faeli worth trusting."

"You are right. He is beyond our reach, with conventional means, that is. However, there *are* unconventional means."

"Magic?"

She inclined her head.

"There are enough vagha in Tulgesh to cast a path, for sure," Geril said, "but we cannot send a path through an ocean. Eldurim is an earth god. The seas are controlled by Aguarehl. Negotiating the magic is impossible; selumari were made by the water goddess, but you cannot cast the needed spell for land."

"What lies beneath the sea, Geril?" Naemyar asked.

The dwarf waved away her question. "Land. Everybody knows that, but it'll never work."

"It *will* work," she insisted. "It has to work, *for all our sakes,* if Harol is going to the Netherwold."

Geril raised a bushy eyebrow. "Do you know something I don't?"

The Netherwold lay at the heart of the World Wound, a rift stretching across the continent of Dereh'Liandor, which was ripped open during the Magestorm Wars. Nekarthis, The Worldbreaker, had built a stronghold around the Netherwold, which was rumored to be a doorway to access whole dimensions beyond Esfah. Myths claimed it was a gate to Rhaudian, the moon, and Leguin, Esfah's dim sister planet that sometimes crossed the evening sky. It was also said it could provide an entry to the realm of the greater and lesser gods and that Nekarthis had planned to entreat Selurehl, father to the god of Death, and seek even greater power. Thankfully, the gnomes had somehow stopped his madness.

Naemyar set her jaw. "Yes… no… I am not sure." She met his gaze and then turned aside to Sheron, the spell caster who stood near Geril. "If you had enough magic, could a path spell take your company from Tulgesh to Derehliandor?"

Sheron reluctantly nodded. "Given enough magic, *anything* is possible. Magic's power comes from the gods, and it is wielded—crafted by our limited understanding of it. But in theory, yes. The sheer volume of magic required…"

"Then say no more," she insisted. "You gather every last vagha you can in the city, and I will supply the rest."

Geril looked at her, knowing that the extremely rare wayfare orbs would have been easier to collect and grant to his party than to amass such magical skill. He was about to argue when she cut him off. "Geril sa'Ghuren. Surely by now you must realize that there is far more to me than what you have come to know."

He shook his head and muttered something about elves and their secrets and then departed, knowing it would take them all day and night to rally his kinsmen. All the dwarves in Balgavarr reaches combined could not cast the spell Naemyar suggested. But Geril headed out anyway. They had to try something, and if nothing else, a common struggle could potentially quell the locals' hostility.

As they walked out, Naemyar summoned Lotep to dispatch a message for King Matrek. They'd need to inform him that the sudden gathering of dwarves was planned and not a hostile action.

CHAPTER TEN

Coryn walked away from the enclave of dwarven soldiers. For the most part, her father's soldiers dealt with the army's needs and logistics. Nobody was fooled into thinking that her appointment as Warlord was anything more than an honorary title.

As a temporary commission, it was her duty to see that Geril's mission for the army's northern forces continued and he trusted no one to accomplish that task more than his daughter. Thus, her position as Warlord carried all the authority of Balgavarr's ruler, but had none of the obligations, which meant the appointment would expire as soon as the war did. Authority without responsibility never worked over the long term—in this case, it had been necessary. But Coryn didn't know enough about the military to direct it efficiently. Besides, she hadn't served alongside these vagha—not in a military sense. Her background had been as a diplomat and an adventurer rather than a soldier. Additionally, she'd spent more of her adolescent years among the frostwings than her own people.

She angled for her companions, who waited for her near the walls of the keep where the Balgavarrian forces had clustered. The leaders under her command would do the heavy lifting and maintain the army. For her part, she'd promised to find out what she could about the undead and tell the military where to strike. They were the axe, and she was the sword arm.

"Now I've just got to find out whatever I can about our enemy," she grumbled, recognizing that the undead still outnumbered them, and this time, they'd be battling them on their home turf. If she didn't find out something useful about the bloodless, or at least how to foil their plans for the mist stones, their trek across the tundra would prove futile—and deadly. Coryn swallowed and hoped that Leisterbane's scheme was not a simple ruse meant to lure new, warm bodies into the wastes so he could further add to his numbers.

A gray shadow marred the white snow where Ra'al stood next to Bastawr and Karou. Coryn looked up as she approached and spotted *Aguarehl's Envy* where it hovered with its air bladder inflated. Captain Taerlon and Fazayou, the leader of the Azure Company, stood with the other selumari. She felt a pang of grief and missed the red elves that she'd traveled so far with, but she was glad for Fazayou. He was her link to Naemyar and what remained of his mercenaries had agreed to go north with them. Taerlon was happy to have their assistance in crewing his airship.

"Are you ready?" Ra'al asked.

Coryn nodded. "The vagha will meet us at the waypoint and we can regroup there to advance on Leisterbane's forces. Hopefully Skrilluk Peak doesn't turn out to be a dud lead," she said.

If Karou could have blanched, he would have. Instead, his fur rippled with agitation. "Something must be there," he insisted. "Some clue."

"I've heard Skrilluk Peak is the home to frost ogres," said Bastawr. "And that it is almost unpassable, even to the winged areosa."

"Both true," said Coryn. "Captain Taerlon, we just need for you to get us as close as you can." She ignored Fazayou, who wondered below his breath if the rumors that frost ogres sometimes ate other citizens of Cyrea were true. Coryn grimaced at his question. She had heard they'd developed a taste for frostwing flesh.

"I can get you close," Taerlon said. "But Skrilluk Peak is precarious by both sky *and* foot."

"Then let's move out," Coryn said.

Taerlon nodded, grabbed a rope that hung from his coral airship, and set his foot in the loop. His crew hauled him vertically into the sky as Ra'al grabbed Coryn. Karou snatched Fazayou into the sky and they boarded the craft.

Far below, Coryn spotted the vaghan army merge with the battle group under Ra'al's command.

The mass of bodies moved north. Coryn hoped they weren't all marching to their deaths.

"I have an alliance with Geril sa'Ghuren," insisted Garesch. Wildkeep had elected to side with the rogue prince and word quickly spread to the other lava elf settlements where outcasts eked out their livings in the wilderness—free of all rule.

"We have already escaped the oppression of Saugor," said Turimnab the representative from the nearby town of Hinterhome. "Why would we voluntarily come under the rule of his son?"

Sharsah stepped forward. "Wildkeep asked those same questions. But we have sided with the prince," he said. "If Garesch can truly keep our enemies at bay—especially his father—then we must support him. Some threats are too big for us to face individually. One or two of our communities will fall against oppression, but if three or more bind together, they form a cord which will not snap beneath the weight as the individual strands will."

Hinterhome's contact crooked his jaw and sighed. "And you can guarantee the dwarves are no threat?"

Garesch shrugged. "I can only say that I have the favor of their leader and the friendship of his daughter. They are wardens of the area you all live within, and they have made reasonable accommodations for those citizens who live abroad. Their own kin have pockets living in Tulgesh, Icehome, and many other places. Certainly, with the alliances I've struck, the morehl living beyond Uruzak will be allowed to remain."

Marnash scanned the hesitation on the faces of the lava elves from Hinterhome, Havendell, and a few others from the nearest communities. "You must all remember what it means to be morehl," his said, his voice carrying grave weight. "As soon as Saugor is certain his son is in open rebellion, he will focus all of his efforts on Prince Garesch's destruction. It is the morehl way, the old way, one which we have all found to be lacking. But that nastiness which we have each rejected reminds us of what will come our way as soon as the king decides to bring his flintlocks to bear."

All the eyes locked on the spell caster who had long been Garesch's mentor. "I fought at the Battle of Balgavarr and was taken captive by the vagha. Upon my return, I watched the king execute any who fled the field rather than throw themselves into destruction for Saugor's glory. He thinks himself a god, not a king. And that is why he must be overthrown. The subterfuge ingrained in our nature serves us in other ways. If we put our wills to this, Saugor will never see us strike from the shadows. He will fall and we will *all* be free."

Hope glistened in the eyes of the gathered lava elves. Sharsah stood. "But we need more. We each only know so many other communities." He held up a map and plotted a couple of Xs on it. "I am aware that it is a risk to reveal ourselves. But I believe in this mission. I am giving the locations of what diaspora towns I know, writing letters of recommendation for the prince's safety, and advising local leaders to hear these morehl out."

Sharsah looked each one in the eye. "If we stick together, Saugor will fall, and we will have the favor of the new king who will leave us to our self-governance."

The handful of leaders stomped their feet against the floorboards in support and each one stood to expand Sharsah's map.

Marnash looked sideways at Garesch. The prince grinned. It was as good a start as they'd hoped for, but they'd need to keep moving to enlist the numbers of support they needed.

Skrilluk Peak towered overhead as *Aguarehl's Envy* hovered like a distant gray blob behind the travelers. Only Coryn, Ra'al, Karou, Bastawr, and Fazayou walked up the snowy approach to the jagged peak. Fierce spears of icy wind lanced out of nowhere at seemingly random times. The shears could have dashed an airborne frostwing into rocks or smashed them to the ground with ease. That made the areosa walk with the rest.

They plodded through the drifts with a length of cord tied between each in the gang, forming a line so that none would be lost. Twice, Coryn lost her grip and slid away, caught by the safety rope.

Winds howled, and the trek took hours. Little could be heard save the shrill songs of an angry wind that mourned like a funeral dirge. During a moment of rest, Coryn spotted the somber look on Ra'al's face and took his hand. "What's on your mind?"

They returned to the trail, pacing slightly ahead of their companions in silence for many steps. Finally, he admitted, "My mother. She's gone. As much as I hated her many lectures, I'd give everything to hear her tell me one more time how I've got to get out and see the world... discover more about the song of the wind." He sighed. "We are both now without mothers."

Coryn didn't try to cheer him up. She remembered losing her mother at a young age. Her younger self, still fresh with pain, had resented the platitudes offered by others. Instead, she merely walked by his side.

In the distance, a towering figure shifted, startling the adventurers. They'd all thought the shape was a snow-covered tree, but it reached out a hand and pointed in a direction up the hill. Intelligent eyes burned beneath the furry shelves of snow that layered upon the creature: an ogre.

The travelers turned at the creature's direction and continued upwards to where a trail seemed to develop. Several sets of footprints had cleared a path through the deepening snow. As the party scrambled to wade through the banks, the trail turned and curved around a sharp wall of stone, which narrowed to hem the path into a funnel. When they finally cleared it, a small village opened at the top of the wind-whipped peak.

Round bodied yurts dotted the area with trails leading to each other. There were piles of wood stores for their furnaces. Wisps of smoke curled up from each one.

A second snowy ogre stood there, looming twice the size of Ra'al. He wore a wide-brimmed woven hat with a chin strap that kept it from flying off his head in the sudden bouts of rushing air. The ogre stood there, blasted by frost clustering into clumps on the creature's fur, as he watched the travelers gather before him.

Coryn kicked the ice from her steel boots and bowed. "We are here looking for your help, mighty frost ogre. We were hoping there are some here who remember the aid rendered to the sages centuries ago. We come in service of Esfah and hope the memories of the frost ogres are as long as legends imply."

The creature studied her for several long moments. Coryn nearly wilted beneath its gaze. Finally, it returned the bow and pointed to a circular cottage nearby and ushered them toward the shelter.

They hurried inside and out of the elements. Once there, the ogre raked the snow out of his hide and shook himself free of remaining moisture as the others huddled around a small but efficient potbelly stove, where a cauldron of stew simmered.

Finally, the ogre removed its hat and bowed to them; they could finally see that he was male. The ceiling nearly brushed his head. "Greetings. I am Tanneyha, and I've not seen a vagha since before the Second Age began. I am the village elder here."

Coryn's eyes sparkled. "Do you know the ogre we seek? A sage took refuge here long ago and..."

"Yes, yes. I am he. Your sage stayed in my care. He gave me something in exchange for my hospitality," Tanneyha said. "He gifted me something he highly valued. Tell me, young dwarf. What do you bring to barter? It must be something that you love greatly."

Coryn's eyes flashed to Ra'al, and she gulped. *Were the rumors true? Does he want to eat Ra'al? Maybe he'll settle for Karou?*

"No," Tanneyha chuckled. "I am not interested in your friends." He nodded to her foot gear. "But those fancy shoes you wear. They look precious... and if we trade, I shall remember your visit because of the sacrifice you made. A part of you will remain in my house forever."

Coryn frowned. Her father had given her those boots when she set out on her adventure before the undead had arrived. *How long had that been now?* "I… I…" She sighed and sent up a prayer to Eldurim and Firiel, entreating them to protect Geril. "You are right. They are precious to me. And we must know about the sages and the mist stones."

She began to unclasp the boots' latches as Karou opened his book and turned the sketched mist stones over to Tanneyha, hoping the drawings would jog his memory.

"Oh my," said Tanneyha. "This is an old book."

Coryn stepped out of her boots and offered them to the frost ogre. Her heart sank as she did so, and the skin on her feet puckered and formed gooseflesh as the cold air hit them.

Tanneyha pinched the treasure between his fingers and offered each of them a bowl of stew. "We must go all the way back to discuss the sages if you are to understand the mist stones and their purposes," he stated, setting his new shoes upon a curving shelf mounted to the wall of his circular dwelling. "In the beginning, the sages were all eldarim, the eldest species that evolved from the power of Nature, of Esfah itself…"

Geril recognized the dwarf who stood alongside Naemyar at the assembly outside of Tulgesh. She'd had him direct the vagha to gather just a little way up the main road that stretched from the elven capital to the Kafnysan Mountains, which ran mostly parallel to the Sareen River. The waypoint was marked by a large boulder and a field of scattered, head-sized stones.

"Greetings, Fargan," Geril recalled his name. The dwarf's sister was recently widowed and Fargan had been a part of the near revolt in Tulgesh after Harol's slaughter had been discovered. Fargan's brother-in-law had been one of the victims, but he'd proved loyal to Geril. Fargan only wanted justice to be done.

Scanning the crowd, they'd turned out several thousand dwarves who lived in Tulgesh, and Geril noted the watchful eyes of coral elf scouts in the distance. No doubt, Matrek had employed magic as well to eavesdrop upon them, just as Naemyar's sailors had done to discern Harol's identity aboard a distant ship.

Fargan bowed low enough that his beard nearly brushed the ground. He held a crown to his head with one hand, as if in salute; he didn't dare place such a powerful item upon his head.

Geril cocked an eyebrow at the artifact. Fargan and several other dwarves nearby possessed them. A few others brandished rings, amulets, and others clutched sightstones: smooth rocks imbued with runes that amplified magic. While the stones were not uncommon, anything of greater power, such as the crown, was truly rare.

The dwarven leader bit his lip. Geril was not a caster, though he'd long ago proved some favorable aptitude for it. Still, with such artifacts at their disposal—likely borrowed from Naemyar's vaults—he knew that they'd assembled enough power to sink Tulgesh into the bedrock if the army chose to do so. But it was still not enough to send his company across a sea and as far away as Dereh'Liandor.

"It's still not enough," Geril told Naemyar, shaking his head. She held a couple of books beneath her arm. "Maybe it's enough to send just one. *Maybe.*"

Naemyar turned her gaze. "I told you I would see this done. And Fargan here has agreed to help."

Geril cocked his head, wondering what Naemyar knew about Fargan that he did not.

Fargan sighed. "Well, if this is gonna cost me my life, we might as well get it over with.

Geril frowned and argued, "If we're using death magic to…"

"It's not that," Naemyar insisted. All magic had some kind of cost. Usually that came in the form of energy by a caster, who often felt tired at the conclusion of a spell. Death magic often extracted life itself, sometimes even killing a victim in exchange for power.

Geril still did not understand. "Listen, I'm not sure that even Harol is worth whatever it is that…"

Fargan's eyes narrowed to slits as he responded. "Tracking that bastard down is *the only thing* that matters to me. And Naemyar tells me that stopping him goes far beyond simple justice for our murdered kin."

Geril locked eyes on Naemyar. "All right.. Level with me. What *aren't* you saying?"

She bit her lip and her shoulders slumped. She kept her voice low. "I fear that Harol is trying to resurrect Nekarthis. An old legend says that his remains still lay at the bottom of the World Wound, at the entrance to the Netherwold, only paces away from the access to the Void."

"Aye. An old children's tale," Geril said.

"Is it?" she asked.

"You tell me," Geril said. "Yer the expert."

Naemyar shrugged. "I only know that he has secured both a map and the means to reanimate the corpse, if the myth turns out to be true."

Worry spread across Geril's face. The threats to Esfah went far beyond the horde of potent weapons. If Nekarthis returned… "Do you think the map is legitimate?"

"I only know that *Harol* thinks the map is real. He picked it up some time ago from a vendor in Frostshoal. I long thought him a collector of artifacts and such oddities, much as I am—that is how he came to be at my party when your daughter visited, aside from the fact that he impersonated a dignitary. My part in this all is something which I am still trying to remedy. During this nightmare with the undead, I am afraid he was able to get his hands on the last piece he needed: a container of death-infested alchemy called Necralluvium."

"What in the Sha'la'dinan is necra... necro..."

"Necralluvium is what ties the corpses into the will of the unnamable one. Death. It is what reanimates the dead. With it, he could potentially revive Nekarthis."

Geril's face sunk. "There is still the problem of getting us there in time, let alone crossing the foulest continent in all of Esfah so we can stop this madman."

"I told you not to underestimate me," Naemyar said. She cracked one of her books and turned a page to make sure she did the rite correctly. With a piece of chalk, she drew upon the large boulder, recreating the sigil traced in her tome. "I will awaken the spirit and commune with it. There is an elemental here. A daemon."

"You are a follower of the Quietudes?" Geril raised his brows.

"No. But I know a few things."

The Quietudes were a philosophy of magic which had largely gone out of style by the time of the Dragoncrusades of the First Age. However, some still remembered and practiced the old ways. They drew power from elemental spirits rather than directly from the gods of magic.

Every spell caster acted as a conduit for power from whatever god they were attuned to. If that conduit was like a trickling stream of power from the gods, enlisting the aid of a spirit was like swapping the stream for a rushing river. Their access port was simply larger. However, elementals were known to be fickle things... and always demanded a price for service, typically even higher than the gods. Quietudes, as a practice, helped one live in greater harmony with the myriad spirits which walked Esfah unseen and allowed a practitioner to befriend them. Sometimes a price could be done for no cost, even, if there was a relationship with the spirits; usually, Quietudes were a way to reduce a spirit's fee or locate them in the first place.

Naemyar finished her symbol and offered a muted prayer. The boulder shook, and those stones scattered all around rumbled as well. When elemental spirits took a physical form, they were known as a daemon, and most daemons were cantankerous, violent things. It was understandable. Most known ones throughout history had been bound into their physical form permanently by mystic practitioners who, if they were not careful, were often killed by those bound creatures they had captured. Quietudes usually prevented that. But some spirits, much like anyone else, could be just plain mean.

Stones from across the field flew through the air, drawn by mystical forces that shifted as the creature assembled itself out of stone. The monstrous figure, a stony, bipedal behemoth, towered far above them. Its size was great enough that Geril ascertained it was much more than a minor spirit. It was some kind of mid-level entity, at worst.

Naemyar stood back and looked at Geril.

"I hope you didn't just piss that thing off," he mentioned.

"He remains unbound," she assured him. Though that would not prevent an elemental earth daemon from smashing them to paste with its mammoth-sized boulder hands if it decided to. It could make the whole situation easier, in fact.

The daemon bent low to regard the little creatures which had awakened him. "Little sparks," its voice reverberated like a landslide. "Why do you disturb me?"

Fargan stepped up boldly. "Good daemon, servant of the mighty Eldurim. I come asking a favor. My friends must cross the ocean to stop an evil creature from satisfying the hated Death god."

The daemon bent low and seemed to sniff Fargan. "I smell vengeance on your mind… tell your friends to use a boat. I return to slumber." The daemon made moves to return to the field.

Fargan boldly took another step closer. "I cannot allow that. Time is critical. They must reach him before the evil one does further harm to Nature."

The elemental regarded Fargan curiously. "I am an earth spirit. Eldurim has no power over the water."

"And that is why we come to you," the dwarf said. "We seek your power to go *under* the seas rather than over or through them. We can cast the spell, but we lack sufficient power. We have the means but not the strength, and we have come to you to bargain for it."

Straightening in surprise, the daemon said, "I am willing to aid you. How many must take the journey?"

Twelve additional vagha surrounded Geril, including a very nervous looking Sheron and Ringuld.

"Very well. However, the price is high," said the daemon. "Tell me your name, that it might be bound to me in service for the rest of your natural life. That is the price. You will serve in the temple of Eldurim until your form expires and your soul is released to The Eternal Lands."

Geril looked at the dwarf, almost begging him not to make such a deal. But he held his tongue. Fargan's life was his to do with as he pleased.

"I am Fargan, son of Thodda of the Hydrak clan: Hy'Fargan sa'Thodda accepts your price." Fargan turned to Geril with a serious light burning within his eyes. "Good luck, and good hunting. May Eldurim protect you."

Naemyar bowed and blessed him likewise. "This is a one-way trip," she said. "I'll send help, a ship. Hopefully it arrives in time to help pick up the pieces of whatever transpires."

"Or erect a headstone?" Geril asked.

"Yes. But let us dare to hope," Naemyar said.

The daemon rumbled, "It is done." Stones flew up to latch around Fargan's neck, reforming to create a stony, smoothed torc with a glowing set of sigils that bound him to the promise and marked him as both an acolyte of Eldurim and a temple servant. "Wizards, you may cast your spell."

As the vagha huddled together in bearded clusters, Naemyar stepped forward, pressed a letter into Geril's hand, and then retreated. "The journey is long, but my letter is brief and the news ill. Read it only with a stout heart whenever you are ready."

Geril nodded and placed it in his pocket. "You will tell my daughter what happened here today?"

Naemyar nodded solemnly.

Sheron turned and provided some brief instruction to the gathered crowd of vagha. A moment later, the assembly began to glow gold, channeling the power of the earth god, Eldurim. The light glimmered brightest where those using artifacts stood. And then the cocoons of stone enveloped the travelers again in their bubble-like enclosures, and they sped through the earth, delving deep within the bedrock and disappearing. They hurtled toward their destination, far below even the seas, safe within the dark orbs of the path spell.

CHAPTER ELEVEN

Seated upon his zombie steed, Leisterbane emerged at the head of his army. A hazy, snow-filled fog parted before the dread lord who moved forward with his army at his back.

The shambling hordes had finally arrived at the first of the mist stones. He'd brought all that he had, undead, both great and small. The ground rumbled beneath the feet of the army and the thundering of wheeled wagons that bore the massive cauldrons holding the necralluvium they'd drawn from the pools within the Heimdarl Crag.

Leisterbane's mount paused before the muddied bones and frozen flesh of his minions, who had toppled the first of the sage's stones. As each ward fell, the next became easier to destroy. And once they were all down, the Great Tree would be undefended and ready to be uprooted.

Satisfaction wormed through his gut. After so many years in the frost-cursed Shadowlands, he'd come to the verge of satisfying his dark god's purpose... and then perhaps he could rejoin Lord Melkior, whose presence rekindled far away.

So long as the one who'd made Leisterbane walked upon Esfah under the power of the necralluvium, Leisterbane would be able to sense him.

As the two armies merged, Rorduk, one of the undead generals, dragged a human into their midst and thrust him to the ground. Avaryth collapsed into a weakened heap of legs and ratty dreadlocks. He barely had the strength to stand, let alone resist his captors.

Behind Rorduk emerged a row of fiends who carried armloads of artifacts taken from the Magestorm cache by the vaghan minion Harol. Leisterbane watched as they dumped them unceremoniously into heaps and dragged the larger pieces to deposit nearby—a pair of blade golems, a rolled carpet of levitation, bundles of enchanted arrows, magic swords, and more.

"There is one piece in particular I know you will enjoy," Rorduk said with a voice like a hungry beast. He drew the dragonstaff blade and turned it over to Leisterbane, whose cold lips peeled back into a grin of vicious teeth.

Leisterbane accepted the weapon with an amused kind of purring and turned his gaze to the human prisoner, who shivered in the dirt. Pointing to Avaryth, Leisterbane roared, "None may eat him."

His voice echoed between his thousands of thralls and Avaryth cringed. Despite the order, skeletal jaws clattered hungrily as teeth clicked against each other. Hollow eyes all around the human greedily scanned his body, lustily consuming his flesh with their empty sockets.

Leisterbane hung the sword from his belt and howled, "Now, get to work on those remaining stones! Somewhere across the oceans, Melkior waits."

Tanneyha sat cross-legged on the plank floor within his home as his guests ate stew. Even Ra'al's infamous hunger was sated by it.

The ogre told them about when Esfah's first races were still young. "The sages had many roles. The first of these was to teach the younger races created by the gods how to treat the planet." His gaze flitted from selumari to vagha.

"The sages established places of education including the famed libraries of Yentosh—though they'd already made many for their own purposes, the sages welcomed the newer ones, believing knowledge would help preserve Esfah's harmony... Yentosh was the first place targeted in the Dawn of War, when the morehl revealed themselves as traitors and servants of Death. Lava elves were still so new that none could have expected the deep hooks Malgrimm had created within them and enticed them with."

As he said the name of the Death god, a rumble sounded in the mountains. The telltale sounds of a distant avalanche echoed, and the adventurers glanced nervously at each other. According to legend, only close servants of Malgrimm could speak his name without invoking him and hastening their own demise.

While speaking, Tanneyha employed his massive hands to work a piece of fur and leather, using implements far too tiny for his hands. It would have been comical, like a giant crafting corn husk dolls for human children, were it not for the weight of the ogre's words. Tanneyha's guests paid little attention to his project.

Tanneyha noted their fear and winked. "The dark one holds no favor here," he said, allaying their concerns and continuing.

"Secondly, the sages were tillers of the monsters, creatures such as myself: primal beings woven from the thoughts and dreams of the gods. We creatures were not always attuned to the elements. Not at first. We became attuned to them through the ages, much like how eldarim clans have made allegiances to gods and other powers. The entire eldarim species are almost exclusively made of acolytes now, separated by the colors of their magic. That is the basic chromadiscylum which they taught at the school in Yentosh, anyhow."

Karou nodded. "It is still taught to students of the arcane. Chromadiscylum is fundamental to the principles of magic."

Tanneyha nodded. "Eldarim and the great creatures were once only white… universally respecting of all chroma. Now few of those remain, and *none* of the great creatures, which you call monsters, remain white. Not truly… not as in the old days.

"The great ones attuned to their surrounding elements. Some say it was power of the terrain reaching out to claim allies, as Death instigated the early wars. Others claim it was the will of the gods, but regardless, the nature of the world has influenced *all* its creatures."

Tanneyha shrugged. "I much prefer to remember how things were in the beginning. We came in a similar manner to the elder dragons, which the earliest eldarim watched fall to Esfah as if tears from the Mother Goddess. The eldarim preceded the creation of the first races by many lifetimes and when the sages formed their initial order, they took companions from among these monstrous creatures, bound themselves to them as friends… family."

Coryn interjected, "Were *you* a companion?"

Tanneyha shook his head. "No," he said simply. "Though I have known many sages in my lifetime."

The dwarf cocked her head. "How old *are* you?"

Tanneyha chuckled. "I am not one of the first ones," he said, but I am ancient enough to have conversed with elder dragons, the ones capable of speech."

He switched back to the topic at hand. "Finally, the sages were protectors of the Great Trees. Although this was not always one of their primary duties. That came later, as a necessary response to the campaigns of the evil one."

His guests leaned forward in anticipation.

"The mist stones were created through ancient magics crafted by the sages;, magics only capable by adherents to the white chroma. I suspect it would be impossible to recreate them. Magic was more powerful in the early days."

Coryn blurted out, "We've got to get to the Great Tree. We want to protect it. It's guardian sage died, and his maps fell into Death's hands."

Tanneyha smoothed his ruffled fur. A look of sorrow shaded his eyes. "Very well," he finally said. "We frost ogres are experts at anti-magic and skilled at crafting dweomernulls. Perhaps they can help get you inside the barrier created by the ancients. Or at least, I can teach you to navigate them. I once accompanied my friend, the sage, on a trip to visit the Great Northern Tree of Ghaeial."

The sound of the earth shifted into a low baritone the further through the crust they traveled. Sounds like gravel running over an empty barrel echoed through the traveling sphere and time stretched long. The scratching rumbles deepened and turned to a crunchy, silt-like growl as the path traveled below the seas.

Though the spell cut travel times dramatically, its speed was not nearly as close as teleportation; only a couple dwarves clustered within each of the spheres. Ringuld was with Geril, among a few others. He eventually withdrew a sightstone to enhance his magic power and funneled his concentration into it. He activated his will and made the stone glow so that he could read the letter Naemyar had written him.

He fumbled with the papyrus document and opened it with the light as his guide. Geril wanted to wait to read it, but dark thoughts continued to niggle at his mind as they hesitated on the path, hoping to emerge on Dereh'Liandor. And none of the dwarves were guaranteed to survive the chaotic moments that might follow their emergence into the hostile continent.

Now was as good a time as ever to visit the elven lady's thoughts.

Dear Geril,

I considered not telling you the news I discovered for fear that it would distract you from your current mission. However, you are entitled to know, and it might be vital for whatever plans you can engineer for your return.

Queen Rashingot is dead.

Ra'al yet lives and Coryn is fine, but circumstances changed at the last second and Rawrgyld's challenge went defended by Rashingot, who fell in battle against the bear master. Her killer now reigns in Icehome.

Rawrgyld has allowed for Ra'al to lead a contingent of warriors to travel north with the vaghan army and root out the undead. They have the support of what selumari survived the siege of Castle Ice and Taerlon has gotten his sky ship flying again. To his credit, he has rebuffed any suggestion of heading south. There is that, at least, and I'm sure Matrek's aggravation on that score will give you at least some small amount of joy.

Esfah changes daily, it seems, and for the first time, I feel old. Perhaps the world is headed in a new direction. Young heroes and champions emerge. Previous generations are passing and something new rises. Despite all the pain and loss in its wake, perhaps that is a good thing.

For the rest, though, much is uncertain. I only know that you should hasten your return once Harol sa'Lahmyn has been dealt with. Times are dark and growing darker still. Regardless,

I shall do my best to guide whatever comes next in your absence.

    -Naemyar

Geril's guts turned sharp and sour. He left Rashingot and Thrag's widow died, exactly as he'd feared.

The dwarf rolled up the letter and stashed it in his gear before letting the magic light fade. He rode the remainder of the way in silent darkness.

After many more hours passed, the crunching sounds of shifting scree elevated in pitch, and Geril prepared himself for the path's emergence. Within a few minutes time, the bubble rose above the ground with a shudder and fell silent.

Geril hacked his way through the protective shell and stumbled out into the brilliant daylight on a hill about a league inland from the Dereh'Liandor shore, which he could see as an azure blue and white line down the slope. The other stony shells bobbled nearby as his companions broke free.

Snapping his collapsible long-look open, Geril raised it to his eye as Sheron and Ringuld joined him. "He is here," Geril said, concentrating on the distant ship moving toward the horizon. It had nearly slipped beyond the long-look's ability to spot it. "I recognize the colors of *Chariot's Wake* hightailing it north."

Geril sucked in a deep breath and then spat. The air was thick with the green aroma of peat and swamp grass, mud, and the fetid stench of decayed bodies.

"What do we do next?" asked Ringuld.

Geril shifted his eyes to the busted eggshell-like remnants of the path spell. They were a telltale sign that dwarves had secretly arrived on the continent.

He bobbed his head at them. "We'll fan out and search for signs of the traitor in a second. But first, go destroy those. A few good whacks and they ought to break apart."

Tanneyha turned to the shelf where Coryn's boots had found their new home and plucked a seed from its display. He held it low to show them. Small in Tanneyha's hand, it was a large kind of nut, smooth and dark like burnished bronze, but with creases upon it where its original gold hue still shone through.

"This seed came from the tree of life, a Ghaeial Tree," Tanneyha said. "The very kind of tree protected by the mist stones. These special trees are very rare and hold up the power of Nature's magic. They are what allow us access to the power of the gods and are why every creature on Esfah has at least some connection to their mystic energies. Think of them like tent poles holding up the outer shell. If one falls, it will go poorly for those inside."

Coryn stared at the seed. "Has Death destroyed any of them?"

Tanneyha nodded gravely. "Only once. While the whole world was distracted with the Magestorm Wars. That is the reason behind the hardening of the Arcana Veil."

Understanding washed over Karou's face. All spell casters knew that magic used to be easier to cast. The Magestorm Wars marked the end of the First Age, but it was a convenient historical end cap to an era when magic came easier and those who did not practice spell craft could not understand the significance. The presence of the Arcana Veil was much like trying to swim while wearing armor and mages had long pondered what would become of their trade should another veil fall—at some point, magic would become functionally impossible. Their tent could collapse.

"Leisterbane is on his way to destroy the one in the Shadowlands," Coryn realized.

Tanneyha's jaw locked and his nostrils flared. "This is a very bad thing."

"Perhaps we can grow a new one and hide it from the enemy?" Ra'al asked, motioning to the seed. He admittedly did not know much about gardening, but he instinctively knew that the loss of the Ghaeial Trees would only benefit Death.

"This is long since petrified," Tanneyha explained. "The tree that birthed this seed was cut down ages ago, but there is more to germinating it than putting it in the ground. It must also be pollinated by the Waters of Lethial, which tap into the same powers in Dereh'Liandor that draw Nekarthis. He established himself there at the nearby World Wound. Because of his evil, those waters mutated the denizens there and created the sarslayan, the reptilian swamp stalkers. I fear that germinating a replacement may prove impossible at this point… and the loss of another tree will spell grave peril for all Esfahns…

"After the arcana veil hardened, the goddess tried to create another of the great trees," Tanneyha said, "but she had been weakened by Death's constant wars. The opening of the World Wound pained her greatly, and so her attempts did not go as planned. Rather than birthing a new tree to undo the damage Malgrimm earlier wreaked through his minions. Her actions instead awakened the efflorah. The treefolk had always been alive, but they were called to greater strengths and services—a new race in their own respect. They hid for hundreds of years before emerging from the forests and engaging the world at large."

"So, the gods *can't* repair Death's damage to these trees," Coryn said. "Got it. The stakes have never been higher."

"Oh, it gets worse," said Tanneyha. "Perhaps you have seen the nasty black gunk? The sage called it necralluvium. It creates the shambling dead, and it has been growing like a plague in the Shadowlands and abroad. It will kill any living thing that comes in contact with it, and shortly thereafter, turn them into a walking corpse. Except for the dragonkin, all living things can be converted."

"Then perhaps we can use the wild drakufreet to our advantage?" suggested Karou.

Tanneyha shook his head. "You misunderstand. The dragonkin are killed, but do not rise again. Their origins are tied to dragon magic and a secret heritage that predates even the Ghaeial Trees. But that is a story that you've not got time to hear."

The frost ogre finished the craft he was working between his meaty fists and turned them over to Coryn: a pair of furry mukluks. "I appreciate your gift, vagha. And I give you these in return."

Coryn turned them over in her hands. They were flawless, and she thanked the ogre for them. The lightweight foot gear would certainly help stave off fatigue as she tromped through the powder.

"Then time is of the essence. We must hurry back to Taerlon and the ship straight away," said Ra'al.

With a grin, Tanneyha pulled out a large toboggan. "There is a much faster way down the slope, you know."

Garesch rode abreast of Sharsah and he followed the crude map they'd constructed. It was meant to lead them to the next hub of scattered morehl villages nestled within the Wilds of Dur'Sona. The trails were mostly accurate, but the distances between them had been uncertain.

Marnash's horse rode only a slight distance behind the two and a parade of lava elves followed them two by two. They'd coordinated plans for a future foray into Uruzak, but a mission to visit the remaining elves who'd been scattered abroad would help embolden their numbers.

They spoke in hushed voices and kept a wary eye. The Wilds were not particularly dangerous, except for when they were.

A dwarven bolt whistled through the leaves and lodged deep in Sharsah's chest. Hot blood spurted red from the wound and leaked steam as the elven leader toppled from his mount.

"Run! We are betrayed," Marnash yelped to those behind him. The morehl stiffened and yanked their flintlocks free, ready for defense.

Before any could move, the ground rumbled, and the air sizzled with vaghan magic. A wall of earth shot up from the dirt, separating the leaders from the defending elves at the rear and splitting the path between the trees. Heavy leaves fell from ironwoods and horses neighed as the vertical curtain of sandstone curved around to trap Garesch and Marnash against it.

A small army of dwarves riding upon ponies emerged from their hidden positions in the forest. "Greetings, Prince Garesch," yelled Skrathos, sneering to reveal his missing tooth. "I am a hunter, and I always get my prey."

Garesch curled a lip and bared his snarl. Marnash steadied him, keeping a hand on the prince's arm and urging caution.

A second, older dwarf rode alongside Skrathos. His grizzled visage was less cruel, but equally stern. He looked more like some disapproving version of Geril, and the elves guessed he was equally committed to their harm as Skrathos, though perhaps less for his own amusement.

The old dwarf bowed ever so shortly. "I am Derihus, son of Balgavarr and hero from the last time your kind tried to destroy our home: I was taken prisoner during the Battle of Balgavarr."

Marnash grimaced. He'd been there; he understood the dwarf's bitterness.

Derihus threw two sets of manacles to the elves. "Put those on. I'm bringing you back to stand trial before the Council of Elders for your crimes."

Garesch puffed out his chest indignantly, though glanced nervously at Sharsah's corpse. "I have an agreement with the Council," he insisted. "I've committed no crimes and you are attacking a diplomatic traveler!"

Derihus flashed him a dangerous look. "But you *are* a criminal," he said in a low voice. "You've been named as a murderer in the death of Harahsus, a noble businessman and relation to Elder Lahmyn."

Garesch shot a confused look at Marnash. The elder elf gave him a worried look, glancing around to see how poorly they were outnumbered. "Do you think this could be my father's doing?" he whispered.

Marnash crooked a jaw. "I'd imagine he knows, but there's enough corruption in Balgavarr these days that he may not be involved… he could just sit back and let events unfold." He paused and added, "I don't think we can take them."

"If ye won't put them on, I'll clap ye in iron myself," growled Skrathos as he urged his pony forward. "Drop your blade or I'll put three bolts in your leg until ye comply."

Garesch fixed Marnash with a knowing look and handed him the legendary sword. He mouthed, *'You know what to do.'*

Skrathos yanked Garesch's wrists violently as he tightened the manacles. "Fat lot of good that'll do." He sneered at Marnash and indicated that another nearby soldier should apprehend him.

The dwarf moved forward. "Drop the sword," he barked, and Marnash complied as he dismounted.

Derihus yanked Garesch closer to his side and watched as his trooper reached for Marnash. The morehl sorcerer muttered a curse and then snatched the sheathed blade as his attacker tumbled forward, dead as a stone. The dwarf's veins had turned black and bulged close to the skin as the lava elf summoned death magic to snuff the life from him.

"Fire!" roared Derihus and a barrage of quarrels lanced out from the vaghan shooters in the trees. Their crossbow bolts lodged in the dead dwarf, who Marnash used as a shield, and then the elf dropped him as the enemy reloaded.

He dashed toward the lowest point of the wall that had trapped them and leaped over it, barely clearing the lip before more deadly missiles skewered the air where he had been. Then, he and the sword were gone.

Skrathos growled and bit his lip, ready to pursue Marnash into the dense wild lands, but Derihus stayed him. "Forget him," the war hero said. "We have what we came for, and it is enough to stoke memories of my bygone fame."

Garesch looked back, searching for any hint of his friend in the trees. Derihus jerked the reins of his prisoner's horse, and then they trotted west toward the Kafnysan Mountains.

CHAPTER TWELVE

Tanneyha towered over the guests, who had stayed a short while in his home. They each wound their grips through the rope at the edge of the large sled. The curved toboggan was sized for a frost ogre and so they sat two abreast of each other, nervously peering down the steep slope.

Fazayou and Bastawr sat beside each other and the dwarf sat half squeezed between the frostwings.

"You're not going with us?" Coryn asked.

The ogre shook his head. "I'll walk down the trail and pick up my sled next time I go round that way." He looked over the ledge. "Besides," he added, peering with mock nervousness over the precipice, "that's really steep."

"Wait," Ra'al said worriedly. "Are you saying that you haven't done this be—"

Tanneyha gave them a shove over the mountainside, laughing as the large frostwing howled. His toboggan caromed between a couple of large and windswept drifts and then straightened onto the path that slung them down the mountainside at breakneck speed.

Coryn squealed, but Ra'al white-knuckled the edge of the sled as it whirled around a sloped edge, helping them turn and riding the rim around an icy loop. The two areosa did not like the way their vehicle kept dropping though the air as it rode over ramp-like banks and then splashed up clouds of fresh powder as they landed. They were used to being in control of their bodies when airborne, and Coryn laughed that her friend was now stuck aboard the ride. He'd been able to follow from a distance the last time when she and the morehl had taken the Kafnysan shipping luge down the mountain.

Finally, the sled slowed and eventually came to a stop near the bottom. Skrilluk Peak reached hazy gray heights behind them, and their army gathered on the icy plains a little way beyond them. Taerlon's ship hovered above it, waiting for their return.

Coryn scrambled to her feet first, walking more nimbly in her new footwear than before.

Bastawr approached her from behind and stared into the distance. "I see them. More gwereste."

Coryn turned to regard him.

"We sent up a call for help," the tigerfolk told her. "The gwereste in the Wilds of Dur'Sona have long felt the sickness growing in the Shadowlands and they've sought redress for ages. I knew some would come... just not so many." His voice carried a note of awestruck thankfulness.

Coryn stared into the distance, but the range of her vision ceased at the hazy white wall where the distant vagha forces advanced north. "I don't see them."

"They are coming," Bastawr assured her. "They heard of the siege of Icehome and the feral folk remember the kindness shown to them by Thrag and the areosa when they were displaced a generation before the Battle of Balgavarr. They will help stamp out this enemy."

Coryn spotted *Aguarehl's Envy* high overhead and shivered in the cold. She withdrew the gnomish puzzle cube and clutched it in her mitten.

"Why do you have that out?" Ra'al asked.

"I'm going in," she told him. "It's warmer in there, and besides, you'll each need to fly one person up to the ship to get aboard." Coryn nodded toward Bastawr and Fazayou. Ra'al and Karou could fly one each, but they could not manage all three in one trip. "I can ride in a pocket this way… just don't drop me in a snowbank somewhere."

Ra'al nodded. "Not *this* time."

The dwarf activated her cube, and it splintered apart like an electrified chain. Coryn stepped through the portal, and it collapsed behind her, returning to its geometric form.

Ra'al snatched it up and secured the gnomish device. "Let's get aboard and start moving," he said, glancing back at the ogre's sled. "It's a long journey north, and I'll be glad to be in the sky instead of… whatever that was."

Coryn's gaze met the steely eyes of Euhysaurom and froze for a moment. She relaxed a second later. Yoo-ee would likely instill terror in any enemy that could be considered prey for dragons… which was just about everything as far as Coryn knew.

Yoo-ee's eyes glanced down at the dwarf's feet.

"You like them? A frost ogre gave them to me," she said.

The trapped creature seemed suddenly disinterested and looked away.

Coryn approached and looked around. Banks of explosive casks lined the walls where she'd stolen them from below Icehome and stashed them for later use. She was still amazed at the scope of the gnomish pocket space; even though Coryn knew she was probably being jostled and flown through the wintry air with Ra'al at that very moment, her interior space was not at all affected by the outside world.

Stroking her chin, she wondered if and how the gnomish technology could be used against the undead. Short of getting them all to fall into the portal and be trapped within forever, Coryn couldn't come up with any practical applications.

She approached Yoo-ee's enclosure, but this time she did not feel the unsettling gaze of any outsiders, mirrored walls or not. Whatever lingering presence she'd felt once before had not returned since the first time.

The last time she was here, aside from coming quickly to stash the explosives, she'd told Yoo-ee that she would free him. So far, that hadn't happened. But at least she could take a few minutes to attempt it again. Earlier, Coryn had figured out some of the gnomish technology when she'd figured out how to escape. The place didn't feel as much like a prison as it did a storage pantry.

Ha. Tell that to poor Yoo-ee, she thought, looking around for some kind of control panel like the one at the rear of the wedge-shaped room.

A voice behind her nearly made her jump out of her skin. "Sweet Aguarehl's spirit!" Fazayou gasped.

Coryn yelped and whirled, yanking her axe to the ready. Yoo-ee's eyes widened at her outburst. She relaxed when she spotted the selumari warrior. "What are you doing here?"

"Ra'al and Hennedy sent me in to get you."

Her eyebrows knit together at the mention of the name. "Hennedy? I thought he stayed behind in Icehome." Because the frostwing was a royal messenger and not a direct member of the military, Rawrgyld had ongoing use of him at Castle Ice.

"He was. But he is here now, and there are things you must see. You've been in here for days… I hope you know how to get out," Fazayou said nervously.

"Days?" Coryn rolled her eyes and scowled, remembering that time inside the cube didn't seem to align with the outside world.

"Sorry Yoo-ee," she said. "But I'll be back." She left off saying *soon*. Coryn had no idea about the creature's perception of time.

The dwarf hurried back to the circle etched on the floor where the portal could be opened. She bent toward the floor and flicked the entry mark, and then the gate opened with a crackle of energy.

Lahmyn leaned forward over the cup of hot black leaf. Elder Bakurun was far more conservative than most vagha and he had a serious way about him, otherwise the cabal leader would have plied him with ale.

"I am uneasy about letting our guard down," Bakurun told him. The wealthy vagha lived in a modest dwelling. He was a dwarf of the people and had never been given to much indulgence. He had only a few paid staff in his home, none of which were personal attendants. "The undead struck Balgavarr hard and they remain in the Shadowlands—the last time we saw them, they were allied with Uruzak and brought the elder black dragon to our doorstep."

Bakurun stood and retrieved the hot carafe and offered it to his guest. Lahmyn put a hand over his cup to signal he was fine. Bakurun topped off his mug and took a sip while Lahmyn addressed his concerns.

"I think quite the opposite," Lahmyn said. "I don't think they will be a problem at all. Not to us, anyway, but perhaps to Icehome."

Bakurun bobbed his head. "Exactly. We must help shore up the areosa and strengthen their defenses. Queen Rashingot still believes that…"

"Rashingot is dead," Lahmyn interrupted him. He said it matter-of-factly. Even if he held no special affinity for the frostwing people, he had no malice, either.

Bakurun could only blink in stunned silence. Finally, he managed, "Oh. I was unaware."

"She and her people, combined with the strength of Balgavarr, chased off the invaders and scattered them back to the icy plains. She died several days later when a ritual challenger to her throne bested her in a duel."

The news seemed to bother Bakurun, and so Lahmyn continued, "Balgavarr Reaches' allegiance died with her. This new king, Rawr-something-or-other, does not seem to think the dead remain a problem, and he is currently very concerned with security. It is time to end our state of war and bring our soldiers home to rebuild Balgavarr Reaches."

Bakurun nodded reluctantly.

"You really think things are safe again?"

Lahmyn stifled a laugh. "When have times ever been safe in Esfah? No. Not safe, but I think the time for war is over and that we will *be safer* if the army is inside our walls rather than beyond it."

A look of agreement spread slowly across Bakurun's face and Lahmyn knew he had him. "I assume I can trust on your vote for this issue the next time the Council meets?"

Under Leisterbane's baleful gaze, the undead redoubled their efforts. Using the guidance of the remaining maps, they located the other mist stones.

Leisterbane grit his teeth and hissed as he glowered at the stony towers. Mystic runes glowed as he split his army into four portions, and they gathered around the massive plinths.

Within their protective boundaries lay a secret glade and the Ghaeial Tree—the very thing Malgrimm sought to destroy. Only so many existed within the world and killing this one would further open the denizens of Esfah to corruption… his master's tool. Further, it's felling would stiffen the arcana veil again and make magic more difficult. Except for those who followed Death. Malgrimm needed no trees; his magic was not connected to life at all—it was rooted in entropy. And so, Leisterbane and his forces would feel no ill effect.

Leisterbane glared at the brilliant sigils whose glow pierced the haze as the undead drew near. The stones warded the area, making it difficult for the enemy to move past, but once they were down…

The undead leader could already make out the vague outline of the towering tree behind the fog where the first stone had fallen.

"Rip down these stones. All of them. At once!" he roared.

A cluster of mages relayed his orders and creatures began digging, hacking, poisoning the ground, and attaching cables meant to topple the erected stones. Leisterbane's long-dead skin cracked like dried parchment as he bared his teeth in a macabre smile.

It will not be long now…

Lordan hovered near the door of a tea shop and stepped out to grab the arm and ear of Detective Perdy as the dwarf walked toward the more active parts of Balgavarr's market.

"Elder, how may I help you?" Perdy asked.

"Information," Lordan said. "Some of the details surrounding Harahsus's murder don't seem to add up."

The detective's face grayed. "I don't know what I can tell you," Perdy stated. "The case is fairly open and shut. Every sign seems to point to the lava elves, who Geril extended clemency to. I gave my full review to the council. I suspect it is the topic slated for the next meeting."

Lordan could feel when he'd been boxed out by other elders. "Who in particular did you send that report to?"

"Elder Trinean, of course. He told me that he was handling it on behalf of the council."

Lordan cursed beneath his breath. Trinean was always in close cahoots with Lahmyn. The murder felt more political with each day that passed.

"The flintlock used to kill Harahsus was special, correct?"

"It was," said Perdy. "A very rare kind: the magic ones they used to make down in the Karaktoan forges in the First Age before they were destroyed. No reloading, just pull the hammer back and fire."

Lordan withdrew a paper from his pocket and unfolded it. It was a copy of the script he'd taken as a rubbing on the flintlock's barrel. The elder had traced the lettering in charcoal. "This was on the gun's barrel. Have you determined what it means? There doesn't seem to be a durned gnomish expert in all Cyrea."

Perdy smiled. "If I didn't know better, I'd think *you* were the detective here." They rounded a corner, and the market opened further. The investigator paused at a kiosk to purchase some produce and other items on personal errands.

"Yes," Perdy finally told Lordan. "I sent an inquiry abroad and a channel in Tulgesh sent a response…"

"Who is your expert?" Lordan interrupted, eager to know more—he'd been unable to put that piece together.

"Lady Naemyar's house," Perdy said. "Her father was quite the lore master and archaeologist with a special interest in the Magestorm Wars. The gremmlobahnd were central to them."

That drew a nod from Lordan, who bade the detective to continue. He already suspected he knew the meaning of the inscription, but he wanted confirmation.

"The inscription reads, 'A Gift for Hirthak.' Hirthak was the…"

"I know who he was," Lordan said. Everyone with an ounce of learning knew that Hirthak was the only Trog recognized *by all races* as a hero. He was "The White Goblin," and had been the troggish champion of the First Age, blessed by the gods and given an arcane flintlock by the same gnome who had made the mystic forges in Karakto before escaping. He'd been chosen as a Champion, but the weapon had been lost to time after his death at the Trial of the Champions, when the heroes sacrificed themselves to end Melkior the Lich's madness.

"Are you sure it is authentic?" Lordan asked.

"No reason to suspect otherwise. It took so much effort to get a translation that I would guess the flintlock's owner didn't even know the meaning. It wasn't kept as a collector's piece like one would think… it was used to kill." Perdy reminded him that the weapon was very functional. "If the owner knew its deep significance and value, he likely wouldn't have left it at the scene."

"An excellent point," Lordan noted. "*Any* of the Karaktoan firearms are supremely valuable. This one chief among all. Why would it be left behind?"

"I would guess there was a struggle," Perdy said. "There were certainly signs of one. The weapon must have gotten lost in the conflict."

"And where is it now, this famous weapon?" Lordan asked. He didn't know if Perdy was receiving bribes or merely overlooked the timeline—the body had been cold and dead for days before the murder was reported. There *had* been time to locate a lost weapon. Lordan tucked that mental note away in case it became relevant again later.

Perdy cocked his jaw, and his face belayed some mild annoyance. "If you ask the other Council members, they could give you my full report. I suspect it will arrive shortly in any event, with the trial coming and all. I just heard this morning that a bird arrived to report Derihus has captured Prince Garesch and is bringing him back to be interrogated by the Council and to stand trial."

Lordan flashed him a worried look. Derihus's re-enlistment had been only a rumor until now, and Lordan had paid little attention to it. The old war hero had fallen largely out of grace in Balgavarr when he'd continually harassed the Hydrak clan at Geril's peak popularity. He'd quit the city to live in relative obscurity when the public responded disparagingly to Derihus's rants. But Balgavarr was in a much different political place these days and his harsh words, anathema to an older generation, found fertile soil with the one that came after.

Perdy finally answered the Elder's question. "Hirthak's weapon was used to murder a member of the Kiyh clan and so we felt it only right to leave it in their possession. Elder Lahmyn is the head of it, and he holds it in trust. He'll bring it to the trial as soon as Garesch is brought before you. I'm certain the lava elf's guilt will be proved there, and the Council will sentence him at your discretion. They'll either execute him or trade him back to Uruzak; I hear Saugor has an interest in reclaiming his son. But that part is above my pay grade."

The elder had spent the last several days scouring the history behind the special flintlocks. The Karaktoan weapons were more artifacts of legend than anything else, and few solid facts were known about them. The most common knowledge was based on myth. Lordan's research, however, had uncovered references to a linking ritual which bonded the weapon to its owner. It could not fire without being first attuned to its master—but the weapon's power came from the life force of the owner. Much like magic came from the gods and was funneled through a spell caster, the flintlock's destructive energy came from the life force of the linked wielder and was funneled through the weapon.

Further study of the incident known as the Karaktoan Revolution in 532FA recorded that many vagha *had* been attuned to the mystic weapons, including the notorious Burgard, a dwarven diplomat from Gundakhor who perverted his station and took a morehl woman for his own. Lordan had stumbled onto the listing in a book detailing Gundakhor's first-age legal appointments... not exactly a thrilling read, but he'd been determined to cross reference every piece of information he could in his search for the rare weapons.

The Gundakhorian book was the only copy in the archives and that data was not available elsewhere. He wanted to keep that fact as close to his chest as possible, and so he removed the tome from the library and placed it under his protection, adding it to his own collection.

Lordan kept his face neutral and refused to smile as the pieces came together in his mind. He didn't really think Perdy was corrupt, but he developed a plan at that moment. He loved the "Aha!" moments in the bardic tales when roguish heroes tricked their enemies. If the Council *did* hold a full inquisition, he'd use the trial to firmly demonstrate Garesch's innocence— in the most flamboyant way possible.

Perdy raised a brow. "Is something funny?"

Lordan smoothed his beard with his hands. Apparently, he'd not kept his face as placid as he'd hoped. Lordan planned to put the weapon in Garesch's hands and have the elf prince try to fire the inert weapon at Lahmyn; it would make the old dwarf piss himself. If he didn't, Lordan would know beyond a doubt that Lahmyn, like his son, was a traitor to Balgavarr.

"No," Lordan said. "Just caught up in my thoughts."

They turned and walked deeper into the market and the elder let the conversation drift into different topics. Lordan did not see the dwarven iron leaf vendor who'd followed at a few paces. The eavesdropper veered sharply off and headed in the direction of Lahmyn's estate.

CHAPTER THIRTEEN

Coryn emerged from the portal with Fazayou and then put the gnomish cube in her pocket. *Aguarehl's Envy* hung only a little way above the ground on its inflatable bladder and the dwarf could tell that their procession had moved far in the last couple days. Below them, the vagha and areosa forces had all gathered near the ship.

"How far are we?" she asked Captain Taerlon, who plotted a course next to Bastawr. The tigerfolk stared at the map and used a talon to pinpoint their destination on an inked canvas rendering.

"Well over halfway," said the coral elf. He narrowed his gaze on the gathered forces below. "And then we got a messenger."

Coryn rushed to the edge of the craft and looked out to see Hennedy standing with Ra'al. Ra'al was arguing with a cluster of his best warriors and looking very frustrated.

She clambered over the side and descended the rope ladder before hurrying to him; Coryn felt the eyes of cold vagha following her as she rushed past. She could feel their nervousness, as if they knew something she did not.

"We cannot refuse the king!" one of the frostwings snapped at Ra'al.

Another growled, "Rawrgyld rules now, and he gave an order. If you or your mother had—"

"I know what the results of the challenge were," Ra'al roared loud enough to make the frostwing recoil. Ra'al tensed enough that even Coryn thought he might have struck. "I was there."

Coryn whispered to Hennedy, "What happened?"

Hennedy stood meekly, keeping a few paces behind the altercation. His expression seemed to resent that he'd been forced to deliver a summons to Ra'al and the army. He handed her a scroll with a broken royal seal. It bore Rawrgyld's signature at the bottom.

She scanned the letter. It ordered the army to return to Icehome and defend Castle Ice from any potential future attacks and warned of rumored unrest among the morehl. Coryn wanted to grin, assuming that Garesch must have had some success, but the tone of the areosan order seemed overly dire. She blasted a snort of rage through her nostrils, knowing that any trumped up lava elf threat was an empty excuse. The morehl had no interest in trying to brave the frigid, uncomfortable north. They'd only ever wanted Balgavarr Reaches because of its resources, and even then, they'd resented its cooler climate. For that matter, any morehl force would have to pass the vagha first.

Coryn rolled the letter up as she muttered curses. "Lousy fake king. He obviously sent the army with Ra'al and then pulled them back as a power play, driving home the fact that Ra'al no longer has any sway... and to make the army resent him."

Hennedy nodded slightly as Ra'al continued arguing with the commanders under him, trying to plead his case. "You may be right," Hennedy said, "except for the part about

Rawrgyld being fake. He *is* the king... however awful that fact might be."

The frostwing commanders paused for thought as Ra'al insisted, "Maybe the morehl *are* moving and it's worse than I can imagine, but this move is illogical. *Festration!* The entire population of Uruzak could be headed for Icehome right now and pulling back would still be the wrong move. The vagha are wardens over the Wilds of Dur'Sona. They'd knock the fire out of the lava elves and that would mean even a paltry force of areosa would be capable of defending. The undead are a far greater threat—and the longer we delay, the more strength they will gather."

Ra'al's commanders looked from one to the other, each soldier estimating the other's willingness to commit treason in order to accomplish a greater good.

"Unless..." one of them suggested.

All eyes turned to the captain, who spoke, "Apologies, but we must realize that with a new King, old alliances might no longer hold."

Danger flashed in Ra'al's eyes, and he bared his teeth, making the dissenting frostwing take a half-step back.

He continued, "Balgavarr's alliance has always been to Thrag and his line. With that line's rule broken, so may be the dwarves' allegiance to Icehome. I think Rawrgyld may be right to worry."

"But the undead are..." Ra'al's voice went unheeded as the frostwings grumbled amongst themselves and then turned to each other. Their minds had been clearly made up: they sided with the throne.

The former prince roared loud and defiantly; he drew a blade. The ringing steel grabbed the attention of his peers. Even Coryn stiffened. "Uh-oh," she squeaked. She'd never seen her friend like this—then again, he'd never been so low as he was now, even in the days before he'd found the song of the wind.

Ra'al jammed the blade into the frozen tundra, where it wavered like a battle standard. He had their attention, but he had to make his last words count.

"At least let me make an appeal for volunteers. Any areosa that would join me in trying to stop the undead should remain with me and Coryn's vagha."

His request earned a few reluctant nods. "We will spread the word," the commanders agreed, and then they trickled back through their ranks.

Ra'al turned back to Coryn with despair written on his face.

Hennedy placed a hand on Ra'al's shoulder. "I am with you," he said, flashing a grin. "And I've brought you something. A delightful bit of treason." Hennedy produced a wrapped package from behind and gave it to Ra'al.

Ra'al unpeeled a flap of the fabric that covered it and snapped his head up. "You stole *Frostquake? This is Rawrgyld's axe.*"

Hennedy shrugged. "It looks like it's *yours* now. You need it a lot more than he does if he's going to hole up in Castle Ice like a scared tundra mouse. Besides, there's no such thing as only *a little treason.* I figured I might as well go all in and give us a chance at stopping Leisterbane."

The idea of treason hit Ra'al hard. He remembered back to the river docks north of Tulgesh at the bottom of the Kafnysan cargo luge. He'd seen an excommunicated frostwing living there in disgrace. Was that Ra'al's fate, he wondered?

"Treason," Ra'al muttered and then watched as his army turned and took to the sky, abandoning the quest and returning home at King Rawrgyld's order. Thousands had left. Less than a hundred remained, all of them wearing forlorn faces. They recognized that they might never be allowed to return home… and that was only if they somehow survived the upcoming encounter with the undead.

"At least we still have the vagha," Ra'al said, surveying their much-reduced force. And then, he sensed a flash of magic as a white-frosted stone shell emerged from the ground. Someone had used a path spell.

The thin bubble of earth rocked slightly as its inhabitant struck from within. Its facade broke and a dwarf wearing diplomatic clothes revealed himself. If the envoy wasn't from the Council, he had to be Balgavarr's best impostor ever.

Ra'al scowled and Coryn cursed as she watched a dwarf who was missing one tooth emerge carrying a scroll. She cursed, *"Sha'la'dinan."*

Coryn shoved her way through the vagha as she made her way to the visitor from Balgavarr. She did not like that their progress toward the great tree had slowed, even if she hadn't been forced to trudge through the snow alongside the rest of her kin.

"Who are you?" she barked, finally spotting the messenger whose most conspicuous feature was a smile that was short by one tooth and a flinty look in his eye. It was the kind of wild look that advertised he liked to inflict pain.

"I am Skrathos," he said, not bothering to bow. "You must be Coryn sa'Geril?"

She did not like his demeanor or his familiarity. "On the field of battle, you will address me as Warlord."

An electric glee rippled across the intruder's face. "I don't think I will," he hissed, producing a document. Skrathos thrust it in her face.

Coryn snatched it and read it quickly. "They can't just strip my rank and title," she argued. "We are in a war."

The dwarf smiled wickedly. "They can, and they did. They ended the war and called the vagha home." Skrathos turned and shouted to the dwarves. "You all hear that? Back to your warm hearths… it's time to leave this gods' forsaken frozen wasteland. Go home! Make more vagha and help prop up Balgavarr's economy once again."

Several cheers went up from shivering lips. As the vagha dispersed, Skrathos was heard delivering orders to some of the casters demanding a return trip to Balgavarr via a path spell.

Coryn was shaking, she was so mad. She and her father had worked so hard for all of this. And Rashingot—she had died for a chance to end the threat Leisterbane posed. She was about to draw her own weapon when Ra'al's strong hands grabbed her.

"No," he whispered. "Not like this. There's got to be another way." The frostwing propped her up on his shoulders so she could address the dispersing crowd.

"The army of the dead is still out there!" Coryn yelled. "Please—don't go. We have to stop them, or they'll come back, or worse, they'll destroy the magic trees and Death will come for Esfah. If we don't end this now, the Reaches *will* fall."

Most of the dwarves muttered nondescriptly and headed back for home. This was no longer Balgavarr's war. It was Coryn's, and Geril's. Without Geril there to rally them, they turned for home.

Only a tiny portion remained. Mostly, they were vagha who had little left to live for, or those who were particularly devout and remembered legends of the world trees. They must have felt a keen religious obligation to stand for Ghaeial's protection. They were about the same percentage as the areosa who stayed to support Ra'al.

Coryn felt like she'd been kicked in the chest, and she didn't know what to do. She looked to her friend, but Ra'al was reeling, too.

"We're so close, Ra'al… and yet, so far."

He looked down at her. "We'll find a way," he insisted. "We'll just have to fight smarter. The gods are with us."

"You really think so?"

"Of course I do," Ra'al lied.

Marnash stewed in his dark thoughts, deep within the public house in Hinterhome. He'd fled there after Sharsah was killed and Garesch taken captive. Turimnab sat across from Marnash.

Turimnab was a younger morehl, a few years Garesch's junior. He was also the elf who had been elected as the representative to speak for the scattered lava elves. Not all of them lived in small dales, many were in mere pockets of two or three families scattered around the Wilds. Still, news of Garesch's plans had spread quickly and Turimnab, the leader in Hinterhome, was asked to represent them to Sharsah so the minority in diaspora had consideration.

Now Sharsah was dead, and Prince Garesch was in vaghan custody. The heat had been knocked out of their updrafts and Marnash stalled. He still tried to see a way forward, but without Garesch, all was lost. The prince was the key.

The older lava elf sat quietly and stared into his cup, frowning at the dark red fluid within. Wine. It was a local blend they'd made from the resources of the Wilds. *These morehl have proven resourceful… resilient and clever. There is strength in them.*

He could feel Turimnab's eyes on him. The Hinterhome leader had watched him for some time.

Finally, he spoke, "What will you do without your prince?"

Marnash looked away, mouth puckering with a sour taste. He didn't want to answer.

Turimnab asked again, adding, "Garesch seemed pivotal to the plan."

Marnash snapped, "I don't know, okay? This has always been about Garesch. He has been the one capable of rallying support. I have devoted my entire life to the prince ever since returning from Uruzak's attack and surviving Morguus Ebraxus. Without him, I…" he trailed off, deep in thought. His dark eyes twinkled for a moment.

"You have a plan?" Turimnab asked.

Marnash's face grew placid. "I have a plan," he confirmed. It had all flooded into him at once.

"Good," said his host. "No offense, but we signed onto prop up the wielder of the Blade of Aeschere, not some sad hedge wizard who can't decide what to do."

Marnash stood, indignant at the younger elf, but then he slouched, recognizing that Turimnab's characterization might have been at least temporarily accurate. These people, the warriors of Hinterhome, Wildkeep, and so many others, had agreed to risk their lives and the safety of their families to overthrow their government: a monarchy that had existed for hundreds of years. Their decision was no small thing.

"Turimnab, I need your help—now more than ever with Sharsah's demise. Can you take over Garesch's speaking tour? We must rally the morehl in diaspora—something you may be perfectly suited for. Can you do that?"

"There is no revolution without Garesch," Turimnab insisted.

"Then I shall make sure we have him. Even if I've got to walk barefoot into the Abyss to make it so," Marnash assured him.

"You can do that?"

"I said I had a plan. But I need someone I can trust to make sure we have an army to return to. Can I trust you? Can you rally the troops?" Marnash asked.

Turimnab nodded. The red of his skin had brightened with the faith the older caster placed in him. "It will be done."

"Then Garesch shall be free." His fingers went to his pockets. One of them had been sewed shut where he'd placed an item he'd secreted away, only to use in the moment of his most dire need. That time was finally upon him, and he cut the stitches to withdraw a wayfare orb. He'd acquired it long ago and sewn it into the batting of his coat after his time spent as a captive at the Battle of Balgavarr. Not even Prince Garesch knew he had it.

Marnash asked, "We are near a vaghan outpost, aren't we? I'm sure you have had at least some dealings with the dwarves indigenous to the Wilds. I think I need their assistance."

"They're not likely to help…" Turimnab began.

But Marnash cut him off. "I only want a small piece of information and I can pay for it. Derihus I have met, but there was another fellow with him, an angry fellow who was missing a tooth. Garesch tangled with him in Castle Ice once previously, but never shared a name. I merely want to know it."

"I think I can supply it," Turimnab said. "It won't take long if you've got some gold."

Marnash nodded. "Also, I need your fastest messenger. I shall dispatch a letter to Lady Naemyar; she is an ally and I trust her. She has a fleet at her disposal—not a war fleet, mind you, but she can surely help shore up some of our needs, provided I can have Garesch returned in time to help in the battle for Uruzak."

Turimnab bowed. "I'll get started right away and reach out to a vagha contact I have in the Wilds."

The hour was very early and there was little traffic in the halls of Balgavarr. Most dwarves still slumbered.

Despite the time, Lordan looked up from his feet and spotted a vaghan attendant hurrying toward him; the young page worked for Warlord Kile—or more accurately, for the Hydrak clan which both Kile and Geril belonged.

The cranky Elder stared him down, ready to give him a piece of his mind. As the page slowed, Lordan unloaded.

"What is the meaning of last night?"

Kile's attendant blinked dumbly and worked his mouth to no effect.

Lordan continued, "Someone called a meeting of the Elders last night and I was not summoned. I don't like being boxed out or the fact that a quorum might have been formed without so much as a notice to me—Geril put an end to that practice back when…"

The page interrupted. "The warlord was at no meeting last night."

Lordan looked at him, suspicion aroused. "What's your name?"

"Hy'Drommie sa'Gorhus," he said using his full formal name, including lineage and clan.

"All right, Drommie," Lordan groused. "Why were you looking for me, then?"

"The warlord has fallen ill, sir. Very ill. He sent me to fetch you."

"Fine, fine," Lordan followed Drommie. "But the council and I must also have words about why I was denied access to the lava elf prince in our prison."

Drommie shot him a wild look of surprise. "Prince Garesch? He's in prison?"

"But I thought the Elders had extended him diplomatic permissions and a branch of friendship?" Drommie pressed.

"As did I," Lordan muttered, glancing sideways at him.

They arrived at Kile's residence and Lordan hurried to the warlord's bedside. Blankets were strewn as if he'd spent the night thrashing in a fever and there was vomit on the floor.

Kile laid in a sweat with ashen skin and vacant eyes. Lordan bent over him and noted his condition, especially his eyes, which were shot through with yellow and just a faint tinge of green.

Lordan sat back, immediately suspicious of poison. The green hue in his blistered veins was the giveaway, and that would fade as soon as the warlord expired, which Lordan thought very likely. "Drommie. Run and fetch a healer before it is too late. Warlord Kile has been poisoned. I'm certain of it."

Drommie nodded and sprinted from the room.

"The intrigue gets thicker every day, it seems," Lordan growled as he mopped Kile's brow with a damp cloth and tried to rouse him.

"Kile. Warlord Kile," he yelled, knowing the dwarf could barely hear him through the fevered fog in his mind. "Kile, I think you've been poisoned. Tell me who you last ate with?"

No response.

Lordan tried again. "Who did this to you?"

Kile stiffened and he grit his teeth together, inhaling a sharp breath through his clenched jaw. His eyes focused on Lordan momentarily, and with great effort, he relaxed his jaw and croaked one word. *"Lahmyn."*

And then Kile stiffened as if every muscle in his body tensed at once before falling limp. Too limp. His body seemed to unwind, permanently, and the light in his eyes went out.

Lordan stood and roared a wordless cry. But he had his evidence against Lahmyn's betrayal, and he rushed from the house and dashed to his own home as fast as his legs would carry him. Moments later, he threw up an inkwell and papers on his desk so that he could record what he'd discovered and present it to both the council and the authorities.

As soon as he dipped his quill in the pool of ink, his ears perked up at a strange clicking sound. Lordan lived alone, and the city had still not yet awoken.

He turned, startled to find the barrel of a flintlock pointed at his face, and then Lordan's eyes focused on the face beyond the barrel. Fires of hate burned in the eyes of the weapon's wielder: Lahmyn. A flash of flame and smoke blasted as the Karaktoan pistol erupted and Lordan saw nothing ever again.

Lordan's body tumbled to his desk with a ruined face. Chunks of gray and skull fragments littered the wall and papers where the Elder had sought to ruin Lahmyn, who neatly polished the weapon with a kerchief and then returned it to a holster he wore beneath his robes.

Footsteps hurried into Lordan's office and Lahmyn turned to find Skrathos. Blood splattered his wrists where he'd missed cleaning it. "Kile's page won't be a problem," he said with a note of dark mirth.

Lahmyn wiped the blood from his minion's wrist and then tossed the soiled fabric on top of Lordan's body. He looked at Skrathos and said, "Take care of the body and clean this mess up. Deliver it all to the dump."

Skrathos nodded.

"I've got another council meeting scheduled for this afternoon. Make sure none of this is still here by then… I've already recalled the army, but I still must ratify the action to do so before it returns, or else I'll need you to clean a lot more homes like this in the coming days," Lahmyn threatened.

With that, the elder turned and left.

With a mighty crack, ancient stone splintered at its base and toppled as long dead creatures pulled upon chains. Simultaneously, Leisterbane's minions plied the mystic stone with levers to upend it. It groaned as it fell and then thundered to the ground. The runic light that had glowed around its runes finally died.

The last ward was down, and the fog cleared away from the arcane glade. As it dissipated, skeletons poured into the breech. They carried axes and other tools. A cluster of them hauled a long saw that was longer than any house. It howled like a banshee as the ribbon metal whined in the blowing gusts.

As the haze lifted, a tree towered skyward. It was bigger around than a small village. Regardless, Leisterbane watched his skeletal workers hurry toward the massive wooden thing. They began chopping in what looked like a futile effort.

Leisterbane grinned. He knew the destruction of the Ghaeial tree would take much time—days, even—but he had planned for that. His minions were tireless, after all.

CHAPTER FOURTEEN

Marnash kicked a thin sheet off his body and sat up with a gasp. Sleep had come uneasily, and he'd been unable to rest. Too many stressors plagued his mind: Uruzak, Garesch's imprisonment, Saugor's shadow, and the fate of his friends in the far north.

When he'd finally drifted off, he dreamed of trogs. Goblins who played with fire, hurling it at them, and a grinning face of death: a bleached white skull.

Marnash hung his feet over the bed and put them on the cool floor. The sensation clarified his mind. It hadn't been a dream; it was a memory. Marnash focused on it, recalled his flight several months ago through Big Wet, a goblin-controlled swampland directly north of Uruzak. He and his companions had crossed it after a hasty departure from Frostshoal, and in their hurry, they had been pursued by goblins.

"The skull," Marnash muttered. "It is the key."

At the very last leg of their escape, they'd been ambushed by continual waves of trogs... but one had used fire magic. In fact, one had hurled a rune-trapped skull with an arcane fireball so that it exploded in a wave of flames after Marnash and his companions had drawn close.

"But trogs can't cast magic drawn from Firiel. The goddess would not allow it." Marnash tapped his lower lip thoughtfully. "Unless there are acolytes in Big Wet," he concluded. An acolyte was someone who shifted allegiances and had forsaken all other bonds to earn the favor of the gods, much in the same way eldarim had done over the millennia, the non-white eldarim at least. An acolyte, eldarim or otherwise, only served one deity, be it one of the pair he or she was born to or one that they chose. It could even be a foreign god or goddess; Marnash had heard of that and the vaghan traitor Harol sa'Lahmyn was an example. Dwarves were not created at birth to be adherents to Death.

Though Marnash refrained from channeling Death's magic because he found it distasteful, he had never become an acolyte of Firiel. But some trogs in Big Wet had done exactly that! It was the only explanation for fire magic in the hands of swamp dwellers.

He looked across the dark room he'd been granted in Turimnab's home. The gentle snores of the household sounded faintly beyond the thin slat walls. Marnash spotted the gleam of Rhaudian's full light shining against the steel of Garesch's blade and formed a plan. It was not a *new* plan. Turimnab was already set to meet with the leaders of other towns and convince them of their cause, but even so, their soldiers would still face overwhelming odds.

Marnash looked at the prince's blade again. It had once belonged to Aeschere, but the champion had forsaken any allegiance to Death and become an acolyte. An inscription on the blade was written in the languages of the first four races, which read *The Right Hand of Firiel*.

None could dispute the blade's origins, but could it be enough to persuade goblin acolytes to join their cause? Big

Wet's allegiance to Uruzak had soured over the decades since Saugor made his play for Balgavarr. But that sentiment might help Marnash's cause rather than hurt it—especially if there truly *were* acolytes.

Marnash stood and retrieved the blade. He had little time, but Big Wet was closer to Hinterhome than Uruzak was… and Marnash was desperate.

He packed hastily and stepped out of the room. Turimnab was seated at the table, drinking a dark infusion loaded with stimulant root. "Surely you're not leaving?" Turimnab asked.

"No, I mean, yes," Marnash said, taking a seat. He explained his foolish plan to rally the goblins to their aid. "For your part, I need you to assemble the scattered morehl and lead the charge on Uruzak."

Turimnab crossed his arms. "I agreed, but you promised that Prince Garesch would be present."

"And he shall be," Marnash reassured him. "But our victory in Uruzak must be certain. I will both guarantee Garesch's release and presence at the battle, plus I shall bring in additional support. Is that the box over there?"

Turimnab nodded. He'd secured a locked box with a cypher like the kind used to send messages from royalty to ambassadors. The elf sighed and handed it to Marnash. "I'll keep my word, but if you fail to show up, I swear by the gods that my ghost will plague you for all eternity."

Marnash gave him an awkward grin, scrawled something on a bit of paper, and set it inside the box. Then, he locked it and tripped the tumblers. "Your dwarf is waiting to hear a response from me?"

Turimnab nodded. "His shift begins at sun-up. If you're leaving now, you'll catch him as he begins."

Marnash stood. "Then I had best be on my way if we are to keep our original timeline."

Turimnab nodded and clasped the older elf's hand. "Then gods' speed to you. Keep safe."

Marnash met his eyes. "And you as well. I will see you again in several days' time."

"And if I don't?" Turimnab asked.

"Then the trogs are not coming… and I am dead. Probably eaten."

Turimnab nodded grimly and clasped Marnash's forearm once and then rapped a closed fist over his breast in salute. Marnash mirrored the gesture.

With that, he ducked through the door and hurried into the night.

Near the main halls of Balgavarr Reaches, Derihus stood at the forefront of a large crowd. He wore his soldier's uniform, complete with medals for service given in years past, including one specific to the defense of Balgavarr Reaches during Uruzak's invasion. His shoulder sash bore an old tear; the fabric was draped down vertically to indicate that he had un-enlisted.

The firebrand whipped a crowd into a frenzy, thanks to the misinformation campaign that Trinean had overseen. While Elder Trinean's nephew Skrathos had earlier led a contingent of loyalists into Icehome to collect Prince Garesch, several other teams worked to renew morehl resentment. The dwarves' grudge glowed like a red-hot ember. It would only take a small gust of air to conjure up the flames of vaghan anger.

Derihus fanned that fire, publicly decrying the recent actions of Warlord Kile and the policies of Geril who had appointed him. "And what has friendship with the lava elf prince brought us besides more dead dwarves?" Derihus yelled.

The crowd roared its assent. Several cried out slogans that Trinean's team had planted. "Derihus was the true hero of the Battle for Balgavarr," and, "The only good red one is a dead one," caused murmurs of assent.

Someone had constructed a podium and Derihus climbed up it to address the assembly. Not far from them stood the doors to the Council chambers, the same place where both Thrag and Garesch previously petitioned and earned vagha support.

"Behind those doors are the representatives of the dwarven clans: vagha your families sent to represent your interests. But our government has failed us and made bedfellows with our enemies." Derihus pointed to the doors. "They ignore the looming threat of a new and secret war. One filled with lava elf assassins. A war that sends our army far away to fight the dead and police the wastelands, though the dangers creep much closer to home."

"But the dead attacked us," cried out a lone voice.

"Yes. They did." Derihus looked down his nose. "And we defeated them. Perhaps if we had a more capable leader at home, our casualties would not have been so severe. A stronger economy that bolstered a civic army has been an avenue Geril sa'Ghuren has rejected. And the resulting complacency is why we were so ill prepared. Friends, we must end this war…"

The crowd took up the chant, "End the war!" Finally, Derihus held up his hands to call for silence.

"Further," he said, "we need a new Warlord, or even better, a new steward. Warlord Kile will only give us more of the same offered by his clan mate, Geril. Hydrak has ruled long enough."

The doors behind Derihus opened and Lahmyn emerged. His peers on the Council stood on the threshold and watched. Lahmyn took to the stage and Derihus offered him the chance to speak.

"Thank you General Derihus. This is perhaps an unconventional means of getting Council news out," Lahmyn said and scanned the crowd. "But we do not live in conventional times. I must report with a heavy heart that Warlord Kile has died."

A gasp rippled through the audience. Lahmyn continued, "Perhaps it was an illness related to the wounds he suffered in battle not so long ago. The physicians cannot be certain of anything except that he has died. With him, the steward's seat is open. Additionally, Elder Lordan has disappeared. He has not answered a summons to the last two Council meetings, and we feel it only right to petition Clan Hydrak for a temporary replacement until Geril returns."

Lahmyn cleared his throat and swallowed. "The Council also wishes it known that your voices have been heard. We have, just now in fact, voted to end the needless war in the Shadowlands. A messenger was sent to call our troops home."

Sounds of approval buzzed in the crowd.

"We have also voted to open the steward's seat—a temporary measure per our bylaws. Upon Geril's return from traveling abroad, a special election will be held to re-seat him or keep his successor in power." Lahmyn scanned the crowd. The dirty vagha scratched their heads and beards, trying to make sense of the legal talk. "I certainly intend to run my name and my first act as steward will be to appoint Derihus as my warlord." He flashed the assembly a manipulative look. "Of course, that is, if I'm elected."

That elicited a rumble of applause.

Derihus stepped forward. "And I can endorse Lahmyn as a civic-minded moderate who wants nothing more than a strong Balgavarr."

Lahmyn held up a fist. "The strength of Balgavarr is its people—and I will make our mountain strong again."

Derihus's crowd cheered.

"Furthermore, as an Elder of the Council, I will personally preside over the trial of Prince Garesch, who sits in our prison even now, for the murder of innocent vagha within our own halls," stated Lahmyn. "And with his conviction and likely execution, we shall also excommunicate any vagha who has proved to be in league with the traitor."

Lahmyn crawled down and left Derihus to drive home the sentiments. He walked back toward the Council chambers and restrained himself from smiling. He knew he had them; he had them all. Within two days' time, he would sit in Geril's seat and then he would undo everything the upstart had worked so hard for.

Balgavarr would be strong. And it would be Lahmyn's.

Marnash hid in the bushes and waited for Soll's early rays to warm the surrounding air. As it came up, he spotted movement in the vaghan outpost. A stout dwarf stood outside the short watchman's tower. He was just old enough to have been young during the Battle for Balgavarr. Whatever he'd done to pull a duty-posting out in the Wilds was anybody's guess.

The tower was made of stone and the top layer had slits for dwarven missilers to aim from while enjoying maximum protection; a short barracks bulged off from the one side.

The dwarf stretched and walked a short circuit as the day's first light burned off the morning haze; Marnash identified him by the scar that crisscrossed his face. As he drew closer, Marnash called out from his hiding place in the trees.

"Hail dwarf. Are you Kiryn?"

Kiryn stopped cold and scanned the foliage. "Aye," he said reluctantly. "Do I know you? Show yourself."

"It has reached the ears of Emperor Saugor that few dwarves hate the morehl as much as you."

Kiryn absentmindedly touched the scar that puckered the flesh across his face. "That much is true."

Though not as much as he loved money, according to Turimnab, thought Marnash. "Then how would you like to kill the elven prince, Saugor's only legitimate son?" Marnash asked.

Kiryn cocked his head and grinned. "Mirryn, is that you? Are you playing a trick on me?" Kiryn approached.

Marnash summoned Firiel's magic and applied it in unconventional ways. He heated the damp and peaty soil stretching through the woods. The heat repelled the moisture and sent it skyward as a fog allowing Marnash to slip hidden to another space.

"No, friend. I am someone who, like you, must see that the prince is dead. He must not endure a trial... what if he is exonerated—what if the Kafnysan Elders are in cahoots? Geril has influence on the Council still."

Kiryn stopped. His face betrayed him: he thought that was certainly possible. "Show me your face."

"That I cannot do. But I have an artifact in my possession, an item meant to torture and kill whoever beholds it. One must only look upon it and the thing will consume the viewer, destroying them in the most agonizing way possible."

Kiryn didn't prove as stupid as he looked. "I heard the whelp was going to overthrow Uruzak. You must be a morehl... did Saugor send you?"

Marnash paused. "I am a lava elf. You are right in that."

"I don't want to help the emperor."

"But you greatly desire to kill his son?"

Kiryn dug at the soil with one foot. "I ain't fool enough to think I'd ever get to put my axe through an enemy king... but his son?" He paused a moment longer and then answered the question. "Yes. I'd kill him."

"Then so you shall," Marnash promised. "There is a messenger box placed upon the tall stone, five cubits north of you. Deliver it to the prince."

"And if I open it?"

"Then you shall die the worst death imaginable. Much like the mystical dawn blade which cuts a soul away from a body and imprisons it for eternity. This device, a soul orb," he made up a name on the fly, "does the same thing."

Kiryn blanched. "King Saugor doesn't play around, I guess."

"No," said Marnash. "He does not. And he does not offer mercy even to his son."

Kiryn snatched the box. "And after the deed is done?"

"Then you shall be paid. Extra, that is."

"I used to work as a jailer in Balgavarr. I can see that the package is delivered," said Kiryn.

"You hear the direction of my voice," Marnash said, "and you have the package. There is a stump here. I will leave a payment upon it in gold. I shall return to pay this amount thrice over once the deed is done. You will know the tool was successful because it will disintegrate the body upon completion. You only have three days to hand over the box before the weapon becomes inert."

"Fine, fine," Kiryn said. His ears perking up at the tinkling of coins being set down.

Marnash entrusted the spiteful dwarf to his own greed and hatred and then slipped away into the fog and the denser part of the trees, angling his path toward Big Wet. He had no intention of ever returning.

Geril and his comrades hurried through a blasted canyon in a wasteland as they headed east, tracking Harol sa'Lahmyn through Dereh'Liandor. Harol made no efforts to mask his presence and opted instead to hurry ahead of any pursuers.

In Geril's party were several skilled trackers, including Ringuld, and they'd found the evidence of his coming to the shores of this hostile continent. The dwarf had taken an unwavering course east and had managed several days' worth of lead time on them.

Geril unfurled a sketch of the continent and turned his eyes to the sharply angled spikes that seemed to scrape at the clouds. The mountains that jutted up from the World Wound looked like mangled and gnarled teeth, very much like those of the misshapen faeli warriors who Death had long ago twisted to suit his own whims.

"How long before we can find him?" Geril asked.

Ringuld looked skeptical. "Almost a tenday at least, perhaps more." He frowned, knowing the journey from here would grow even more arduous. "His trail seems to indicate he is driven by intense purpose."

"Of course it does," Geril muttered. "He is a zealot on a religious journey… a pilgrimage to awaken his dark priest, Nekarthis."

Ringuld nodded measuredly. "Yes. He is moving directly, but not quite so speedily as one with a deadline to keep."

Geril followed along with Ringuld's assessment. "So, we still might be able to overtake him yet? He is moving methodically." Geril and his hunters stood in a copse of bracken upon a gentle hillock. He scanned the surroundings. The north side was broken and muddy where fens stretched, and the horizon burned green with lush jungle foliage. The south was blasted, tar pits bubbled, and steam geysers ruptured like blisters between bald cypress and stubborn thorn-moss.

"Goblins and sarslayans to the north and scalders to the south," Geril sighed, noting their party's current position on the map. They were in Treglyteholm and a dark line north indicated the long-dried up Lethial Riverbeds, which was the traditional boundary to the Snekdenn Bayou.

The dwarf's stomach turned. They stood in the very creche of life, on the northern side of Dereh'Liandor, known as Annor. Here was where the priests claimed that The Mother, Ghaeial, Nature had awoken to godhood when she heard Tarvenehl's voice and in that instant, she loved him. Here was also the home of the eldarim, who crawled forth from the primordial muck of the Autumn Sea and walked the land for ages unknown before the remainder of the gods created the elder races.

The weight of being in such a powerful location dragged at Geril's crew. None had ever thought they would see this place in their lifetime—and to see it in such a state of decay wrung the energy from their cause like dew from a fleece. This place was infested with hopelessness.

"Trogs, reptilian swamp stalkers, and faeli barbarians," Geril mumbled. "Perfect... so we can assume that Harol, even as an acolyte of Death, is probably taking care to not be discovered?"

Ringuld nodded. "If we can gain a few leagues on him every day, we can hope to catch him before he gets to the Netherwold."

In the middle of the mountain range ran a rift that had cracked open during Nekarthis's siege upon Esfah, the conflict known as the Magestorm Wars. The massive fissure became known as the World Wound and at its bottom was the Netherwold: the seat of Nekarthis's power and his final resting place. What it could do had passed into legend, but if Harol thought he could harness it for great evil, then he had to be stopped. The rogue dwarf had already proved far too terrible to be left to his own devices.

"So, we just have to move faster and more secretively than one lone dwarf," Geril said. That would be difficult to do in a group of twelve.

"That problem is one I can solve. Both problems, actually," interjected Sheron, whose fingers seemed to sparkle with magic. "I am pretty creative when it comes to spell craft…"

A sharp *thawp!* interrupted the moment and one of Geril's scouts quickly re-nocked his crossbow as a trog scout collapsed, gurgling and choking on viscous yellowed blood. The intruder clutched his neck, trying to staunch the flow where the quarrel had lodged in his throat.

"There! Seven more of them," the dwarf shouted.

The vagha opened fire on the enemies, who were just as startled to discover dwarves on Dereh'Liandor soil as the dwarves were of being discovered. A hail of bolts peppered the goblin patrollers, who quickly succumbed to them. Their leader whirled on his wolf mount and attempted to flee.

Ringuld took aim and loosed a bolt which streaked out and pierced the scout's heart. He fell from the mount and the wolf dashed into the distance, riderless.

"Quickly," insisted Sheron. "Retrieve whatever bolts you can and stack the dead in a heap. I'll summon fire to incinerate whatever I can of the carcasses. With any luck, the trogs will assume the patrol was ambushed by faeli raiders." The scalders were capable of summoning fire magic and would likely be the first suspect.

Geril nodded to his men, and they hurried about the task. Within twenty minutes, they were skulking away from the scene and back onto Harol's trail.

CHAPTER FIFTEEN

Marnash lowered the shroud of mist that he'd conjured to help him remain hidden in the swamps. The elf had moved with almost reckless abandon, hurrying through troglands of the Big Wet. He'd found the same general location where he and his former companions had traveled when they'd crossed from Frostshoal to Balgavarr.

He slowed when he found tracks and other evidence of trog activity nearby. Ahead, two goblins stood taking turns smashing a mudfish with a club just beyond the thick mists. Marnash let the billows part and emerged. The trogs' hands went to their weapons and Marnash held out the weapon: The Blade of Aschere.

Speaking in the troggish tongue, Marnash commanded, "Show me to your chief and to your mages."

The goblins blinked vapidly and then snarled. One of them dashed toward the morehl caster, but Marnash fired a bolt of death magic. It shot toward the target, trailing a wispy plume of ethereal black, and the goblin fell dead as a stone.

Marnash cocked his head to the other one, who grew much more compliant. He spoke again in the goblin tongue; Marnash had learned it long ago when he'd been enlisted in Uruzuk's army. His duties had forced him to communicate regularly and at length with the forces of Big Wet.

"To which of the four tribes do you belong?"

The trog shook his head and held up three fingers on one hand and two on the other. "Not four. There are now six tribes."

"My question remains the same," Marnash insisted. "I passed this way many months ago and my party was attacked near here."

"Uruzak no longer holds any alliances with Big Wet. You are all traitors and users…"

"Not all of us," Marnash said. "I am not a subject of Uruzak. Saugor is not my king."

The goblin stared at him quizzically and then shrugged.

Marnash continued, "This is a sword of legend. Do you see the inscription it bears?"

The goblin's eyes widened. Most trogs, unless they traveled abroad, could only read a few words, and none of them were able to comprehend the text etched into the blade. But Marnash saw the recognition in those eyes: this goblin could read… and he knew what the sword represented.

"Am I correct in thinking your tribe has forsaken its old gods and devoted itself to Firiel?"

Reluctantly, the goblin nodded.

"Then we share an alliance, at least as children of Firiel," Marnash insisted.

The goblin grinned and took two steps back. He spoke in the morehl tongue, which threw Marnash off and revealed that this trog was more learned than expected. "I already told you, our old alliances are dead. It was Uruzak who forced our clan to adopt Firiel as our patroness—his reverence manifested as a cruel joke." The trog's yellow eyes glanced aside to the trog's companions emerging from the trees.

Marnash's resolve wavered, and he took one step back.

"We have no true alliances," the trog continued. He gestured to the lava elf intruder and ordered, "Take him."

Thirty goblin warriors rushed toward Marnash, who made no move to defend himself. He'd already committed his way to diplomacy. But the denizens of Big Wet had made no such promise and a large trog carrying a club-like stick cracked Marnash across the head and sent him sprawling to the mud. He looked up just in time to see the butt end of that truncheon come crashing down, and then everything went black.

Lotep, Naemyar's selumari servant, entered the lady's sitting room and delivered her a letter.

"Thank you, Lotep," she said as she broke the seal.

Lotep waited near the door until Naemyar either dismissed him or sent him on an errand.

Her eyebrows arched, and she pursed her lips. "Pity," she said and then set down the letter.

Naemyar knew Lotep was always listening. She often spoke freely around the majordomo, and he sometimes provided her a sounding board, though there were some secrets she knew she could never trust with him. "This girl sounded so promising," she said and looked at Lotep.

"Problems abroad, my lady?"

"My son. He was finally engaged to be married. The young woman and I have been communicating. But the marriage is apparently off." She frowned.

Naemyar had left her husband, King Leidergelth of Niamarlee, many years ago and returned to her family home and business in Cyrea when her father's health fell ill. He had died shortly afterwards. When she'd been young, he had toured his daughter around the world via ship. Of course, it was more than just a tour. He'd been scouting to find her the best suited husband; that tour was her first introduction to Ghuren and Zephras Thunderfist, the Hydrak clan leaders and warriors who had preceded Geril. Geril had noticed her then, and they could have met there, for all Naemyar knew. She didn't remember and hadn't taken particular care to make acquaintances in every area she visited, especially those places so close to home; she'd never intended to remain in Cyrea and found her husband in Niamarlee.

Niamarlee had agreed with Naemyar; she'd loved Leidergelth and even endured the man's close friends, Furtaevell and Raeyalla. The latter had clearly loved her Leidergelth for many years—an intimacy that yearned for much more than the proximity of friendship. Likewise, Furtaevell loved *Naemyar*. Naemyar was wedded to the crown prince, who shortly after took the throne, and Raeyalla married Furtaevell. Many years later, Raeyalla died, murdered by a band of goblin raiders around the same time that Naemyar had returned to Cyrea.

While Naemyar and Leidergelth had been fighting over several irreconcilable differences, they were not the true cause of her withdrawal, as all had suspected. She had never told even her estranged husband the real reasons. Though their interpersonal issues had contributed to the turmoil, as is often the case when unyielding personalities are bundled in wedlock, the reasons were far more Naemyar's than Leidergelth's. She kept secrets from even him.

She truly *had* loved him, once. Him among others. But Naemyar could not bear him knowing about her father's allegiance to the dark one. Perhaps Lotep suspected it, but the circle of living individuals who knew was extremely small.

Naemyar frowned as the memories of Leidergelth and Furtaevell rushed back; the families had been so close for all their years. But Naemyar's son and Raeyalla's daughter had broken off their engagement.

"The wedding's cancellation… it distresses you?" Lotep asked.

"Of course it does."

"I ask because there has been no action from your son, Prince Mantieth, to contact you. I would think things are cold between you," Lotep suggested. "You did not return for his coming-of-age celebration."

Naemyar cocked her head. "Yes… and no. If he had written me, I would have attended. I have not stopped loving him. He is my blood." She sighed, not knowing how to explain it… then she realized she was a queen. She did not *have* to explain it.

But Lotep had a point. Things had grown cold between her and her son. And her only contact regarding the engagement had been with Elorall, Raeyalla's daughter.

"Bring me a parchment and quill, Lotep. I think I shall invite Mantieth for a visit. He's not been to Cyrea since he was a child. And this way I should not risk the necessity of interacting with my husband."

Lotep bowed. "Certainly, my lady." He paused at the door and then spoke hesitatingly. "There is another thing, Ma'am. It concerns security and may be relevant with all the letters coming and going."

Naemyar waved her hand, bidding him to continue.

"There is a spy in your house."

"Yes," she said placidly. "One of the frehlasuhl servants works for my husband. I imagine it rankles him to pay coin to a grey elf." Naemyar smiled. "Leave him be. I have spies of my own in Leidergelth's employ."

Lotep cocked his head, unsure of the rules of these shadow games she and her husband played with half a world lying between them.

She explained, "We may not want to be in each other's company, Lotep, but passion still burns hot. We keep tabs on each other, and I would feel quite insulted had he not attempted to infiltrate my staff." Naemyar could see that Lotep still didn't quite understand the depth of it.

A smile quirked at the edge of her lips. "It's how I know Leidergelth still loves me."

The majordomo bowed, keeping his face neutral, and he departed to fetch his lady's quill and paper.

Leisterbane stared at the three black flames before him and grumbled with animal sounds. Only two of his minions had answered his summons and he knew that the third of them, the dwarf called Harol, must have felt excruciating pain while resisting the death knight's arcane call. The undead knight poured more intensity into the summons for a sheer love of inflicting pain upon the dwarf.

The flickering flames that represented his other two conspirators, both elves, waited patiently for their third. They understood Leisterbane was punishing their companion for his refusal to join the arcane parley. They also knew Harol was otherwise preoccupied.

Finally, Leisterbane tired of the game and turned his attention to the red and blue-skinned elves. "The dwarf is an unnecessary redundancy," Leisterbane stated. "His plan to awaken Nekarthis is a doomed effort. Selumari, you are in Tulgesh. Report."

The coral elf bowed. "Redundant or not, Harol may likely be doomed. Geril sa'Ghuren tracked Harol across the world and has enlisted aid to pursue the dwarf and kill him. He has at least some idea of what Harol intends for his trek to Dereh'Liandor, according to rumors."

"Impossible," seethed the morehl conspirator. "Harol enlisted aid from the fastest vessel in the area. He hired passage with the pirate Ry'Ober."

"Is her ship faster than a path spell, Emperor Saugor?"

"As I said: impossible. No dwarf can pass deep enough to undercut the ocean," insisted Saugor. "Not even with magical means."

The blue elf raised a brow. "I have learned many secrets at my post. And I am certain Geril Dragonsbane managed exactly that."

"Leave the fool to his own demise," ordered Leisterbane. "I am on the verge of victory; soon, the north-most world tree will fall, barring any gross interruption. Your jobs were to prevent exactly that sort of interference. Report."

The blue elf reported. "Aside from a lone airship from the Tulgesh fleet and a few rogue coral elves who refuse to follow orders and return home, the selumari will provide no resistance. They will not see the harm you inflict until after the damage has been done—until *after* you have weakened the connection between Ghaeial and her children."

Scowling at his counterpart, the red elf responded. "The daughter of Dragonsbane may still prove a minor nuisance, but her party has been split. I stoked the fires of dissent and manipulated my son's hatred of me. Garesch was inspired to revolt and his entourage have parted ways to usurp me." Saugor grinned. "Exactly as I knew they would; the power hungry vagha of Balgavarr's Council of Elders war among themselves. They've arrested Garesch while crossing the Wilds. His execution will be soon, and it will be swift—but in the meantime, it creates such a distraction that it may be years before the vagha realize how little of a threat the whelp actually was and how they've erred. That is, if they can ever see past Councilor Lahmyn's forked tongue."

The dark one spoke, "The children of Dragonsbane and Rashingot will never arrive here. I have a surprise in store for them. Some old acquaintances, perhaps." Leisterbane's eyes burned brighter as he turned them to Saugor and took stock of the elf's devotion, even unto filicide. "And will you sire a new child or claim a bastard as your new heir?"

"Neither." Saugor bowed his head. "I intend to rule forever. You promised me as much. You claimed our obedience would make us barons in Malgrimm's coming kingdom. What need for an heir will I have once I am immortal? Once I'm remade in my god's image?"

Leisterbane said nothing. And Saugor made no movement, though the death knight caught the faintest aroma of fear. The morehl had given the correct answer—anything else would have made the bloodless champion reluctant to honor their pact; when the time came, he would have simply killed Emperor Saugor. If Malgrimm wished it, he still might.

He turned his head and looked at the flickering image of the coral elf. That one still worried him. The selumari was too cocksure... too arrogant. As if the elf knew something Leisterbane did not and still had cards to play, should the game's favor tilt.

Saugor and Harol were known acolytes of Death. But Tulgesh's cultist had still not yet been revealed, and the spy had access to persons in very high positions of power. Leisterbane's blue lips cracked as he spread them thinly. He knew he could use that knowledge in the future, provided the shifty elf still played this game of shadows. He chortled slightly, knowing that he'd chosen his cultist conspirators for many reasons, but their honesty had never been one of them.

"And rule you both shall as stewards under a new age of darkness. Hail Malgrimm," he said and then severed the link as they both repeated the mantra, *hail Malgrimm*, in the background.

Leisterbane turned and stared daggers at the mighty girth of the Ghaeial Tree. He muttered a black curse as his tireless minions hacked at it with myriad tools. Skeletal forearms splintered and broke and axe-heads blunted as the mystic topiary defied Leisterbane's efforts to harm it. A twelve cubit saw blade lay discarded in the distant snow; its teeth had all been sheared off when they'd tried to cut through the tough exterior. Most of the animated corpses now carried picks or shovels.

The death knight smiled as piles of frozen dirt and stone towered nearby and his bloodless underlings cut tunnels deep into the soil. Foremen, commanders given greater freedom of will, oversaw them, screaming curses and threats. "Delve deep, you worthless scraps of flesh. The only way this tree is coming down is to hack at the roots."

Leisterbane turned and cocked his head at the shackled human he kept nearby, like a pet. The man was emaciated and shivered constantly. His hair had grown out in wild tufts.

Avaryth scratched at the dirt, pulled a worm from the cold soil, and greedily devoured it. He wilted beneath Leisterbane's gaze.

Leisterbane knew how he would kill this tree. And this man would play a critical role to that end.

Aguarehl's Envy moved slow. Far more slowly than Taerlon liked. The added weight of their mission's futility seemed to accumulate almost as much as that of the dwarf fighters who had stuck by Coryn and the areosan defectors.

There were far too few of both. One overloaded airship could scarcely make a dent in the undead army, but they were determined to try… if only they could make it to the mist stones.

A fierce snowstorm had whipped up. It nearly blinded the vessel's crew as they tried to weave between the blasts of blistering cold air currents. Attuned to Ailuril, goddess of the winds, they felt them coming and reacted as they could, retracting sails and wind fins and trying to respond in such a way to harness them, but the efforts drew long, and they'd almost come to a standstill.

Taerlon's navigator logged each time they were pushed off course or turned from their marks and plotted them on a map. Bastawr stood over the charts with his friends and the captain.

"We've gotten well past the Heimdarl Crag," Taerlon said, showing them by drawing a course on the map. "But whatever this wind is, it's not natural. Someone is using magic to keep us at bay." He looked at the gwereste. "You are sure we're still going to the right spot?"

Bastawr pointed to an X with his talon and nodded vigorously. "I am certain of it. We move slow, but we're on course."

"Well, we can't wait around forever." Taerlon issued an order to his crew. "We're going to increase elevation and try to get over this storm. Tighten your coats and breathe deep; the air is going to get thinner."

Coryn scraped ice from the inside of the porthole windowpane so she saw the deck of *Aguarehl's Envy*. The Shadowlands were frigid, but this cold snap they sailed through made it almost unbearable. The crew working the riggings had thrown wool blankets over their shoulders like shawls as additional insulation. She knew her dwarves, mostly crammed below decks, were huddled for warmth, using whatever scant fire magic they could draw upon to keep their weapon hands warm.

"Ra'al?" she wondered aloud. "If this is magical, can't you try to dispel it?"

The big frostwing cocked his head as if she'd just smacked him with common sense. Taerlon and the others all looked at him.

Ra'al nodded. "I should have thought of it sooner. But we can certainly try." He headed straight out into the blowing storm and shouted for his frostwings.

Hennedy and Karou joined him almost immediately. Areosa, with pelts ranging from blue to black and mottled greys and whites, seemed to arrive out of nowhere.

Flying in the gale had required much more effort, and they'd taken the flight in shifts while their fellows hung from the sides of *Aguarehl's Envy* by makeshift slings and rested. Filled with dwarves, the craft had no more room below decks.

Coryn watched from the window. She shivered with a chill that permeated even the captain's cabin and traded a nervous look with Bastawr, who stood next to her. The gwereste was the only other person who had been with her since the beginning. Things had seemed so much simpler then: find and destroy the undead. Now, political intrigue had whittled their forces down to almost nothing when even the blades of their enemy had failed to cause such attrition.

She and Bastawr watched Ra'al walk the length of the deck. Nervousness lit in her eyes.

Bastawr flashed her a knowing look. "I am certain he'll manage this," the tigerfolk insisted. "Marnash had great faith in him."

"That's not what my biggest fear is," Coryn said. "It's the nature of magic that worries me."

Bastawr cocked his head.

"Death magic couldn't conjure an ice storm like this. Someone *else* is doing this to us," Coryn said and frowned. "Someone who can conjure spells attuned to nature instead of Death."

"Or in addition to it," Bastawr whispered knowingly.

Coryn nodded and momentarily locked eyes with Ra'al, who spoke to his peers outside. She and her Ra'al were practically siblings and could often speak without words. Coryn knew he'd had the same thought.

The cluster of areosa standing on the deck gathered in close and focused on each other. They began to glow with a rippling aura that shimmered but barely, and then something pulsed with an azure flash.

In almost an instant, the fierce winds died. The blowing snow that had blinded them like a white wall crumbled and a quartet of areosan magi flapped their wings in the distance with surprise written across their faces.

Karou gasped. Apparently, he hadn't made the connection. But worse, he seemed to recognize the faces of those in the distance that had.

Coryn opened the door and exited to the deck now that the supernatural cold had dissipated. She furrowed her brow, furious that any frostwing would stand against them in their efforts to destroy an enemy that had so recently tried to wipe out Icehome.

"Now!" Ra'al roared.

The defected areosa who followed Ra'al summoned spears of ice and hurled them through the air. A blanket of jagged death rained down upon the frostwing spell crafters who had impeded them. Frozen missiles caught them unawares and overwhelmed them. Javelins of ice pierced them and they tumbled to the ground far below, with wings flapping in chaotic, uncontrolled falls.

Ra'al's face hardened. He hadn't wanted to kill his own kind, but their mission was too important to let Rawrgyld's interference slow them further. He pulled a few of his soldier's aside. "Gather the bodies and bring them aboard. We cannot leave them behind as evidence. As far as anyone will ever know, these four joined our cause but fell in the battle we all know is coming."

Two winged soldiers nodded. "You really think any of us will survive this?"

Ra'al paused and then reluctantly shrugged. "We must continue to hope."

Standing next to Ra'al, Karou swallowed. "I knew those casters. They were greedy, quarrelsome sorts. Ambitious… always looking for ways to trade their skills for wealth. And none were particularly moral."

Ra'al thanked him for his input. They could only hope that there weren't more of their sort.

No sooner did Ra'al's troops follow their orders and descend to recover the bodies than Ra'al sneezed. Then again, violently. And then he collapsed to his hands and knees and vomited all over the deck, clearly wracked by pain.

Coryn shouted and ran to his side, but he held up a hand to stay her. His eyes were filled with fear.

"I've never smelled something so…" Ra'al choked, unable to even speak. His hand clutched the artifact Marnash had given him to help channel magic abilities.

Ra'al staggered to his feet and snorted, trying to clear whatever odor he could from his nostrils. He concentrated as the morehl caster had shown him, and then he broke the arcane abilities of his enemy, shattering the invisibility of the ethereal undead.

Standing calmly beyond the deck as if it had no need for ground, a cloaked figure cocked his head curiously. Grave cloth shrouded him except for the bony hands which clutched a scythe. Eyes glowed within the thing's semi-transparent body.

Next to Ra'al, Karou almost whimpered. The magi were far more well versed in the arcane. Karou's voice cracked. "It's a minor spirit of Death."

"Can I kill it?" Ra'al asked.

Karou looked at Ra'al as if he were crazy. "It's an unbound spirit, Ra'al! A sliver of Death's very power personified. Goblins worship these things as gods in their own right." He gulped. "This thing could kill us all in a matter of moments."

Ra'al narrowed his eyes, never tearing them away from the thing. "It's in our way."

Something about the way the minor death spirit postured indicated it would not let them pass, even if they tried to chart a course around it.

"If it's got a will and mind of its own, then it appears to have given its allegiance to Leisterbane," said Karou.

"If it's got those things," Ra'al growled, "then it sounds just like anything else I've killed." He pointed a talon at the powerful fiend and yelled, "Hey, ugly! Get out of the way or I'll do to you what I'm planning to do to your master."

The spirit brandished his winnowing scythe and roared with an other-worldly sound. Its weapon seemed to shimmer with a fell light, rippling with chaotic, ungodly power. Its eyes fixed on Ra'al and they blazed with hate.

Ra'al looked aside to Karou for confirmation. "This thing is undead, right?"

"Yes," Karou said. "Moreover, it's never even been alive, like a daemon or demi-god. This might be one of the single-most deadly creatures the enemy could send."

Ra'al swallowed his fear. "Then let's hope my plan works."

CHAPTER SIXTEEN

Leisterbane's forces unloaded the cauldrons near a gentle slope where his zombie crews had dug furrows into the earth. Standing near the massive vats made of tempered metal walked a timeless human, whose eyes seemed to glow with a violet light. His age had halted, though he bore the obvious stains of millennia spent in decay.

Was he older than Leisterbane? After growing old through the First Age, one stopped bothering to care. Peregrine carried a boon: a blessing from the Dark One, and Malgrimm only ever gave gifts with a high expectation attached to them. Lord Death had commanded Peregrine to join Leisterbane's army, even if Peregrine was something of a free operator.

The ancient man of sorrow had claimed the Darkhold Gem and carried it for thousands of years, ever since the early days of Nekarthis. Everywhere that Peregrine went, the gem went, and it created a festration—an arcane bubble encompassing a dead zone—a kind of inter-planar rift into cursed space as if it channeled Hell itself. Hell had many names.

Void. The Abyss. Sha'la'dinan. Morumar. Nether. The Dark. Beyond Lethial. Regardless, they all meant the same thing: a reality where Malgrimm's power held sway.

Peregrine's presence amplified the necralluvium that bled from these festrations. He tapped the metal kettles that towered half again as tall as he was. They were large enough to drown many persons at once and his fist made a dull thud against it. The rows of vats were filled to the brim and their tops fitted with chained collars so that they would all tip at once, given enough leverage.

Leisterbane stepped around him and briefly wondered what Peregrine would do after the tree was destroyed. Would Malgrimm release him from his service, or would Death send them both into some new mission? They'd lived in close proximity for generations, but rarely crossed paths. A henhouse could only do with so many cocks, and Peregrine had come into his own these last several hundred years as he began to understand the power of the Darkhold Gem.

The death knight walked into a cave that his minions had dug and descended. His boots crunched upon broken, frozen scree. The permafrost ran several cubits deep and then the floor leveled out and he found soft soil to quiet his feet. Ahead, a curtain of roots draped across the passage. Leisterbane stepped through.

A square tunnel yawned open, and Leisterbane entered. He had no need for light to see. Even in the total blackness, his eyes worked perfectly. Noting the straight, precise cuts and workmanship, he recognized the subterranean structure and its origins as eldari. The original sages had been eldarim, Esfah's Old Ones, and when he had been still alive, Leisterbane had heard legends of eldari temples dug below the Ghaeial Trees. He wanted to see it for himself, though in those days, people still thought the Great Trees to be little more than myth.

Leisterbane walked through. His steel-shod boots clanked upon the tile floors. The discovery left him feeling hollow; his mind felt the dissatisfaction of the dreams from his old life contrasted against the greatness promised by Malgrimm.

He wandered in the dark for several minutes with his eyes roving, taking in the sights. The Ghaeial Tree's roots came through the ceiling and curved along it. They clung to the walls before trailing to the floor and then along the wall and floor tiles, where they drilled deeper still.

The roots partially obscured relief carvings depicting the emergence of the eldarim, the great wars between them, and the emergence of the dragonkin after the great corruption of Harkamis, eldari sire of the drakufreet. Inset wooden doors had moldered to scrap and dust covered the floors. The place was a sarcophagus containing history that predated the First Age.

Leisterbane ran a hand along the thick, corded vines and felt them. They were not guarded by the armored bark like the tree above. Using a knife, he cut a length of its fibrous flesh. It turned the blade away, but the sharp edge did some damage, at least. An axe or stronger blow would have more effect here.

He grinned. Slashing it all away was not his intent; that would take ages and a massive excavation effort. The necralluvium was the key. Once poisoned, the tree would become vulnerable.

Leisterbane took one last, long look at the hallways and the myriad rooms splitting off from the straight corridors. They hid untold treasures, and many forgotten secrets of the Shadowlands tucked away by the sages. They would be lost to time, consumed by Malgrimm's unrelenting march of purifying decay.

"As it should be," Leisterbane hissed.

He turned on his heel and then departed, leaving all the forgotten wisdom behind to rot.

Prince Garesch paced in his cell, deep in the bowels of the Kafnysan Mountains. Ever since the dwarf, some forgotten hero named Derihus, had captured and thrown him in the vaghan prison, they'd all but forgotten about him. If it wasn't for the occasional dwarf gawker peeking at the humiliated prince in his hole and dropping comments that they expected an execution any day now, Garesch might have guessed that they *had* forgotten about him.

Presently, he leaned his head against the stone of the far corner and unlaced his trousers so he could relieve himself. Someone rattled the bars of the view port to get his attention.

Garesch sighed and paid him no mind. Unless he heard the click of a key in the heavy lock, he had no interest in whomever was at the port.

A dwarf chuckled behind him and seemed to take perverse glee in how low the prince had been brought.

Once he was finally finished, Garesch took his time tying his trousers and then turned to find a dwarf. This one was unfamiliar to him. A scar turned diagonally across his face, splitting a crease between beard hairs on lips, cheek, and chin.

Garesch crossed his arms. "I don't know you. And I'm not in any mood to talk."

"I'm Kiryn. Your father's agent sent me with a care package." Something about the way he said it informed Garesch that it was not a full truth.

Kiryn slid open the door's slot just above the door and used his foot to push a box through. It skidded to a stop in front of Garesch and then the dwarf flashed him a mischievous grin.

Clutching what looked like a handful of pebbles, he unfolded it and the tiny stones interlocked to form a kind of cloth that vaghan artisans called a rockblanket. The lava elf knew of them, but he hadn't known they came in compact forms. Kiryn hooked it over the bars so that he could not see in, and the prince could not see out.

Garesch waited a few moments and listened. Kiryn's footsteps indicated that he'd departed, though whatever precaution he'd intended by blocking vision seemed out of place. Regardless, the prince retrieved the box.

It was of morehlian construction, and it had a lock that could only be opened by solving a complicated numeric sequence. He bit his lip and attempted to open it. All members of the royal family throughout history had been given unique codes to access locked messages. He tried his code; success would prove the package originated from his father.

"Probably a message sent to gloat. Surely he knows of my attempted insurrection… he's probably surprised it took me this long to finally launch a campaign," he muttered.

The code failed. Garesch examined the box. It was of a lower quality construction than something that would be sent by the royal houses of Uruzak. He grinned and tried the code that he and Marnash had agreed to use.

With a subtle click, the mechanism triggered within and the door to its compartment released. Its lid swung open to reveal a scrap of paper and an opalescent sphere. Garesch reached for it and felt the thing radiate power. He pulled his hand back and retrieved the note instead. A familiar scribble had drawn text in the high speech of the lava elves.

Focus on the Sword of Aeschere, it read.

Garesch understood what it was. His crafty old mentor had somehow kept a wayfare orb secret from him until now. He squeezed the artifact in his palm and felt it radiate power through him. The orb's call echoed in his mind, asking for a heading.

Concentrating on his sword, an item that he'd bonded himself to by his claim upon it and the thing's impact upon his destiny, the wayfare orb pulsed with a massive burst of power, and then disappeared, taking its holder with it and leaving behind an empty cell and only a puff of ozone smelling vapor.

The minor death spirit stretched out his hands to beckon to other minions from Leisterbane's army. Ra'al's heart twisted as the floating spirits revealed themselves where they'd been hiding in the cloud banks and mists. Ghostly apparitions, specters, and others hung there, defying gravity as if that natural force did not apply to them. This was the army they had repelled from Icehome, only with addition of the heavy hitter: a black spirit known as a Minor Death.

"We are here to answer the song of the wind with a tune of our own—a Dirge of Blood!" Ra'al howled to his countrymen. The areosa standing aboard the deck of *Aguarehl's Envy* roared and unfurled their wings. They took flight even as Taerlon, his crew of coral elves, and what remained of the Azure Company with Fazayou in the lead, rushed to take their places.

The Minor Death was unimpressed by them. Its burning eyes remained fixed on Ra'al. The dark spirit screeched and held its scythe high.

"Destroy them all," Ra'al shouted to his flying troops. Now that they'd been revealed by the tool in Ra'al's hand, the enemy could be seen and harmed by his frostwings.

Areosa hurled shards of jagged ice at the ghostly forces. Frozen spears pierced the creatures and they burst apart like watery bubbles cresting the surface, exploding with final blasts of dark energy.

They were outnumbered, but Taerlon and Fazayou's crews redirected all their energies to the battle, relying solely on the air bladder of *Aguarehl's Envy* to keep them afloat. The coral sky ship coasted to a slow, yawing slide.

Karou joined the selumari casters and the blue-skinned elves radiated power, drawing on the magic within them and their connection to the goddess, Ailuril. The casters harnessed the eldritch forces and called lightning.

Raw flashes of pure energy tore through the cloud banks and vaporized the enemies at their flanks. The selumari howled as they poured all their concentration into the spells, just as the areosa did the same to summon their spears of ice.

The Minor Death's burning gaze took in the destruction of its minions. Then it turned its gaze back to Ra'al. Standing behind him, Coryn yelped slightly.

"Get back," he barked to her.

She complied even as the spirit surged forward with supernatural speed. It crossed the distance in the blink of an eye and stood on the bow, towering over the nearby coral elves. The fiend stretched out a hand to them and a whole cluster of them tipped over, stone dead. Several fell over the rail and pitched end over end, tumbling gracelessly until they collided into broken heaps of flesh upon the jagged tundra below.

Fazayou leapt for the creature, sword at the ready, but the minor death shimmered as if phasing out of existence for a moment and the Azure Company's leader rushed forward too far, spilling over the edge and into a free fall.

"Fazayou!" Coryn screamed, losing sight of the elf in the gathering mists below.

Ra'al spotted where the thing had reappeared and roared his challenge, splaying his empty hands to his sides. He pointed at the minor death and called it out. "Come and get me, you undead bastard! I'm the one you want—and I'm the one that is going to destroy you."

The minor death turned his head in a macabre, impossible way, as if it had no neck. And then it tensed like a fenhound, ready to pounce. It streaked toward the unarmed Ra'al in a blur, trailing a black and ethereal glow, stretching its bony clutches for the frostwing.

Ra'al ducked just enough to snatch Frostquake from where it hung behind his back and slashed the mythic weapon in an arc across the fiend's belly. It exploded in a gout of black power and a clap of thunder that knocked Ra'al backwards, as if he'd mixed opposing alchemies together. The force knocked him to the deck boards and leveled anyone standing nearby, but to no significant damage.

The air quieted after the minor death dissipated, leaving behind a small pile of ash. For many seconds, nothing made a sound except for the creaking of the ropes that held the air bladder in place.

Winking at Karou, Ra'al grinned and broke the silence. "I'm glad you were right. Same goes for Hennedy. I'm just glad Rawrgyld's axe is so effective against the dead."

Moments later, Hennedy alit to the deck, setting down Fazayou, who he'd snatched from the air. "You're lucky I came with," he said and flashed Ra'al a smile. "I don't think any of the apparitions survived. With any luck, we won't have to face them again."

Ra'al turned to Taerlon while the captain took stock of their casualties. "Do we still have enough wind to get us to the mist stones?"

The selumari captain grimaced but nodded. "It shall be more difficult. The death spirit slayed many of our remaining casters. It will slow down our speed, but we can arrive in a few days, I think."

Coryn huffed, unused to being sidelined for an entire skirmish. "Then let's get on with it. I can't let my father do all the heroing."

Taerlon tilted his head in a grave manner. "You'll slay your dragons yet, Coryn sa'Geril. Let us hope we can survive long enough to make the return voyage.

Garesch blinked. When he opened his eyes, he thought he was blind. The brightness of Soll burned overhead; after so many days spent imprisoned below, Balgavarr felt like someone had driven a needle through each eye.

"It's about time you got here," barked a familiar voice as Garesch shook his head to clear his sun-spotted vision. He shielded his eyes and traced Marnash's form. The ground crunched beneath his feet with familiar, crusty notes.

The old spell caster held aloft the Sword of Aeschere, returning it to the morehl who he felt divinely chosen to rule. Nearby, Uruzak towered in the distance.

Garesch looked at the orb. It had turned a dark color, rendered as inert as a stone now that it had been used. Until it could be recharged, it had no practical application. Besides, it wouldn't allow them access to Saugor's inner sanctum even if the orb had been one of the legendary artifacts that could be used repeatedly. Saugor had warded his most private areas with dweomernulls to cancel magic.

"The war has started?" Garesch asked, surveying the battle in progress. His forces assailed the slopes of Uruzak already.

"Indeed it has," Marnash stated, pointing to the arrayed forces on the slope nearby. "I knew you'd arrive soon. But you wouldn't believe what it took to get the trogs on board, but they now make up three quarters of our army. Turimnab stepped into Sharsah's shoes and helped rally the diaspora after... you know."

Garesch cocked his head as he hung the sword at his belt. "What did you promise the trogs?"

"Not much, actually. The difficult part was getting an audience with a tribal leader." Marnash explained how he'd been dragged unconscious to a tribe in Big Wet, which controlled the lands on the far east. They were the closest to the sea and to Uruzak. The other goblins had not known how to handle their peers who channeled the power of the fire goddess, and so many troggish clans simply ceded land to them, allowing the fire casters to expand. "They simply want the best part of trade rights… and fifty percent of the plunder inside Saugor's vaults, whatever that might be."

Garesch nodded slowly. "There is not much there by way of gold. Not anymore. Saugor's previous wars depleted much of the treasury."

Marnash grinned. "I'm well aware of that." Saugor had tied up much of what remained of the empire's wealth in other speculation abroad. His abandonment of local trade and industry had plunged the lower castes into abject poverty and continually drove the middle class lower each year. "I agreed, provided that every family gives us their fourth born from every litter for the next seven generations to work for five years before being released. They'll work the mines and forges and help us improve the economy. That will, in turn, benefit their home clans who have favorable trade."

The prince nodded, seeing the logic. Trogs birthed in litters of seven. Their greatest asset was fast breeding and maturation. The problem was that goblins grew too quickly to learn the value of self-preservation before they became interested in activities that killed young goblins. Typically, only half a creche survived to adolescence and trogs were superstitious about the middle child, believing them cursed and the most prone to killing themselves and their siblings. If they trained trogs to work and supervised them, they would turn into the most industrious and long-lived of their birth order.

Sounds of the battle reached Garesch's ears. He assessed the carnage on the slope below with a long-look he borrowed from Marnash. "Who leads my father's forces on this side of the slope?"

"Don't worry about that now," Marnash said. "You must get to your father and kill him. It is our only path to victory and has been our plan since before we ventured to Tulgesh all those months ago."

Garesch knew that. It was the only way. If an heir permanently deposed his parent, the remainder of the lava elves would fall in line and serve the new emperor. It was barbaric to outsiders but had been a custom for as long as any could remember. Still, Garesch had to know who his army faced.

"Tell me, Marnash. Saugor has an army for each of the slopes. Who leads the army we face?"

Marnash spoke. "Merod the third."

Garesch flashed him a worried look. "He is one of Saugor's best generals—and he is certainly the cruelest of them all."

"I told you not to worry." Marnash pointed and Garesch spotted the general. Some ways down the slope, a large troll stood over the fallen body of Merod III. He raised his meaty fists in triumph. Steam still rose from the morehl general's blood that splattered the creature's hands and forearms. Merod III wore a distinct set of armor to distinguish him as a member of the emperor's praetorian guard, who had been elevated to an even further position.

Up the mountainside, a cannon-shot boomed, echoing across the battle. A moment later, the immense ball of steel obliterated the troll, tearing through him and dashing his torso to pieces in a grisly, random pattern of sickly yellow and green ichor. The creature's lower half flailed about as if it did not realize the rest of it had died.

"Quickly," Marnash insisted, and Garesch followed him. They hurried to Merod's body and crouched, fearing they might make a good target for snipers wielding flintlocks.

"I still don't know how you plan to get to my father. Reinforcements aside, we are badly outnumbered until I can kill him and take the throne." Garesch flashed a glance over his shoulder to the bay, where he could vaguely make out the sails of an incoming ship from the Tarvenish Ocean. "Is that your doing? More reinforcements?"

"My doing. Yes... but not reinforcements. I'll explain later," Marnash explained. "I have a plan, but no time to explain it. Strip Merod. We will need his clothes."

The old spell caster caught the prince and spoke in a serious tone. "For this to work, we must be fully committed to our cause. Our bodies, our blood, all of it."

"Yes, yes. Of course," reassured Garesch as he concentrated on stripping the general's raiment. They'd already flung themselves into a civil war against Saugor. He didn't understand why his loyal adviser thought he needed to be reminded of—

"Gods above and below! What are you doing?" Garesch cried.

Marnash used a knife to cut a traced outline on the flesh of his own face and then peeled away the skin. It made a sick, wet sound, and the caster screamed as he peeled his own face off with a pained grunt. He'd circled his eyes with the blade so that he'd keep his eyelids but cut below his nose so that only half his face was torn free; an ear went with it as he jerked the flesh away with a tug and he gasped with a labored breath. Muscle and tendon lay exposed to the open air.

"What are you doing?" the prince repeated.

"Showing you the level of my commitment," Marnash said. His words were slurred by both shock and the fact that half the muscles which controlled his mouth were slashed free. His face was a mask of steam as the hot blood vaporized where it hit the air and leeched moisture into the sky. "Now dress me," he pointed to Merod's armor. His voice came as a ragged, pained gasp, "And do exactly as I say."

A moment later, the wounded morehl with half a face staggered toward Uruzak's entrance, dragging the prince in tow.

Far behind them, the stumbling legs of the obliterated troll calmed, and a new top began reforming where the ragged remnants of flesh knitted back together to create the body of a new troll, letting it rush back into the fray.

CHAPTER SEVENTEEN

Ringuld reached past Geril and grabbed Sheron, pulling him back into the foliage. He pressed a finger to his lips and crouched down into the lush undergrowth, keeping his peers behind him.

Geril noticed the movement, too. He motioned to the rest of his vaghan entourage, and the party crouched in the bracken, keeping silent.

They had tracked Harol for several days, pursuing him through slough and across pockets of savanna. The trail had never gone cold, and they knew they grew closer every day.

A loud hissing intensified in the glade beyond them, and a scaly humanoid appeared. He carried a crude, double pronged spear. Though he looked more like a snake than a biped, complete with a body that terminated in a tail and trailed away for several cubits. He had shoulders that jutted out slightly, in contrast to his legless body. Baldrics guarded his shoulders, and their bony bulges allowed the creature to wear a harness made of tooled leather straps. The piece attached to affix to a lower girdle and belt where a wavy kriss hung in a partial scabbard.

Ringuld mouthed to his group, *'Swamp stalker'*. As a species, the sarslayan had emerged first from the bayous of Dereh'Liandor and they were precariously close to that area now. That Harol would cut through sarslayan territory only proved his madness.

The first swamp stalker was soon joined by another, and then another, until there was a small cluster of them. The vagha could probably take them, especially since they maintained the element of surprise, though none of them had ever faced these creatures in combat. That meant casualties were likely, and a lost sarslayan patrol would bring further scrutiny. Thus far, stealth had preserved them. Sheron's spells had combined an element of the dwarven stoneskin spell and they'd camouflaged their bodies with leaves and green cuttings.

Hissing and gnashing, the swamp stalkers spoke with each other in their strange tongue. Ringuld watched them with great interest, following their conversation with a look of concentration on his face.

Swamp stalkers spoke the common tongue, in addition to their own, like most creatures of Esfah. The species had also been something else, once. Perhaps the eldarim knew more about their origins. Ringuld suspected they may have once been eldarim cultists before the original sarslayan found the mutative powers in the Waters of Lethial. Now, they were a mix of interbred reptilian things and those poor mutated souls captured and reborn by their dark rituals.

After a brief argument, what appeared to be the youngest and most cocksure of the sarslayan creatures was overruled. The rest of the hunters turned and skulked away.

The vaghan intruders waited until they were certain the coast had cleared. "I think we're safe now," Geril commented.

"We are," Ringuld assured him. "The young fang wants to pursue *the intruder*. They were onto Harol's trail, too. But the older warriors overruled him, claiming he was too difficult a prize to take and would cost them many lives they can't afford to waste. Apparently, the stalkers are fighting both the trogs and faeli on different fronts."

Geril shot him an awed look. "You speak sarslayan?"

Ringuld nodded. "I learned it in the academy."

Balgavarr's leader looked surprised again. "They teach that there?"

The captain told him, "Patrols on the western edge of the Kafnysan range, where Zephras Thunderfist first made a name for himself by holding the tower, has had several encounters with the stalkers."

Geril tightened his hand on the haft of Old Thunder at the mention of his grandfather.

Ringuld continued, "The sarslayan mostly keep further south and are a bigger nuisance to the selumari of Tulgesh. But they sometimes disturb our shipping lines along the Sareen River and are well entrenched in Deepmire. Our soldiers captured one of their number and forced him to teach us their language. We assume they will be an eventual threat, hence the priority for some of our younger troops to at least learn their strange tongue. I assumed you knew all of that."

"I should commend Warlord Kile. Perhaps he told me, and it slipped my mind. I entrusted most of the military's endeavors to him." Geril sighed. "Council business took up far too much of my attention." The thought struck him that he could have spent more time with Coryn in her formative years had he refused as much civic engagement as Balgavarr had thrust upon him.

"The sarslayan indicated they have a village nearby," Ringuld told him. "They seemed afraid of Harol."

"Then hopefully they'll fear us, too," Geril growled. "Because I intend to lodge Old Thunder in that traitor's skull within the tenday." His confidence rallied the spirits of his vaghan company. "You say the coast is clear?"

"I think so," Ringuld said.

Geril looked at Meron. The wizard nodded to indicate he didn't sense any sort of magical threats.

"Then we'll redouble our efforts," said Geril, looking past the glade beyond their hiding spot. And then he moved out, again in pursuit.

Deep in the bowels of Uruzak, the door to the imperial throne room opened beneath a slow, methodical grasp. A red-skinned hand dripped hot blood along the edge of the portal and a slender morehl staggered into the room. Blood stained his uniform, both the red of lava elf and the muddy yellow of trog—ilk who came down from the northern fens.

Saugor leaned forward upon his throne and watched the door open. "General Merod. You do not look well," he noted, pointing to indicate the destroyed portions of the elf's face. "But at least *some* of the color on your vestments indicates some success against our enemies. Though I can scarcely believe that our agents in Big Wet would turn against us. Tell me, Merod, how goes the war and then I shall summon a healer." The emperor curled a lip as if he enjoyed the surprise that the sudden arrival of the trogs presented. "I can scarcely believe they'd pose this much threat without my son to lead them."

The bloody elf cocked his head. "So, you *did* know about Garesch's fate at the hands of the vagha?"

The emperor cackled but remained seated upon the black throne that had been molded from ebon, volcanic glass. He tilted his head. "Marnash," Saugor said, recognizing the voice of his former subject. "You finally reveal yourself. I always suspected you were involved in luring my son and heir away from me. I should have killed you after you returned from the failed campaign in Balgavarr Reaches."

Four praetorian guards leapt into action and darted from behind their hiding places in the throne room. Marnash's hands flew to a pair of loaded flintlocks, and he snap-fired, dropping two of them.

Then, another two shots rang out as another bank of blue smoke filled the entry. Garesch entered the hall, picking off the other two guards who had moved to kill his friend.

The prince drew his blade and held it menacingly, pointing the Sword of Aeschere at his father. He glanced aside at the two servants cowering behind the throne. "You two will bear witness to this. I have come to claim the throne and end Emperor Saugor's madness. Too long has he devoured our people with his personal avarice."

Garesch's words did little to assuage their fears. Servants under Saugor lived in constant terror. The emperor was a capricious and demanding master; for all they knew, the son could be the same.

"So, you have found yourself a fancy blade," Saugor hissed, drawing his own: a blackened vorpal blade that glinted with an evil light. Once unsheathed, everyone in the room could feel the blade's thirst. It craved blood, screamed for it— demanding it like a nursing babe. Emperor Saugor sneered and motioned for his son to engage with his weapon. He taunted his younger kin.

Garesch rushed toward him, slashing his blade in a whirlwind motion. Their steel collided repeatedly. Blades sang like a violent melody.

With every step that the prince took, he cut closer to his father. Saugor's eyes widened. Too long he had sat complacently upon the throne, ruling by force of will, but letting his strength grow weak and his training grow lax. The emperor's eyes sparkled with sudden fear. He realized that his son's strength had surpassed his own.

Garesch gave him no quarter and showed no mercy. Still fresh to the fight, he struck heavy blows repeatedly. His father proved no match for the ferocity that Garesch, who nursed years of bitterness toward Saugor, brought to bear. Without his protectors there to intervene, the emperor was at the mercy of the prince.

Nearly backed against a wall, Saugor struck with the last of his energy and Garesch easily parried it. He returned the blow with a left hook that stunned his father. Garesch knocked the ravenous blade aside, and it skittered across the floor where Marnash picked it up. Behind him, the old wizard teetered on his feet with failing legs and fleeting strength.

"Mercy?" suggested Saugor. His voice cracked and a fearful light shone in the emperor's dark eyes.

Garesch smacked him across the face with the pommel of a sword. "Mercy? What right have you to request such a thing?" He threw the vorpal sword behind him and punched his father in the teeth, splitting the emperor's lips. "Never have you shown a scrap of it to your countrymen, and none shall you receive," the prince roared. He rammed his blade into his father's abdomen, angling it upward and toward the emperor's heart. The tip of Aeschere's weapon pierced it, and a gust of steam belched from the wound.

"This brings me no joy, Father," Garesch cried.

Saugor sank to his knees, clutching for the hilt of the blade of Aeschere. He gasped. "No. You lie. This… this is in our nature. Power. You shall lust for it. Yearn to watch the light die in the eyes of your enemies as they press in all around."

Garesch pulled close to his father. "You say that only because you have always been surrounded by your enemy, and never by allies. Never by friends."

Saugor's face shook with fear; a dribble of blood seeped past his lips. He'd never thought of that, and now, with his life pouring out in a pillar of steam, he wondered if his son had found a better way.

Footsteps echoed in the hall. A squad of praetorian guards entered the room and Saugor sneered. "Guards, kill these intruders!"

Steel rang as blades came to bear. But a wavering voice called out from nearby. One of the servants spoke. "I have borne witness," he claimed. "This was a duel for control of the throne. The son has unseated the father."

Saugor gasped as Garesch twisted the blade. His eyes went feral, and all rational thought left. The emperor looked down as Garesch withdrew the blade, slashing through more flesh as he did so. "Such a fine blade," Saugor said. "And it wasn't even magical. The sword… the sword of Aeschere…"

With a lurch, Saugor collapsed to his knees and then tumbled into a heap face down upon the floor. A dwindling column of steam rose from the body as a puddle of blood pooled around it.

The cluster of praetorian guards all took a knee and bowed their heads, pledging fealty to the newly won emperor. "All hail *Emperor* Garesch," said the ranking officer. The rest of the guards repeated his phrase as a mantra.

Nearly staggering with the effort, Marnash grabbed the nearest servant by the collar. "Where did Saugor hide the dweomernull?"

As the servant pointed to a nearby stone embedded in the wall behind the throne, Garesch barked orders.

"Call off the attack. Sound the alarm for a cease fire and report to those battling on the slopes that Garesch has prevailed over Saugor." Garesch spoke with imperial authority.

A praetorian guard ran from the room to fulfill the orders.

Garesch pointed to a servant. "You. Inform the ruling families and the upper castes, and then inform the proletariat. Make the announcements so that word spreads quickly, and then invite our kin into the throne room. There is much yet to do, and we don't have time for the pomp and ceremony normally associated with a coronation."

The servant paused. "But surely you want the rulers and military leaders to swear fealty to the new order?"

"Surely," Garesch said. "But the rest of it will have to wait. There are bigger forces at play than scorned heads of self-important families."

Marnash yelped and growled as he slashed the fallen emperor's magic blade through a stone engraved with dweomernull. The power of the anti-magic stone shattered, and the magician sank to his knees, clearly in more pain than he was in moments before. The adrenaline had ebbed away, leaving behind only agony and fatigue.

Garesch rushed to his friend's side.

"Quickly," Marnash said, "before Saugor's spark goes out. I must perform a spell and extract the cost for healing."

Garesch flashed him a startled look.

"I am using death magic." Nodding measuredly, Marnash closed his eyes and whispered, "Saugor's spark is strong. I sense it even now, seething in the space between Esfah and the Abyss. Severing it for the sake of this spell solves two problems."

Marnash stole the energy being released in the former emperor's death throes and whispered an incantation. He groaned as the pain flooded him, stitching pink, new flesh back across the face that he'd voluntarily cut away to gain entry to Uruzak's interior. He'd hid his true self by wearing a mask of horrific pain, and only by enduring more of it could he reclaim his visage.

As soon as his face healed, the wizard tipped to his side. A deep sleep overtook him, and his chest rose and fell like a winded sprinter, but Garesch was certain Marnash would recover. Though his friend would still feel pain for more than a tenday as nerves regrew; they were always the last to form.

"Rest," Garesch said softly. "Your sacrifice was not in vain. We did it. Uruzak is ours, and we will fight for a new and better tomorrow."

Emperor Garesch stood, and the second servant bowed and pointed to Saugor's corpse. "What shall we do with the body, my lord?"

"Dispose of it," muttered Garesch.

"The family crypt?"

"No." Garesch shook his head. He worked his tongue and jaw as if he had a bad taste in his mouth. "Throw it on the rubbish heap beyond the wall."

The servant bowed low and went in search of a cart to haul the corpse. Before he left, Garesch called out, "One more thing."

Averting his gaze, the servant paused for instruction.

"There was a ship in the harbor. I believe that it was selumari, and if I know Marnash, who always tried to plan for every angle, it is here for a reason. Please send it my summons," Garesch ordered.

The servant nodded and then departed to go about his tasks.

Derihus stood upon a massive cleft rock and watched the line darkening the distant path up the slopes of the Kafnysan range. The vagha's northern forces slowly trickled back home upon weary legs.

Wearing the full regalia of the dwarven warlord, he knew the sight would come as a shock to the soldiers who had just been recalled. Fresh from the battlefield, they knew nothing of the shifting political winds within Balgavarr Reaches.

However, his dress would indicate his position; all soldiers would recognize that, and the site held certain significance.

The cleft rock had been the first entrance to Balgavarr in its earliest days, when the dwarves had first settled here after voyaging up from the Birthlands, according to the legends, anyway. The split stone hid the first entrance; all roads since it was first sealed up had passed by it.

Behind and a little lower than Derihus stood what remained of the council. Though the army was bone-tired and yearned for the comforts of their own homes, they understood they should pause here and wait for an address of some kind. Those at the front waited for the stragglers in the rear to catch up.

Skrathos stalked up the step that led to the flat stone they used as a platform. Behind his scarred face, he wore a dour look. The head jailer followed after him.

First, he whispered to his uncle, Trinean, and then he leaned in to speak with Lahmyn to share whatever secrets he'd come to tell. They consulted with the jailer and Lahmyn's face turned even darker.

Lahmyn dismissed the jailer, and the dwarf looked relieved to be excused. The council members in Lahmyn's faction clustered together into an angry knot. The outside elders who had been allied with Lordan looked very nervous. Thadrus and Daemurlin remained stoic and removed, but Dusut and Gloretulin visibly recoiled from the stronger faction as its mood turned like sour milk.

Finally, Lahmyn calmed his party and walked to Derihus, taking him aside. "Warlord Derihus, you had prepared a speech for those returning home. You should alter it."

"Is it not a day for patriotism, Elder Lahmyn?"

Lahmyn sneered beneath his beard. "It is always a day for that, Warlord. Especially when it concerns our soldiers. But our prisoner is gone—escaped or stolen. We are not certain… and without an enemy to rally against, our position weakens."

"Gone?" Derihus balked. He knew how secure the subterranean prison was. It was the strongest cage they had.

The elder's fury rolled off him in waves. "He had to have help. It was those traitors, his companions, who remained in the north. I am certain of it."

Derihus's nostrils flared. "It must be. Nobody escapes the dungeons of Balgavarr Reaches without aid."

Lahmyn stiffened his jaw. "Address the traitors directly, Warlord. Welcome home the patriots and issue a command to all our sentries. Any person who defied the council and threw in their lot to help Coryn sa'Geril is a traitor to Balgavarr and should be apprehended and convicted of treason." The elder seethed, "With or without her, there *will* be a trial. She and her father will be ruined because of this. I swear it."

Derihus nodded. He watched the elder turn on his heel and rejoin the remainder of the council members. The warlord thought over his speech and composed a few new lines. Coryn, Geril Dragonsbane, and the rest of those in the north could never again set foot in the Kafnysan range or its foothills without facing charges as a conspirator, and the penalty for such a verdict, which Lahmyn undoubtedly controlled, would be death.

Emperor Garesch walked before a line of his soldiers. The lava elves had bowed and sworn fealty to him. The young ruler had no time to ponder the fact that his renegades in the diaspora had each done the same for his father at one point or another. All morehl typically did so on their name day when they entered society and claimed their citizenship as a member of Uruzak.

Arrayed in flowing robes fitting of his station, his top adviser followed close. Marnash was still recovering, and he sipped from a stoppered vial every hour. The stimulants kept him going despite his injuries. His face remained a mottled mess of tender pink muscle in contrast to the deep red of his more mature flesh, but he looked otherwise healthy. Proper rest would see to a full recovery. If the battle between Nature and Death ever allowed them a moment's peace, that is.

Garesch and Marnash knew they could not delay in helping their friends. If the undead prevailed in the north, things would become all that much harder in Uruzak.

The emperor wore padded leather and a cape. His outfit was one that bespoke his position but remained functional for battle. *This* emperor did not plan to rule from a throne—he charged into battle and dealt with his enemies personally. At his hip hung the sword, which his people began simply calling *Aeschere*, and on the opposite side he'd slung a flintlock. He'd considered not wearing it as it was one of the rare types, claimed from the ancient forges of Karakto, and that seemed to somehow give credence to the dwarven coup, but he dismissed any implication and wore it anyway. He was Emperor now, and the firearm was his—given to him on his name day by the father he'd just executed. Though he'd only carried it in the past during political functions, he saw *everything* now as a political activity, and carrying it meant something to the morehl. It meant Garesch would surpass his father.

The line of red-skinned elves standing at attention was spaced far apart. Behind each one sat a trained wyvern. The scaled beasts pawed at the ground or shifted beneath tackle and barding. Like the suchia dragonkin, they had scaled wings, but unlike the drakufreet, wyverns had only two legs and were more closely related to snakes than to the dragons. They did not breathe fire, but like adders, they were venomous and contained poison sacks in their long tails, which terminated in a barb like a scorpion.

As he walked past them, he dismissed the wyvern riders, ten of them in all. The warriors retreated to their mounts, climbed into the stirrups, and took to the sky. They were faster than eagles, if pressed, and the emperor had insisted they do exactly that: arrive as soon as they could and assure his friends that help was on the way. Then, aid in the fight against the undead.

With the last of the wyverns arcing skyward, Garesch and Marnash hurried down the stairs on the eastern side of the mountain, where it broke away into the water and a port the morehl had established long ago for its trade partners. Garesch curled a lip and shook his head at the irony.

Lava elves were not prone to sea travel, but he'd been fascinated by it ever since he was young and had at least some prior experience during his travels. From the same docks he now walked, Garesch used to watch ships come and go as a child. He'd spent a great deal of his youth reading about ships that no morehl would ever dare pilot. Captaining his own vessel was a guilty fascination, though he'd abandoned it in favor of less imaginative studies.

Garesch's footsteps echoed aboard the dock planks, and he was grateful he'd learned about ship craft, but also that he'd given it up. He was emperor now, and his political studies were what would save him—and his country.

Naemyar's fastest ship waited for Garesch. The selumari had been in Frostshoal when they received word from Naemyar. At Marnash's request, she'd dispatched them for the morehl's needs. Garesch blushed slightly, though it was imperceptible beneath his crimson skin. It meant a lot to him that she had so much faith in his victory she'd ordered the ship to Uruzak.

Already a cluster of lava elf spell crafters, sharpshooters, and heavy warriors had boarded the vessel. It was not large and so they could only take so many, but the coral elf sailors assured him that they could cover scores of leagues, cut around the islands where Frostshoal was found, and deposit them on the banks of the Shadowlands where they'd be able to make their way inland on foot.

"We might even arrive ahead of those wyverns you sent ahead," boasted the captain.

"She's that fast?" Garesch asked.

"She is. Especially since we've jettisoned any extra weight. We have several wind crafters," he said, indicating the selumari magicians, "and that should make up for the weight of your troops."

Emperor Garesch stepped aboard, and the sailors did not waste any time casting off. Summoning arcane winds, the ship soon streaked northward, gliding upon a glassy sea that lay smooth, like the calm before the storm.

Marnash and Garesch looked back as Uruzak faded to gray in the mists behind them. Garesch hadn't even been emperor for a full day, and already, he was leaving the kingdom. His companion put a hand on his shoulder and nodded in solidarity. "We shall return soon," said the sorcerer.

"I only just got here," Garesch muttered, "and already I abandon it."

"We'll be back soon," Marnash promised.

But in his heart, Garesch knew that they would not *all* come back.

Aguarehl's Envy floated above the clouds as it headed toward its destination. A magnetic compass had already gone haywire and then straightened out after they'd passed the pole. They kept straight, though the mist stones were no longer north of them. *Everything* was now south by degrees.

Coasting further into the heart of the Shadowlands, the mists began to part. Coryn stood on the bow where the winds blasted her hair and her ruddy locks had begun to form dreads.

A massive tree towered below, contrasting against the flat plains. Its broad leaves stretched skyward, and its stout base protruded from the soil like a vaghan tower, only four times as wide.

Upon the white blanket of snow, the enemy stood clearly visible. Gouts of fire splashed from huge bonfires where the pyres of industry burned and swaths of undead scorched the base of the tree to little effect. They'd engineered machines to dig and to smash. Wooden towers and ramrods chiseled at the bark. They'd only just begun to carve a hole into it.

"I see the mist stones," Coryn pointed, identifying them.

Bastawr stood by his side and nodded solemnly. "We have arrived."

Coryn's eyes welled up as she took it all in. Everywhere she looked, blackened flesh and bleached bone of the undead army wriggled like masses of ants.

"There's no way we can beat that," she whispered.

Ra'al sighed behind her. "Maybe not. But we have to try." He put a hand on her shoulder, wishing again for the annoying song of the chirpy little sparrow. "Remember what we are?"

Coryn looked up at him and recognized the complete change in her friend from when they'd first ventured out of Castle Ice so many months ago. He'd been a reluctant adventurer then, and now he stood tall with the song of the wind coursing through him. He was the very image of his father, who they'd only ever known through song, folktale, and art.

When they'd left, it was under the guise of collecting the descendants of Cyrea's past heroes and protecting the continent against the evils growing in shadow. Coryn's hand gripped the haft of her axe. "We are heroes. We are the children of heroes. The gods are with us." Her voice possessed a cheery lilt.

Ra'al grinned. Coryn's spirits had returned and Ra'al shifted from foot to foot, much like Coryn did whenever she grew excited and his diminutive friend grinned, even though certain death loomed on the horizon.

Bastawr raised an eyebrow, sensing the shift in mood.

"Cyrea's heroes," Coryn repeated, nudging an elbow into the gwereste. She looked from her frostwing friend to the selumari captain nearby and called out, "Hey Taerlon, are you somehow related to Matrek in Tulgesh?"

Captain Taerlon called back. "Distant cousins, actually."

Coryn grinned and leaned forward at the ship's railing, eager to engage the enemy. "That's good enough for me. There's no way we can lose."

Taerlon stared ahead, into the heart of darkness, and issued orders. "Bring us around. Lock onto that tree as a waypoint."

Aguarehl's Envy turned slightly, and they plunged forward, knowing the enemy would spot them any minute.

Hanging over the edge, Hennedy held a collapsible long-look to his eye. "What in the world are they doing?"

"Trying to destroy the tree, obviously," said Fazayou.

"No, not that." He handed the coral elf the looking lens and pointed. "*That.*"

At the base of the tree stood an impressive creature who could have only been Leisterbane. He held aloft a greatsword. Next to him, a helpless human had been tied down and laid against the tree.

Leisterbane swung his blade through exposed neck and the pitiful human's head tumbled to the snow with a spray of gory crimson. A vibrant light shot skyward like a sprite fired from a cannon and then it went out, followed by a subtle boom like distant thunder.

Fazayou looked at the rest of the crew. "Oh no."

CHAPTER EIGHTEEN

The lava elves had sailed a couple days and with each one that passed, the salt spray tasted weaker, and the water felt colder. It hadn't taken long to pass by Frostshoal with the ship's arcanists summoning winds to push the sails.

But something felt wrong this morning. Garesch could sense it. He slept with the rest of the soldiers, huddled together for as much warmth as they could secure in the cabins below deck. His ears twitched, and he realized what bothered him. He heard none of the sounds of whistling winds as they rushed past. The scraping of wave against shallow hull did not sound so driven as before.

The emperor dashed up the ladder and into the low, fell light of the morning. The sky was bloody red as Soll crawled for altitude on the horizon. Not a single selumari was in sight.

Sails remained full and caught the natural wind, but the intense driving force directed by the coral elves was gone. None of the sailors remained aboard and Garesch scanned the waters, searching for them, but he saw none.

Panic erupted in his gut, and he turned to stare ahead. The ship rushed forward still, unguided, but pointed directly for a jagged maw of stones where the Shadowlands' coast crept outward. They protruded up from white-capped furrows like sharpened incisors.

Garesch roared an alarm, calling for all hands on deck. He found the warning bell and smashed it hard enough to crack in the frozen air.

The lava elf shouted orders to morehl who poured above deck with weapons readied, assuming they had been boarded. They found their emperor behind the wheel, cranking the rudder as hard as he could while directing untrained soldiers in sailing techniques.

Marnash joined Garesch. "Sabotage?"

Garesch nodded. "It certainly appears that way. But we can't be certain." He glanced around again at the frigid waters. "Perhaps they were murdered… or something else? I'm just glad I read so much on sailing in my misguided youth."

Marnash raised a brow as the ship careened further toward the danger ahead. "You think someone maybe paid them to abandon us?"

"We'll speculate later. Let's just survive, and be glad that nobody knew I am one of the handful of morehl who know how to sail."

Marnash squinted, looked down at the map, and then stared forward. He pointed ahead. "Do you see that gap in the reefs? Don't turn away, angle toward it instead."

Garesch looked at him like he was crazy.

"That's as good a place as any to guide the ship," Marnash argued. "That was the plan, to travel on foot once we were near the pole?"

"Yeah, but we'll be wrecked for sure. I'd like to keep the boat for a return voyage," Garesch said.

"Trust me. This is faster. The map shows a frozen river there. It runs most of the way to our destination."

"Yeah, Marnash. *Frozen* river."

The wizard's hands crackled with flames, and he shouted for the spell casters to join him at the front of the ship.

"Crazy old elf is gonna get us all killed," muttered Garesch. "And that was supposed to be *my* job." He adjusted their heading, and the winds carried them through the jagged spires of ice capped stone where they protruded upwards like leviathan's teeth.

Marnash and his group flung blasts of flame ahead of them, opening the mouth of the river. The ice was not terribly thick; the flow running beneath it kept the top from forming too deeply, and they were able to keep a span ahead of them melted. Working hard, they opened the water just ahead of the selumari craft's speed and made the river passable.

Emperor Garesch kept a light hand on the steering mechanism and just hoped his soldiers could keep a hold of the wind in the sails. As far as he knew, there were no oars. But as long as the gods smiled and kept opening opportunities, he kept sailing through them… hoping it was not part of some larger trap.

"Everyone, hang on!" Captain Taerlon yelled as he cranked the controls to bank the airship. The undead had spotted them and tried their best to knock the ship from the air. So far, they couldn't get their trebuchets or other war engines to fling anything dangerous to a high enough altitude. And then they spotted the lance thrower.

The giant contraption was modeled to be a massive crossbow meant as a defense against dragons and other large flying beasts. *Aguarehl's Envy* was no beast, but it *was* a perfect target, and with the air bladder deployed, it was far too bulky to make a sharp enough turn that could elude any competent marksman. But the undead were not competent, and Taerlon was a very good pilot.

A jagged spear launched toward them like a bolt of lightning. It streaked forward them and missed. The margin was narrow, but there were no casualties and the bolt pierced only air. It streaked just over the prow and those stationed there ducked nervously.

"Get that bladder down," the captain barked, "and deploy the fins. Wind casters, we need support!"

Another lance jolted past. If they didn't get *Aguarehl's Envy* transitioned into a more mobile mode, the undead would eventually score a hit.

Selumari magicians hurried to their posts. They would summon enough wind to keep the ship airborne, regardless of deflating the air bladder, which provided enough buoyancy to keep them afloat without magic. Cutting the bladder would make *Aguarehl's Envy* far more mobile and considerably faster, but it would tax the spell crafters.

The overhead balloon was still inflated when a third javelin fired from the missile launcher pierced it, tearing straight through. Elven efforts to deflate it were rendered moot, and the thing flopped like a fish out of water as the warmer air inside it vented rapidly, creating a cloud of vapor above the ship.

Taerlon's crew had deployed the fin-like wings and patagial membrane sails that caught the eldritch wind. *Aguarehl's Envy* lurched forward and down as it surged like a raft caught in rapids. The ship's speed picked up and the captain soared through the burning air, dodging projectiles flung by catapults as the undead tried to knock the coral airship from the sky.

On the deck below, Ra'al reached through the glowing portal Coryn had created with her gnomish device and pulled out barrel after barrel of explosive powder. He handed the casks to the areosa, who carried glowing punks between their teeth to use as lighting for the wicks they'd rigged.

One by one, the frostwings snatched a charge and took to the sky. Seconds later, the explosions began. Icehome's forces swooped over the masses of enemies with fuse-lit bombs. Some dropped them indiscriminately from on high, others were more targeted. Trebuchets and lance stations erupted in flames and crumpled as the casks detonated, flinging shrapnel that shredded the bloodless ones nearby.

Finally, Ra'al pulled Coryn from the strange other space where she'd safely stashed the hidden barrels. Still more explosions cracked the ground below. Areosa spear throwers began to rain down frozen missiles upon the dead who had little recourse. Few bloodless retained enough dexterity to engage in ranged combat.

But the dead channeled the power of their god, Death. Mid-flight, frostwings began to fall, flapping lifeless wings behind them that trailed like festival streamers on Turambar's Day. Death crafters hurled their dark magic at the interlopers, draining their lives in an instant.

And then a horn split the air and the magic of the dead fizzled and failed in gray burps. Tanneyha and a quartet of frost ogres broke the spells of the enemy as they arrived on the edge of the battle, un-slowed by the unfavorable winds of the areosan traitors and able to tread direct paths that none other could walk.

A cloud of skeletons charged for the ogres and Tanneyha blew his horn again while his companions swung clubs and scattered their skeletal attackers. They flung them leagues at a time and sent bones raining across the hillside where they'd come.

After a third blast, a giant pack of white wolves rushed over the hill. The wolves split into smaller packs and tore at the enemy flanks. And then the wyverns arrived. Nearly a dozen of them swooped over the battle. Their riders wore heavy coats and eye goggles that had begun to freeze over. The riders and beasts soared past the airship and skipped overhead of the dead, blasting them with flintlocks from overhead. They tried to pick off the necromancers first.

Tanneyha and his clan mates continued breaking the undead's spells and Coryn waved to the frost ogre as *Aguarehl's Envy* soared past. Captain Taerlon deftly piloted the vessel, swooping low and around the great tree.

Fazayou called out when he'd spotted the undead leader. "Leisterbane's killed some kind of hostage," he pointed back to the enemy leader. "I've got a bad feeling about this."

"We'll come around again," Taerlon roared, cranking on the wheel. The plan was simple: eliminate Leisterbane and the undead should scatter. Without any real direction, the hordes of zombies and skeleton warriors should disperse, unguided—far less of a threat without a guiding mind to focus their efforts. "Destroy Leisterbane and save the world." If there were more leaders than Leisterbane, they'd locate them next and repeat the process until the dead became compliant enough to wander away.

Coryn, Ra'al, and Bastawr huddled against the railing, along with a whole host of soldiers who were prepared to leap down, blades drawn, in the hopes of eliminating their arch fiend. *Aguarehl's Envy* turned tightly, encircling the Ghaeial tree at high speeds.

And then something giant, black, and scaly flew through the ship, smashing the hull to pieces like an anvil dropped into a puddle. Deck boards dashed to pieces and vagha were flung to the wind. Some landed upon clusters of the hungry dead, who tore the soldiers apart with their steely grips and gnashing teeth. Others fell to the dirt. Some survived the fall; others did not.

Coryn rolled to a stop in a patch of open ground and looked up at the thing which had just destroyed their ship with sucking ease. On black wings, an ebony drake soared through the sky, roaring victoriously. She froze, identifying the beast, and a chill wind pierced Coryn to her bones.

She clutched her hand around her weapon and whispered, "It can't be… it's Morguus Ebraxus!"

Leisterbane turned his unfeeling eyes skyward as the coral airship coasted around the great tree. He sneered at the elven craft as it passed him and then grinned at Avaryth's severed head, which rested at his feet. The dragon had been summoned.

By their nature, dragons were forces of pure chaos, something both separate from the gods and supplemental to them. Tears of Ghaeial. Eldarim had methods of controlling them, but even a black dragon would attack Death's forces unless they took proper measures. Leisterbane grinned; he had secured those measures.

Peregrine, master of the darkhold gem, stepped toward the death knight. "Leisterbane, you are sure this will work?" Even after all these centuries, the undead human still had a sense of nervousness about him.

Leisterbane nodded once. "Dragons are not mere forces of power. They are also sentient—possessing memories and thoughts. I have summoned Morguus Ebraxus, who harbors a fierce hatred of vagha—and now also of the areosa. He is not one of the elder dragons, not powerful enough to speak with us directly, but he will attack the vagha and their allies first."

The death knight tapped the illuminated spot on Peregrine's chest where the dim violet light glowed just beneath the dead human's skin. "And I also know a spell that will turn his hatred in our favor."

Peregrine cocked his head and watched his peer remove an ebony ring from a pocket and slip it onto his finger. It dated to the Magestorm wars, no doubt, and with the added strength of the festration, Leisterbane summoned enough power to cast a spell that would make his old master, Melkior, jealous.

Both the bloodless leaders turned their heads when the black dragon streaked through the sky like a crossbow quarrel and eviscerated the coral airship. Its crew scattered like wind-blown chaff as the craft busted in two. Morguus Ebraxus circled back to survey the wreckage.

"Do it now," Leisterbane ordered.

Peregrine blew a horn and signaled his minions. They'd been prepped already for the call, and they used massive levers to dump the chained cauldrons of necralluvium into the tunnels. Three of the four banks of vile ichor tipped and poured into the holes. A fourth cluster failed to trigger, and the levers broke, but the effect was immediate.

The great tree turned a nasty shade of gray and many of its ball roots withered. In some spots, they even pulled up from the ground, dangling tendrils like painful nerve endings quivering at the end of an extracted tooth. A pulse of psychic energy blasted off the pained tree. It had no effect on the dead, but Leisterbane knew the living would feel it like screaming in their mind. He had no idea what it might do to the dragon.

Morguus Ebraxus flapped his wings and searched for his next enemy to attack when the ten wyverns streaked toward him and encircled the beast in tight arcs. Roaring, the dragon used two powerful limbs to snatch the thick branches of the Ghaeial tree and then batted the creatures from the sky, first swatting a few with his powerful wings. Those that ducked were caught by Morguus Ebraxus's tail. The crushed beasts twirled in wild loops to the dirt below. They croaked and groaned with broken wings and legs; their complaints turned to shrieks as the zombified hordes set upon them with hungry mouths.

Only one wyvern got away, slipping above the tail. It turned a tight loop and flapped its wings, speeding a doomed escape. Morguus Ebraxus snapped out with his jaw and bit the flying creature into three pieces, swallowing its rider whole.

Leisterbane grinned and then triggered his spell while the dragon was distracted. A pinpoint of light zapped out and contacted the dragon. With dazzled eyes, the creature saw an illusion created by Leisterbane. The tree appeared to the drake as if it were a massive vaghan tower. Morguus Ebraxus took the bait and poured a stream of caustic, black fire onto his enemy, both burning and afflicting it with toxic breath. Hunks of bark blasted off. Near the base, patches of it sloughed off like diseased skin.

The tree turned an even sicker shade of color. At its base, the axe and saw wielding undead rushed forward again to attack the sickened tree. They hacked and cut away with mechanical abandon. Skeletons on the far side attached great lengths of chain to upper branches. Entire hordes of skeletal steeds pulled on those chains to apply force like a lever, but there was not yet nearly enough to cut away—that would take time.

With Morguus Ebraxus still working away on the illusory enemy, Leisterbane turned his gaze to the three remaining frost ogres. He didn't know how or why they were in league with the laughably small resistance, but he knew their specialty. He could not risk them breaking his spell and freeing the dragon. With a clear mind, Morguus Ebraxus would attack the dead if they were the closest target; it might single them out first, if he realized he'd been tricked by them. Dragons were as vengeful as they were dangerous.

Leisterbane stared menacingly at Peregrine. "Tear this tree down. I will protect our efforts and dispatch the ogres." The bloodless leader turned to point at a few of his undead generals and their waiting forces. "Rorduk, Brehdran, Duhlk. With me!" He leveled an accusatory finger at the frost ogres and the wolves that harried their flanks.

Already, the hillock where they'd come from was littered with the corpses of fallen wolves and interspersed with the remnants of twice-dead soldiers. Two fallen ogres were already being feasted upon by distracted zombies. Leisterbane grinned as the canine warriors kept coming. Soon there would be more dead littering the countryside, and with Peregrine present, his army would grow yet again.

CHAPTER NINETEEN

Harol chugged up the mountainside. He knew he'd find the busted cliffs where the World Wound began on the other side of the steep ridge. At the bottom of the steep drop lay the Netherwold, the foundation of Nekarthis's stronghold.

The dwarven cultist felt more at home in the mountainous rise and with solid stone beneath his feet. He hated that—hated how familiarity with his heritage brought him comfort. Everything about Balgavarr Reaches disgusted him. Harol sa'Lahmyn yearned to have more in common with the dead; he'd already completely changed his nature as an acolyte, and he consciously rejected all identity outside of the Death god and his kingdom. *But unconsciously?*

Still, the path up the mountain brought him some measure of security, and that helped him move easily and quickly toward his goal. None of the natives had given him any trouble as he journeyed through Dereh'Liandor. They kept their distance, as if recognizing he was on some kind of unholy pilgrimage.

Harol slowed his gait and paused in the shade of the mountain slopes. He dug in a pouch and produced some seedcake to munch on. He did not have much food left, but he knew his dark lord would sustain him. As he quietly chewed and reflected on his mission, he glanced down the side of the twisting mountain path where it weaved between magmic openings. There, lava pools bubbled to the surface, melting stone to slag that cooled in rhythmic cycles like tidal pools.

He spotted movement from the corner of his eye. Harol cocked his head, but he couldn't spot it. Then, as he turned his head away, he caught it again in his peripheral sight.

Harol snapped to attention and scanned the road. He growled as his eyes failed. Then, he found the culprits on the edge of his vision: Geril sa'Ghuren and a company of hunters.

The cultist hissed a curse, uncertain how they'd gotten here so fast. Harol knew spells, but he was not a particularly skilled thaumaturgist and lacked finesse; Harol's magic tended more toward the blunt, powerful, and dangerous. Self-taught as a black magician, he knew only what he knew, and that was it. And so, when he spotted Sheron's artful casting, he couldn't help but be impressed with the mystic camouflage that his pursuers wore. There was no way Harol could replicate it.

"Some kind of variant of the stone skin spell," he muttered, noting their position. They'd be able to catch up within a day at this rate. He squinted, intentionally looking past them so he could locate the shifting color of their movements. "And they're fast… sped up by magic."

Harol took out two metal figures from a pocket. The baubles looked like toys, barely larger than a dwarf's fist. But Harol knew better. He'd enchanted them for exactly this purpose with one of the few simple spells he *did* know from the Purlieus Chromadiscylum, the colorless kind of spell craft which even an acolyte could harness.

Setting them down on the trail, Harol reversed the spell that had shrunk the items to pocket size. Two blade golems grew tall and stood at the ready. Harol activated them. They towered larger than any dwarf, or even most humans, covered in edged weapons, and made from the same stuff as the blades protruding from their bodies and armor. Centered on each of their heads glowed a single crystal eye.

Both the blade golems stared at their master, who had activated them. They had limited intelligence, and their thoughts were always attuned to their purpose.

"Hide," Harol instructed them. "When the moment is right, reveal yourselves and kill my pursuers."

The golems turned their heads mechanically and searched for Harol's hunters. They found them after a few moments and a light seemed to shift within their crystal eyes. Slinking backwards, the two protectors wedged their bodies into craggy apertures on the stony approach, hidden by cleft and shadow.

Harol grinned, and then he turned back up the slope and redoubled his efforts, abandoning any thought of stealth. Only thinking of what lay at the end of his journey.

The explosion slapped Ra'al against the side of the great tree like an insect swatted out of the air. He slid down the trunk and gasped for breath, feeling for broken ribs. His ears rang so loudly that he could scarcely hear his own voice as he shouted for his friend.

"Coryn? Coryn!" Hot blood trickled down his scalp, and he crawled to his feet, succeeding on his second try. Ra'al pulled his axe from his pack, Rawrgyld's axe, but he'd decided he would never return Frostquake. Ra'al extended the claws of his free hand.

The frostwing cut down three zombies that lurched toward him with hungry intent glowing in their eyes. Ra'al was wounded, but not so much that he couldn't defend himself.

A nearby vagha limped away from a pack of zombies. With a busted femur protruding from his skin, he couldn't quite muster the necessary speed to escape the zombies. They dragged him to the ground and tore away flesh pinched between rotten, yellow teeth. The dwarf died seconds later, screaming loud enough to pierce the ringing in Ra'al's ears.

There was nothing Ra'al could have done to save him. Panic struck, he thought: *That could be Coryn's fate!*

He scanned the ground frantically, searching for any sign of her and then he spotted Coryn. She lay face down on the ground. A cluster of enemies closed in on her helpless body, but Ra'al was too far away to help.

And then, she spun around and brought her axe to bear, hacking them to pieces as soon as they got close enough. She smashed the black spot from the base of their skulls to ensure the hungry enemy could not rise again. *She'd baited them in!*

Ra'al grinned. *Typical Coryn.*

Her eyes met his, and they hurried together to form up defensively. Bastawr clawed his way through a group of skeletons and rushed toward them to join their rank.

"We've got to find Leisterbane," Ra'al roared, searching for scouts who could help them. Any of his frostwings who had been airborne when the dragon struck could be deployed on a search mission. He looked up and saw a trio of them gliding toward them.

Ra'al flared his wings and tried to meet them in the sky, but a busted wing made him cry out and falter on the ground. Looking up, the trio of areosa disintegrated when Morguus Ebraxus spat a line of flame at them. Smoldering bones fell into a charred rain of chitin and clattered around them.

"We've got to kill the leader. It's the only way," Ra'al insisted.

"But that won't take care of the dragon," yelped Bastawr over the din of the battle and chaos. "None of our plans accounted for a drake."

Coryn's resolve set upon her face, and she gripped her axe handle tightly. "You leave Morguus Ebraxus to me. My whole lineage, it seems, has been devoted to killing him."

Gliding low to avoid the dragon's eyes, Hennedy carried Karou in his arms. The spell caster's wings were limp, and he gasped in ragged breaths. A gaping chest wound gushed blood where something had punctured his flesh during the wreck of *Aguarehl's Envy*.

"I saw Captain Taerlon," Hennedy insisted, collapsing near his friends. Coryn put pressure on Karou's injury while the others defended them against an oncoming wall of decaying enemies.

"Where?" Bastawr demanded.

Hennedy pointed. "The other side of those skeletons."

Bastawr launched himself toward the enemy, all fang and tooth and claw. His stone knives cracked bone and slashed through necralluvium tendrils until he busted through the group and found Fazayou. The blue elf's sword flashed as he kept the monsters at bay, but barely.

Taerlon laid on the ground, rocking in pain and missing his left leg. Something had torn it off at the knee and the selumari had done his best to seal the stump with a tourniquet. However, the smell of the green tinted, pulsing blood had driven the undead into a feeding frenzy.

Bastawr picked him up and let Fazayou cut a path back to the others. They were so deep enough inside the ring of the bloodless that escape was unlikely. They were also precariously close to the massive tree, and the undead nearby were more concerned with using axes against *it* than the intruders.

The group were rats in a maze—a deadly, deadly maze. A maze of shifting walls made of hungry corpses.

Bastawr and Fazayou cleared the soldiers and found the others. A few dozen vagha and half as many areosa had done likewise, plus a handful of the Azure Company's survivors. A trio of the selumari laid glowing hands upon Karou, providing just enough relief to let the magi's one working lung keep him upright. He coughed up globs of blood but wiped his chin and nodded to them, certain he'd be able to pull his own weight until the end, though *anyone's* survival looked unlikely.

The disjointed clusters of survivors regrouped, and none dared speak to their hopeless situation. This is what they had each signed on for: a suicide mission and a surgical strike against Leisterbane. They wore grim faces of determination, like weightlifters mid-set, pushing unbearable loads. The only sounds came from those who growled against the pain, defiant regardless of their agonizing wounds.

Ra'al howled, still searching for information. "Leisterbane. Has anyone spotted Leisterbane?"

Leisterbane squared off against the largest of the frost ogres as his generals led squadrons of undead into the fray against the wolves. Only one of the frost ogres remained. The other two mystic creatures had already fallen to their wounds, and an overgrown carrion crawler already claimed the body of the closest of the fallen.

"I am Tanneyha of Skrilluk Peak. I have guarded the north since before your kind came to Esfah," the ogre yelled, his voice nearly out of breath. He whirled a stick like a club and spun a circle, clubbing down swaths of enemies. "I have befriended sage and traveler alike, but I shall not let you have this tree."

The wolves howled and shrieked behind them as the undead found their marks, tearing a pack apart and painting their bleached bones red with blood. Tanneyha crouched and turned three-hundred-sixty degrees, with one end of his staff in the snow. He completed the circle and then used the stick to make another sign taught to him by an old sage. The snow glowed.

Leisterbane pointed his blade at Tanneyha. "Your time has come and passed, old beast. The same is true for the First Races, even the selumari whose flesh I possess." The bloodless leader cocked his head at his generals.

Rorduk, Brehdran, and Duhlk each possessed a devilish light behind their eyes: the light of intelligence. They were free operators, and the threesome each cast their spells. Black bolts fired like darts, trailing streams like smoke as they shot toward the ogre.

The ebony fingers of dead energy splashed harmlessly against the circle, making it spark in a shaft of vertical light where the crafty ogre had created a dweomernull sigil in the snow.

Tanneyha acted quickly, moving and casting with a fluid grace that made it seem like one smooth dance step. With a grin, he kicked a foot through the snowy furrow that made the symbol, dispelling it. And then, he fired back with the same spell, shooting out a trio of black bolts that caught the generals by surprise.

Rorduk, Brehdran, and Duhlk collapsed in heaps of flesh, mud, and frost as entropy suddenly accelerated and caught up with their bodies.

Leisterbane sneered and pointed his blade at him. He would not be caught off guard like the others, and he advanced on the last of Skrilluk's reinforcements.

Tanneyha was twice the size of the warrior who threatened him, and the frost ogre leapt forward, trying to smash him with his club, but Leisterbane sidestepped it and hacked at the ogre, opening a gash in his thigh.

Stepping back, Tanneyha regarded the knight with frigid eyes and began summoning the cold to him. The ogre's eyes misted over with frost, a sign that he planned to try freezing the death knight.

Suddenly, a loud draconic screech rent the air behind Leisterbane, followed by the sound of cracking wood and the rustling of leafy canopy.

Tanneyha turned his eyes only for a split second, his attention stolen. And Leisterbane smiled. It was more than enough time.

"There he is," shouted one of the vagha. "I see him. I see Leisterbane!" He pointed to the spot where wolves harried the undead's flank.

Coryn gasped when she saw two of the ogres fallen behind Tanneyha, and her ogre friend facing off against Leisterbane.

A loud crack split the white noise of battle and woodcutters' axes as a gout of dragon's flame tore through the battered tree. Chains rattled as the steeds on the far side of it pulled from the top. A fissure in the wood splintered with a deafening groan.

Tanneyha looked away momentarily and Coryn yelled, "No!"

Leisterbane slashed upwards, splitting the furry hide that covered Tanneyha's chest and exposed muscle and bone. The ogre gasped in surprise, and the death knight plunged his left arm within the gore, snatching him by a rib and hauling himself closer. He gained enough angle to plunge the blade deep into Tanneyha's organs.

The ogre fell to his knees where Leisterbane slashed again, sending a spray of carotid blood into the sky. Tanneyha doubled over and clutched the wound, but Leisterbane whirled and slashed again and again at the massive creature's neck. On the third stroke, he finally succeeded, and the ogre's head rolled free. The ancient creature's blood poured red upon the snow.

Coryn screamed and her companions bolstered themselves, preparing to fight their way toward the undead warrior and bring all their forces to bear. They had one shot at ending this madness and saving the tree. She roared and held her axe high. The vagha matched her rage-filled howl.

First Leisterbane, and then the dragon, she pledged to herself, rushing forwards. Her companions surged alongside her.

Someone in the rear shouted, "More sails. There is another ship!"

The explosions started before Coryn knew what was happening. A flare of red flame blinded her, and she recoiled, shielding her eyes. The ground suddenly gave way in all the chaos, and she felt herself falling.

Marnash and his sorcerers threw fireballs from the edges of the boat. The fiery orbs streaked toward their target and detonated in rings of flame, flash boiling the ice and busting it into manageable pieces. The icy fields of the broad river boasted only middling chunks, and the ship sped as a natural wind gust drove it by the grace of the gods.

Garesch steered as best as he could, but many of the floating chunks bounced off the front of the hull. The wood had cracked and dented, but the integrity remained whole.

Marnash hurled a large, fiery orb ahead of them and it seared a steaming gash for nearly a league, melting a course leading up to the tree towering ahead of them and rising above the light mists. The fact that they could see it indicated the stones they'd once tried to keep secret had all fallen.

Banks of undead milled absentmindedly about the plains as the ship surged past. Once in the thick of it, and with a black dragon trying relentlessly to incinerate the Ghaeial Tree, the morehl fire casters cast their magic offensively. They scorched ranks of walking corpses, blasting the dead and scattering flaming debris.

Garesch stood upon the high point of the quarter deck and tried to locate his friends amid the blazing eruptions. Clouds of fire sprang up and some of the war machinery Leisterbane had used against the tree crumbled, but the emperor could not find them.

Gray and blue smoke filled the air as his troops blasted the nearest fiends to pieces with ball shot.

"Come on, come on," Garesch hissed. He squinted and searched for them. "There!" he yelled, pointing for Marnash to see. "I see Ra'al and Bastawr."

Marnash dashed up the jib boom and balanced upon it as best as he was able. "I see them. They are running toward something… *toward Leisterbane?*"

"Do you see Coryn?" the emperor asked, trying to pilot the craft to a gentle ice docking. With the favor of the gods and more than a fair amount of luck, they might be able to use the ship to escape if his friends' fates turned even worse.

"No. I do not see her," Marnash yelled back.

The caster looked back in time to see another of his caster's fireballs knock out the skeletal remains of a trebuchet. Collapsing in a heap, the structure upended a bank of giant metal cauldrons, tipping and dumping their inky contents into a waiting hole, which drank in the fluid like a thirsty mouth.

CHAPTER TWENTY

Geril refused to let his burning lungs hold him back or admit that his stamina waned slightly as he'd grown older. Ringuld clambered up a stony escarpment and scanned the ridge, searching for Harol. They'd made good time in the mountains, catching up incredibly quick once on their favored terrain. Sheron's camouflage had proved even more effective on the rugged slopes, and the dwarves even had trouble spotting each other at two paces.

Sheron tapped his friend on the chest and handed over a vial of noxious smelling stimulant. Geril accepted it and uncorked the stuff. The fumes burned enough to awaken a mammoth from a drunk slumber. And the tincture had less than a drop of dragon piss in it.

Geril glanced sidelong at Sheron. The wizard was even older than he was, but the stuff had kept him on his feet and moving at the pace of a young vagha, and so, he pinched his nose, opened his mouth, and threw his head back to drink the vile potion, aiming directly for his throat. He didn't want the stuff touching his tongue.

The vial was tiny, and the effect was immediate. Geril's eyes widened, and his sinuses cleared as if he'd just snorted a dose of fire sauce.

Ringuld hopped down into their midst. "I spotted him go over the ridge. He's beyond sight now," the younger captain said. "If we hurry, we can capture him within the hour!"

Nodding, Geril still sucked for air. After another lungful, he nodded and steeled himself for one final sprint. A hardened resolve burned in his eyes as he drew Old Thunder. "We can't let him reach the Netherwold, and I'll be more than happy to make that Death worshiping bastard pay for his sins."

Geril dashed forward, with his crew following behind. They charged upwards with renewed vigor, not bothering to look over the steep ledge of the mountain trail. It fell away for hundreds of cubits before the tops of the tallest trees began. Their canopy spread out below the cliffs like a carpet rolled out by a hearth.

Dwarves knew mountains. They understood to respect their sharp curves and steep falls. Ringuld suddenly tackled Geril in complete defiance of vaghan ideals regarding cliff-side safety.

Neither rolled over the edge, but Geril cursed as a sharp blade skewered the air where his head had just been. He and Ringuld scrambled to their feet, weapons ready as two blade golems emerged from hiding.

"How in Sha'la'dinan did Harol get one golem up here, let alone two?" Geril lost a step as he parried the first golem's attack.

Ringuld caught the second one's arm cross ways with an axe, preventing it from slashing down and eviscerating him. The vagha in the rear roared and charged ahead.

Geril's opponent whirled and slashed one of them across the throat. A geyser of hot dwarven blood shot into the air. The soldier reached under his beard and clutched at his throat momentarily before pitching headlong over the ledge and into the greenery far below.

"Go!" one of them yelled. "We'll handle these walking turnip graters. They're no match for vaghan axes!"

All the same, Sheron intensified the stoneskin spell upon himself and three others. The effort cost them their camouflage, but they assumed Harol had set the trap because he knew their position already.

Geril and Ringuld dashed further up the slope while Sheron and three others charged through the gap where the two golems blocked further traffic. Even with the spell coating them in a thick skin made of living stone, the enemies each managed to skewer one of the dwarves. Sheron and his remaining shield mate hurried forward to catch up with the others, leaving the shrinking remnant of Balgavarr's finest to deal with the mechanical warriors.

While the rearguard engaged the golems, those nearest the peaks ran ahead, huffing and puffing, knowing that at any moment, they would finally face down the greatest failure Balgavarr Reaches had ever produced: the traitor, Harol sa'Lahmyn.

Coryn rotated in the air and darkness. Then, she landed in the tunnel with a meaty thud that knocked the wind from her lungs. She gasped and sucked in a dusty breath before trying to get her bearings.

Sounds and light from the battle overhead bled through the ceiling where she'd fallen through. She didn't understand what had happened, only that she'd fallen into some kind of pit and her friends were left without her.

Scanning her surroundings, she saw that she'd landed in an underground temple interwoven by the Ghaeial Tree's roots. Coryn crawled to her feet and examined the room. It looked like most temples she'd visited before. This one was abandoned to time, but it looked somehow more polished. Ornate reliefs decorated the walls; it must have been magnificent in its day.

The room held only few items and furnishings. Some chains dangled on sconces and scraps of moldered fabric, which might have once been tapestries. A stone table sat at one end of the room with a decaying wood door on the other.

Coryn looked at the roof, which crumbled where the Ghaeial Tree's roots seemed to have crawled upwards, retracting from the above threat. It had weakened the soil and ceiling. "That must be why I fell in," she muttered.

She wandered toward the table and saw that it might have been an altar. Coryn didn't know much about religions beyond the basics that all vagha knew. Upon the table sat a kind of box. Try as she might, Coryn couldn't find an opening, and it was heavy. It seemed to have a kind of interlocking joint where it might have attached to something else, or something might have attached to *it*. For all she knew, it was an ancient idol or eldarim tool.

Markings on the metal block looked gnomish. Coryn retrieved her puzzle cube and compared them side by side. "Definitely gnomish." She stuffed the mysterious artifact in her pack for later and took one last look around. There was no way she could escape the way she'd come in, and so, she headed for the door.

The wooden plank half-collapsed and half-stuck as she tried to open it. Coryn forced her way through and staggered into the long hallway. Skeletons screeched and snapped their attention toward her. They rushed at her and the vagha produced her axe, hacking away at the first ones to arrive.

Behind the mindless drones, a larger creature stalked toward her: an undead knight. He retained ragged bits of flesh and decayed armor. Something intelligent burned within the fiend's eyes and Coryn understood he must have been one of Leisterbane's generals. He would likely give her more trouble than the rest.

"Alright then, you bloodless filth, give it your best shot!" Coryn mowed down the underlings as the general stalked methodically toward her. Slowly, he drew his wicked and jagged bastard sword.

The dwarf chopped the legs from a zombie in front of her and then separated its head from shoulders once she'd cut it down to her size. A dull rumbling and a sound like wind echoed through the hall. The creatures kept on coming, ignoring it.

Coryn narrowed her eyes to slits as the chief fiend continued his approach. And then, Coryn realized the sound was not wind. She recognized it from her travels near the Sareen River. "A waterfall? Maybe a rushing current?"

The general cackled and was not deterred, as if he understood what was happening. Coryn recoiled from the sight. A flood of writhing, black necralluvium rushed through the tunnel, blanketing everything in splattered black death.

Rats and small mammals who had taken refuge in the halls squeaked and ran ahead of the flow. As soon as a drop of the fluid touched each one, they died with a screech and were immediately consumed by the flow.

Coryn's opponent surged for her, mere steps ahead of the corrupting river of black. As he reached for her, she disappeared into thin air, dissipating like a flash of smoke. A small metal box clattered to the floor as if the dwarf had somehow turned invisible and dropped the item.

As the necralluvium rushed past his ankles and coated everything in black, the cube seemed to vibrate with an energy that repelled the stuff. The necralluvium could not touch the odd cube. The bloodless soldier grasped the cube and then turned in a circle. He sniffed deeply, searching for the scent of the vagha, but could not find it. It was as if she had simply ceased to exist.

He turned and splashed through the murky pools toward the tunnel's exit. He'd claimed a prize to deliver to Leisterbane. Perhaps he would know what it meant.

"Coryn! Where is Coryn?" Ra'al roared, scanning the tops of heads as the undead pushed in around them. He ducked beneath a spear aimed for his head, turned, and then chopped through the skeletal creature. Frostquake hit the bloodless, and it exploded in a trembling pile of bones.

The areosa bared his fangs and returned to the task at hand. He had to pause his concern for his friend—they had to take out the leader. He locked eyes with Leisterbane, whose face glowed with amusement as he stalked back toward the intruders corralled by his forces near the great tree. Leisterbane was still splattered with frost ogre blood, and behind him, the remaining wolf packs howled, signaling their retreat to the wilds in Tanneyha's absence.

Ra'al recognized the look on his enemy's face: joy at claiming an easy victory. It was the same look that Rawrgyld had worn when he had killed Ra'al's mother.

Leisterbane's forces gathered behind him, and the magicians stretched out their withered hands, clutching painted, glowing bones and other fetishes, preparing to cast their spells. Their leader had his blade at the ready and walked purposefully toward the would-be heroes clustered beneath the shuddering tree that creaked in tortured waves as the undead tried to fell it. The death knight's hand glowed with the eerie illumination centered around the ring he wore. The same strange glow intensified around the dead wizards' bone fetishes as they summoned eldritch power to mold with their incantations.

Ra'al saw the spell coming. He leapt over the wall of rotting bodies and his own troops, who barely held the line. The frostwing winced as the wind caught his busted wing. He ignored it, focusing all his pain, all his anger, into breaking through to engage Leisterbane.

Black trails of ethereal power trailed the spell like smoke. The wave of necromantic energy hit Ra'al like a hot wind. Vestigial effects washed over him and glanced off like water. Both the spell breaker at his neck insulated him as well as his areosan nature, providing some resistance.

Without the additional help from an artifact, Karou, Hennedy, and the remaining frostwings succumbed to it, as did the remainder of the allied forces; they fell into a trance and collapsed, staring ahead with vacant eyes as if asleep. Ra'al heard screaming and saw the distant morehl being overwhelmed with enemies from the corner of his eye. More bloodless spell crafters assailed the vessel in the same manner.

Ra'al grimaced and pulled his wings back to his body. He ignored the grinding pain and took to the air momentarily, landing atop the enemy and crunching several dead below his girth. He whirled Frostquake, eviscerating the nearest bloodless. They collapsed with violent effect and Ra'al thought he detected a look of surprise, perhaps even fear, on Leisterbane's face.

The undead nearest him parted, clearing a path between Ra'al and their master.

"I have your friends, frostwing," he growled. "They will soon join my ranks, as shall you. You shall all become loyal soldiers and generals in my army."

"Never," Ra'al cried, brandishing the weapon that disrupted undead. Behind him, the tree cracked with a sound like a sundered mountain.

Leisterbane sneered. He jammed his blade into the ground. It stuck like a battle standard and the fiend took two steps back, splaying his arms wide and exposing his chest, taunting his opponent. "Even if you destroyed me here and now, my master's dark shall still be accomplished." He turned and focused his attention on the tree. The dragon poured more streams of energy into the base as the teams of dead cavalry yanked on their chains, nearly dragging the tree far enough to snap. He focused none of his attention on the axe wielding frostwing.

Ra'al raised his weapon and charged. "This ends now!"

Barely one step away from Leisterbane, a burrow exploded up from the soil and an enormous carrion crawler burst from below. The pale worm opened a mouth that writhed with thrashing tendrils like snakes. They slapped across Ra'al's hide like electric eels, forcing his muscles to spasm and lock up.

Ra'al collapsed muzzle first to the dirt and dropped Frostquake. He shook with spasmodic seizures. He felt his body flip over as bony hands turned him.

Leisterbane's serious face momentarily greeted him, and then disappeared. Ra'al could see only the sky as the undead dragged him across the rugged terrain.

CHAPTER TWENTY-ONE

Geril and his entourage crested the top of the ridge, where it opened like a burst thorax. A cavity stretched away on the other side, opening into a ravine that split the world as far as the eye could see in either direction: the World Wound. A chasm dropped away into darkness, too far below to be visible.

At the top, Harol stood waiting for them.

Geril's eyes widened, and he tackled Ringuld, returning the favor and saving the younger dwarf's life. A black missile of death magic shot out from the cultist's splayed hand like a deadly finger of the Death god. It trailed a vaporous line to the acolyte and wafted just overhead.

The magic finger slammed into the chest of the next dwarf in line and the soldier pitched head over heel, toppling as dead as a rock, despite the stone skin. Sheron, who brought up the end of the line, ducked into a roll and hid from the acolyte.

They paused for a long moment, as if at a standstill. The trio of hunters from Balgavarr hunched behind boulders and waited for an opening.

"You've finally got my attention, Geril sa'Ghuren, the great Dragonsbane," came the evil one's voice. A gleeful lilt permeated it. "Do come out and play."

They heard the rustling of Harol drawing something from his pack.

Geril stalled and kept him talking as he and his companions tried to work out a plan with hand signs. "You're going to die here, you know that, Harol?"

"I've been trapped in a mere shadow of life now for decades, Steward of Balgavarr. Ever since you banished me from the Reaches." He chuckled. "You think me a monster, Geril, but *you made me*."

"Bah! Ye made yerself!" Geril groused with his back to the stone.

"I was merely a dabbler with the dark until you had me cast out of the light. And now, here we are. I, the acolyte, and you, trying to stop me." He laughed again, this time, a hearty belly bark. "You think my death will stop what I am doing here? *I yearn for it,* Dragonsbane. When I am dead, Malgrimm shall repay my loyalty and I shall rule forever as a Duke in the glorious hell he shall establish!"

"Yer frackin cracked," Geril barked. "I've known it for ages. So did your father. Tell me, did he know you were a crazed cultist? It's all part of a plan he devised to kill me, isn't it? Lahmyn's hated Clan Hydrak all his life…"

"Father knew nothing of this!" Harol snapped. "He figured out what I truly was, but that came later. And he is no fool. Though he's abandoned me to your judgment, I am certain he will play it to his own advantage."

Geril believed the traitor. But that didn't solve the Lahmyn problem he was sure to have waiting for him at home.

"Now, come out and play… come out and die, Dragonsbane," Harol giggled.

Geril locked eyes with his companions and steeled himself, coiling muscles like a spring ready to unleash. He nodded, and the trio sprang into action. Geril darted out on one side of the boulder and Ringuld went on the other. Sheron popped up at the same time.

Harol snap-fired a crossbow from the hip and the bolt lodged deep in Ringuld's thigh. Ringuld collapsed and rolled onto his back with a pained roar.

Sheron bared his teeth in deep concentration as he countered spell after spell the acolyte tried to cast at Geril. Death crafts fizzled one after another as the dwarf raised Old Thunder high overhead and swung it with a killing blow.

Harol abandoned magic. He was good at spells he knew, but Sheron was a properly trained wizard, and the cultist knew he couldn't match arcana against him once Sheron had figured out he had a limited bag of tricks. The renegade brought his own axe up and parried Old Thunder.

Geril's weapon fell harmless to the side, still clutched in his right hand. He twisted his hips and slugged Harol in the nose with a hard roundhouse fist, cracking the cultist with a solid left.

Staggering back two steps, Harol teetered precariously close to the ledge. He got his feet underneath himself and tasted the blood from his broken nose as it painted his whiskers.

Geril didn't give an inch. He stepped forward and struck again, swinging Old Thunder as if he were chopping wood.

Harol reached for a shield slung to his pack and got it up just in time. But the force of Geril's blow sundered it and the round plank fell into two halves.

Geril hefted the axe once more, ready to either cleave his enemy into two equal hunks of flesh or knock him over the ledge and let gravity ravage him. Harol recoiled and leaned back; Geril's axe missed by a hair's breadth and lodged in the stone.

With the ground crumbling beneath his feet, Harol overextended and brought his own wild blow to bear. His feet shifted his balance and his axe collided with Old Thunder's steel axe-head and smashed through it, shattering it into seven pieces of jagged metal. As the ground gave way, Harol reached out and snatched Geril by the beard, hanging on for dear life as his feet tried to find solid purchase on the shifting soil of the cliff that was now evaporating like mist.

Geril fell to his hands and knees as Harol's footing slipped away entirely. Sheron yelled and Ringuld scrambled to his feet, but both were too far away to help.

Harol clutched two fistfuls of whiskers and cackled. "How about it, Dragonsbane? Shall I take you over the edge with me? We can go to greet Malgrimm together!" He tugged as he dangled there, trying to haul his enemy into the abyss with him.

One of Harol's hands still clutched Geril's beard and with the other, he drew a dagger. Harol reached up and plunged it into Geril's chest.

Geril roared with pain and reached aside with one hand. Snatching a shard of Old Thunder in a fluid motion, he rammed the jagged splinter of steel into Harol's neck.

His enemy's manic grin fell slack, and Harol released his grip on Geril's beard. Trailing a stream of blood, Harol sa'Lahmyn's body went limp and then tumbled end over end into the darkness.

After a brief paused, Geril turned from the crumbling lip and flashed a pained grin to his companions. "I think… I think I'll be alright."

And then the ledge gave way and Geril plunged over the side, with Ringuld and Sheron screaming after him.

They rushed to the edge and scanned the blackness. There was no sign of Harol, but Geril lay on a stone escarpment just over the side. He'd only fallen about forty cubits—plenty distance to break a stout vagha, but it was survivable, too. Geril's stern constitution, and stubbornness, could keep him alive yet.

"I've got you! I've got you, my friend," Sheron called down to him, trying to assure himself that all would be okay. He moved recklessly, urgently.

Ringuld stayed him with an arm, compelling him to not slip and fall himself. Ringuld shook his head. "No. Look."

It was too late. Geril had landed upon Harol's dagger and the fall had rammed it deeper within his chest. It protruded out of their friend's back and a pool of blood leaked around him.

Sheron hung his head and sobbed. After a few minutes, he gathered his wits and concentrated. Using earth magic, he solidified the stone below and shifted its forms, making it rise. The platform where Geril had landed slowly came up to their height and then tipped, gently sliding their comrade's body toward them.

The three remaining vagha who had stayed behind to battle the blade golems rushed up the slope and arrived in time to find the mourners tending Geril's body. They dropped their weapons and knelt, ignoring the cuts and wounds they'd earned in their victory over the golems.

After a few long seconds of silence, their peers joined them and they looked over the ledge, searching the blackness once more for Harol's body. Sheron illuminated several stones and dropped them over the edge. They fell a long way, and eventually, covered enough space far below to make out Harol's broken body lying in twisted repose at the bottom of the ravine.

Ringuld turned and walked away to see to Geril's burial. They could not take him with them.

One of the other dwarves asked him, "And what of the traitor's corpse?"

Without looking back, Ringuld ordered, "Leave it for the carrion eaters."

Someone flipped Ra'al's stunned body over and dumped him across a heap of bones. Now, his dazed body could watch what happened next. Already, he could feel the creature's chemical restraints weakening. In a few minutes, Ra'al might be free. But it would be too late.

His companions had been arranged in a line with the great tree at their back. The morehl had been dragged to the end of the single-file line, awaiting execution.

Before them stood Leisterbane, who tossed Frostquake unceremoniously onto a massive heap of assorted Magestorm weapons. Many of the death knight's generals joined at his side.

Leisterbane locked eyes with Ra'al and allowed himself an opportunity to gloat. "I told you. Your companions would join my side and serve Lord Death."

One of Leisterbane's minions approached and placed a cube in the knight's hand. "The girl who leads the vagha is gone. And I have this to offer you."

Leisterbane held up the gnomish cube.

With just enough muscle control returned to his face, Ra'al roared. His heart tore from the agony of losing his best friend—the cube confirmed the demon's words. He'd never seen any others like it. *Coryn! Coryn is dead!*

"Interesting," Leisterbane murmured, still holding it. He turned and nodded to one of his minions further down the line.

The decaying toady grabbed Fazayou and clutched at the blue elf's mouth. Still too stunned by the magic to speak, Fazayou growled and moaned, trying to clench his teeth shut, but the undead forced his fingers into the elf's mouth and pried it ajar. Despite him wriggling and tensing up, the fiend incrementally forced Fazayou to his side and tore a stopper from a vial with his teeth.

Fazayou's eyes widened with terror and his tongue flailed. All the same, the dead man poured his contents into the selumari soldier's mouth. The viscous goo landed on his uvula and the change was immediate; Fazayou's skin blanched and veins on his skin bulged and blackened like dark spider webs. His legs stiffened with spasms, and he jerked repeatedly like a drowning man.

And then, he fell silent and limp. A few moments later, Fazayou stood and fixed his former companions with cold, dead eyes. They'd filled up with unfeeling blackness.

He was one of them now.

Leisterbane chuckled, low and menacing, as he basked in this rare moment of hubris. He inhaled deeply, drinking in the sweet musk of his captives' fear. His nearby generals did likewise, feeding upon the cluster of living folk who would soon become their allies.

"Who do you serve?" Leisterbane addressed his question to Fazayou.

The corpse-like elf answered. His voice sounded raspy, like a wheezing death rattle. "Only Lord Death," Fazayou said. "I serve Malgrimm."

Down the line, eyes bulged with horror as Fazayou's former companions realized what would come next. The corpse who had converted Fazayou pointed to the next captive in line, a dwarf who trembled beneath the undead's gaze. "Take... eat," he whispered to Fazayou.

The elf fell upon him like a feral beast and sank his jaws into the vaghan meat, tearing with his mandibles and thrashing his face as he bit into the dwarf's neck. The creature Fazayou had become flung blood in every direction.

Through his nose, Leisterbane inhaled deeply, tasting the sweetness of abject terror. Behind the row of hostages and those feasting upon their fear, Morguus Ebraxus inhaled and screamed at the sky; the great tree shuddered and then gave way, snapping and bending even further as the driven teams of skeletal mounts redoubled their efforts to tear it down.

Tears welled up in the eyes of his victims. They knew as well as Leisterbane that the tree would fall at any second.

CHAPTER TWENTY-TWO

Coryn huddled against the glass wall that enclosed Yoo-ee. She squeezed her legs, drawing them close to her, and shivered. She didn't have any idea what to do.

She kicked the last explosive cask that had rolled near to her where it had been left, forgotten behind the plinth near Yoo-ee's enclosure. Coryn looked up and realized the dragonkin-like creature was looking down at her expectantly.

"I don't know what I'm supposed to do, Yoo-ee," she argued with it. "If I touch that black stuff, I'll die. Instantly, like those rats... and for all I know, our cube is submerged in the stuff. I'm trapped in here... just like you."

Yoo-ee's face looked angry. He head-butted the transparent wall hard enough that Coryn thought it would shatter. The creature's golden scales shook, and his eyes bored into a spot on the back of the plinth.

She saw several gems there, each a different color. She reached out and touched them, and they lit up one at a time.

Once certain combinations were lit and a new color was pressed, their backlighting switched off and reset.

Yoo-ee cocked his head and Coryn furrowed her brow, concentrating on it. "I don't know how I missed this before," she mumbled. "I was stuck in here for ages the first time."

Coryn stared at the colored, square-set gems. They were stones much like the ones in the puzzle that guarded the Magestorm weapons cache she'd accessed with Ra'al and accidentally exposed to the traitor, Harol.

Biting her lip, she tried a color combination, touching an amber tile and one of ruby to indicate the colors long associated with the vagha. They lit and remained static.

Coryn searched everywhere for some kind of new button, keyhole, or unlocking mechanism on the pane that would free Yoo-ee. Finally, she slumped, distraught.

"Sorry, Yoo-ee. I guess that's just one more promise I can't keep. You'll probably be in there forever." Her voice cracked and her eyes welled up.

The creature smashed his forehead into the barrier again to shock her out of her despondency.

Coryn touched another of the colors and the panel went out. "See? See… I can't do anything with this." She activated two more colors until she got a pair to light up.

Yoo-ee thundered again, his mighty forehead slamming against the clear wall. Carefully, so that Yoo-ee could see her, she touched the ruby and amber again. Yoo-ee seemed to relax but was otherwise positioned to smash his head again.

Coryn stood and turned toward the far wall of the pie-shaped chamber. She took a few steps toward the exit and then *wham!*

She turned back, realizing Yoo-ee was communicating with her. She reached out her hand and pointed toward the mirror-like side wall and Yoo-ee tensed, about to bang his head. Coryn spared the creature's face and pointed back to the middle before he had to face-plant again. She turned her arm in the opposite direction to the other wall and Yoo-ee followed the same pattern.

Finally, Coryn's finger pointed directly at the plinth again and she stepped toward the post, which bore an engraved plate with the name Euhysaurom. *Yoo-ee.*

"This thing?" she asked, resting her hand on it. Instead of the glowing spectral image of the gremmlobahnd which had appeared before, this time, the projection was of a vagha. Coryn realized the stones on the back changed the figure and the language it spoke.

Uttering his question in an old dialect of the vaghan tongue, it asked, "Shall I release the creature to combat the Drekloch?"

Coryn didn't know what that meant, although she understood the words. She spoke in her native tongue, which she used far less often than the common one. "Yes."

The image of the dwarf evaporated, as did the clear wall which held Yoo-ee. The golden beast stretched and then bounded out of the space where it had been held for eons.

Coryn panicked slightly as the massive beast bore down on her. For a fleeting moment, she wondered if the creature had been imprisoned here for good reason. It caught her and pressed her to the floor with a heavy claw. Suddenly, a voice echoed in her mind. It was not audible, but it resonated inside her.

Calm yourself. You are bonded to me now.

Coryn blinked and stared at Yoo-ee with wide eyes. "Y-Yoo-ee? Is that you?"

My name is Euhysaurom, but you may call me that if you find it is easier.

"You're… in my head?"

I can communicate directly with you when we are touching. It is no small thing to be bonded to a dracolem.

"A what now?"

Dracolem. It is what I am. I am... created by the gremmlobahnd to fight off a creature of evil. The Drekloch. I am the only thing that can keep it at bay.

"None of that makes sense to me, Yoo-ee. You look like a dragonkin."

The drakufreet. Yes. I was patterned after them, meant to look like them to better blend in. But I was created, not hatched.

Coryn raised a brow and Yoo-ee removed his talon, letting her rise. "Like a golem?"

She put her hand on Yoo-ee so he could respond. *Yes... but no. A dracolem is so much more. Now come, we must go. I sense a Drekloch is free on Esfah, though I know not where.*

"Didn't you hear me before? I can't open the door, or I'll be killed by the black stuff."

Yoo-ee named it. *The necralluvium cannot touch me. I am not of Esfahan materials. Like the gnomes, I came from Leguin, and that was so very long ago. I can protect you, but you must open the door.*

Coryn tightened her lips, upset that it seemed Yoo-ee was not listening. And then he nudged the explosive cask toward her, and she formed a plan.

Leisterbane's lips parted, and he exposed his teeth, baring them menacingly. He raised his hands in victory as the Ghaeial Tree finally broke. With a thunderous crash, it fell toward the misty plains.

Pushing more of his will into the illusion spell, Leisterbane's ring glowed again, and he hid his army and captives behind the spell. The last thing he wanted was for the drake to turn on them in his moment of victory.

Morguus Ebraxus mounted the fallen tree, thinking that he'd toppled a mighty prize of the hated vagha. He perched there with a mighty roar and lorded over what he thought to make his new lair.

A flash of light blipped quickly, and Leisterbane searched for its source. Finding none, he turned back to drink the fear of the living as he relished in their anger. With his victory secured, they would be ripe with flavor now more than ever.

He found all eyes locked on him, expectant. Defiant. Leisterbane did not understand: their fear had evaporated. And then his foot struck something hard, which nearly tripped him. He turned to find a wooden cask somehow dropped at his feet, as if it had spontaneously come into existence.

Leisterbane cocked his head and used a toe to turn the small keg over. "Strange. I sense no magic upon this thing."

And then, he saw a glowing ember race down the last length of wick. The powder keg exploded, tearing Leisterbane apart along with the corps of spell crafters who stood nearby. Leisterbane's limbs and torso were ripped free in a splatter of gore that incinerated most of his lower half.

The death knight's severed hand fell and lay next to the metallic cube his minion had collected. The ring he'd worn remained upon his finger, but the faint glow shimmering about it died.

Chaos erupted all around as the illusion spell failed. Beyond them, Morguus Ebraxus shrieked with anger and took to the sky. He rained down caustic breath upon the undead, understanding that they had tricked him.

The heroes shook themselves free as their enemies' spells fell in the absence of the casters. Taerlon screamed as he tried to fend off the zombified Fazayou. The captain crawled backwards on his elbows and one remaining leg as Fazayou closed the distance, hands greedily clawing for him.

Suddenly, the former ally exploded in a heap of entrails as Bastawr chopped through him with Frostquake. Taerlon thanked him and took Bastawr's hand. Then, the tigerfolk handed him a shield and a rapier to defend himself and leapt back into the chaos.

A trio of vagha raided the pile of Magestorm weapons, tossing items into ready hands. Freshly armed, the freed warriors charged into the fray, some even before they were properly armed.

The gwereste found Ra'al and shook him to his senses. The areosa was not enthralled by the magic of venom, and he responded sluggishly. Bastawr tried rousing him to little effect.

Marnash rushed to his side and withdrew a stoppered glass tube from a pouch. "Hold your breath," he warned before yanking the plug free.

Bastawr remembered the effect of the dragon urine the last time he'd had a call to use it. He turned to help Garesch with their defenses as the morehl caster held the container near Ra'al's face.

He stoppered it again as Ra'al recoiled, neatly toppling as he tried to get away from the vile odor, suddenly invigorated. Bastawr thrust Frostquake into his hands and then drew two long daggers.

Before the pungent aroma of dragon's piss could fully dissipate, it caught the nose of Morguus Ebraxus, who roared and turned to belch more fire at the bloodless armies. He angled for the living, his eyes locked on the scattered vagha nearby.

Ra'al cursed. They had been wrong. While many of the bloodless seemed to shut down, the majority of them did not. The tree had fallen regardless of their efforts, and now, the drake saw his opportunity to sterilize the tundra in caustic flame. Ra'al knew that they could no longer prevail—not with both the undead and Morguus Ebraxus trying to kill them.

"Everyone, run!" he shouted. A pang of grief burned through Ra'al's heart. Coryn had insisted she would kill

Morguus Ebraxus, but Leisterbane's forces had killed her. As he turned to shout more evacuation orders, his eyes caught the gnomish cube his friend had carried. *If Coryn was dead, then who had blown up the death knight?*

A gout of black breath spewed in a line toward Ra'al and the dwarves, and then the gremmlobahnd's cube unfolded in an explosion of light. Coryn and the massive, golden beast that she'd called Yoo-ee suddenly blipped into existence.

Ra'al stared a moment, blinking. He'd only seen the creature once while it had been still in captivity the one time Coryn had brought him into the cube.

Yoo-ee turned his winged shoulders into the blast and shielded Coryn below her. Morguus Ebraxus pulled up and shut his mouth in surprise, veering off to assess the new challenger.

Coryn's face lit when she saw Ra'al and her friends still alive, and then it darkened when she spotted Fazayou's remains. It grew worse when her eyes turned to the destruction of the great tree.

Ra'al shouted, "We've got to get out of here!"

CHAPTER TWENTY-THREE

The undead split their attention. Most of them turned to the dragon, while only those closest to the living made attempts against them.

Taerlon limped toward the weapons cache and dragged free a carpet embroidered with shades of aquamarine. He rolled onto it and then snatched a bow engraved with mystic sigils. The carpet levitated, giving the crippled selumari a dose of security as he rained down arrow after arrow on the fiends below him.

He looked over and discovered Coryn. The dwarf still lived, and she rode on the back of a winged dragon of her own. Taerlon shook his head; it was not a dragon… but it wasn't quite a dragonkin, either. Right now, he didn't care so long as it could help them escape.

Nearest her, Ra'al issued calls for retreat. Word spread quickly, given that there were so few of them remaining.

Coryn's draconic creature turned, revealing that its side had been scorched by Morguus Ebraxus's flaming breath.

Scales puckered and slagged where its flank had melted away, hide and natural armor turned to molten material.

Taerlon blinked. He could have sworn that he saw clockwork machinations within, where the creature's hide had been burned away. And then, the liquid metal skinned over the wound and stitched itself closed, regrowing plates that resembled golden scales.

Coryn whirled her axe and yelled, "Come on, Yoo-ee! We have to distract Morguus Ebraxus so the others can escape."

"The boat," Garesch yelled, pointing. It floated in the narrow ice gap, though many bloodless still stood between them. The lava elf yanked his flintlock pistol from within his imperial robes. The bloodless had not bothered disarming the morehl on the boat once they'd been subdued with eldritch power. They hadn't intended to keep them around long enough to allow for any escape.

The emperor's muzzle flashed repeatedly, and he knocked down a cluster of walking cadavers. Their remains quivered and began reforming. Garesch had been firing rapidly, though imprecisely. He wanted to open a path, rather than take the time and focus to aim precisely enough to destroy his enemies. The base of the skull was a small target.

Coryn sailed over head and dipped just low enough that Yoo-ee could use claw and tail to rake a furrow through the forces of the dead. "Come on," yelled Marnash, who hid behind a small, mixed company of morehl and vagha leading the way. Once bitter enemies, they were now battle-bound against a common foe. They pressed toward the boat and through the heart of the undead.

With his limp wing trailing behind him, Ra'al defended Hennedy, who half carried the severely wounded Karou. Ra'al swung Frostquake and kept the bloodless at bay. He hoped that as soon as they arrived at the ship, Marnash could heal him so Karou could help summon enough wind to push them beyond Morguus Ebraxus's reach.

A few steps further, and Ra'al staggered. His death sense triggered like it never had before: worse than even the minor death. His nose went blind entirely, and his body tingled, wanting to vomit.

Marnash noticed Ra'al's reaction and caught his eye. Also caught up in a strange sensation, he explained, "We are caught in a festration. Whatever you do, do not die here, where Death's power is at its peak."

Taerlon picked up two of the morehl in the rear, rescuing the stragglers from the dead, who seemed suddenly more menacing than ever before. The source of the dark energies lay ahead of their dwindling forces, between them and the ship.

The captain, more familiar with sail ships than any of the others, called over the edge of his flying carpet, "We'll fly ahead and ready the boat!"

Garesch nodded his approval and Bastawr pointed to Morguus Ebraxus. The dragon flew a large arc around the edge of the battlefield, picking off any of the bloodless who wandered away mindless and uncontrolled. The dragon intended that none should survive, dwarf or otherwise. "Do not draw the dragon's attention," he warned.

Taerlon flashed a signal that he understood. He kept the aerial ride low but saw that Coryn and Yoo-ee were flying smaller circles, ready to try and provide interference should the drake turn his attention back to the escapees. The carpet streaked away like a shot and bore the advance team to prep the vessel.

Charging through the festration, Ra'al realized the ground had blackened and cracked inside the bubble of evil energy. He swung his axe, and the weapon failed to function as it had before. It no longer powerfully devastated the undead. Here, the weapon was merely an axe. Still, he fought with a ferocity worthy of the frostwing heroes he'd grown up knowing, if only through bardic song. Ra'al felt he sensed the greatest of them, his father Thrag, smiling down on him—only now, his mother was at his side, too.

He battled his way through and found the remains of a lone human barring his path. The undead man stood defiant, but with sad and intelligent eyes. Something below his skin seemed to glow with fell shades of violet.

Ra'al snarled and charged for him, slashing his axe with wild abandon. The former human stepped away, keeping just beyond Ra'al's reach. It regarded him curiously, and when Ra'al finally had a step on him, the festration itself defended the fiend. Spikes jutted up from the ground to block Ra'al's blows.

Speaking in an ominous voice, the creature spoke, "You cannot leave here. It is all futile. Death always wins. Death takes everything. Resign yourself to the only true outcome and I shall make you a general in his army." He looked around for Leisterbane, confirmed the former leader was dead, and commented, "In *my* army."

The frostwing roared defiantly, "Your voice lies! My father and mother have passed beyond life—but they are untouched by Death. They are immune to its touch, and they are *still alive in me!*"

The creature recoiled at the implication, and Ra'al's strength surged when he saw the reaction. He crashed through the vertical spikes and hacked both the demon's arms off before the spires shot upwards all around, entrapping Ra'al.

Sneering, the fiend knelt low. Inky, black tendrils of necralluvium hung down as strands of the stuff reached upwards. They intertwined, and the arm stitched itself back to the socket. "Long have I served Malgrimm, and for almost as long has Leisterbane held thrall over poor Peregrine. Now, Leisterbane is gone, and it is my time to prove my worth to the Master of the Abyss."

Peregrine reached for the other arm when a massive beast fell upon him from above. He collapsed beneath Yoo-ee's weight and the dracolem used his tail and hind legs to smash the stone columns imprisoning Ra'al.

The frostwing lunged with his axe and beat back the undead coming to aid Peregrine.

Yoo-ee shifted his weight and a horrific cracking sound came from Peregrine's chest. The undead's voice shifted tone as if Death's thrall had slipped.

"Renata… Renata, my love, where are you? I can finally join you. Renata, it's me, Peregr—" *crunch*.

His body broke beneath Yoo-ee's paw. When the dracolem pulled it back, little was left of Peregrine's ruined body except a smear of sticky black and torn scraps of skin and bone. A glowing amethyst gem lay in the center of the mess.

Ra'al hissed and smashed Frostquake through it. The gem exploded into fragments and the festration dispelled. As it did, the mind holding together the bloodless ceased to do so. Hordes of zombie and skeleton soldiers turned and began to wander toward the wastes, unbound and unchecked.

Morguus Ebraxus was no longer picking at the fringes. Coryn searched the sky frantically for the black drake. "What happened to him? Where is he, Ra'al?"

And then they heard him. Morguus Ebraxus flapped his wings, hovering just a few cubits above the ship that had ferried Garesch and his soldiers.

The drake sucked in a chestful of air and then spat a stream of flame into their last hope of escape. It lit like a dried pine in a flash fire. The undead threat had deescalated, but they now had the dragon's full attention.

Coryn stared as the flaming vessel crumbled. "What do we do now, Yoo-ee?" Her voice trembled as the dracolem spoke to her in the telepathic link. Coryn listened, then whispered, "You can do *what?*"

Taerlon's bones, and those of his surprised companions, sank below the surface along with the flaming wreckage of the ship. The remaining stragglers stared glossy eyed at it while it slipped below the waves. Their hopes went with it.

CHAPTER TWENTY-FOUR

Ra'al bore up the wounded Karou as Hennedy led the remaining few frostwings against the dragon. There were only a handful of them left. Luckily, they knew the drake would concentrate most of his attention on the dwarves, but they had to distract the beast long enough for the others to form a plan. They buzzed near the dragon like flies, flinging javelins of ice and trying to keep his full attention from turning to the vagha.

Coryn's dwarves had proved stout enough that nearly twenty remained. Their forces were roughly equivalent to Garesch's company. Sadly, none of the Azure Company remained; it had died with Fazayou.

After pointing to the toppled and destroyed war engines, Coryn leapt to the nearest pile to address them: it was the pile of Magestorm items. Most of them were not attuned to powers she could control, at least, not without training or learning to barter with spirits such as practitioners of the Quietudes did. That made them useless. However, her eyes spotted a weapon handle stamped with a sigil that looked like a mountain and she pulled it free, discovering a battleaxe with power tied to Eldurim, the earth god.

Yoo-ee walked behind her as Coryn rallied the dwarves and held the axe aloft. "A sign from the gods," she shouted, uncertain if that was true, but sure that she needed to inspire courage in the remaining vestiges of her team. "The undead are destroyed here, though at great cost—a cost that we do not fully yet realize—as they took the tree with them. But our role is not yet over. I command you each to get home alive."

Directing them back to the few remaining war machines, she said, "Those ballistas look usable. We are vagha. Moreover, we are dwarves of Balgavarr Reaches and that is Morguus Ebraxus, our mortal enemy! If he survives us, he'll surely turn south and attack our mountain home with prejudice."

Her soldiers roared their approval, eager to bring the down beast. They rushed off to right the few tipped ballistas. They affected quick repairs if necessary, and prayed to Firiel, Avanna, Tarvanehl, or whoever might listen, asking that their missiles would strike true.

As they rushed off, one dwarf paused and eyed her. "You aren't helping, Warlord?"

She looked down at him and brandished the axe. "Oh, I am—*I'll have this drake's head.* I swear by Thunderstrike here. You all will be my diversion."

He nodded, beard wagging, and then rushed to the ballistas, just happy that the young dwarf had a plan.

Coryn watched him go and then watched as they got three of the machines operational. The areosa scattered when Morguus Ebraxus began using his breath against them. With an opening to fire, the vagha shot their weapons. The lances streaked home, and the first weapon bounced off the drake's shoulder.

Morguus Ebraxus snarled and turned his scaled shoulder into the next two. They harmlessly bounced off his armored hide, which boasted thick scales.

As they reloaded the large machines, other dwarves aimed crossbows and fired mostly useless bolts at the dragon. He batted his wings, blinding the dwarves with a gale force that pelted them with snow and frozen topsoil.

"It is time, Yoo-ee. Do it now." She laid a hand on his side.

It is dangerous. We are bonded; I must keep you safe. I told you about my special ability so you could escape from here... this power only works for my kind... but I can make an exception for one person.

"And leave Morguus Ebraxus to return to the Reaches and slaughter everyone there? Fat chance! Now you said you could make a portal that will send me anywhere I want to go—make that happen."

Yoo-ee shot her a distinctly disapproving glance, but then touched her with the crest of his head, as if nuzzling a hatchling. The metallic skin that had stretched to reform over his blasted side pulled away from Yoo-ee's crown and enveloped Coryn, coating her in a sheen of liquid metal the color of Yoo-ee's scales. The patch where it had come from remained uncovered, with the dracolem's alloy skull exposed.

He closed his eyes as if in concentration and summoned an energy gate. It opened like a rippling pool of light that crackled with raw power.

The ballistas and crossbows fired again, one last time in unison, and Morguus Ebraxus sloughed them off. He flared his wings wide and sucked in his breath, ready to incinerate his northern enemies once and for all. As impotent missiles rebounded off his armor, Coryn charged for the energy gate with all her speed; she held her mystic axe high.

"I am the daughter of Geril Dragonsbane and the great granddaughter of the mighty Thunderfist, and I will kill my dragon," she roared as she plunged through the portal, disappearing as easily as if a coral elf diver plunged beneath the surface.

Before Morguus Ebraxus could expel his lungful of caustic plague breath, a bright disk of light bloomed open in front of the dragon's breast and Coryn plunged downward through it with all her gathered momentum. She fell, further aided by gravity, and hacked Thunderstrike downward and into the dragon's belly.

Coryn's axe struck with the force of a boulder fall, splitting him open vertically and spilling Morguus Ebraxus's guts across the broken scree and the crushed bones of the dead strewn below.

The dragon cried out with a raspy screech of pain muddled with surprise. And then he choked on his own chemical spew of fiery death magic before his split body and stilled wings succumbed to the grip of gravity.

Coryn crashed against the bulk of the mighty beast and rolled down its muscular leg, narrowly missing the razor-sharp talons of Morguus Ebraxus's foot. Then, she smashed onto the ground and rolled several paces away. The dragon crashed to the tundra near her with a noise like dull thunder.

Her great grandfather Zephras Thunderfist had died in battle, killing the mighty drake and saving Balgavarr Reaches. The body of Morguus Ebraxus had fallen upon him and crushed the brave dwarf posthumously.

She groaned and checked herself to see if she still lived. Her legs spasmed slightly from the jolt of energy the gate had sent through her when she'd passed.

Silence reigned for a few moments, and she used that opportunity to reach out and test each of her joints and ensure that nothing was broken. She felt pain, but she had busted bones before and could tell that this was a different kind. Coryn would be sore, but she lived, and was relatively well.

Footsteps crunched nearby, and she rolled over to find all her vagha companions had come around her and fallen to one knee. When she sat up, one of them called out, "Coryn Dragonscourge!" The remainder took it up as a chant.

Ra'al came over and rested his hands upon his best friend's shoulders. "You did it. You really killed the dragon."

"Pssh." She blew it off as if it was nothing. "I told you I could do it." Coryn touched a hand to Yoo-ee and the strange creature reabsorbed the skin that had enveloped the dwarf for a period. "*We* did it," she told the dracolem. "And I don't know how I survived all that lightning-like energy, but let's never do that again."

Yoo-ee snorted his agreement.

Sheron used his earth craft to form a sarcophagus and a last resting place for the body of Geril sa'Ghuren. With his magic, he inscribed the stone with his finger as easily as a quill draws ink. There Sheron recorded the great deeds and history of Dragonsbane upon the casket.

Ringuld and the other survivors lowered Geril's body into his final resting place and then Sheron transmuted the stone below into mud so that his body descended into the earth, leaving the appearance of an empty burial box in case any of Death's followers thought to revive him with their necromancy in the future. Such an abomination would be an affront to everything the great dwarf had stood for. Without hacking off the hero's head, there wasn't much else they could do to ensure that would never come to pass. Creating an empty coffin would make a distraction that would hopefully deter such an activity later.

They placed the broken remains of Old Thunder in the box where the body might have otherwise laid. Similarly, they buried the other dwarves nearby with slightly less ceremony, simply descending them far below the soil and beyond the reaches of the enemy.

"And what do we do now?" Ringuld asked.

Sheron turned to the south. "We make for Hyperannor. It's the region south of the Netherwold. The fringes are dangerous, where Annor meets Hyperannor, but we can skirt through the mountains near where we landed and hopefully, we'll elude the faeli who control the Firequags." He gave them a look of relief. "We are safer in the mountains than trying to cross through the depths of the World Wound, and Goral is in Hyperannor. It is a dwarven stronghold. Surely one of us can call upon members of a clan there and they'll help us return to Cyrea."

The vagha agreed somberly, turning their noses to head southwest along the mountainous terrain at the edges of the World Wound and beginning the arduous trek to Goral.

After exploring the wreckage of *Aguarehl's Envy*, they found enough rations and supplies to sustain the survivors on the long walk south. Unfortunately, it was only because so many of them had died in the conflict.

None felt excitement at the prospect of trudging south, especially as exhausted as they were. But neither could they wait in the shadow of the destroyed Ghaeial Tree. Its image was too sad for them to bear.

"First, to Icehome, and then to Balgavarr Reaches before an escort can accompany the lava elves back to Uruzak," Coryn suggested.

Hennedy shook his head. "I do not think we can return to Icehome. Certainly, we must be banished for defying Rawrgyld's orders to return." He sheepishly looked at the Frostquake, which he'd stolen, and pointed to it. "Also, there's this."

Ra'al said nothing. He brooded behind the others but knew that they wouldn't have succeeded without every advantage they'd used, and that included Frostquake.

"And Balgavarr Reaches is out of the question," said Garesch.

Coryn tilted her head. "But it's my home…"

Marnash flashed her a sympathetic look. "Your home is overrun from within, Lady Coryn. I do not think your father is welcome there, either. Political winds have shifted." He explained what he'd learned about the coup of elders in Balgavarr while he prepared for the siege against Uruzak and while Garesch was locked away.

Coryn's face remained neutral, which her companions knew indicated that she was deeply bothered by the turn of events.

"That only leaves Uruzak," Garesch said. "I will open my hope to you, my friends. It is, I think, the only option."

"No," piped up Ra'al. "We go first to Icehome; we will not be denied entry, and I must strike a blow against Rawrgyld while I can."

"Ra'al," Coryn said, "I don't think you can challenge him so soon for…"

"You are right, Little Sparrow, but I must learn this game that he insists I play. And I have a play to make." He pointed toward the horizon. "You may not be able to see it. I know that *I* can no longer, but I'm certain they are there before. Areosan spies; they are heading back for Castle Ice. I caught only faint glimpses of them earlier. They are probably from the same cluster of magi who tried to prevent us previously. They will report to others what has happened here." He puffed out his chest. "Only a hero stands a chance to challenge the king, and then, only when the time is right."

"You have something in mind?" asked the newly-crowned morehl emperor.

"I do. You have heard the tales of Davian Whisperwynd?" Ra'al drew on his knowledge of ancient stories from when he'd once intended to pursue bardic interests. That seemed a lifetime ago now.

Yoo-ee nudged his head down to Coryn as if he were a giant pet wishing to nuzzle. The dwarf raised her eyebrows, turned to her companions, and brandished her metallic cube.

"Everyone ought to fit fine within here and I'll ride Yoo-ee back. We ought to be able to cut down our travel time significantly."

Marnash eyed his tall, winged friend, and then sent some of his morehl to retrieve lumber from the wrecked war machines or whatever else they could find. "We will build a fire, then," he said, "Bind your wounds and hasten your healing. There is plenty of time for us in the meanwhile."

"Time for what?" Ra'al asked.

"To let the spies return and allow your fame to grow," Marnash explained, grinning.

CHAPTER TWENTY-FIVE

Ra'al entered the mostly wrecked outskirts of Icehome several days later. True to his word, Marnash had helped him recover. First, he used his magic to heal Karou, and then the frostwing caster used his gifts to aid Ra'al's busted wing.

Coryn had flown atop Yoo-ee and the pair had set down a few leagues away from the areosan capital. The survivors exited the gnome-space and walked the rest of the way into town so that they could be seen coming. They wanted to make an entrance, for Ra'al's sake.

The frostwing walked the main path through the city as if it hadn't been so recently violated by the bloodless. The commoners watched his approach and gathered around, acting like the small procession of warriors was a parade. They also spoke in hushed tones of awe.

Ra'al forced a smile, happy that Marnash was right. His fame *had* grown. It didn't even matter to the regular folk that his true mission had failed. None of them knew about the tree.

They had destroyed the undead leaders and defeated a black dragon, and that was all the people really needed to know.

Word spread quickly and the people of Icehome rushed to watch and welcome them. The memories of the areosa were not so short that they would forget a former prince so soon, even if he had spent most of his life riding his mother's windwake. Until now, that is.

Soon, the whole town, it seemed, gathered to witness Ra'al's return. News must have spread to the king and Rawrgyld emerged from the doors of Castle Ice. He played it calmly, but Ra'al detected the disappointment on Rawrgyld's face; he'd likely assumed that Ra'al would have thought better than to return and face the king's wrath. Even returning could have been construed as continued defiance by members of the military who knew how Ra'al had pushed north against Rawrgyld's explicit orders.

Ra'al turned to face the people as he climbed the steps where Rawrgyld stood; Nanku the bear sat complacently next to the king. Ra'al's ears perked up as people chattered. *Looks just like his father... Thrag would approve of his son... succeeding despite the odds, like Rashingot...*

Rawrgyld stared at him as if he were the usurper, oblivious to the fact that *usurper* was an appropriate title for the newest frostwing king.

Coryn and the rest of Ra'al's companions remained on the ground behind their friend, who clutched the stolen axe. Ra'al narrowed his eyes, not oblivious to the fact that his mother's sword hung at Rawrgyld's side in an open sheath; it hadn't even been cleaned and the dead queen's blood still encrusted it near the handle, as a reminder of how he'd come into the throne.

It is also how you will lose the throne, thought Ra'al.

Before Rawrgyld could speak, Ra'al turned and raised his voice to address the crowd, stealing the King's option to strike first in the war of words.

Keeping a regal posture, Ra'al held Frostquake aloft and said, "I want to publicly thank Rawrgyld for supporting the northern war efforts and gifting me the mighty axe, Frostquake. I have put it to good use in my efforts against the undead and will continue to do so as I safeguard the Shadowlands." He slung it behind his back, indicating to the king that he was keeping the weapon.

Rawrgyld smiled wryly, knowing he couldn't directly call a newly-minted hero a liar in front of the people without losing face. A sparkle in his eye responded. *Turnabout is fair play, I assume.* He offered an olive branch, which might have been a trap. "I hope to additionally offer to Ra'al, son of Thrag, the same position his father held in Icehome's army: Devastator, an elite warrior status."

Ra'al shared a knowing look with him. *I won't fall for your trap... I want the whole of what you took from me. The throne will be mine.* "I cannot accept. A position in the army would only hold me back." He elevated his voice. "I claim the path of ahronin. A master-less warrior who serves only Mother Ghaeial. A wandering hero unbound by edicts, orders, or service, except that to Esfah."

Rawrgyld cocked his head, continuing their private dance. *Well played, young warrior, but you walk a dangerous path, and I will have you yet.* "Surely young Ra'al will consider my offer. The life of the ahronin is a difficult one, and there is room in my court for a warrior duke. Devastator, and servant of the throne, surely any young female would love to join herself to him?"

Below, Coryn crossed her arms and spat a raspberry.

"I have heard the songs of Cyrea. It is the song of the wind, and it is a dirge of blood. I must obey its siren call," said Ra'al. He leaned forward and clasped Rawrgyld's forearm, hard enough that his talons bit the king's flesh.

Rawrgyld did not flinch, but he extended his own claws to give Ra'al as much as he took. Ra'al did not flinch either.

Ra'al spoke at a volume that only the king could hear. "Know this, Rawrgyld: You are insulated from a challenge for only so long. And now that I am recognized as a hero, I must only wait for you to fail and falter. Then, Thrag's throne will return to me, and I will put you into the ground and salt your bones."

"I suspect as much," Rawrgyld spoke quietly. "Though I'm quite surprised you survived the trials of the north. Perhaps you will make my time as king interesting."

"It will take a much stronger trap to ensnare me than the one you laid, pretender. You will miscalculate again, and I shall return to smash a crown of my own."

Rawrgyld raised a brow. "Fail *again?*"

"You should have only poisoned me with a half dose—I would have still fought your challenge while ill. And you might have killed me easily instead of slaying my mother and incurring my eternal wrath."

Rawrgyld's eyes revealed his surprise. He told the truth when he said, "I did not poison anybody." The king leaned forward. "Though her death brought me great joy, it was *you* I intended to murder all along." Rawrgyld took Ra'al's grip and then turned to raise their interlocked hands in victory, drawing the crowds' cheers. They recognized their second hero of the Shadowlands in only a few months' time.

The two locked eyes. "We shall meet again," Ra'al insisted, and then he descended the stairs toward his waiting friends. He had every intention of leaving Icehome, for who knew how long. Emperor Garesch clapped his friend on the shoulder as Ra'al met them in the court, and the group turned and walked away from Castle Ice.

"Yes, Ra'al" Rawrgyld muttered to himself. "We certainly *will* meet again."

EPILOGUE

The cabal of red elves skulked through the under-tunnels of Mount Uruzak. Two walked in the front and two in the back. Each carried an end of the rolled-up tarp and the carrion that they'd unearthed at the midden heap. Foul denizens of the shadows stalked the deepest holes of the volcanic mount. The lowest castes operated here, where their presence would not blight the more sensible lava elves stationed on the higher levels where the civilized morehl lived. Here, in the sub-barrow, lived only the destitute, and the banished, and those with no means.

Often, the wealthy entered the slums to search out the unseemly and the desperate for experiments or to play out taboo sexual fantasies. Here was also where they banished any frehlasuhl, though there were not many gray elves in Uruzak.

The hooded foursome found an empty hovel and laid their burden within. It fell with a meaty thud. They unrolled the pack and exposed the body. A red-skinned hand flopped over the edge of the tarp.

"Are ye gonna eat him? Can I have some?" came a soft voice of an abandoned child hiding below a destroyed table and leaning along one wall.

One of the four secretive lava elves chased the youth out of the cave, brandishing a dagger and promising he'd be devoured next if he ever came back. The elf returned to find his necromancer friend holding his hands over the corpse of the body with his head turned, as if listening.

"Emperor Saugor is stubborn," he said. "His spark of life has not yet left this plane; it is only banished from his body when life's link was severed. I know a spell which can recall him."

Hastily, the necromancer laid out his reagents and lit incense.

"A pity you did not kill that child," said the death crafter. "His blood would have increased the spell's efficacy."

After many hours of chanting and spell craft, Saugor's body awoke with a start. He sat up and gasped.

"My throne," he croaked with a dry throat. "I will not give up my throne to some upstart child I mistakenly fathered."

One of the cultists pulled back his hood and grasped Saugor by the shoulders. The emperor recognized him as one of his servants. "You must wait here in hiding, my Lord. Your servants are working to create the right opportunity—a chance for you to strike and take back your throne."

Saugor stiffened his neck and glared at his loyal servants. "And strike I will. Now leave me. I have higher callings which I must honor."

The cultists who had revived him bowed and departed. Before the last one left, Saugor ordered, "Return when you have found me some food and drink."

He nodded and then leaned several planks against the hovel's entry in lieu of a door.

Once he was alone, Saugor sat cross-legged on the floor and opened his mind as he called out with the spell he had been taught. Only the highest-ranking cultists knew it. The dark communion was a variation on the contact spell Leisterbane used to reach out to his trio of supporters.

The blue elf and a dwarf responded to Saugor's call. The elf was the same, but the dwarf was someone else, not Harol. Not even kin by the look of him.

"Saugor—you are alive?" the selumari said. "Reports of your murder had reached me in Tulgesh."

Saugor grinned wickedly. "Rumors of my demise were greatly exaggerated."

"Truly, evil never dies," quipped his blue counterpart.

"I *was* dead, but now I am revived." Saugor paused to address an itch in his mouth. He curled a lip and pushed against a tooth that pained him. His gut knotted with hunger pangs. "I shall live again, as will my empire... only this time, without Leisterbane insisting that all actions fall in line with his purpose. We can take a more nuanced approach, as we Nekarthans prefer."

The other two bowed their heads, showing their approval.

"Subtlety and intrigue is our game," the vagha interjected, "but we must also be prepared to strike."

"Explain," said the selumari.

"I have heard rumors that the Champions of the Gods, the Gods' own, have come again to Esfah. Certainly, Ghaeial fights to keep the seeds of life blossoming even as we find success in our endeavors to prop up the Masked Ones. We must do something to stop these Gods' own," claimed the dwarf.

"Yes," said the blue elf thoughtfully. "I was warned of this by my lover, the drider Sshkkryyahr. It was she who introduced me to the cult of Nekarthis. Sshkkryyahr claimed the Gods' own would be reborn by the gods before the third age."

The vagha looked down his nose at the elf. "Selumari, it was one of these supposed Gods' own who struck down your lover in Undrakull."

The blue elf hissed.

"I am far away, but I have uncovered a relic that will help our plans," he continued. "And I have secured more than the relic, but the key required to use it as well."

Saugor narrowed his eyes. "Speak plainly." He wiggled the painful tooth, which seemed to have come loose.

The vagha wore an unmistakable look of smugness. "I have found an heir to the Deathbard of Dereh'Liandor." After a pause for dramatic effect, the dwarf continued, "And I hold the reforged instrument of Nekarthis himself."

"And your madcap plan actually works?" asked the coral elf.

"It does," said the dwarf gleefully. "We shall use this tool only once we know we can control it to great effect. Before these Gods'own pretenders learn of our existence, we must redouble our efforts to locate the fourth of us."

His peers each nodded. They all knew the stakes.

"We are the masked ones," said Saugor. "We are patient. We wait in the shadows until the fourth of us is discovered, and then we shall leave the shadows—and blot out the light."

"We agree and decree it so," said the coral elf.

The dwarf chanted, "By the power granted to us by the four totem faces of Death: Malfeus, Noxigant, Ghastamant, and Surfeibese. The Masked Ones."

Saugor released the spell and sat for a few moments in the darkness. He repeated the line and mused, "Truly, evil never dies."

Lying at the bottom of the World Wound, where light barely penetrated the depths, the blood drained from Harol sa'Lahmyn's broken corpse. Though the dusty soil drank in the thick, red fluid, something else leaked as well.

The glass tubes Harol carried in his pockets had shattered, leaving behind only busted fragments and cork stoppers. Their contents, the sludge-like necralluvium, had seeped out and through Harol's clothes. It crawled until it came in contact with flesh, and then it attached itself to him. It absorbed into Harol's body and stretched out through the vagha's veins like needles, searching for the central nervous system.

Soon after, the bloodless dwarf stood and searched the darkness. There was nothing nearby but blasted stone that rose in vertical sheafs for as far as he could see, and the ground was a wrecked landscape of twisted stone and blasted scree. Harol searched his memory. He recalled scraps of who he was… what he had been. He remembered.

The creature stalked through the shadows, heading west until he found the easiest route up the jagged cliffs. Weeks of wandering passed until he found himself again in the fens of Hyperannor. Mists rose in the mornings and evenings, hanging in the air like humid grave shrouds. He was vaguely aware of the odor surrounding him; Harol understood that he smelled like a cadaver.

From the trees, he spotted two bright green eyes hunting in the darkness. The light of Rhaudian reflected off them like mirrors.

"Finally, I will end you, and prove to the village why I am the greatest warrior," he hissed, "and not merely some young fang. I'll take your vaghan head to the elders and they will elevate me."

The sarslayan youth launched himself at the walking corpse, sword drawn. But the undead expected him. The young fang coiled himself around the strong enemy, but the bloodless used his hands and broke the creature's spine with a wet, snapping, sound.

He dropped the writhing creature, who flailed and gasped for breath. And then he bent over the swamp stalker and hissed, "Tell me about this village of yours." And then, he withdrew another of his glass vials, the only one to have survived his fall. He let out one drop, letting it fall into the creature's agape mouth.

The reptilian warrior gasped, screeched, and breathed its last as the veins of black shot through its body.

"We shall go there together, you and I," said the former Harol. "Together, we shall show them the glory of our master, Malgrimm."

The thing rose, looked at his new undead master, and then led the way.

Coryn fidgeted with the block of metal she'd claimed below the Ghaeial Tree in the tunnels. In the months that followed their return, she'd moved to a nice apartment, which she shared with Ra'al in Uruzak. She had shown the strange item to everyone with any working historical knowledge of lore related to the gremmlobahnd. None of them could read a lick of gnomish and could do little more than identify its origins. It *was* gnomish, but beyond that, little was certain.

She and her friends had only just begun to grow restless. The trek down to Uruzak from the Shadowlands had been difficult. At least the travelers had been able to re-provision in Icehome so they hadn't had to march on an empty stomach. She remembered how her father had once warned her of exactly that—adventuring was not for the comfort seekers. Her mind wandered to Geril, wondering when she might hear from him. Not likely until he returned to Balgavarr and straightened out the corruption within the council.

As she stared at the gnomish cube, there came a gentle knock at the door. In came a selumari messenger, wearing a jacket that identified him as a sailor from Riechus Aqualines. Coryn brightened as she realized Naemyar had many connections beyond her own and was a historical expert in her own right on certain topics. *Certainly she could provide some help!*

The coral elf handed over two scrolls and then departed. Coryn noticed that one had been resealed with a different kind and color of wax. She cracked it and read. It had been from Elder Lordan, who had disappeared from Balgavarr seemingly overnight during the campaign for the Mist Stones. Coryn had only learned of it recently while trying to contact her family's allies on Balgavarr and lobby for a return.

The letters' contents were addressed to Naemyar and outlined what he'd learned about Karaktoan flintlocks and how they linked to specific power users… and how they could not fire if they were not attuned. He also included a carefully drawn copy of the rubbing he had taken of the weapon's barrel. *More gnomish writing.*

Lordan had asked for her to help him translate the text and shared his suspicions that Lahmyn was, at the very least, framing Garesch for the murder. He implied a suspicion that Lahmyn may have even been the trigger man.

Coryn opened the second letter, assuming that it was also from Naemyar and would give context on why she had forwarded the message from Elder Lordan. The opening line confirmed that, and she read the rest softly to herself.

"I know you have had a difficult time in the Shadowlands; I had heard you were now staying in Uruzak under Emperor Garesch's protection. Forgive me, I would have delivered this news to you in person, except my business has kept me excessively busy as of late—and I cannot keep this news from you any longer. I recently found company with a few Balgavarrian dwarves, including Sheron and Captain Ringuld, who had caught a ride to Tulgesh from one of my ships departing Annor Dereh'Liandor. Coryn… I'm so sorry to tell you…"

Coryn fell silent. Her lips too frozen to read the news of her father's fate. She fell to her knees and let out a spine-chilling wail, followed by sobbing. She hadn't cried like that since her mother's death.

Ra'al rushed in from the other room. The frostwing sank down to her side and tried to comfort her. "Coryn? Coryn, what's wrong?"

She couldn't find the words, and so, Ra'al scanned the letter. His eyes found the report. Harol had been brought to justice, but Geril sa'Ghuren, her father, had died protecting Esfah from him.

Ra'al held her, stroking her hair, and let her cry into his fur. He knew the feeling; he'd also lost both his parents. And he knew that, sometimes, there were no words that could come. Sometimes there was only the song of the wind.

The End

Appendices

The Shadowlands
Icehome
Frostshoal
Briney Main
Gyrea
Wilds of Dur Sona
Karinyana Mountains
Balgavan
Deep Mire
Tulgeth
Thurisa
Plains of Sesham
Uruzak Mountains
Plaguelands

Glossary of Terms

Abyss - the home of the Void, a realm where silence reigns aside from pockets of terror and chaos where unknown gods reign. This is a similar concept to Greek myths of an underworld.

Ailuril - the second born of the Esfahan gods. She is represented by the color blue and has power over the air elements.

Aguarehl - the fourth born of the Esfahan gods. He is represented by the color green and has power over the water elements.

Amazon - the race of mankind said to have been deposited whole upon Esfah as one of the few races created by Tarvanehl himself. Amazons are the warrior caste of human race.

Areosa - commonly known as the frostwings, a frigid felinoid, winged race with magic resistance.

Bloodless - another common name for the undead.

Deadzone – synonym for the Abyss, except from the point of view of the trogs or morehl. Within their respective religions, versions of the afterlife differ wildly and as often as they align in geopolitical goals, neither could imagine spending an eternal afterlife in the company of the other.

Death - the half-brother god who is the child of Nature and Void.

Dragons – these beasts come in two forms: Drake and Wyrm. Drakes have wings, and wyrms do not. Though the dragonkin are a kind of subspecies, they are not the same thing, no matter how similar they are. They used to live hidden across Esfah, but were nearly eradicated in the Dragoncrusades. Dragons have eternal spirits and when they die, they return to the plane where they now dwell. Dragonmagic came in two forms and it summons them from this realm or from nearby (the older form of this magic which has now been forgotten since these mythic beasts have largely gone out from Esfah.)

Drakufreet - the dragonkin come from the same realm as dragons and appear as a type of draconic hybrid race.

Eldarim – a human-like race that emerged over eons from Esfah's primordial soup and predated the gods-made races. The eldarim are versatile and have proven the capacity to breed with many of Esfah's races. They are called eldarim, meaning "from the earth."

Eldurim - the firstborn of the Esfahan gods. He is represented by the color gold and has power over the earth elements.

Efflorah - the race of treefolk.

Esfah - the world and one of two planets revolving around Soll.

Empyrea - known commonly as the firewalkers, a war-loving mercenary race.

Faeli - commonly known as scalders or steam dancers. These creatures are fickle and capricious and were once captured and tormented by Death.

Festration - a kind of location so tainted by evil activity that the very land itself has become corrupt and avails itself to wickedness.

Firiel - the third born of the Esfahan gods. She is represented by the color red and has power over the fire elements.

First Age - everything from the beginning of creation to the year 863.

Frehlasuhl - also called the Forsaken or Mudbloods. They are the offspring of selumari and morehl unions. They cannot breed with each other to have children, only with one or the other race, but they are rejected wholesale by both.

Ghaeial - the mother goddess known more commonly as Nature.

Ghwereste - called the "feral folk." These are a hybrid of animal and man created at the dawn of the Second Age.

Kreethaln - there are three of these mystical artifacts made of an unknown metal. Little is known about them except that they each possess some kind of arcane power. Their names are Life-bringer, Wisdom-giver, and Spell-crafter.

Leguin - a sister planet to Esfah that also orbits Sol; it can often be seen in the night sky appearing above the horizon like a bright star.

Lich - a powerful undead spell caster. Lichs often possess necromantic capabilities, though their created undead are maintained by force of will, rather than by other means, such as the Necralluvium.

Morehl - commonly called lava elves. They have red skin in addition to their elf-like features and their blood is said to smoke when exposed to air.

Necralluvium - a kind of magical potion with a seeming life of its own. This black filth can kill the living. The dead that are exposed to it become animated.

Rhaudian - the name of the moon. It circulates Esfah twice in a daily cycle.

Sarslayan - commonly known as swamp stalkers. These snake-men emerged in the Second Age as a result of Death using magic to twist the creations of his half-brother Aguarehl. They create more of their kind through magic conversion rather than by reproduction.

Second Age - everything after year 863 of the First Age. This began when Ghaeial walked the face of Esfah and surveyed the damages of the myriad of wars. The 864th year is year 1 of the Second Age.

Selurehl - the name of the second god to emerge after Tarvanehl, usually known as Void.

Selumari - commonly called coral elves. They have blue skin in addition to their elf-like features.

Shara – what the eldarim people refer to themselves as when they communicate with each other. It means "little god-in-the-making."

Soll – the sun.

Tarvanehl - the creator god who came first, according to all mythology and story; he is often known as Father Time, or simply The Father.

Teldrim - a race of extinct horse lords that bore many similarities to the Amazons. A creation of Tarvanehl, these were remarkable because the race could intermix with any other. They were eradicated by Melkior shortly after their emergence.

Trog - a synonym for goblin. trogs much prefer to live in boggy areas and tend to pollute the land.

Vagha - commonly known as dwarves.

Void - sometimes used interchangeably with the Abyss or, the power or person of Selurehl who is frequently referred to as Void just as his son Malgrimm is more widely regarded as Death. Context determines the meaning.

Warchief - a title of rank among the vagha. Below the king is a Warchief who leads Warlords and Warcommanders under them. It might commonly be understood as a sort of general.

Timeline

Included is the general timeline of major world events in Esfah. Please note that, during the time before the Mother, Ghaeial, became a goddess and the First Age began, prehistory spanned a scope of time measuring eons, and in that time, verily, only *Time* existed. Despite the sage's attempts to capture much data and ancient knowledge, they did not begin tracking time and dates until the first passing of the Daybringer. The first three years of history might very well have been hundreds or even a thousand years as the gods (and the earliest race of eldarim) kept time differently.

Prehistory N.D.

Tarvanehl exists and creates within the realm of Void/Abyss and Esfah and Leguin are born; Ghaeial realizes she is a goddess and falls in love with Tarvanehl.

Turambar courts Leguin.

Selurehl, third of the brother gods grows angry.

Eldurim, the firstborn (earth) god-son of Ghaeial and Tarvanehl is born.

Ailuril, the second born (wind) god-daughter of Ghaeial and Tarvanehl is born.

Firiel, third born (fire) god-daughter of Ghaeial and Tarvanehl is born

Aguarehl, fourth born god-son (water) of Ghaeial and Tarvanehl is born

Malgrimm, the cursed bastard son (Death) is conceived and birthed after Selurehl's violence upon Ghaeial

Eldarim are birthed by Esfah and slowly emerge from the mire of her lands and water, evolving over long periods of time. They call themselves the Shara in their own tongue.

The First Age

03FA the Daybringer Comet passes Esfah for the First Time, the Sisters of Fate are birthed of Turambar and Leguin, Dragons and the Drakufreet are created during the schism of the god-children.

04FA Earliest creations of the gods: "monsters" are formed

15FA selumari are created

16FA vagha are created, trogs are created

17FA morehl are created

19FA The Dawn of War. morehl invaders overthrow the first selumari

22FA Humans arrive on Esfah via Tarvanehl's intervention

28FA Davian Whisperwynd leaves Maris-ta-Sehlim

32FA The proto-empyreans are birthed in the whirlwind

42FA Gundraokh Shatterfist finds the Bands of Turambar and renames the city of Orelod to Gundakhor

96FA Sshkkryyahr the Dread rises to power

103FA Malgrimm attempts to create a new powerful, destructive force within the Shadowlands, but the Areosan's magic resistance helps them maintain mild independence from the Death god and he abandons them to the frost plains.

143FA Undead created, Melkior is defeated upon the Raithlan Plains by the gods' chosen Champions

167FA Dilution of the eldarim race and the reduction of the Dragon population via the Dragoncrusades that eliminated nearly all the natural dragons of Esfah; the spells that compelled natural dragons that still remained in the realm became forgotten after this date in favor of those drawing eternal dragons through the interplanar rifts

341FA Existence of the empyreans is discovered when they aid the elder races in the first major Undead uprising.

447FA *Book of the Land, 1st Ed.* is published and immediately begins revisions

520FA morehl city of Karakto falls to the selumari

532FA morehl discover cursed bullets and retake Karakto

544FA Large load of Eldrymetallum discovered on the Karakto slopes

562FA Final version of *The Book of the Land* completed after 23 quintennial installments

836FA The Magestorm Wars erupt with the tectonic cataclysm that opens the Netherwold and nearly splits Dereh'Liandor in two; the Arcana Veil stiffens

842FA Disappearance of the gremmlobahnd and the genocide of the drakufreet

863FA Final battle of the Magestorm Wars ends the first age, the faeli are birthed in the Firequags and captured by the forces of Death and subjected to torments in the pits of the World Wound.

The Second Age

01SA Ghaeial walks the earth and surveys the damage of the elder races.

03SA Ghaeial creates the ghwereste

79SA The plagues of the World Wound at its evils continue and the first of the sarslayan emerge from the nearby Snekdenn Bayou

153SA The areosa race emerges from the Shadowlands. They are known mostly as rumors, but their existence is verified to the outside world.

209SA Whether the faeli escaped the torments of the World Wound or were released, none know, but they were so twisted by the centuries of abuse that they have become more children of Malgrimm than Ghaeial

233SA Under Ghaeial's wishes, the sylvan efflorah, existing as trees since even before the humans came to Esfah, picked up their roots and first emerged from forest and grove

829SA Zephras "Thunderfist" dies defending in Cyrea defending Balgavarr from a dragon

967SA Geril sa'Ghuren "Dragonsbane" born

1021SA Geril sa'Ghuren rules in Balgavarr

1082SA Coryn Sa'Geril is born

1119SA Daybringer Comet makes its pass by Esfah

1122SA Kholkoro Wicebrow writes her commentary *Kholkoro's commentary on Book of the Land*

1127SA The famed "Adventurer King" Hy'Mandr sa'Meril is blinded

1139SA Melkior is revived

1142SA Daybringer Comet makes its circuit

About the author:

Christopher D. Schmitz is author of both Sci-Fi/Fantasy Fiction and Nonfiction books and has been published in both traditional and independent outlets. If you've investigated indie writers of the upper Midwest, you may have heard his name whispered in dark alleys with an equal mix of respect and disdain. He has been featured on television broadcasts, podcasts, and runs a blog for indie authors.

As an avid consumer of comic books, movies, cartoons, and books (especially sci-fi and fantasy) he basically lived out Stranger Things as a kid in the 80s. He lives in rural Minnesota with his family and three wild frostwings where he drinks unsafe amounts of coffee; the caffeine shakes keep the cold from killing him. In his off-time he plays haunted bagpipes in places of low repute.

You can connect with him via the following links:
http://www.authorchristopherdschmitz.com

Follow me on Twitter:
https://twitter.com/cylonbagpiper
Follow me on Goodreads:
www.goodreads.com/author/show/129258.Christopher_Schmitz
Like/Follow me on Facebook:
https://www.facebook.com/authorchristopherdschmitz
Subscribe to my blog:
https://authorchristopherdschmitz.wordpress.com
Favorite me at Smashwords:
www.smashwords.com/profile/view/authorchristopherdschmitz
My Amazon Author Profile:
http://amazon.com/author/christopherdschmitz
Follow me at Bookbub:
www.bookbub.com/authors/christopher-d-schmitz

DRAGON DICE

Dragon Dice™ is SFR Inc.'s core product. We are constantly working to create a quality game that everyone can enjoy. Dragon Dice™ was originally created by Lester Smith and produced by TSR© in 1995. After several years, TSR, now owned by Wizards of the Coast, had put Dragon Dice™ on hold to work on other projects. In October of 2000, SFR Inc. purchased the rights to Dragon Dice™ and now will continue to support and create NEW! products for the game.

Dragon Dice™ is strategy game where players create mythical armies using dice to represent each troop. The game combines strategy and skill as well as a little luck. Each person tries to win the game by outmaneuvering the opponent and capture 2 terrains. Of course, eliminating your opponent completely is another acceptable way of winning.

Get online today and "Roll your way to victory!"

http://www.sfr-inc.com